MW01104606

*W*ind
*W*ater

Also by Jeanne Williams

*W*ind
*W*ater

JEANNE
WILLIAMS

St. Martin's Press ❧ New York

Design by Nancy Resnick

Library of Congress Cataloging-in-Publication Data

Williams, Jeanne
    Wind water / by Jeanne Williams.—1st ed.
        p.   cm.
    ISBN 0-312-14765-1 (hc)
    I. Title.
PS3573.I44933W56   1997
813'.54—dc20   96-31039
                                                CIP

First Edition: April 1997

10 9 8 7 6 5 4 3 2 1

This book is dedicated with love and admiration to Belle James, consummate artist with flowers, whose work has given me—and many others—so much delight. Her lifelong love for windmills may have something to do with why she is still going strong at ninety!

Author's Note

Windmills are beautiful things against blue skies, promising water in parched country. They've always been part of my landscape, but it wasn't till I read *Blades in the Sky* by T. Lindsay Baker, published in 1992 by Texas Tech University Press, Lubbock, Texas, that I realized there was quite a lot to erecting and maintaining windmills and how vital they were and still are in many places to the plains. Baker's book is drawn from the records and memories of B. H. "Tex" Burdick, who ran a windmilling company out of El Paso. Dozens of his vintage photographs illustrate the text. It is filled with triumphs, disasters, and the men who set up mills from west Texas through New Mexico.

When I asked Dave Webb of the Kansas Heritage Center in Dodge City if he knew of any good material on windmills, he lent me ten years of *The Windmiller's Gazette*, edited and with many articles by the same T. Lindsay Baker who wrote *Blades in the Sky*. With photos and sketches, these were a treasure trove of information. Dave also referred me to an excellent history of American windmills, *Wind-Catchers* by Volta Torrey, The Stephen Greene Press, Brattleboro, Vermont, 1976. Dave, an author himself, and peerless educator, has generously helped me with sources for a number of my books and I am grateful.

The range war in my story was waged with windmills. Without them, the plains could never have been settled. I might have located this book in many places but I chose my favorite setting, the region where I was born, once called No Man's Land, the narrow strip, now the Oklahoma Panhandle, that stretches between Texas and Colorado to New Mexico.

I've loved the Valley of the Dry Cimarrón ever since my uncle, Lou Salmon, took me there several years ago and we drove between hills and buttes greened sparsely with juniper and oak. This country below the great Black Mesa is vividly recalled in *Girl on a Pony* by LaVerne Hanners, University of Oklahoma Press, Norman, Oklahoma, 1994. Other books that give the history of that small but fascinating area are *No Man's Land* by Carl Coke Rister, University of Oklahoma Press, Norman, 1948, and *No Man's Land* by George Rainey, privately printed by the author, Enid, Oklahoma, 1937.

Carrizo, now Kenton (and maybe then, too; my sources don't agree on when the name changed), was known as the Cowboy Capital for men from the adjacent parts of three states and New Mexico Territory. Now you can buy a cold drink at the general store—if you're lucky enough to find it open. The Nature Conservancy and Oklahoma State Park Department manage Black Mesa for its unique ecosystem. There's a five-mile foot trail to the top.

For an account of how wild animals, predators and prey, refuged with people who'd burned a backfire for safety, I'm indebted to J. C. Chatfield of Scarsdale, New York. He wrote to me that his father on that day stopped a man from shooting a deer, saying nothing would be killed in that sanctuary.

Lynne May, my friend and neighbor, who admires, understands, raises, and trains mules, gave me fascinating insights on their behavior, including their songs.

John Wylie of Austin, Texas, read the manuscript with special attention to water-well drilling, and kindly sent me much information on early practices. The account of the future General John Pope's attempts to drill wells from west Texas through New Mexico is given in *History of Oil Well Drilling* by J. E. Brantley, Gulf Publishing, Houston, Texas, 1971.

Alden Hayes, friend, neighbor, and previous owner of my

home who replaced the windmill with an electric pump, talked firsthand about maintenance. Uncle Lou and my cousin, Jack Salmon, investigated the remaining tower and showed me how the winch positioned the wheel. Alden also told me about building fence, which is much harder with our rocky soil where a post-hole digger won't work. It would have worked on those High Plains, so for instruction in using one, I turned to Don Worcester of Aledo, Texas, whose graduate students came to believe that Ph.D. stands for "post-hole digger."

The damage hail wrought to cattle, horses, and crops is documented in many places. A couple of minutes of hail could completely destroy a year's corn or wheat. However, there was truly a rural neighborhood whose people, after losing all their crops and a number of cattle, gathered up the big hailstones and, just as the wedding party in this book do, made ice cream.

Jeanne Williams
Cave Creek Canyon
Chiricahua Mountains, Arizona
June 12, 1996

*O*ne

*E*ven though these late April days could get downright hot before noon, nights were chill on the high plains of No Man's Land, edged by Colorado and Kansas on the north, New Mexico to the west, Texas south, and the Oklahoma District on the east. Julie poked her head enough out of the tarp protecting her bedroll to see Cap Mc-Cloud lean out of his bed to start the fire with cow chips, withered soaptree stalks, and thistles he wrapped in a tarp each night to keep dry from dew or frost.

A little beyond camp, the capped casing of the well above which they were going to erect a tower and windmill thrust eight or so inches above the slush and tailings left by the well driller. Colonel Jess Chandless, the most powerful rancher in this unclaimed region, had engaged Cap to put up windmills at a dozen wells.

The crew had hauled materials for this windmill but Chandless would have his men pick up the other tower and mill parts at the railhead in Tyrone about seventy-five miles northeast, not far from Liberal, Kansas. After the Kansas boundary was set as the southern quarantine line for tick-carrying Texas cattle, the spur had been built so cattlemen could ship their cattle from No Man's Land.

The windmillers were running a little late on Chandless's

mills. A rawboned former schoolteacher, Cora Oliver, had intercepted them three days ago. She'd hired a well-drilling outfit to dig her well and ordered her mill and the tower parts from a Liberal supplier. Would Cap put up the mill and take some of his pay in eggs and butter and such? He would, so the crew had located Chandless's well just before dark last night. Now, with the skill born of thousands of such mornings, Cap got the fire going, adding slats from a windmill packing-crate for staying power. What clothes he hadn't slept in, he pulled on beneath his tarp, then sat on top of it to lace up his boots.

His rust-and-white-spotted hound, LeMoyne, poked his long muzzle out from under the tarp, mournful eyes reproaching Cap for rousing him. LeMoyne never tried to crawl under the blankets, but he claimed equal rights to the tarp.

Columbine gave her plaintive good morning bray. Absalom added his gruffer notes. To hush the duet, Cap had to go caress them. They were big mules, bred from the same gray sire that Cap proudly boasted was descended from Royal Gift, the jack sent to George Washington by the King of Spain and the pride of the first president's breeding program. Columbine's mother had been a Percheron and Absalom's a Belgian.

Having soothed his team, Cap ground coffee beans in the grinder permanently attached to the chuck box facing out from the back of the wagon. He never ceased to be grateful that Arbuckle had found a way to roast the beans and coat them with a sugar and egg glaze so they'd keep fresh a good while and didn't have to be roasted right before they were used. He filled the two-gallon coffeepot from the water barrel, dumped in about three-quarters of a pound of coffee, and set it on to simmer. Cap was particular about coffee. He would use only Arbuckle's and the pot had to be scrubbed clean every night.

"By supper, that'll be strong enough to carry the pot away," he chuckled to Julie. "Good morning, honey."

"Morning, Cap." Julie smiled, yawned, stretched, and pulled on her own clothes under the shelter of the tarp.

At twenty, she was old enough to appreciate the way Cap greeted each day with a grin so broad you'd think he'd never

2

seen the sun rise before. That was in spite of serving in some of the bloodiest fighting in the War Between the States and carrying shrapnel in one leg.

She was lucky it had been Cap who'd heard a baby wailing from a silent covered wagon nineteen years ago, lucky that he'd dared the cholera that had killed her young fair-haired mother and father, and two brothers. There had been other wagons in the party but they had apparently fled when the deadly contagion struck.

"You can't much blame 'em, Julie," Mike Shanahan had told her when she questioned him. The captain's onetime sergeant didn't mind bragging on Cap and was more forthcoming with details of her rescue than was Cap. "Cholera spreads fast. Nothin' can be done for it. Runnin' didn't save the rest of them. About a day's journey on, we found three wagons of dead folks." The stocky redheaded Irishman's grim look faded into a proud smile. "Let me tell you, darlin' girl, that when I was shot nigh in half at Shiloh, Captain Bob stood over me and fought off the Rebs till he could carry me away. I've followed him into a hail of Minié balls that whistled like all the devils in hell and I've been with him when he stormed positions that it looked like no mortals could take. But I never saw him do a braver thing than climb in that cholera wagon and take you gentle and easy out of your poor mother's dead arms."

All Julie could get out of Cap was, "Even in that bad sickness, your mama was a pretty lady and your daddy looked like a man I'd be glad to know. I'm sorry I didn't get you some keepsake, honey, but the truth is I wanted out of that wagon as fast as I could make it. I wish we knew what your folks called you, but I gave you my own mother's name. It's the prettiest one I know."

So Julie felt that for her especially, life was a gift with each day a present to be unwrapped, admired, and savored. When she was about seven, Cap tried to leave her in Fort Worth with a preacher's wife so she could go to school. Her protests were so tearfully vehement that the good lady took the precaution of locking her into her upstairs room.

The window could open, though. Discarding her new dress

for the boy's clothes she'd always worn, Julie shinned down a cottonwood tree after dark. She knew Cap was traveling the westward road toward Fort Griffin, the rowdy buffalo hunters' hangout, which she knew from several trips. Hungry and footsore, she walked through the moonlit night and caught up with the wagon at noon next day when Cap stopped to rest the mules.

"You got to learn to be a lady, honey," argued Cap as she sobbed against his chest. "Shan and me can't teach you that."

"I don't want to learn anything you can't teach me!"

"But, Julie, when you grow up—"

"I'll be a windmiller just like you!" She glared at him through her tears. "I don't want to be a—a stupid *lady* and live in a house."

Cap wiped her eyes with a bandanna and said helplessly, "You need to go to school, sugar."

"Why? You can go on teaching me to read and write and I'm learning 'rithmetic from helping measure girts and such and making out our bills and ordering supplies." She held on to him tight and played her ignoble but effective ace in the hole. "I don't have any family but you and Shan, Cap." Rance Gillespie, the third member of the windmill crew, wasn't offended by being left out. He'd just been with the outfit a month and it only took him another month to decide he'd rather cowboy than put up windmills. Through the years, that third member of the crew changed half a dozen times, once because he fell from the tower and broke his neck.

Cap, obviously torn, smoothed Julie's tangled hair till Shan grunted. "Come out of that, you little fraud!" he admonished. "Cap, she's got you hornswoggled and hogtied, but who's to say the colleen's not right? I'd rather put up windmills in a tornado than work like women do out on the plains."

So Julie stayed with the outfit. By the time she was sixteen, leggy as a colt, but tough and strong for her slender five feet seven, she could dig a level hole for an anchor post, the job most heartily detested by windmillers, nail together wooden towers or help assemble steel ones, and use the block and tackle to raise towers or heavy parts and lower the sucker rod and pumping cylinder.

When they stopped in town for supplies or to pick up wind-mill parts at railroad depots, never had she regretted running away from the nice preacher's wife in Fort Worth. She tossed her single braid of tawny hair and ignored the frowns women directed at her clothing and the sniggers and pointing of girls her own age.

What did they know about capturing the power of the wind to bring water up from the earth, cool sweet water that was life for humans, beasts, and crops? Their lives were bounded by town or homestead or one ranch—what could they know of the wild regions she traveled, across the South Plains and west over the Staked Plains rising from the Caprock to the mountains of New Mexico, or across the High Plains from Colorado and Kansas into Texas and the Unassigned Lands, formerly part of Indian Territory, that only a week ago in this spring of 1889 had been opened to homesteaders?

"We cover about the same country the Comanches and Kiowas did," Cap said once. "When the buffalo were killed out, there wasn't any way the Indians could live in their old fashion." He shrugged unhappily. "I've seen some of their artistic work on settlers and freighters and soldiers but I could never blame 'em much for trying to hold on to their style of living. It was mighty free and fine."

Free and fine. That was how Julie thought of her life. She couldn't imagine trading it for the confinement of a soddie, or even a big frame house with polished wooden floors and running water supplied by a windmill. Now and then, a handsome young cowboy or homesteader hung around more than necessary but the outfit could put up a tower and windmill in two to four days so they kept on the move. There was never time for shy grins and awkward courtesies to progress further. Sometimes Julie regretted that a little, but when, on a lonely farm, she saw an exhausted woman her own age with a baby on a hip and one or two at her skirts, Julie thought herself fortunate.

Cap scraped some coals to the edge of the fire and set the greased cast-iron Dutch oven in them. He dashed water in his eyes, washed his hands, and began to make sourdough biscuits while Julie performed her ablutions and nestled a big skillet in the coals.

They had fresh eggs for a welcome luxury, part of Cora Oliver's pay for her windmill, along with butter, cottage cheese, and a ten-gallon can of buttermilk. Cash money was scarce. The windmillers often counted sacks of beans, onions, potatoes, and other food toward payment. Out on the plains, fresh garden and dairy foods were better than money.

"Nothing between here and the North Pole but a bob-wire fence and that's blown down!" grunted Mike Shanahan, turning up the collar of his sheepskin coat to meet the brim of his battered felt hat.

He was digging a trench to hold lard, bacon, eggs, butter, and buttermilk. Covered with wet sacks, these things would stay cool even through the heat of the afternoon. Julie chopped potatoes left over from supper in the skillet, added sliced onions, and took a half dozen eggs from their straw cushioning. She broke these into the skillet, added salt and pepper and stirred the mixture to keep it from sticking as she picked over beans, rinsed them well, and set them on to cook in a large kettle. Seasoned with onions, canned tomatoes, and dried chilies, they'd be edible by noon but by supper, they'd be perfect, and good for breakfast, too, when a new pot would be put to simmer.

The rich fragrance of coffee and biscuits was cheering as the warmth of the fire. Facing the sun just starting to burst from clouds of gold and rose on the horizon, Cap bowed his head.

"Thank you, Lord, for these high, wide handsome plains, the water beneath them, and the wind to bring it up. Bless all your creatures and help us put up strong towers and good mills that'll help folks and animals a long time. You lived in a desert country once so you know what water means. Amen."

"Amen," murmured Julie and Shan.

They had quelled their first hunger and were enjoying final golden brown biscuits and cups of coffee when LeMoyne sniffed the wind, gave a soft growl, and rose to stand sentry by the wagon.

A small figure showed on the rim of the prairie with a smaller figure on either side and an even smaller shape rang-

6

ing ahead. LeMoyne rumbled but Cap, rising, quieted him with a scratch behind his ears.

"Early in the morning for company. And it don't look full-grown at that, excepting maybe the dog. We got enough left to feed 'em, Julie, or do we need to break out the dried fruit and open some cans?"

"I made enough potatoes and eggs for noon," Julie said. "And there's eight biscuits." Those had been intended for a quick lunch, too, but it was unthought-of not to invite anyone stopping by to a meal if it was that time of day.

Well, the outfit would just eat beans and cornbread. At least, thanks to Cora Oliver, they had delicious butter. Shading her eyes, Julie said, "That one in the middle could be a small man, but those are boys with him. They'd probably like some dried apples and peaches."

"Might as well put up our bedrolls before scorpions or tarantulas homestead in 'em," said Shan.

By the time they had attended to their camp chores and Julie got out some dried fruit, the visitors were close enough to be seen as three boys in heavily patched overalls and peculiar jackets of spotted cowhide. The eldest was perhaps sixteen, the others maybe twelve and fourteen.

All were towheaded, freckled, barefoot, and had blue eyes. The snub nose of the youngest was less snubby in the middle lad, and vanished into a straight, rather long nose in the angular face of the tallest boy.

He got a grip on the ruff of a gray-yellow dog of indeterminate ancestry, though it looked like the result of a coyote's beguiling a domesticated cousin. It gave sharp little yips of excitement but managed to contain them when one of the boys called, "Hush up, Sunny!"

Giving the drab-colored animal that shining name showed the triumph of love over reality. Cap quieted LeMoyne with a word and offered his hand.

"Mornin'!" he greeted. "How's about some breakfast?"

"Thanks, mister," said the tallest, shaking hands. "But we've come to talk business. We've had breakfast—"

"Just a hunk of cornbread!" protested the snubbiest-nosed youngster.

7

"Not a big hunk, neither," muttered the in-between.

"Shut up!" hissed their elder, turning dull crimson.

"We're through eating," said Cap. "Those sourdough biscuits and spuds mangled with eggs will taste a lot better now than when they're cold."

The smallest boy tugged at his brother's elbow. "Aw, Davy! Please—"

Julie started filling hastily wiped plates. "Sit down," she invited. "Would you like coffee or milk or both? The milk'll go sour before night if it's not used up."

"Real milk?" The smallest snub-nose twitched. "Not evaporated?"

"It came from Miss Oliver's cows. You must know her."

"Heard of her," granted the biggest boy. "She saved up her pay from school-teachin' in Kansas so she's got some cash which most of us don't." He amended quickly, "Anyways, not much. I sure would like some coffee, ma'am, and milk in it, thank you kindly."

Only when he hunkered down did the others sit, too, crossing their legs, and requesting milk *and* coffee, chorusing "Please, ma'am" at their elder's frown. "I'm Dave Collins," he said. "Jon's next to me. Jerry's our runt."

Jerry mumbled through a mouthful of biscuit, "Mama named us out of the Bible. David and Jonathan sound good, but Jeremiah! Sufferin' horntoads!"

"Folks wouldn't know if you didn't tell them," Dave said between blissful munches.

LeMoyne had dined last night on a jackrabbit he'd caught, and thriftily buried some bones. Now, without protest, he let the new dog exhume his pantry and settle down to chew. In fact, he seemed to watch his visitor feast with the pride of a good host, behavior that proved the coyote-colored beast was female. LeMoyne, though he'd wag his tail amiably until attacked, soundly thrashed any male dog who challenged him, but as Shan said, he was "a plumb fool for the ladies." The scroungiest of them could, with impunity, take a bone right out of his mouth and snarl at him or even bite without retaliation.

From the way the boys demolished the crew's prospective

lunch, those breakfast chunks of cornbread had been mighty small. Julie filled a pan with dried fruit. It quickly went the way of the potatoes and biscuits.

To be sociable and encourage their guests to eat their fill, the windmillers each had another cup of coffee and a few chewy wedges of dried peach and apple. At last, Dave gave a replete sigh. "Haven't had anything so good since . . . since— well, for a long time."

"Since Mama died," put in Jerry. He snuffled and rubbed his face against his peculiar spotted garment.

"Huh!" said Jon. "We didn't have any eggs or milk since we left Colorado!" Both brothers scowled at him. He added swiftly, "Mama sure made good wild-plum pie—when we could find any plums. And she flavored up prairie chickens and jackrabbits real good with wild onions."

"Hate to hear you've lost your mother, boys." Cap filled their cups again. "When did that happen?"

"Right after Christmas," Dave muttered. He ducked his head but Julie saw a tear roll down his cheek. Anticipating the next question, he smeared a sleeve across his eyes and looked up defiantly. "Our dad got hurt so bad he died while he was working in a mine last spring. Timbers caved in on him. We were trying to save up so we could get a farm but paying the doctor and burying Dad and buying a team and mules and a plow and such took just about all the money."

"So you came to No Man's Land," said Cap.

Dave nodded. He would make a handsome man when the flesh filled in around his bones but for now he was gangling and big-eared. At least his voice stayed on a deep, pleasant level. "Mama knew there was plenty of land down here even if we can't homestead proper till the government decides what state to tack the panhandle onto. We've got a dugout a couple of miles over there." He nodded toward the west.

Three boys living in a hole dug out of the side of a slope? "Don't you have kinfolks somewhere?" Julie asked, at the same time wondering if *she* did. What would have happened to her if someone other than Cap had rescued her from the cholera wagon?

"Dad ran off 'cause his dad, who was a widower, used to

get drunk and beat him up," Dave said. "His sister and bigger brothers run off before that. No one ever heard of 'em again. Mama's father and brothers got killed in the war. Her mother married a mean old farmer who—well, Mama was scared of him. She and Dad met at a dance and ran off that very night to get married." The boy shook his head. "We don't know if our grandparents are living or dead back in Missouri, but we don't intend to find out!"

"Can't blame you." Cap was himself a runaway from a stepfather who'd lashed him hard as he did the horses. "But mightn't it be better to throw in with someone like Miss Oliver, the teacher lady, who needs some help at her place?"

"It's *her* place." Dave's long jaw thrust out. "We'd be lettin' our folks down, 'specially Mama, if we don't make a go of our farm." His blue eyes met Cap's. "We can't do that without water."

Jon nodded. "We got here in time to break sod and plant corn last year." He spoke around a mouthful of peach. "But every day that ornery old wind blew hot and hard out of the southeast. Blasted the crop like you'd set a torch to it. The drought finished what was left."

"If we could have watered the corn, we'd have had plenty to eat and feed our stock and some to sell," Dave mourned. "Only crop we had was buffalo bones and bones from the cattle that froze in the 'eighty-six blizzard. We got about ten dollars a wagonload for 'em in Liberal. That's all that got us by, along with jackrabbits, prairie chickens, and wild plums."

"And our cow, old Bessie, who went and died," Jerry lamented.

Shan raised a bleached eyebrow. "Didn't the government ship in salt pork and beans and stuff?"

"Yeah, but Mama wouldn't take it," Dave said. "She used to laugh and say, 'Lord, you take care of the poor folks and us rich devils will look after ourselves.' "

"She must've been quite a lady," Shan admired.

Dave gulped and nodded. "You bet she was, mister. When our cow died, 'stead of carryin' on, she tanned the hide and made us these coats."

He regarded his pridefully. It was clear that no other coat

he might have in his life, however expensive and tailored, would be as valued. "We punched holes in the hide with nails so Mama could sew up our coats with sinew," Jon said.

"You and your mama did a mighty fine job," complimented Cap. He rubbed his chin. "Are you close to the creek or river?"

"Colonel Chandless runs his cattle along the creek *and* river," Dave said bitterly. "That's why we had to settle three miles from running water. Exceptin' what little rain goes into the barrels and cistern, we haul water from the creek. We can't water crops that way."

"So you don't have a well?"

The boy's fair head lifted proudly. "We do now! We were digging it out by hand. Got to thirty feet and still no sign of water—"

"But then Trace came along!" Jerry's eyes grew worshipful. "He's got a steam engine! Only took him and Cibolo a couple of weeks to drill down three hundred feet."

"They put in a casing," said Jon and looked hopefully at Cap. "Now all we need is a tower and windmill. We could maybe build the tower—"

Cap shook his head. "That's a real tricky thing, son, 'specially digging holes for the anchor posts. They have to be plumb level or the posts won't come together right at the top."

Dave's color heightened as he answered the question no one had asked. "Trace says we can pay him out of our crops, a little each year."

"He says it's like putting money in the bank," Jerry beamed. "This makes him kind of save up, you see—"

"Jerry," growled Dave, reddening more. "Trace just said that to make us feel better." His tone to Cap was man-to-man business with no hint of pleading. "We'd like to make the same deal with you, mister. Till you and Trace are paid off, we won't use any crop money outside of what we just got to spend."

"I won't take that deal," Cap said.

Julie caught in her breath. "Oh, Cap!" she began.

"Look, Captain," urged Shan, "don't you reckon we can do this?"

"We'll put up a windmill." Cap's face and voice forbade argument. "But you've got to promise to get yourselves shoes before winter, new overalls, and whatever else you need, includin' a good milk cow."

Dave was now beet red. "Mama wouldn't want us beholden."

"Sure, laddie," put in Shan, "she'd want you to eat and not get your toes frostbit."

"Of course she would!" Julie scratched the coyote dog behind her ears and scraped out the skillet for her. She smiled coaxingly at Dave. "Why don't we shake hands on it? You pay us whatever you can out of your crops, but get what you need first."

Dave gazed at Cap, who nodded. "That's our deal, son." He put out his hand.

Jon pushed his brother. "Shake!" he hissed.

Taking a deep breath, Dave thrust his hand into Cap's and clasped it vigorously before shaking with Shan and Julie. Jon and Jerry, solemn but eager, did the same. The dogs wagged their tails. Sunny gave a yip of approval.

"Lucky we haven't unloaded the parts yet," said Cap. "Soon as we break camp and hitch up the team, we'll go set your mill up."

Dave glanced at the capped well and said reluctantly, "Maybe you better do Chandless's first."

"We're putting up a bunch of mills for him," Cap shrugged. "Like you say, his cows are spread out along the water. They're not thirsty."

"But the mill—"

"It's mine," said Cap. "Chandless's other mills are coming in by rail. He can easy order another to make up for this one."

In half an hour, the wagon creaked westward. LeMoyne and Sunny raced through the short grass. Julie walked ahead with Jon and Dave while Jerry rode between Cap and Shan.

The grassland stretched out of sight in all directions, broken only by flowering stalks of soaptree yucca and a distant fringe of trees that marked the winding of a creek. Cattle were drinking there, and grazing on either side.

This was such a vast expanse that you'd think there'd be room for settlers. Land wouldn't do them any good, though, if they didn't have water. Julie gave silent thanks that the unknown Trace had drilled a well for these boys. He must have a good heart. What was he like?

Two

The first thing Cap did when starting work at a new location was unharness Columbine and Absalom, rub them down, grain them, and turn them loose to graze. The second thing was to spread out a tarp and arrange his tools on it.

"If you just drop your wrenches and things where you've used them, they get lost in a hurry," he told the Collins boys. "Saves trouble and aggravation in the long run just to spend that extra few seconds to put a tool back on the tarp."

It had taken less than an hour to reach the Collins place in a gentle valley. Except for freshly plowed land and a field of sprouting corn, there was little to make it visible against the broad sweep of prairie. Two scrawny mules foraged on the far end of the slope into which a shelter had been delved. A stovepipe sprouted from the faintly greening turf which, Julie knew from having been in other dugouts, must be supported by pole rafters made from cottonwood or longer-lasting wood hauled in from somewhere else.

Mud-chinked logs closed in the front of the dugout except for a window covered with an oiled hide that would let in a little light, and a door made of poles nailed together with ax-hewn slabs at top and bottom and running crisscross.

Dried chips, yucca stalks, and other weeds were heaped to

14

one side of the door. On the other, a scarred enamel washbasin and water bucket sat on a crate. The towel fluttering from a nail was the color of the trampled soil. An upended galvanized tub leaned against the wall next to a pitchfork, shovel, and hoe. A battered wagon hunched between the dwelling and another, shallower dugout that was obviously a winter refuge for the mules and departed cow, which had logs stacked between uprights on either side to make a small pen. A heap of bones gleamed dully from one side of the pen. A sod-breaking plow was tilted against the other wall to protect it as much as possible from the weather.

It spoke well for the widow Collins and her boys that they had tried to shield their animals from the weather and were protecting their implements as much as possible. The endgate of the wagon hung down to give access to two spigoted barrels that, from the faded lettering on them, had once held vinegar and molasses. One barrel drained into another that had been cut in half to make a watering trough for the mules. The missing half was probably inside, serving as a table. Wood was too precious and scarce for homesteaders to burn.

Three saplings planted with deep, wide wells around them showed no sign of budding. Following Julie's glance, Dave said, "Mama loved trees. We dug out these little cottonwood saplings for her and gave them all the rinse water from washing clothes and dishes, but it wasn't enough. At least Mama never knew they'd died." The boy gulped and his voice wavered. "When her fever got high, she'd talk about how pretty the trees would be and how they'd give us shade and something green to look at."

"Yeah, they're goners," said Jon. "But look at the wheat!"

Wheat, which must have been planted the autumn before, thrust hopeful green stalks from one field adjoining several acres of freshly plowed and planted earth.

"When we planted corn last spring," Dave said, "the sod was so tough and full of roots the mules couldn't hardly pull a plow through it, but we hacked out enough to poke seed corn between the clods. The grass roots pretty well rotted since then and plowing was a lot easier this year. We worked in lots of mule manure. Planted a patch of potatoes last month. With a

15

windmill, we ought to get good crops even if this is another dry summer."

"You don't have your fields fenced," Cap said.

"Can't afford it, sir."

"Can't afford not to, son." Cap used that word so often that Julie felt a pang.

Did her beloved foster father miss having a son, a child of his flesh? Had taking her to raise in some degree kept him from having a real family? It felt real to her—she, Cap, Shan, and LeMoyne—but after all, she wouldn't know the difference. Cap hoisted down the crate with the blades before he turned to Dave.

"No use planting and watering for Chandless's cows. I'm surprised they haven't already been at your wheat."

"We'll keep watch and run 'em off," Jon suggested.

"Going to do that all summer? Anyhow, if it gets dry and they're hungry enough, the three of you, even with your dog, won't be able to keep all of them out of your crops."

Dave's thin shoulders drooped. "Then we won't be able to pay you or Trace, either. I guess, sir, you don't want to put up a mill for us. Sure can't blame you."

"We'll put up your mill." Cap handed Julie the still-warm pot of beans which she placed near the fire Shan was starting. She fetched the coffeepot and started digging the trench for keeping perishables cool. Knowing Cap, she was sure he'd find a way to help the Collins boys.

"I want to protect my investment," he told them, all the while unloading parts. "I'll lend you the money to get enough posts and barbed wire to fence your fields."

"We could cut posts about ten miles from here where the cedar starts," volunteered Jon, looking eagerly at his brother.

"By the time you did that and strung your fence, the cows would most likely have cleaned you out, lads," put in Shan. "The captain's right. You need to get that fence up poco pronto." Approvingly, Shan added chunks of old, hard-packed manure that he'd spaded up. "Must have been sheep here once. They pack their droppings hard with their hoofs. Burns hotter and better than cow chips."

"Yeah," said Cap. "I've heard that during the Civil War, the

Baca brothers from New Mexico drove thirty thousand sheep onto the range around where Kenton, the cowboys' whoop-up town, is now. They lost animals to wolves and Indians but did real well till a gang of forty or fifty outlaws built a stone fortress over by Black Mesa—that's the long, flat-topped dark mass you can see on the northwest skyline. Looks like a squished-down thundercloud. It's sixty miles long without a break in it."

"We've cut cedar over there," Dave said. "Rough country. We saw what was left of a stone fort but the storekeeper in Liberal said it was built by Kit Carson to protect the Cimarron Cutoff route of the Santa Fe Trail from Indians and those Robbers' Roost outlaws."

"Carson did build Camp Nichols," Cap explained. "It was used less than a year. Robbers' Roost, some say, was blown up by a six-inch cannon from Fort Lyon, Colorado. What happened for sure was that some Colorado state troops caught a bunch of the robbers and hung them high."

"What happened to the sheep?" asked Julie.

"About 1871, cattlemen started moving in." Cap shrugged. "The Bacas and their partner, Juan Bernal, moved their herds into the Sangre de Cristo Mountains. The story is that the cattlemen paid them twenty-one thousand dollars to leave."

Dave snorted. "Chandless's 'move-along' man, Lute Hartman, offered us fifty dollars to clear out. Mama told him no. After she died, he came back just like a buzzard. Said Chandless had upped the money to a hundred because he felt sorry for us."

"Looks like you turned him down."

"You bet! But after last year's drought and this starvin' winter, he bought out lots of folks for a mule or cow or a little cash. Most of 'em headed for the Run on the Unassigned Lands that took place a week ago."

Cap raised an eyebrow. "Why didn't you? Might have got a place near water."

"I'm not eighteen, sir. Even if I am kind of the head of the family, I don't know if we could file on a claim." Dave hesitated. "Anyway, after hearing what Trace had to say about it, I'm glad we didn't."

Trace, who had drilled these boys a well on credit that was doubtful, to say the least. "What did he say?" Julie asked.

"Said the Unassigned Lands had sure as the world been assigned to the Indians till a couple of years ago when Congress broke up some of the reservations and made Indians take individual allotments of a hundred sixty acres."

"That's for the head of a family," Cap supplied. "Single people get eighty acres, minors get forty, and if the allotment's on grazing land, the acreage doubles."

"Bet some Indians won't take allotments," Shan put in.

"If they won't choose an allotment within four years, the agent picks it for them," Cap said dryly. "The pious argument is that Indians won't become civilized—to our way of thinking—as long as they lead a tribal life on tribal land."

Shan gave a grim chuckle. "The Irish still aren't civilized to the English way of thinkin' and they've been trying for hundreds of years!"

"No wonder I haven't got anywhere with you in twenty-six, then," joked Cap.

Dave laughed but sobered quickly. "The land left over from allotments is being opened to homesteaders, like in the Run last week. Because of treaties made with the Five Civilized Tribes when they were forced to leave the East over fifty years ago, the government can't just grab their land in Indian Territory, but commissioners will push till they have to give in. Trace's mother is Choctaw and he was brought up in the Choctaw Nation. They already farm and ranch and are a sight more civilized, Trace says, than plenty of homesteaders."

"So, even when you're old enough, you wouldn't feel right to file on land you figure really belongs to the Indians," Cap summed up. "We're on what used to be Comanche and Kiowa hunting grounds but the buffalo are long gone and it's quite a lot different than claiming land the government said would belong to the tribes for good." Cap frowned. "I still wish you youngsters would think about throwing in with Miss Cora Oliver or someone who could give you a home in return for your help."

"We've got a home." Dave's tone was offended. He glanced

protectively toward the dugout. "May not be much, but it's ours. We can't just walk off from what our folks wanted the family to have. We'd be letting them down."

The boy's clear blue eyes met Cap's unwaveringly. After a moment, Cap put his hand on Dave's shoulder. "Well, then, let's get to work on your mill."

Tightness eased out of the way Dave held his body. Like a puppy, his feet and hands were large in proportion to the rest of him. "Just tell us what to do, sir."

"You can finish unloading and open up the crates. You and Jon can take turns digging one of the anchor holes. But tomorrow bright and early, I want you boys to drive to Tyrone or Beaver or Liberal and buy enough wire and posts to fence your crops."

"But—" began Dave. He saw the glint in Cap's eye, and amended, "We'll do that, Captain, and we'll pay you back, with interest, if it takes till I got a long white beard."

Everyone concerned shook hands, including a solemn Jerry. Cap began to painstakingly measure distances from the casing to the locations of the anchor holes while Shan opened the crates that held the vanes and head and the rest of them unloaded the tail, casting, and angles for the tower which were bundled up in fours.

The iron block with the tackle or pulley for lifting the tower and heavy parts stayed on the wagon but picks and shovels were leaned against it.

"How does a windmill work, Captain?" asked Jerry, squatting beside Cap who was marking the last anchor hole.

"Have you seen a water mill?"

"Sure. We took our grain to one back in Missouri to get it ground into flour. It was fun to watch the water turn the big wheel."

"Well, son, the wind is like a big river, and the wheel of the windmill catches the power of the wind and sends it to the head of the windmill which changes the power into an up-and-down motion that runs what we call the sucker rod. The sucker rod, going up and down, drives the pumping cylinder which is underground at the level of the water."

"Why does the tower have to be so high?" asked Dave. "Folks who have mills are always grumping about having to climb up to oil them."

"Like I said, the wind's like a river. There's a strong, steady central current down the middle but at the edges you get whirlpools and turbulence. The wheel of a mill needs to be higher than houses, barns, trees, and anything that causes rough winds."

"Besides," Shan added, "the platform needs to set high enough to pull the sucker rod for repairs. That's why most towers are at least thirty feet high."

"It must have taken a real smart man to figure all that out," Jon marveled.

"Lots of men worked on the invention through the ages." Cap loved history. The little house he rented on the outskirts of Amarillo had more books in it than anything else. They were, of course, seldom there for more than a week between jobs. "The Persians may have made the first windmills well over a thousand years ago. The Crusaders brought the idea home with them around the year 1100, and pretty soon there were windmills all over Europe. Most of them had towers of stone or wood like those you see in pictures of Holland."

"Wouldn't think you'd have to pump water in Holland!" Dave said.

"They didn't. Mostly, the mills ground grain. It was a glad thing for women when they didn't have to grind their flour by hand. It took several hours to make enough for the day. In the same time, the mill ground enough to last for months."

"It saves womenfolk a sight of work," allowed Shan. "But there still isn't anything as tasty-tender as tortillas made from cornmeal fresh-ground in a metate."

"Sure!" hooted Cap. "You'd keep a poor woman grinding for hours to make your tortillas a little better!"

"Indeed, and I would not!" retorted Shan. "Still, what I said is true, and you know it, Captain."

Arguments over trifles like this tended to keep the two from blowing up over important matters, but the Collins boys looked scared. Julie poured two cups of robust coffee, brimmed them with milk, and handed them to Cap and Shan.

"Drink up before we start to work," she ordered. "Dave, Jon, Jerry, would you like coffee, milk, or milk with coffee?" The boys all chose the mixture as did Julie. A morning cup of Cap's brew was all her nerves would stand. LeMoyne followed Sunny as she showed him the bone pile and other interesting spots. Columbine and Absalom, who didn't have to be hobbled since they never wandered far, ambled in search of anything thornless and green.

Cap put down his enameled cup with a contented sigh at the coffee's vigor, shed his sheepskin jacket, put on his work gloves, tossed Dave an extra pair, and took up a pickax. "We've got a couple of other rules, boys," he told the Collins youngsters. "Never leave a pick or shovel stuck handle-up in the ground. Someone can fall off the tower and gut themselves or get hurt real bad."

Jerry's eyes widened. "But there isn't any tower yet, Captain!"

"There will be. Easiest to form one habit than remember when you need to change it. *Always* leave long-handled things resting flat on the ground by the tool tarp. Other rule is when anything heavy gets dropped from the tower, yell 'Headache!' to warn people below."

They all followed Cap to the well, Dave with the third pick, Julie and Jon with shovels. Cap let Julie do most things she felt like trying but he drew the line at her wielding the heavy pick on dense sod. "You can shovel all you want once the roots are chopped out," he'd admonished when she got strong enough to think she could swing the pick, "but you're a woman and I won't have you strainin' your insides."

"How about *your* insides?"

Shan chortled as Cap floundered for words. "What he means, colleen, is that women are made mysterious and wonderful so they can have babies. The captain doesn't want you messin' up those special parts."

After that, Julie hadn't argued, though she was privately sure she could chop at the sod without blighting her chances of motherhood. She didn't think she wanted babies, anyway, or marriage, either, unless it was to another windmiller. She

21

glanced at the dark cavern where the boys' mother had died and repressed a shudder.

"If there were an old tower or something high enough to fasten the other end of our cable to, we could put the tower together on the ground and lift it into place with our block and tackle," explained Cap. "As it is, we'll build the tower from the ground up. Either way, these anchor holes have to be just right. We'll make 'em five feet deep, and since we have to get down in them to dig, they'll be about two feet by four. When you get down to your shoulder, Dave, let Shan or me finish. The bottom has to be exactly level with the other holes."

"Don't I get to do something?" Jerry pleaded.

"When we start on the tower, you can carry tools back and forth," said Cap.

The smallest boy's lips trembled. Shan dropped a bracing hand on his shoulder. "You'd help a lot by keeping the fire fed, laddie. And maybe you could spade up some more of that good, pounded-hard sheep dung and gather soapweed stalks and such."

"Just don't go so far you can't see the stovepipe," Dave warned. "You'd still be lost if Sunny hadn't found you the day you were supposed to be picking wild plums and got interested in arrowheads instead."

"You act like I'm a baby!"

"Don't act like one and I won't." Dave sent his brother a stern look and swung down the pick.

Jerry gave an offended sniff, but he did add chips to the fire, empty the fuel bucket, and start digging up slabs of the sheepmen's legacy. As soon as Cap broke up the matted turf of her anchor hole, Julie moved in with a shovel.

There were no rocks in this soil but it was still hard work. Within ten minutes, all the diggers shed their jackets and pulled their hat brims lower against the climbing sun. What had been strenuous labor while the hole was shallow grew increasingly difficult since each spadeful had to be tossed out of the excavation.

"Don't try to keep the hole small, Dave," Cap advised. "You need room to work. Two feet by four is about right."

Julie was glad to let Jon spell her while she got a drink but she finished the bottom of the hole that had to be at exactly the same level as the others. Cap ensured this with his steel measure and practiced eye.

"Looks good," he allowed, after earth was taken here, added there, and tamped down hard. "Now for the anchor posts."

A one-foot length of steel was bolted horizontally to the bottom of each anchor post. Julie settled hers in the center of the hole and then positioned the first section of her quarter of the tower, and the girt connecting it to Shan's, leaving the nuts and bolts loose enough to permit adjustment.

Squinting at Dave's work, Cap said, "All right, son, we're at the most important part of building a tower. We've got to be absolutely sure the legs are perfectly square and the exact same distance from the well and from each other. Just a smidge off will make it mighty near impossible to match up the bolt holes at the apex. Even if they can be forced, the tower won't be as strong or last as long. Here, Jon, will you hold the end of the tape right here at the center of the well casing while I check the legs?"

Cap's and Shan's legs were precisely right. Julie's had to be moved half an inch closer and Dave's set back a fraction. The boy whistled. "Sufferin' cats, sir! I bet not even a doctor who's carvin' into someone's innards is this careful!"

"Well, I sure hope he will be if he ever carves into mine." Cap chuckled as he rolled up the tape and got his straightedge and level. He placed the straightedge across the horizontal girts, one by one, and peered intently at the bubbles in the instrument to make sure the girts were indeed level. One post had to be lowered a tad, another raised.

"Now," said Cap, producing the tape measure, "we check all the distances again. Takes a few minutes now, but it's worth it."

After a few minute adjustments, he nodded in satisfaction. "Square as square, folks. Let's tighten the nuts and bolts and fill in the holes." He handed Dave a steel bar. "Use this pretty often to tamp the earth down good and solid. Then we'll eat before we tackle the rest."

The beans in the big blue kettle were done enough to chew,

though they'd improve with the afternoon's simmering. Since the boys had devoured the biscuits meant for noon, Julie hastily stirred up cornbread and spread it thin in the greased Dutch oven for faster baking. Canned peaches topped off the meal. The boys consumed them so avidly that Julie opened another can, and blessed the fact that there was no need to be sparing; Cap always carried more provisions than they expected to use.

Cap declared Jon and Jerry "camp bosses," which meant they were in charge of doing dishes and providing fuel. Jerry, beaming with importance, handed tools to Cap and Julie as they stood on a stout plank laid across the girts as close to the north tower legs as possible.

Jon, grumbling because he wanted to take Dave's place on the southerly plank, supplied tools to his brother and Shan. Julie and Dave used ropes to hoist the next sections of corner posts and hold them steady with rope and hands while Cap and Shan bolted them into place. Next they secured the horizontal and diagonal girts.

"We'll be too high from now on for you boys to reach us," Cap told Jon and Jerry. "We don't want to drop any tools on your heads so you better go make sure we've got plenty of fuel."

Two freckled faces fell. Shan leaned toward them confidentially. "Lads, long before this old tower falls down, you'll be tired of climbing up it to oil the head and make repairs."

"*I* won't get tired of it." Jerry's eyes gleamed as he stared at the ladder.

"You won't either of you climb up without my say-so," Dave said.

"Huh!" snorted Jon. "You're not the boss of me, Dave Collins!"

"I am as long as I can lick you," Dave said equably. It seemed to be a battle he had waged before. "I promised Mama to take care of you and I will if I have to pound you into the dirt."

Jon gave him a furious scowl but yanked Jerry's shoulder. "Come on, squirt! I'll have a windmill outfit when I grow up and you can work for me—but not ol' Dave!"

The crew used the ladder built onto one of the tower legs to climb to the next level, carefully position the planks, and build the next section. "Got to get the nuts as tight as you can," Cap told Dave, giving one an extra tug with a special long-handled wrench. "Most tower problems come from the nuts loosening up and falling out. It's smart to check them every few weeks and tighten any that need it."

As the tower narrowed, Cap and Shan worked alone, which gave Julie time to make biscuits in one Dutch oven, and what they called "Dutch oven cobbler" in another from a mixture of stewed dry apricots and peaches with a biscuit dough crust. Dusk was gathering when the legs of the tower were bolted together at the top.

Knowing what was needed next, Julie climbed the tower with an iron weight tied to a rope. Cap hung this from the center of the joined legs. They watched intently as the weight swayed back and forth a few times before hanging steady.

"Right smack above the casing, Captain!" Shan clapped his old friend's shoulder. "You've done it again."

"We did." Cap grinned.

They descended and dropped their tools on the tarp which Cap folded up and stowed in the wagon. "Tomorrow we'll put up the mill and you'll be all set," he told the Collins boys. He wrinkled his nose. "Do I smell rabbit?"

"Jon got one with his slingshot," Dave said. "I fried it with spuds and onions." All the Collins boys beamed their pride at adding something to the meal.

"Smells scrumptious," said Shan.

They washed off the grit and sweat of the day and settled around the glow of the fire. Its warmth felt good in the rapid cooling after sundown. Jerry started to reach but Dave caught his hand as Cap bowed his head. "Thank you, Lord, for helping us build a strong tower. Guide us as we put up the mill and bless its work of pumping water for these boys, their animals, and fields." And then he added his favorite words from the Book of Common Prayer: " 'O ye Winds of God, bless ye the Lord: praise him and magnify him forever.' "

The Collins boys, as if remembering something they had almost forgotten, chorused "Amen" with the others. Lids came off Dutch ovens, kettle, and skillet. Sunny and LeMoyne lay down, watching for scraps.

Everything tasted wonderful, the more because of the boys' keen enjoyment. "First cobbler we've had since—" Jon broke off.

"Since Mama died," finished Jerry. "Wouldn't she be tickled to see us puttin' away such a dandy feed?"

"You sound like we're mules," chided Dave. "Hey, Jerry! Don't reach for more of that cobbler! You've already had two helpings."

"Finish it," urged Julie. "It tastes better tonight than it will tomorrow."

She divided the remaining crust and fruit between the boys, who polished their plates to the last crumb. They volunteered to do the dishes. Julie let them but she personally scoured out the coffeepot.

The boys lingered by the fire, clearly in no hurry to go to their dugout. "Our folks would sure be happy to know we've got a windmill," Dave said. "We'll pay you back every dime with interest."

"We're not losing sleep over it," Cap shrugged. He stretched and yawned. "And speaking of sleep—"

"Why don't we sleep outside, too, Davy?" wheedled Jerry. "It's not *real* cold."

"The air's a lot sweeter," said Jon.

Dave glanced at the windmillers. "You folks don't mind?"

"It's your place," laughed Cap. "But you better get to sleep before Shan starts snoring or you'll think there's a train coming through."

"How would you be knowing that, Captain?" demanded Shan. "I can't remember a night when your snoring didn't put me to sleep like a mother's lullaby—or a dadburned sawmill!"

Julie, following Cap's and Shan's example, unrolled her bedding on top of a tarp with the head facing away from the wind. Then she tucked the end of a second tarp beneath the foot of the bedroll and burrowed snugly, pulling the tarp over her covers and head. She was asleep so quickly and soundly that she never knew who snored first, or if anybody did.

Three

The boys devoured eggs, ham, gravy, fried potatoes, and biscuits next morning as if they'd been starved for a week. Somewhat to her surprise, Julie found herself enjoying them. Because she was a windmiller, they treated her with a respect real kid brothers would have lacked, and did the dishes before gathering to watch Cap and Shan attach the vane to the head.

"Want to help us manhandle this into place, Dave?" Cap invited. "Julie, maybe Jon and Jerry will help you bring over the wheel sections."

The wheel fitted with sheet-metal blades was a small one, eight feet in diameter, but it would have to be lifted in quarters with ropes, so Julie brought those, too, and got one section ready to haul aloft. When the head and vane were bolted to the apex of the joined tower legs, Cap sent Dave down.

"The captain says it's windy enough that I'd better pull on one end of the wheel part while he's hauling it up," Dave said.

"That's so the blades won't get caught in the wind and bang against the tower," Julie said. "All right, you hang on down here. I'll take the other end of the rope up to Cap."

It was considerably more windy at the top of the tower than on the ground. Even though she stood on the wooden platform built for oiling and repairing the mill, Julie held on to the tower.

"Get down before you blow away, honey!" Cap shouted as he leaned down to take the rope from her. "Shan and I can do this."

She climbed down, jacket and braid whipping in the wind. The vane above, its notched edges looking like the feathered part of an arrow, turned as if eager for the wheel to be in place so it would be part of a working mill.

While Cap hoisted the section, Dave held it in line with another rope till Shan grabbed it and wrapped a leg over one end till Cap could untie the rope and take the other. They wrestled it into place, connecting it with the head that would capture the energy of the wind-driven blades and change it into the up-and-down motion of the sucker rod that powered the pump.

Cap was ready to pull up the last section when he paused and shielded his eyes. Julie, at the same instant, caught the sound of hoofs, and turned.

In the glare of the mounting sun, horsemen rode at the gallop. Five—six—seven. This was not the style of cowboys at work and there were no cattle in sight. Alarm ran through Julie. She wished Shan and Cap were on the ground, not thirty feet up, outlined starkly against the sky.

Instead of coming down, Cap began to raise the quarter wheel. "Hold 'er below, son!" he called to Dave. "Quite a breeze we're having!"

A volley of shots thundered. The wheel section veered crazily above Dave's head, then crashed to the ground as the bullet-frayed rope gave way. Rifles and pistols still in hand, the strangers reined in their horses which seemed to be spooked by the firing, an indication that they weren't used to it.

Their riders looked eager to shoot again, though. They reminded Julie of a pack of hounds scenting prey. Roving, excited stares ranged in disappointment over the boys and woman, dismissed them, and fixed on the men poised on the tower.

A sunburned, bulky-shouldered man with a ropy ginger

mustache raked an appraising glance over Julie before he sent his horse forward a few lengths. "Is one of you Cap McCloud?"

"I am." Cap's tone was icy with controlled anger. "Do you just come shooting at folks you don't know?"

"I'm Lute Hartman, Colonel Jess Chandless's foreman. I don't have to know the name of anyone who tries to put up a windmill on his land."

"It's not his land!" Dave's thin, big-boned face was white. He knotted his fists. "He's hogged the water but he can't claim everything!"

Hartman showed tobacco-stained teeth. "Reckon he can and does, sonny. Some folks around Beaver have set up what they call the Territory of Cimarrón and elected some officials but it don't amount to a hill of beans since Congress won't recognize them. The only law in No Man's Land is this." He raised his rifle a little and squinted up at Cap. "How come you're puttin' up a squatter's windmill instead of the JC's like you're hired to do?"

"The Collins are no more squatters than your boss, Hartman. He's just squatted on a sight more land is all."

Hartman laughed. "He pays the wages of eighteen men. I just see two of you besides these kids and a tomboy girl."

"That's all it takes to put up windmills."

"Not on land Colonel Chandless claims."

"These boys have to have water or their crops won't make it."

"That's the whole idea," grinned Hartman. "Long as squatters don't have windmills, the boss is willin' to let 'em starve out. He'll even buy their two-bit claims. But there won't be any windmills."

Cap shrugged. Silhouetted against the sky, he only reached Shan's chin. To Julie he had always seemed the tallest man in the world but her heart contracted now for he looked vulnerable, almost as if he were trapped in the shining web of the tower. "I put up a mill a few days ago, Hartman. I'm putting this one up, too."

The foreman shook his head. "I'm giving you a chance to get down from there, take the tower apart, and get yourself over to set up those mills for Chandless. He'll pay cash, remember?"

"I've got along without his money so far. Guess I can make it a little longer."

"You're throwing up a deal for a dozen mills?"

"Oh, I'll put 'em up. Soon as I finish here." Cap peered down at the fallen quarter wheel. "Don't look like you've bunged it up too bad."

"I can fix that."

Sensing the foreman's intent, Julie sprang forward and shielded the blades.

Hartman swore and raised his rifle. "Get down from there! Now!"

Cap didn't move. Julie flung herself forward as the rifle barked, trying to knock it aside. Hartman's horse reared. She went down. The horse's plunging hoofs missed her by inches.

"Fool girl!" yelled Hartman.

Scrambling up, she scarcely heard him. On the tower, Cap swayed, reached for a girt, and fell.

The fall seemed to last forever. So did the scream that left her throat raw. She reached Cap in the same moment as Shan, who had slid down the leg as was his fashion when in a hurry. Cap's neck was twisted at an angle. There seemed to be nothing left of the back of his head but blood and awful things that filled her hands when she tried to lift him.

His eyelids fluttered when she called his name. He looked at her and smiled, tried to lift his hand. It fell on LeMoyne's muzzle. The bewildered dog whined and licked his master's limp fingers. A shudder wracked Cap. Then he was still. So still . . .

"I didn't go to do that!" Hartman's voice cracked. "I fired at the damned wheel! It—it ricocheted—"

Shan, breathing hard, tears in his eyes, muttered, "Oh God, Captain—" Giving himself a shake, he put an arm around Julie and tried to lift her up. "Come away, colleen. This is no sight for you."

She repulsed him, cradling Cap in her arms, heedless of the blood and ooze of mangled bone and brains, rocking him as she would a child.

"Ma'am," said one of the shamed, shocked cowboys. "Ma'am, we're sorry."

"It ricocheted," said Hartman again. "Goddamn bullet ricocheted."

"You fired it." Julie looked up at him over Cap's body. She longed to kill the man with her own hands. LeMoyne, sensing her feelings, bared his teeth at Hartman and growled deep in his throat.

"He should of come down like I told him." Hartman sounded aggrieved.

What would Cap want? What could she do for him? How could she give his death a meaning, make it something besides an accident? Her gaze fell on the last wheel section.

She lowered Cap gently and covered him as much possible with her jacket. Rising, fighting dizziness, she said in a tone she didn't recognize, "Shan, let's put up the mill."

Hartman reined in front of her. "Now, ma'am, you can't do that!"

"Are you going to shoot me?"

Contrition faded from Hartman's eyes. "You know we can't do that, young lady, but we can drag the tower down later and smash up the mill."

Dave had run to the dugout when he saw Cap was dead, and returned in time to hear the foreman's threat. Now he pulled a revolver from under his spotted coat and aimed it at Hartman. "Clear out of here, mister! If you come back tryin' to wreck our mill, I'll shoot you faster than I would a chicken hawk."

"Big talk for a kid with peach fuzz on his face."

The sound of the shot sent the nervous horses skittering.

"You whelp!" Hartman grated. "You need a good hiding!"

"You won't be the one to give it to him." Shan, by the wagon, leveled his shotgun. "Dust out of here, Hartman, or it won't be no accident when I shoot you."

"Aw, Lute, let's go," urged a dark young cowboy. "These folks are all upset."

"Yeah," muttered another. "If there's more shootin', the lady and kids could hurt."

"If squatters get away with puttin' up one mill," growled

Hartman, "there'll pretty quick be another and another till there'll be no stoppin' it."

The black-haired rider turned his horse away. "You may get paid enough to fight women and kids, Lute, but I don't."

When he saw his men were leaving, Hartman blazed a wrathful look from Shan to Dave and Julie. "I'm warnin' you! Don't set up that mill!"

He swung his big red roan after his men.

With the threat of him gone, strength drained from Julie. She sank down by Cap, gathered him to her, and wept.

It was hard to put Cap into the earth when Julie couldn't yet believe that he was really dead, but it was necessary to keep scavengers from flocking to him. "We buried Mama by that thicket of wild plums yonder," said Dave. "Will that be all right?"

Julie nodded and fought to control her voice. "I'm glad Cap won't—won't be alone."

It seemed fitting to bury Cap in his work clothes, wrapped in his favorite quilt. Julie, Shan, Dave, and Jon carried him to the grave Shan and Dave had dug, on a gentle slope by the flowering plum thicket that kept the boys' mother company. Flowers bloomed before the bushes leafed out, but fresh new leaves were starting to green the branches. Mrs. Collins's grave was marked by a slab of white limestone that her sons must have brought from a distance. On it was carved:

MOTHER
LOUELLA COLLINS
1855–1889

Thirty-four years. She had died before seeing her sons grown-up, died before seeing her dream for them come true.

Cap's grave was as deep as the anchor-post hole for a big windmill, six feet, but it was longer and a little wider. Shan and Dave got down in it to ease the body to rest. Julie soothed LeMoyne who whimpered and crouched at the edge of the grave.

Cap wouldn't have wanted living creatures deprived of the fruit that would follow the flowers, so Julie broke off only a few small branches to strew over the quilted form.

Cap! This isn't true!

Blind with tears, she knelt and scattered a handful of sod. Dave and Shan filled in the grave and mounded it, tamping it down to discourage curious beasts. *Just as you tamp around an anchor post,* Julie thought.

They stood with their hats off while Shan paid a halting tribute to the man who had saved his life, the man he had followed for twenty-four years. "The captain dug his own anchor holes and dug 'em level. He put up good mills on good towers, hundreds of 'em, that'll pump water many years to come for the good God's critters, humans and animals." Shan choked up and gulped before he could go on. "Captain Bob was the best officer I ever had and the best man I ever knew. God bless him forever."

Julie couldn't talk about what Cap had been to her without ruining herself for the task she had vowed to complete that day. She faced the sun, the breeze that rippled her hair. " 'O ye Winds of God, bless ye the Lord: praise Him, and magnify Him forever.' " In half prayer, half exhortation, she turned toward the unfinished windmill. "Help us get this mill working just like Cap would have done!"

She started for the tower. The others followed her. LeMoyne lay on the mounded sod. Sunny, who had watched from a little way off, trotted up now, touched noses with her friend, and curled up beside him.

Several blades were dented by their fall and two were pierced by bullet holes, but Shan pronounced the section usable. It was important to Julie, a kind of tribute to Cap, to help mount this last part of the mill, so Dave held the rope below while Shan pulled the section up. Julie untied the rope. Together, they got the unwieldy part securely mounted, completing the wheel. Next, they climbed down and, with Dave's help, lowered the bottom length of the cypress sucker rod with the simple attached pump into the hole and screwed on four more twenty-foot rods till the pump was immersed.

Half of the last rod protruded from the casing, so one more length reached the head. Shan connected it and said proudly, "A good oiling and she's ready to work!" He gave Julie a hug. "You can just bet, colleen, that the captain knows we finished what he started."

She nodded, unable to speak. Her eyes blurred as she looked all around that high country where there seemed to be nothing but wind and sun between the earth and God. "I don't know about heaven," Cap had told her once. "What I hope the good Lord lets me do is be part of the wind and light and rain."

Julie took off her hat and closed her eyes. Shan had finished oiling the head and wheel. Hearing the first humming of blades, the first up-and-down lift of the rod, the flow of water out of the pipe into the tank—surely, it was like hearing the cry of a baby entering the world with its first breath. Cap thought it was the sweetest sound in the world, the rush of water where there had been none.

The sun caressed her face, the wind brushed her hair as might a loving hand. She could almost see Cap smiling. Then she opened her eyes to the new mound by the plum thicket. Convulsed with grief and outrage, she gripped a steel girt to keep from falling, leaned her head against it for a moment.

"Julie!" Shan caught her arm. "Are you all right?"

"I will be." She steeled herself to think of what should be done next. "Shan, after we eat, why don't you go with Dave to get the fence posts and wire? It must be about a three-day trip and the sooner you go, the sooner you'll be back."

Shan gave her weighing look. "You sure you'll be okay?"

How could she explain to him that she needed time alone, time to weep? She and the younger boys would dig post holes that afternoon but after supper, after they were asleep, she could go down to Cap's grave and give way to heartbreak without worrying anyone.

"I'll be fine," she promised.

She got out Cap's record book. Through her tears, she wrote down the dates and location and other information for this mill. The last one Cap had worked on. The first he hadn't finished.

Shan left his shotgun. "I'll feel better if you have it, Julie. Don't look for Hartman to bother us for a while but you never can tell who may ride through this lonesome country." He glanced from her to the younger Collins boys. "Don't work too hard while you just have shovels and a pry bar, kids. We'll buy a couple of post-hole diggers—they'll do fine in this soil—and get a wire-stretcher, too."

After he and Dave rumbled off in the wagon, Julie and Jon took turns driving a long iron bar into the earth, raising it with both hands and bringing it down hard. The bar had a sharp chisel edge on one end and was pointed on the other. The tighter the earth fitted around the post, the better, so the goal was to keep the hole as small as possible.

As loose earth accumulated, Jerry scooped it out with a can. When Jon or Julie tired of plunging down the bar, the other used it on the next hole while the weary one worked with the shovel. Julie had never built fence before but she had often seen it done. To hold the posts snug enough to keep the wire stretched tight, the holes had to be about two feet deep, except for those holding posts that got a lot of strain.

"We'll let Shan and Dave dig the gate and corner holes," Julie panted. "The posts have to be buried three feet deep."

"And braced, to boot," nodded Jon.

A tower's anchor post had to be deeper and wider but at least you dug one and were through. Post holes—well, Julie didn't even want to know how many it would take to protect the crops.

She welcomed the hard work, though. Wielding the bar vented her anger and grief and tears mingled with the sweat dripping from her face. Besides, she was doing something useful, something that would help these boys who worked almost as relentlessly as she did. The morning chill had long vanished and the sun beat down in a foretaste of full summer. All three diggers were grimy with dust and sweat.

"I'll be glad when Dave and Mr. Shan get back and can

help!" Jon, red-faced and breathing hard, leaned on the shovel. "Boy howdy, ma'am, you sure can bring that bar down!"

"I'm ready to have a drink from your new well and rest awhile," Julie said. She found a smile. "Please just call me Julie."

"But, ma'am, Mama told us—" Jerry floundered.

"Pretend I'm your cousin or sister," Julie suggested.

The Collinses' horses, drawn by the scent of water, had come to drink, and grazed close to the windmill as if hoping to keep an eye on this plenteous supply. Julie and the boys rolled up their sleeves and splashed their faces and hands, then cupped their hands beneath the pipe and drank.

Drawn cool and sweet from almost a hundred feet down, this water tasted nothing like the alkaline stuff in the creeks and rivers of the region. "It tastes so good!" Jerry gasped between swallows.

"Won't rust out our innards like Mama said the alkali would." Jon ducked his fair head in the tank and laved his face again. "Miss Julie—I mean *Julie*—you can just bet every time we take a drink or use water, we'll remember you folks. And we'll fetch the captain a pretty white stone like Mother's and carve his name on it."

Julie nodded, too choked up to speak. Sorrow and loss overwhelmed her but with a clear part of her mind, she knew Cap had died while making it possible for these boys to survive on the land for which their parents had sacrificed so much. She could never be reconciled to his death but at least it happened while he was doing what he loved to do.

She wanted to go on with his work and was certain that Shan would. They'd have to find another windmiller to make up the crew. One thing sure, they wouldn't set up Jess Chandless's dozen mills even if they needed the money. They didn't. Cap had tidy sums drawing interest in Amarillo and Dodge City banks.

Glancing at the boys as they walked back to their labor, Julie remembered Cora Oliver, the teacher whose mill they had erected three days ago. In spite of the droughts and disasters that had made hundreds of settlers abandon their claims to make the Run for a homestead in the Unassigned Lands, there must still be scores of people who had stayed, like Miss Oliver and the Collinses, families that needed water to survive and make a living.

We can set up their windmills—work on credit, even supply the towers and mills. When we're through fencing here, we'll locate some other folks to work for, folks who intend to stay in spite of Chandless. If enough of them stick it out, he won't have things all his own way. That will avenge Cap better than anything. It's what he'd do if he were still alive. . . .

Her mind raced as she worked. Would Shan think she was crazy? She didn't think so. Anyway, he had his own savings, and those wouldn't be affected. Of course, their customers would somehow have to get their wells dug, but apparently the outfit that had drilled the Collinses' well would do some work on credit, and the rig couldn't have got too far away.

With two more stops for drinks and rest, the three worked till sundown. Sunny spent the afternoon running back and forth between the workers and LeMoyne, who lay like a statue on Cap's grave, muzzle between his forepaws.

Julie had taken a bucket of water to him about mid-afternoon and left it near when he took no interest. Now, after putting cornbread to bake, she carried fresh water to the grave and coaxed LeMoyne, courteous but unenthusiastic, into drinking from her cupped hands.

"Poor old boy." Her eyes blurred as she scratched behind his long ears. "Do you know Cap's gone?" LeMoyne gave his tail a sad thump. She hugged him and said, "I'll be back in a little while. Maybe you'd like some cornbread?"

Another polite but forlorn thump. Sunny galloped up, touched his nose, sighed, and flopped down close to the mound as if she understood it was reserved for chief mourners. "Good girl. Maybe you can get LeMoyne up from there. At least, you're company."

Julie didn't think she could eat at first but after a few forced bites, she was ravenous. A high cold moon silvered the tower and blades of the windmill. "I'll be glad when Dave and Mr.

Shan get back." Jerry finished off the canned peaches and took a handful of dried apricots. "And I bet they'll be glad when they see how many holes we dug!"

"Still be plenty to go around," Jon said. He yawned prodigiously. "Beg pardon, Julie. Soon as we do these dishes, I'm hittin' the hay."

"Me too," said Jerry. "Julie, can we spread our bedrolls close to yours?"

"Sure. But I'm not turning in for a while. You boys pick a spot and I'll bed down beside you. Put your feet toward the wind or it'll blow down your neck."

When the dishes were done and food stored in the chuckbox, it only took the boys minutes to fetch, unroll, and get into their bedding. Possessed by a strange, protective feeling, Julie tossed a tarp over them and tucked it well under their feet. They were tough little guys but there was something vulnerable about all of them, even Dave, that made Julie think of young animals that had been weaned too soon.

Jon whistled for Sunny. She came a bit reluctantly but curled up on the tarp between their legs. Julie got the shotgun, a blanket, and a chunk of cornbread. The white flowers of the plum thicket glimmered as she neared Cap's grave. She put the shotgun down and persuaded the dog to accept a few bites of his favorite delicacy. Only a few.

"Look here, hound," she chided. "You aren't going to be one of those noble beasts who starves on his master's grave. I won't let you." Suddenly blinded, able at last to mourn in private, she sank down beside the dog and buried her face against his neck. "Oh, LeMoyne! Cap's gone, he's gone!"

LeMoyne whimpered and licked her cheek. Julie wept till her head throbbed and she was drained. It was cold but she wasn't yet ready to go back to camp. She doubled the quilt and wrapped it around her, hunching her knees against her face, close to LeMoyne as much for mutual solace as for warmth.

Cap had loved the wind. In this high, wide country, it would be with him in every mood from blasts to lullabies like the one that now whispered to Julie. She could almost hear Cap lulling her with that song she had loved from babyhood.

> *"Blacks and grays, dapples and bays,*
> *When you wake, you shall have*
> *all the pretty little ponies."*

Strained muscles relaxing, she drowsed. The clop of hoofs moved into her consciousness as part of the song, part of a comforting sense that Cap was with her, that he was still alive. Then the sound was so insistent that, accompanied by the creak of a wheels, it drummed through the haze of exhausted sleep.

LeMoyne was up, drawing in scents carried by the wind. He growled deep in his throat. That quashed Julie's thought that Shan and Dave had turned back for some reason instead of going to Tyrone.

So who was it? Hartman wouldn't drive a wagon. Hushing LeMoyne, Julie made for camp. In the dull glow from the fire, the boys were motionless, tarp-covered mounds. She dropped her quilt on the chuckbox and dropped down behind the adjacent windmill crate, resting the shotgun on it.

Moonlight shone on the barrel. She dragged an edge of the quilt over it, tented the quilt to conceal her head, and waited.

*F*our

*T*he rumbling neared. Too loud for one wagon and team, surely. The boys slumbered on. LeMoyne, roused from mourning by possible danger to his charges, made soft warnings in his chest as he guarded Julie's happenstance barricade.

Horses and two wagons materialized, shadows that assumed more substance the closer they came and the louder they sounded. "Hold it right there!" Julie called, voice husky with strain.

The drivers halted their teams. "No need to get excited," came a deep voice with a pleasant Southern lilt. "We're just well-drillers looking for Cap McCloud. From the looks of the new windmill, we've found him."

"Trace! Cibolo!" Jon had finally woke up. Skinning into his overalls, he ran barefoot toward the wagons. By standing between them, he managed to clutch a hand of each driver. "Whillikers, I'm glad to see you! Cap—" He broke off, glancing at Julie.

Feeling a little foolish, she rose from behind the crate, but she held the shotgun. Most likely the strangers were trustworthy but she was on guard after what had happened that day. While she collected herself to speak to the men, she studied them and their wagons.

Even in the pale light, she could see that the giant driving the coal-and-water wagon was dark as the shadows. The other man's wide-brimmed, light-colored hat was pulled low, but a rather bent nose had wide nostrils and the lips in a hard jaw had a surprisingly tender downward curve.

Her long braid, or something else, made him know she was a woman. He took off his hat and nodded. "Ma'am, I hope we didn't scare you."

She couldn't tell the color of his eyes but the straight eyebrows were dark, and thick hair that could have been dark red or brown fell over his broad forehead. His wagon held what must be the steam drilling rig, a contraption with a boiler and various beams, rods, pulleys, ropes, and wheels.

"Cap was killed this morning." In spite of great effort, her voice broke.

"Oh, Lordy!" The stranger tossed the lines to Jon and sprang down. "Did he fall?"

"He fell. But he was shot first."

"Shot?"

"Lute Hartman, Jess Chandless's foreman, fired at the windmill. The bullet ricocheted."

The man shook his head and bowed it. "I don't know what to tell you, ma'am. I sure am sorry. There isn't any law in No Man's Land."

"Even if there was, Hartman would probably get off. I'd have to say it was an accident." She swallowed hard but her words came thick as if through blood. "But what gave Chandless the right to try to stop us putting up a mill? Or the right to land that can't be legally claimed by anyone?"

"His right is what he can get away with." The man looked up at the wheel that was turned out of the wind. "Hartman must've been knocked back on his haunches. He left the mill up."

"We finished attaching the blades to the wheel after he was gone," said Julie.

"You three?" Dark eyebrows raised toward tumbled hair.

"No. Shan, Cap's helper, and Dave Collins and I did it. Shan and Dave went to Tyrone to buy fencing stuff."

"We're going to fence our crops so the cows won't eat 'em down to a nub," Jon put in.

"Well now, that's a great notion, but do you think Chandless will leave the fences up?"

Julie hadn't thought about that. "Do you think he'd get that mean with three orphan kids?"

"Do you think he won't?"

"He offered to buy them out," Julie admitted. "I guess he could argue they're too young to make it on their own."

With a sinking feeling, the taste of defeat sour in her mouth, she realized that neither windmill nor fence would be safe unless Chandless could be persuaded—or forced—into letting them stand. She stared at the white blur of the plum thicket and could just make out the new mound beside it. Iron resolve filled her.

"Maybe neighbors will help stand guard. Maybe someone could watch Chandless's headquarters and bring word when a bunch of cowboys seems to be heading out to do something but gather calves."

"Maybe."

"When Shan and Dave get back, we'll figure something out."

"Will Shan carry on with the windmill business?"

"He and I will. We'll need another person."

"Pardon me, ma'am, but I never heard of a woman windmiller. Are you Cap's wife?"

"He found me in a cholera wagon and raised me. I never wanted to do anything except help put up windmills."

Again the brows rose, but he smiled suddenly, and put out his hand. "Maybe we should swap names. I'm Trace Riordan. My partner's Cibolo Martin."

His hand was warm and muscular. Julie caught herself wanting to hold it longer than a greeting allowed. Then the warmth was more than that of his hand, a tingling flush like slow lightning, something she had never felt before. She jerked away almost rudely. "I'm Julie McCloud. And of course you remember Jon and Jerry."

"Sure do," chuckled Cibolo.

"If you're staying in the business," Trace said, "maybe we could throw in together—dig wells and put up the towers and mills."

"Right now we're stringing fence as well."

He shrugged. "Reckon we've done some of that, huh, Cib?"

The giant nodded. "We've done some of most everything, it seems to me."

"I'd better tell you," warned Julie, "that I intend to put up mills on credit for folks who need them, starting with this land Chandless wants to hog. I can't think of a better way to use the money Cap saved."

"Most ladies would buy a nice house in a city and get the duds and furniture to go with it," Trace Riordan said quizzically. "Buy a carriage and fancy team and all."

"That is absolutely the last thing in the world I'd like."

She hadn't even thought of changing her life now that Cap was gone, now that she would inherit what he told her he'd put aside for the future. "Won't always be able to climb towers and do the work," he'd told her. "Maybe then we'll buy a little farm." He'd checked himself with a laugh. "Shucks, you'll be married by then. Wherever you are, I'll settle close and enjoy your young 'uns."

"I don't think I'll get married. Not unless he's another windmiller."

"Reckon that could happen. But when you fall in love, Julie girl, I reckon it won't matter much what he does."

It would matter a lot if he expected her to stay put on a farm or ranch or in a town house, but it all seemed so far off that Julie hadn't argued. Now, remembering her duties, she asked the well-drillers, "Have you had supper?"

"More or less."

"Less," corrected Cibolo. "Cold biscuits and side meat. Don't go to any fuss, ma'am, but if there's anything left over, it'd hit the spot."

"I'll heat up the cornbread and beans and there's apple cobbler. Why don't you camp here tonight? When Shan comes, we'll talk business." She realized that underneath everything, she *had* been afraid. The presence of two strong men was worth the trouble of brewing up fresh coffee. "We're digging post holes. You're more than welcome to help with that!"

"For apple cobbler," allowed Cibolo, "I can do most anything."

Jerry and Jon tagged the men and helped unhitch the teams and hobble the horses while Julie built up the fire and got the late supper going. The prospect of joining forces appealed mightily to her, especially when they were sure to have serious trouble with Chandless, especially when Trace Riordan could make her feel so different, so vibrantly alive.

That seemed disloyal on the very day of Cap's death, but Cap had taught her to be honest about her feelings. "You don't have to tell everybody how you feel," he'd advised. "But don't ever lie to your own self, honey. Sometimes you can't or shouldn't give in to your wants, but you can manage them better if you know what they are."

Trace and Cibolo polished off the cornbread and consumed most of the beans. In spite of having eaten only a few hours before, Jerry and Jon looked so wistfully at the cobbler that Julie scooped the last of it into tin plates for them. She'd make another tomorrow, maybe of dried peaches.

"Did you drill Chandless's new wells?" she asked. "We were supposed to put up mills for a dozen of them."

Trace gave her that lopsided grin that rather matched his slightly skewed nose. "Big ranchers get enough of the water out here without me helping them to more."

"That's the onliest rule we got." Cibolo had reddish brown skin, a long thin nose, tawny eyes, and tightly curling hair that must have given him his name which was Spanish for "buffalo." "We don't drill for anyone who claims more than a section of land or runs more than a hundred head of cattle."

Jon put the question Julie was thinking. "If you're not working for rich folks, do you always get paid?"

"Generally do, sooner or later."

" 'Course, we've taken pay in everything from butter and eggs to quilts and knitted socks," added Cibolo.

"We've done all right. We own our outfit free and clear." Pride glowed in Trace's voice. "That dandy little American portable drilling rig can dig a well a thousand feet deep like nobody's business!"

"It ought to," countered his partner. "To pay for it, we sure kicked down many a well with a spring-pole."

"What's that?" asked Jerry.

"A device the Chinese may have figgered out first. It's been used thousands of years."

"Sounds like an awful lot of work," Jon grimaced.

"Sure, but you can dig a well eight hundred feet deep that way."

"How come you'd rather dig wells on credit for folks like us instead of getting cash from the rich guys?" Jerry puzzled.

Trace's face closed for a moment. Absently, he touched the break in his nose before he shrugged. "A man named Rousseau said something like, 'The fruits of the earth belong to everyone but the earth belongs to no one.' "

"Chandless wouldn't agree with you." Bitterness left a metallic taste in Julie's mouth. "He wants the land, and water, too."

"That's why I want to help small farmers stand up to him," Trace said. "I'm half Cherokee. My Riordan grandpa came from Ireland in the famine years and married a Cherokee. Their son married a girl whose daddy was from Scotland. I grew up in the Cherokee Nation over in what's left of Indian Territory. Our people can use what land they need but it all still belongs to the tribe. Now the government wants to make each person on the tribal rolls take an allotment."

"So the land can be opened to white homesteaders?"

"That's the reason. The *excuse* is that Indians will never progress till they have their own property and start thinking like white men. That is, planning how to cheat their neighbors, refusing to share with those in need, and getting rich."

"Some of your folks don't need teaching," Cibolo grunted. "They had slaves in Georgia and the Carolinas and brought 'em along to Indian Territory like they did my grandparents."

"Your grandparents were slaves?" Jon asked, wide-eyed.

The matter-of-fact statement startled Julie, too. There had never been many slaves on the High Plains, never many people of any kind. Slavery was something in the past and hard to imagine, though you knew it had existed, like the vast herds of buffalo and free-roving Comanches and Kiowas whose dominion this had been till about a quarter century ago.

"Both sets of my grandparents were brought from Georgia with James MacManus's prize livestock. My folks were born his slaves and grew up and married, still his slaves. I was born a slave in 1863, but of course I don't remember much before I was growing up on my parents' farm. The federal government made slaveholders deed land to their freed people." He snorted. "It'd take Yankees to think you could whack off some of a rich man's fields, plunk them as had been his slaves down there, and expect 'em to get along."

"Especially when the government grabbed more Indian land because some like Stand Watie fought for the South," added Trace. "Some fought for the North, too, but most just wanted to tend their crops and creatures and keep clear of the white men's fuss. Any old excuse will do when the government wants to take more Indian land."

Jon stole an abashed look at Cibolo. "Do your folks still have their farm?"

"Not in the Cherokee Nation. The government appointed guardians for the colored people who weren't considered able to handle their own affairs. Well, the guardians did such a bang-up job of it that within a few years most of my people had been cheated out of their farms. My family homesteaded in Kansas. That's where I grew up." His laughter held a wry edge of old hurt. "My brother and sisters were the only black kids in the little country school. We ate and played together. The other kids acted scared of us. The teacher broke a paddle on the only boy who ever called us names but we still felt like we didn't belong—didn't like to go to school. Our folks made us, and at night we'd teach them what we'd learned."

"You talk real good," said Jon wistfully. "Better'n us. There wasn't any school at the mining camp. Mama taught us all she could but she never got much schoolin', either."

"You can learn without school," suggested Cibolo. "All it takes is books."

"We don't have none," said Jerry.

"You can learn a lot of words out of a Sears or Ward's wishbook," Trace encouraged. "And I reckon I have a book or two you might like."

"What happened to your brother and sisters, Cibolo?" asked Jon.

"Lydia's a music teacher in Kansas City. Alice has a millinery shop in Wichita. Bill stayed in the cavalry after I got out. Guess he'll make a life of it even if he never can be an officer."

"He can't?" chorused the boys.

"Well, in peacetime not many white enlisted fellas rise through the ranks, but a colored man never can. Bill—he's a sergeant major—nursemaids the shavetails fresh out of West Point and makes officers out of them."

"That's not fair!" cried Jerry.

"Not much about the army is. Once you know the rules, it's not a bad life. Beats chopping cotton or lots of the work men like me can find."

"How come you quit it, then?"

"Jerry!" Jon glared at his younger brother. "Don't be so doggoned nosy!"

"I didn't exactly quit. Just sort of disappeared." Cibolo smiled and sighed at the memory. "My sergeant and I were courting the same young lady at Fort Huachuca out in Arizona Territory. Hard likker and words led to harder fists and—well, while Sarge was sleeping it off, I faded into the chaparral. I'd always kind of wanted to see the place where I was born— kind of ponder that I *wasn't* a slave, that what I made out of my life was up to me." He sighed again. "So what did I do?"

"What?"

"I dropped in on the MacManuses, just to see the family that'd owned my folks and me, too, when I was a baby."

"Did they—" Jerry winced. "Ouch, Jon! Don't you be kickin' me or I—I'll tell Dave!"

"To make it short, a MacManus who was still wet behind the ears called me 'boy.' " Cibolo shook his head. "No sense in it, I'd been called a sight worse, but it made me crazy. It took the whole bunch to drag me off that young MacManus."

"And the whole bunch to whip you, too," said Trace.

"They dumped me where the road to their place crossed the

main one. Guess I was lucky they didn't toss me in the brush to die."

"I was lucky, too." Trace grinned at his companion. "When I came along that spring mornin' five years ago, and managed to get you in my wagon, you looked like something the cats had mauled a few days before they dragged it in. I didn't think you'd last the day out. You did and I got myself one tough partner."

Cibolo patted back an enormous yawn. "Are we tough enough to take on Jess Chandless?"

"Reckon we'll decide that when Miss Julie's partner gets back." Trace yawned, too. "Us menfolks'll do the dishes, Miss Julie."

"Just for that, you get pancakes for breakfast," she promised.

She picked over beans and set them to soak while two men and two boys made short work of the dishes. LeMoyne had gone back to his vigil on Cap's grave. Ashamed at having been diverted, Julie went down to say a good-night prayer for Cap, one she composed from his favorite.

> *"O ye Sun and Moon,*
> *O ye Stars of Heaven,*
> *O ye Nights and Days,*
> *O ye Light and Darkness,*
> *bless ye the Lord:*
> *praise him and magnify him forever."*

And Cap, may you live on in every good and beautiful thing. May I live and work in a way to make you proud of me, put up mills for folks who need them, and show Chandless he can't claim land and water any more than he can own the wind.

She knelt by LeMoyne and held him till her swollen eyes wouldn't stay open. When she returned to camp, the boys were silent mounds again with Sunny between them. Cibolo and Trace must have spread their bedding on the far side of their wagons. Feeling blessedly safe because of their presence, she spread her bedroll, undressed beneath the covers, folded her clothing under her pillow, pulled on the heavy ribbed cotton union suit she slept in, and pulled quilts and tarp over her head.

It was the first night since she'd run away from the preacher's home in Fort Worth that she'd gone to sleep without knowing Cap was nearby. She couldn't believe he was never coming back, that never in this world, this life, would she see him. She had thought her tears used up but now they stung her eyes. She tried to pray his favorite prayer, but the words faded in her grief. She damned Hartman and Chandless and all their kind, vowed to fight them in the way that mattered most, by setting up windmills that would help small settlers make a living here.

O ye Winds of God . . . She repeated it silently, over and over, until at last she slept.

The smell of coffee and biscuits deliciously woke her. Gracious, she had slept sound! Cap was already up. . . . Then a voice, strange yet reaching deep within her, spoke softly. "Let's keep it quiet, boys. Be good for Miss Julie to sleep all she can."

Drowsiness fled in an instant. *Cap! Oh, Cap* . . .

Stifling the anguished cry that rose to her lips, she wished she could sleep again, be oblivious, but that was impossible. She was alive. There was work to do and Cap to avenge.

Not in blood. He wouldn't want that. But with windmills that would be his memorials all over these plains, proud towers that meant the end of Chandless's dominion. With speed born of long practice, she dressed beneath the covers, put her union suit under the pillow, and emerged.

Trace Riordan's smile warmed her more than the barely risen sun. "We'll have your pancakes tomorrow morning, Miss Julie. I was up and figgered I might as well start breakfast."

"Smells wonderful."

All the others had stowed their bedrolls. She made haste to do the same, trying not to wince as every nerve and muscle in her body shrieked from the effects of digging post holes. There wasn't time to undo her braid, comb and replait her hair, so she washed her face and hands and joined the group around the fire.

She had a chance to observe Trace as he scooped up plates

of what looked like a mixture of eggs, tomatoes, and thinly sliced onions and potatoes, and handed her the first one. He didn't always wear his hat in the sun. Streaks of bright copper showed in rich brown hair, as if gliding fingers had run through it. She rebuked the crazy impulse to do that herself. His eyes were green and gold and brown, depending on the light, unlike Cibolo's, which were warm bronze.

"Please," said Julie. "Cap always said a prayer in the morning. If you don't mind—"

The men nodded and Cibolo gave a flash of ivory teeth. "Sounds like a great notion."

So Julie invoked the winds of God, but there her voice frayed. She couldn't, not yet, maybe not ever, voice Cap's request that they raise good windmills, bring wind water to a thirsty land.

"Amen," Trace finished softly. The others echoed him.

He set the Dutch oven where everyone could reach it and held the lid while the breakfasters helped themselves. Then he poured coffee and handed the boys a can of Borden's evaporated milk. "Better make it half and half," he advised them.

He was right. It was a brew Cap would have approved— *No, this is not the time to cry. Tonight. You can cry tonight.* The lump in her throat made it hard to swallow the first few bites, but the concoction was appetizing, the biscuits almost as crustily tempting as Cap's, and by some alchemy, the warming food eased her aching body, even, a little, her aching heart.

When the dishes were done and camp tidy, Trace said, "Why don't you make that cobbler you promised, Miss Julie, while we get a start on those post holes? We've got a couple of shovels and pry bars."

"I can do my share."

His green eyes warmed to sun-flecked hazel. "I'll bet you can. But we'd all a sight rather have cobbler. Jerry, why don't you scout up some prairie coal? The pile's gettin' low."

While the men and Jon started holes, Julie put peaches to simmer in a kettle, soaked a split biscuit in beaten egg, and carried this to LeMoyne. He lifted his head from between his paws and gave his tail a diminished wag. He loved eggs and seldom got any but he only gave a civil sniff at Julie's offering and lowered his head again.

Softly coaxing, Julie broke off a piece and held it to his mouth. Egg dripped on his paw. He gave her a reproachful look, cleaned his paw, and then, after a moment, accepted the tidbit. Bite by bite, he ate the biscuit. Sunny gamboled up in time for a nibble. She touched LeMoyne's nose, whined, frisked enticingly, crouched low, and pleaded. When nothing got him up, she flopped beside him.

"Keep after him," Julie told the half coyote.

Back in camp, she added onions and dried red chile peppers to the big kettle of murmuring beans, and steeled herself to go through Cap's belongings. His clothes should about fit Dave. From the raggedy quilts and blankets of the Collins boys, they could make good use of the bedroll.

Cap would like for his things to benefit the boys. It would be self-indulgent to bundle them up and drop them off for distribution in some town because seeing Dave in Cap's hat was bound to wrench her heart till she got used to it.

She'd already given Shan Cap's watch. She'd keep his tape measure and level; the well-worn Book of Common Prayer; his *Meditations of Marcus Aurelius* and Walt Whitman's *Leaves of Grass;* the record book of twenty-three years, of the hundreds of windmills he'd set up all the way from the Mexican border to central Kansas, from New Mexico and Colorado to Indian Territory. Cap's body might rest by the wild plum thicket not far from his last tower, but his memorials were scattered all over the South Plains, pumping the water of life.

One change of Cap's was in the canvas laundry bag but she took his other clothing, including his hat and warm jacket, gathered up the bedroll, and carried everything to the Collins dugout.

Heavenly days! It was a veritable den. A rancid odor came from the skillet and kettles on the cast-iron stove. A braided rag rug could scarcely be told from the dirt floor. Bedrolls and clothing were heaped on the ticking-shuck mattress and more garments, ropes, harness, bridles, and gear hung from the iron bedstead. A torn ruffle straggled forlornly from a gingham curtain, now half torn from its cord, that Mrs. Collins must have hung across the cupboard of apple crates, and there was precious little in the cupboard.

A kerosene lantern rose from the litter smothering the packing-crate table. Upended apple crates served as chairs. One, by the door, held a bucket of water with a dipper in it, a tin washbasin, the yellow rind of a bar of homemade soap, and an incredibly filthy sack towel clung to a nail driven in the door frame.

Mrs. Collins's dreams, her hope to make a comfortable home for herself and her sons, showed in the faded curtains at the single window, in the abused rug, in the stained cheese-cloth fastened across the ceiling to keep dirt and spiders from falling quite so frequently into the home. Julie hoped the woman could somehow know that the boys had friends now, that they had a good chance to prosper.

But this—this—hog wallow! There was going to be a great cleaning and washing before Julie moved on, and the boys were going to help. From the door, she looked toward the sprouting fields.

The fence would go a lot faster with Trace and Cibolo. Shan would be powerfully glad to see them. Her ears caught a sound. She shielded her eyes and gazed toward the far-off reverberation.

Horses! A number of them. Lute Hartman again? The men and Jon had heard, too, and were leaving their work. Julie hurried to get the shotgun. Trace and Cibolo passed her. From beneath their bedrolls, they produced a rifle, a shotgun, and two mean-looking revolvers. Julie was reaching for Cap's shotgun when Trace caught her wrist.

"Miss Julie, take the boys and wait in the dugout till we see if there's going to be any trouble." It was a command. "Take the shotgun in case you need it, but stay under cover."

"You don't have a quarrel with Chandless yet. If it's his men—"

"As far as I'm concerned, we're already partners. Agreed, Cib?"

52

"You bet." Cibolo dropped a hand on Jon's shoulder. "Escort the lady to the house, will you? And stay out of sight."

Julie took the shotgun and marched, not sure whether it was more irritating than pleasant to be protected, but grateful that she didn't have to meet the unknown callers by herself.

*F*ive

A spring wagon with a fringed canopy jounced behind a team of handsome buckskins as the driver urged them on. Shrieks came from women clutching their hats, each other, and the seats of the bright vermilion equipage striped with black. Fortunately, they were so surrounded with boxes, trunks, and bundles that there was little chance of their being dislodged.

The driver had lost her hat, and hairpins, too. A mass of long black hair flew in the wind. She pulled on the reins and brought the team to a gradual stop beside Trace and Cibolo.

The pursuing horsemen, six of them, reined up, too. They didn't act hostile. Several had rifles in saddle scabbards but didn't reach for them, and they all took off their hats to the women they'd been after.

"I'm going to see what's going on," Julie told the boys. "You can come when it looks for sure like there won't be any trouble."

Shotgun pointed downward, she joined Trace and Cibolo in time to watch a laughing black-haired man bend gracefully in the saddle to present the driver with a gorgeous wine-red velvet-and-satin hat.

"Sorry the veil's a little snagged from the yucca it caught

54

on," the stranger said. "Lordy, Rose, why'd you lead us on such a chase? We just wanted to have a talk—"

"There's nothing to talk about, John Mallory."

"When did I stop being Jack?"

She twisted her hair up and tried to hold it in place by pulling the hat on as securely as she could. "When you tore after us this morning instead of wishing us luck." Her voice was chill. The reckless smile on the dark stranger's handsome hawk-face must have melted many women but this cream-skinned beauty produced a tiny derringer from the sleeve of her garnet satin dress. "We're through with the life. We're going to claim land and farm."

"*You?*" gasped John Mallory. His gaze swept over the three other women, stylishly and expensively clad, who were trying with varying degrees of success to rearrange their hair and hats. "I never heard of such a daft notion! Who'll do the plowing? Who'll plant and harvest? Who'll—"

"We will. We were all raised on farms."

"Maybe. But if you liked farming so much, how come you left?"

"None of your business." The woman called Rose lifted a firm chin. "All you need to know is that we're going to find land we like, settle, and file on it once it's legally open."

He emitted a soft whistle and settled his expensive fawn Stetson on the back of his head. "If you really mean it, Rose, of course I wish you luck. But Kenton sure won't be the same without you."

"Miss Rosie, ma'am—" The scrawny redheaded young man with a large nose and Adam's apple glanced from her to a dainty blond woman who seemed little more than a girl. "If Letty craves a farm so much, I—I'd be proud to marry her and work the best I can on the place we'll claim."

"Ask her, not me, Danny," shrugged Rose.

He swallowed and fixed imploring brown eyes on Letty, who glowed a becoming pink. "I'm not much, Letty, but if you'll have me, I'll try to make sure you're never sorry."

Her blue eyes misted. It was a moment before she could speak. "Oh, Danny, I—I'll try to make sure *you're* never sorry!

Can we neighbor with Rose and Madelaine and Barbara?"

He rode in close and grasped her hand. "Sure, honey, if that's what you want."

John Mallory's mouth quirked down. "Well, kid, I guess I see who's going to do the plowing and heavy work for all the ladies. If you get fed up, you know where to find me." His sardonic gaze shifted from the women to his other men. "Any more of you hankerin' for double harness?"

"Aw, Jack, lay off!" A big, yellow-haired youngster whose blushing face was still cherubic with puppy fat, appealed with wide blue eyes to the slender woman in green with light brown hair and hazel eyes. "I sure am . . . obliged to you for everything, Madelaine, but—"

"It's all right, Billy." Her smile was good-natured, if a trifle bitter. "You paid for everything you got. Anyway, I'm no cradle-robber."

His head veered up at that but he didn't answer. Red to his earlobes, he studied his saddlehorn as if he had never seen it before. The oldest of the men, hard-faced, with straggly ash-colored hair and mustache, narrowed pale gray eyes already squinted from years in the sun.

"Since you've returned Rose's hat, Jack, I reckon we'd better just ride back to Kenton." Expressionless eyes traveled from one woman to the next. "Good luck, ladies."

He turned his horse, but John Mallory was staring at Trace and Cibolo. "We haven't met," he said. Playfulness fled his voice and eyes. "I think you're the guys I've been looking for the past couple of years."

"We haven't been hiding." Trace frowned slightly. "I'm Trace Riordan. This is my partner Cibolo."

Mallory gave his head a sharp jerk. "You're the one. You killed my best friend, Owen Matthews. Two years ago this summer, in a fight over a dance-hall girl."

"Matthews was doing things to that woman I wouldn't see done to a mean mule."

"Matthews drew first," put in Cibolo.

"Jack, you know Owen could be rank, 'specially when he was drunk," intervened the graying man.

"I don't care what he was or what he did, Owen saved my

life." Mallory's eyes dueled with Trace's, which had gone deep, fathomless green. "Shall we get it over with?"

"Hold on, Jack," said Rose. "We need wells dug. From the look of this rig, we've found a driller."

"You expect me to worry about that when you're running out on me?"

"I never said you can't come calling." Rose's already vibrant color mounted.

He whipped around. "You mean—"

"I mean, let's start over, Jack." Under Rose's assurance, there was suddenly an uncertain, wistful note. "As if—as if you had just now met me."

His brows met in a rebellious scowl. Then he laughed, doffed his hat, and inclined his dark head. "I sure am proud to make your acquaintance, Miss Kendall." Compliance with her wish, or mockery? He swung toward Trace and the smile faded.

"I'd like to oblige these ladies but—"

"I won't leave the country without giving you a crack at me," Trace promised. "I'll be glad to dig the ladies whatever wells they need. Cibolo and I are throwing in with Miss Mc-Cloud's windmilling outfit so we can put up the mills, too."

Julie stepped forward, still holding the shotgun pointed to the ground. "Are you a friend of Jess Chandless's, Mr. Mallory?"

His eyes played over her, making Julie embarrassingly aware of where her shirt and trousers closely touched her body. In contrast to his bold gaze, Mallory's voice was courteous velvet. "I've eaten a lot of Chandless's beef, ma'am, but not exactly at his table."

"His foreman, Lute Hartman, killed Cap McCloud, the man who raised me, because he was putting up this mill for three kids who're trying to make a go of it." She halted, forcing back tears. "My partner and I are helping fence the crops to keep out Chandless's cattle. With Trace and Cibolo, we mean to dig wells and set up windmills for any settlers who want them."

"To get back at Chandless?"

"That's part of it. But mostly, it's something Cap would have done." She looked up into weighing dark eyes. "Mr. Mallory, folks out here have to have wells if they're going to make a living."

His lip twitched. "Are you hinting that a well-digger is a more desirable citizen than some of the rest of us?"

"I'm just saying he does something good. It sounds like your friend was killed in a fair fight. I hope you'll forget your grudge."

"When hell freezes."

"Well then, can't you at least wait till the wells are dug?"

Mallory glanced at Trace, then back at Julie, and sighed. "Look," he said as if to a backward child, "do you think Chandless will let the windmills stand or leave the fences up?" The same question Trace had asked.

"He'll leave ours up," declared Rose. "Lute Hartman is tough but he won't kill women—and we'll sure shoot at him and his men."

Dark eyebrows climbing, Mallory studied Rose and the other women before he chuckled. "*You* may get away with it, Ro—I mean, Miss Kendall. But how about these boys? Or that hatchet-faced ex-schoolmarm, Cora Oliver? Or that old bachelor a couple miles west? Or any of the folks who aren't pretty ladies?"

"We'll fight Chandless!" Jon said in a voice that started deep and then squeaked.

Mallory shook his head. "Son, you got as much of a chance with him or Hartman as a rabbit does with a diamondback."

"Hartman can't bluff me." Danny pushed out his thin chest for Letty's benefit.

"He won't be bluffing," Trace said. He looked at Mallory. "But there's Cib and me and Danny and, I'd reckon, Julie's partner, Shan. We can give Hartman plenty of grief. If we can find a few more men, Chandless will have to import gunmen to run the settlers out. I don't think he'll do that. The days for that kind of shenanigan are over."

"You may be right," shrugged Mallory. "He's got no more legal claim on the land than any squatter. He won't want to cause enough stink to make the federal government take notice." Mallory turned in the saddle and shook Danny's hand. "Good luck, kid."

The boy's Adam's apple bobbed. "Jack, I thought—"

"That I'd take a hand in this game? I've got no use for the likes of Chandless but I'm not real keen on sodbusters, either, present company excepted, naturally." He grinned deliberately, challengingly, at Rose. "It might be different if Miss Kendall was to ask."

"Pretty-please with sugar and cream on it?" she snapped. "I'm not asking favors, *Mr.* Mallory. It might be different if you did one without being asked."

He gave her a long, slow smile before he turned to Julie. "I'll do this much, Miss McCloud. I won't settle my score with your new partner, Riordan here, until you've dug your wells and put up your windmills."

"I won't leave without seeing you," Trace said.

Mallory nodded. He bowed to Julie, swept around with a flourishing salute to Rose, and led off his men at an easy canter. Danny watched them a bit forlornly, till Letty squeezed his arm and drowned him in her smile.

"We—we're going to have a place of our own, Danny! I can't believe it!"

He was like a rather spindly flower opening and responding to the sun of her happiness. "You can believe it, darlin'." He took her hands in his, controlling his horse with his balance and knees. "And we're gettin' married just as fast as we can."

Rose surveyed the pair with amusement, sympathy, and exasperation. "We'll come along to see the deed done," she decided. "But first let's pick our claims. When this does open to homesteading, we can file on a hundred sixty acres apiece. If these quarter sections adjoin, we can locate our houses in the middle of the section—start with one, and all live in it while we build the others."

"One's all we need to start with." Madelaine's practical tone contrasted with her elegant garments. "We've got to get some sod broken and get in a corn crop." She explained to Julie and the others, "We'll have our savings but the sooner we start producing something, the better."

"We can't plant wheat till next year, when the roots in the sod have rotted," added Barbara of the silvery eyes and hair. "But we can poke holes in the fresh-broken sod and plant castor beans and broom corn besides regular corn for us and the horses."

Danny sighed. "I've walked many a mile behind a plow and team. Left home 'cause I was sick of it." He glanced at Letty and his smile returned. "It'll be different now. I'll be doing it for us."

"Danny." Rose's tone was motherly though she couldn't have been more than seven or eight years his elder. "Let's have this straight. The rest of us will appreciate having you close in case we need you, but your responsibility is to Letty. We'll hire someone to break our sod this first year. After that, we should be able to plow." She gave him a smile so dazzling that his jaw dropped. "We'll trade work with you, neighbor, but we won't take advantage."

"Aw, Miss Rosie—" stammered Danny, but he did look relieved.

"It might be a thought to pick claims next to this one," Trace said. "You could maybe share one stretch of fencing with the Collinses, plan your fields so they can have as much shared fence as possible. Of course, till there's a government survey, you can't be real sure about boundaries but those can be straightened out later."

"We're in the northwest corner of our claim," Jon said. "I can show you where we kind of figure our property lines are." His voice squeaked but he added gallantly, "We would sure be proud to have you ladies for neighbors."

Rose and her friends smiled on him. "The pleasure will be ours."

"Why don't you unload your belongings before you choose your land?" Julie asked. "Until you have a shelter built, and a well and windmill, you might be best off camping here with us."

After a searching look, Rose nodded. "Thank you. We'll accept with gratitude. Let me introduce my friends, Letty Sutherland, Madelaine Thomas, and Barbara Galway."

Trace and Cibolo nodded. With Danny, they helped the

women down, and began unloading the wagon. "I can open up some cans if you're hungry," Julie offered.

"We had breakfast," said Rose. "And we've got some plain dresses, sunbonnets, and shoes in those trunks. We've been planning this for quite a spell. What made us decide to make the break now is—"

She broke off. Barbara finished. "I'm going to have a baby. I didn't want to give it away and I couldn't keep a child while I—"

Rose touched her hand. "We'll all help with the baby, dear. It won't ever have to know a thing about family except that it's got three aunts that are crazy about it."

"It's a good thing we kind of got shoved," said Madelaine. "Otherwise, it's easy to drift."

Jon watered the horses while the women plundered their baggage and retired behind the wagons to change. Trace and Cibolo returned to digging holes. Julie made crust, patted it into a Dutch oven, and poured in the peaches, topping them with more crust and sprinkles of sugar and ginger. As she was burying the iron pot in embers, the women emerged.

They were still uncommonly pretty, but slatted sunbonnets shadowed their faces. Cotton had replaced satin and silk, sturdy laced shoes their elegant slippers. Alluring curves were somewhat disguised by modestly cut and shaped dresses covered by aprons. Julie noted, however, that bonnets, aprons, and gowns were made up in colors and patterns that complemented each other and suited the wearer, except for Rose's dark gray chambray. But the severe lines and color only emphasized her blooming figure and beautiful skin.

Shades of light blue and lavender sateen flattered Barbara's moonbeam hair and crystalline eyes. Letty's blue-and-white gingham gave her a fresh, schoolgirl look. Apricot calico lent a matching glow to Madelaine's complexion.

"You go along with the ladies and Dan, Jon, and show them your boundaries," Trace said. He seemed to have put his vowed encounter with Jack Mallory completely out of mind.

He, Danny Shelton, and Cibolo helped the women into the wagon. Julie built up the fire around the beans and went to work on the post holes.

Shan and Dave rattled in about noon with fence posts, wire, staples, and three post-hole diggers. Shan sized up Trace and Cibolo in a penetrating glance as Julie explained the proposed alliance.

"We may all need partners before we're through with Chandless." Shan shook hands with Trace and Cibolo, and Dave did the same. "That fence will sure go faster with two more men," Shan chuckled. "If we'd known you were going to be here, we'd have bought more post-hole diggers."

"We'll have more fence to string," Trace grinned back, "so the next trip to town, we'll invest in a couple more of those contraptions." He waved a hand toward the jaunty wagon rolling toward camp. "Here's our new settlers."

Almost simultaneously with the introductions, the women announced that they had staked their claims. "Three of them corner with this edge of the Collinses' land," explained Rose. "Since someone had to locate away from this common center, Letty and Danny took land in between the Collinses and Cora Oliver."

"From what we hear about Miss Oliver, we thought she'd take more kindly to a married couple than one of us others," said Madelaine. Her hazel eyes shone. "Driving in those stakes was the happiest, proudest time of my whole life!"

Shan looked at her in such bedazzlement that Julie thought it a good thing he hadn't seen the brown-haired beauty in her finery. "Oh, you'll be prouder and happier, ma'am, when you move into your house and hear your windmill pumpin' away for you."

The women nodded, though, being reared on farms, they knew no gambler ever took such risks and wagered more than did people who planted, cultivated, and prayed for a crop, especially on these high plains where high winds, drought, and blazing sun could shrivel hopeful green things even if hail didn't pound them into the ground or grasshoppers gnaw them to the roots.

It took courage to break away from a life of comparative luxury. Julie had only a confused idea of how the women had earned their livings though she knew they had done things with men that should be only for married folk. Cap had stammered out an embarrassed explanation when a twelve-year-old Julie had rushed to him, terrified, and said she was bleeding. There were lots of questions she'd like to ask now but she had a feeling that these women wanted to forget most of what they knew more than Julie wanted to know it.

"We need to trade our fancy wagon for a plain one and several plows, cultivators, and such," planned Rose, as they ate dinner. "I can't bear to part with Duke and Valentine, but they're not workhorses. We'll keep them for riding and buy a good team."

"I've got money saved," said Dan, patting Letty's hand. "I'll buy a team, too. That ought to take care of all our work, and we can share machinery."

"You'll come to town with us, won't you, Danny, and help choose the horses and buy what we need?" asked Letty.

He looked at her fondly. For the first time, Julie caught a glimpse of the man he would be when he finished growing. "You bet I'll come, darlin'. Don't want you out of my sight more than has to be from now on. Shall we hunt up a preacher?"

Letty blushed. "It—it may sound funny," she almost whispered, "but Danny, do you suppose you could—could come courting?"

His look of amazement changed quickly to tenderness. "Letty, from now on you're goin' to have whatever you want if I can anyways manage it. Sure, I'll court you!"

They smiled blissfully at each other. Then Danny sighed. "Sure never thought I'd spend good money on a plow, but if farmin's what you want—"

"It is," said Letty.

As soon as Valentine and Duke had rested and grazed awhile, they were harnessed again to the vermilion wagon and the women set off for Tyrone with Danny riding alongside.

Surveying the trunks, hatboxes, and carpetbags stowed near the chuckbox, Trace said, "Let's throw a tarp over that plunder and get to digging post holes. Pretty women are sure nice to look at but right now I kinda wish they were husky fellas with strong backs and weak brains."

"I don't." Shan lifted his eyes to heaven. "It's like paradise, four beautiful critters all at once." He saw Julie's frown and added, *"Five* beautiful critters, I meant, colleen."

"Blarney," she retorted, glanced at her chapped hands, then, involuntarily, with a twist of her heart, at Trace. "Compared to them I'm a plain old sunflower in a bunch of roses."

"Sunflowers have bright faces," Trace said. "They stand up to winds and weather that'll blight roses."

"I don't think these roses are going to blight." Julie looked from the shining blades of the windmill down to Cap's mound where LeMoyne lay with Sunny close by. "I hope they make a go of their farms and show Chandless that he doesn't own this country."

Five extra mouths had devoured the food she'd meant for supper. While Trace, Shan, Cibolo, Jon, and Dave went to the field where fencing materials had been unloaded, Julie put on more beans and began stewing dried apples for another cobbler.

Six

The posthole diggers had two steel blades about nine inches long that curved till they almost met. The blades were driven into the ground by steel shanks that were then pulled apart to close the blades and lift out the earth. As Trace, Cibolo, and Shan plunged the diggers into the ground, Julie, Jon, Dave, and Jerry put the rough-trimmed cedar posts into holes that were already dug, and used pry bars to work around the post and settle it in deep and snug. Then they filled in the hole, tamping the earth down as hard as possible several times.

"Be sure to pack plenty of dirt around the posts," Trace said. "If you leave a hollow, rain will soak down into the hole and loosen the post."

"We sure don't want that to happen!" Flushed with exertion, Dave leaned on his pry-bar for a moment. "Once this dratted fence is up, it better stay that way!"

Cibolo laughed from his lean belly. "Fences are like windmills and babies, Dave. Always need tendin' to. But it's the only way to keep cows out of your crops." He shaded his eyes. "We've got company."

They all followed his gaze. Three riders came from the north. "Not the right direction to be Chandless's men unless they're comin' from a line camp," Shan said.

"Doubt his cowboys are ridin' mules," put in Cibolo.

"Probably just neighbors, but it wouldn't hurt to get a drink of water and take a rest up close to our artillery," Trace said.

Up at the windmill, which was pumping, they splashed their faces and drank from cupped hands held beneath the pipe. The men drifted toward the wagons and waited in easy reach of their weapons. It was almost time for Julie to get supper, and unless the strangers proved unfriendly, they'd have to be invited. She fed the fire, washed her hands again, and started making cornbread.

By now the visitors were close enough to confirm Cibolo's keen eyes. The men were mounted on mules who were in no hurry. Their long ears flopped in rhythm with the joggling elbows of their riders. The men's awkwardness in their saddles proclaimed even louder than overalls and work shoes that they were indeed not cowboys.

Trace and the others moved away from the wagons as the strangers came to a shambling halt. "A good evening to you, gents." Shan acted as camp host. "Won't you light down and have a bite with us when it's ready?"

"Thank you kindly," said the oldest, whose beard was more gray than black. "Our womenfolk are expectin' us home before too late. We hauled freight for a Carrizo storekeeper in exchange for a pretty fair windmill a customer left him to settle up a big bill before he moved back East. We wondered if we can figger out some way to get a well drilled and the windmill put up."

"On credit," supplied a man who much resembled the other, except that his beard was black. "We sure don't have cash."

"Jack Mallory stopped by and said there was a windmill and well-drillin' outfit here." The youngest man had the same spare, tough build as the others, the long nose and thin, craggy face, but he was clean-shaven. "He also said you was buildin' fence which seems a powerful waste of time when anyone can do that—includin' us."

"We're the Halls," said the oldest man. "I'm Laban. Thad and Rafe here are my sons."

Shan and Trace exchanged glances with Julie. Rising, she introduced herself and the others, then invited. "At least have a cup of coffee and let the boys water your mules while we talk things over."

The three unfolded from the most dilapidated saddles Julie had ever seen and thanked the Collins boys, who took a mule each to the tank. As bargaining proceeded over fragrant coffee, the Halls exchanged dismayed glances when they learned three single women were settling nearby and would need their fields fenced.

"My Lorena's pretty jealous," Rafe said.

Thad sighed. "She's not as bad that way as Millie."

"When it comes to green-eyed, touchy, and suspicious, your mama has your wives beat six ways from Sunday," Laban told his sons.

Rafe rubbed his chin. "With the baby coming, we'll need a lot more water."

"You wouldn't think two girls could get their clothes dirty as fast as ours do," said Thad.

"Reba sure would love to have water for a bigger garden," Laban mused. "And she pines for an orchard like we had in Missouri."

"Talk it over with them," Julie urged. It seemed likely that soon or late, the Hall women would learn about their new neighbors' previous occupation, but if they got to know them first and saw that Rose and her friends truly wanted to make a new life, maybe their past wouldn't matter so much.

Laban's heavy eyebrows met in a troubled frown. "Reba's going to take it hard, our puttin' up fences for other folks when we can't afford to fence our own crops."

"Our company can lend you the money for fencing." Julie was sure Cap would approve this use of his savings. It was her vengeance, to help the settlers stay. She didn't care if this battle took every penny of her inheritance.

The Hall men chorused, "You can?" Laban, eagerness fading, quickly asked, "How much interest do you charge?"

Julie glanced at Shan. "We haven't had time to figure out the best way of doing business but I hope we can manage without charging interest." She paused. It was as if Cap was putting ideas in her head. "To start with, maybe we can keep track of the time you put in fencing this field and the women's crop land. That will be credited, say at two dollars a day per man, against your fencing materials, drilling your well, and setting up your windmill. When you sell your crops, you can pay what you can afford till the balance is taken care of."

"What if there's a drought like there was last year?" demanded Laban. "All through June, that old wind blew out of the southwest, plumb withered everything right down to the ground."

"We'll have your windmill up in time to irrigate," Shan promised.

Laban persisted gloomily. "Even if we get fair crops like we did in eighty-six and eighty-seven, we may not clear much by the time we haul them to the Kansas towns. I sold good wheat those years for fifty cents a bushel."

"Let's just hope you get good crops and good prices before we run out of money," Julie shrugged.

The younger men looked hopefully at their father. After a moment, he spread his calloused hands. "Might as well go bust in a big way as a piddlin' one," he grudged, and almost glared at Julie. "I know our womenfolk sure won't turn down a chance like this. We'll be over by sunup to work on the fence."

Trace chuckled. "You're welcome to it, sir. I'll start digging your well tomorrow if you'll give me an idea of where you want it."

"In between the barn and the house," said Laban. An indulgent smile softened his hard features. "Reba's heard you can churn butter with a windmill. She's rarin' to try it." He rose from hunkering on his heels. "Want we should sign something turnin' our claims over to you if we can't pay off in— oh, five years?"

Julie quoted Cap. "A handshake from an honest man's worth more than all the gobbledygook lawyers can think up."

The grown-ups shook hands all around while the boys brought the mules. As the Halls jogged off, Trace grinned at Julie in a way that balmed her sore heart. "I'm sure glad to get back to digging wells instead of post holes."

"What if Lute Hartman shows up at the Halls' while the men are over here?" Julie worried.

"Hartman may pull in his horns when he sees he's not dealing with farmers."

"What if he doesn't?"

Trace lifted a shoulder and gave a careless laugh. "Then Jack Mallory may not get his chance at me."

"It's not funny!"

"It sort of is, if you think about Carrizo's sporting ladies turning farmer. And it'll be even funnier if that good-lookin' Rose turns hell-raising John Jack Mallory into a sodbuster."

The admiring warmth in his tone as he spoke of Rose sent a prickle of envy through Julie as she glanced involuntarily at her broken fingernails and work-toughened hands. Once Rose started farming, she wouldn't be able to keep her nails prettily buffed and manicured, and that creamy complexion would probably weather . . .

Cat! She stirred the beans so hard some splashed into the fire and sizzled. "How long will it take you to dig that well?"

"A few days if it's good drilling like this and we don't run into problems. Then we'll come back to dig the ladies' wells."

"What if Hartman tries to stop you?"

"He'll have to kill us to do that."

At her distressed look, Cibolo gave a deep, rich laugh. "Don't fret your mind, Miss Julie. Trace and me don't kill easy or we wouldn't be here."

She looked at Cap's grave and prayed no others would join it. But she was also determined that Cap would not have died in vain, that the kind of people he'd best loved to set up windmills for would get the water that meant life in this parched country.

After supper, Cibolo got out a harmonica. As the enthralled Collins boys gathered closer, he brought a train chug-chugging past, echoed the lonesome wind, the jingle of spurs, the cloppity-clop of a team and squeaking wagon.

Shan's tenor often beguiled nights in camp. He joined in on songs he knew and soon the Collins boys were singing along on the choruses.

"Oh beat the drums slowly and play the fife lowly . . ."

Cap's favorite, "Streets of Laredo."

Blinded by tears, Julie slipped away from camp and made her way to Cap's grave. LeMoyne was already there. She put her arms around him. His tongue slathered her cheek. She hugged him tighter.

The Halls showed up at dawn in a wagon holding their bedrolls, supplies, and a couple of post-hole diggers. "Our womenfolk will do the milking and such while we're workin' here," said Laban. He grinned at Trace and Cibolo. "They're so tickled about having plenty of water handy that they'll feed you even better than they do the preacher when he gets around every few months."

"Maybe we won't dig that well too fast," Cibolo chuckled. "But we sure have enjoyed your cooking, Miss Julie."

"You'll get it again soon enough." He and Trace had their teams harnessed to the wagons. Julie was amazed at the wave of desolation that swept over her. She had only met Trace the day before yesterday. How could he have become so important to her?

It must be because he'd come, strong, laughing, and full of life, when she had just lost Cap. He watched her now with a puzzled frown. Her face must reveal something of how she felt, but she couldn't force a smile.

"Hartman's not likely to kill me," she said, "but he won't mind shooting you. You don't have to do this, Trace. It's not your fight."

"Sure it is. My business is finding water for folks who need it."

"You could dig wells plenty of other places."

"This is where I am."

"Trace—"

"Look, Miss Julie, if I don't dig the wells, I'd have to hunt up Jack Mallory and give him his chance at me."

"That's crazy!"

"I gave him my word."

Trace took her hands, held them close in his warm, strong

ones. She felt an overwhelming urge to move into his arms. How wonderful it would be close against him, resting and comforted. Suddenly, though, a golden fire deep in his eyes roused in her a hunger for something altogether different from rest, something sweet, wild and frightening.

She stepped back. Trace let her go. "Please," she said. "Please be careful."

"I always am. You be careful, too, young lady. Chandless's men probably wouldn't kill a woman on purpose but if bullets start flying, get out of the way."

"Like you will?"

"That's different."

"Not really. I'll shoot if I have to and I expect to take my chances along with Shan and the rest of you."

His eyebrows climbed and he shook his head. The sun struck red glints from his mass of wavy dark hair. She longed to touch it, smooth it with her hands. "I didn't aim to be partners with a crazy woman, ma'am. Maybe—"

"Whether you dig the wells or not, Trace Riordan, I'll keep putting up windmills."

He studied her. Slowly, he nodded. "Then, partner, let's both be careful."

He climbed into the wagon with his precious steam engine. Waving back at the Collins boys, he and Cibolo rumbled off. Julie poured coffee for the Halls, who had unhitched and hobbled their mules.

"What did your wives think about our deal?" Julie asked.

"They're tickled pink." Laban's stern expression melted in a grin that broadened his thin face. "Couldn't believe we're getting fences, too."

"What did they say about your building fences for some real pretty ladies?" Shan teased.

Thad blushed and Rafe looked sheepish. "We didn't say they were *pretty*." At Shan's chortle, Rafe added defensively, "After all, we haven't seen the women. Might be homely as a mud fence."

"They'll knock your eye out, any one of 'em, but that Miss Madelaine—" It was Shan's turn to color. He picked up a posthole digger and the others followed.

* * *

Two days later the dull rumble of wheels instead of the thudding rhythm of horses signaled that a wagon was coming. The workers put down their tools and went to meet the buckboard Rose was driving. It was drawn by two sleek mules. The bed was loaded with supplies, including a plow and other implements. Madelaine and Barbara held on to the seat as the buckboard bounced along. The handsome buckskins were fastened behind. Dan drove a second loaded wagon, Letty at his side. His horse was hitched behind the wagon.

Slowing down, Rose called, "We'll unload these things at my claim and set up the tent we're going to live in till we can build houses." She indicated a bundle of poles and blue-and-white striped duck. "Then we'll come back and get the rest of our stuff."

"Have dinner with us," Julie invited. "We've found some fence-builders for you."

"Splendid!" Rose gave a demure wave at the men who gazed avidly at the newcomers though they kept on working. Then she frowned. "I just hope we can afford to pay them. We ordered a windmill from Dodge City. We'll have to pay for it when we pick it up next week."

"We'll work it out," said Julie, and briefly explained the Cap McCloud Cooperative. "So pay in what you can afford," she concluded. "We'll use it toward buying fence for the Halls that they'll pay off in labor."

"I'll bring a check when we come back," Rose promised, and laughed. "I'm glad you're keeping accounts. I'm tired of it!"

Even in their plain dresses, the women were visions of charm and femininity. The Hall men and Dave Collins stole fascinated glances at them when the women weren't looking, and when they were, paid strict attention to their food. Shan didn't even try to glance away from Madelaine. The first time the brown-haired beauty encountered his worshipful eyes, she gave him a bright, practiced smile. The next time, she blushed and looked down.

"Danny's going to start plowing in the morning when the

mules are rested," Letty said with a proud smile at her future husband. "Isn't it lucky he knows how?"

"So lucky I almost can't stand it," Dan sighed, but he patted Letty's hand and added bravely, "This afternoon, I'll help set posts."

Rose, who had slipped Julie a check for five hundred dollars, smiled at the Collins boys. Dave ducked his head and colored to the roots of his fair hair. "Is it all right if we haul water from your well till we get our windmill?" she asked.

"We'd be glad to pay something—"

"Lordy, no, ma'am!" Dave blurted. "You just help yourself to all the water you want."

"We'll find some way to even it up," Rose promised.

Dave helped Dan fill two ten-gallon milk cans with water while the women loaded their wagon with the belongings they'd left at the camp. When they drove off toward the bluish white patch that was the tent, Dave gazed after them before he tousled his brothers' heads. "Hey! We've got neighbors!"

Jon smoothed his ruffled hair. "Be sort of nice to see a lamp shine that close at night."

"Do you think they might—might like some boys?" Jerry ventured.

Dave stared at him, then scowled ferociously. "You mean, would they let us move in with them? You just put any such notion out of your head! We're hangin' on to this land Mama wanted us to have and we're going to make something out of it—and ourselves!"

"That's all right for you, Dave," muttered Jerry. "You're almost grown-up! But you and Jon don't cook very good and our clothes need patchin' and my socks are wore out and the quilts are falling apart and—"

"Aw, don't be such a bellyachin' crybaby!"

"I'm *not* a crybaby!" Jerry wailed. He rubbed his fist across his eyes before he struck out at his oldest brother.

Jon got between them. "Calm down, Jerry," he soothed. "The brown-haired lady, Miss Maddy, has a sewing machine. She said she'd patch our clothes and make us gingerbread if we'd rustle cow chips for them. Why don't you go do that?"

Jerry blinked, caught a joyous breath, and shouted, "I'm gone!"

Off he sprinted, Sunny at his heels. Dave gave Jon a vexed look before he slowly grinned and gave a philosophical shrug. "Guess it's just as well not to have him mopin' around underfoot." He glanced at his shirt. The elbows were out and a couple of safety pins had replaced the buttons. His bare knees showed through tears in his trousers. "Miss Maddy really said she'd fix our clothes?"

Jon nodded.

Dave considered. "Makes sense to help each other out," he admitted. "But we're stayin' on our land."

The fence-builders went back to work. Julie did the dishes, put together a stew for supper, and took water and gravy-soaked biscuits to LeMoyne. Kneeling by Cap's grave, she shed tears on the dog's rough coat. He gave a faint thump of his tail and licked her hands, finally accepting the biscuits as if not to hurt her feelings.

"Oh, LeMoyne," she whispered. "I still can't believe he's gone. But he wouldn't want you to mourn like this. Why don't you go with Sunny?"

LeMoyne whimpered. She gathered him close and stroked him till her tears ceased and she could join the men. It wasn't long till Jerry panted up, freckles brown against his flushed face.

"Miss Maddy and the other ladies want to know if they can eat with us tonight. They'll bring ham and cole slaw and gingerbread with whipped cream!"

"They can come!" yelped Dave, and there was a chorus of agreement.

Julie was glad when the sun dropped low and she could quit tamping earth around posts, in order to get supper ready. The ladies' contributions would turn stew and cornbread into a feast and she didn't have to make a cobbler or pudding.

As the fence-builders quit work and were washing up, the women arrived on foot with their offerings. Shan gave a long soft whistle. "You ladies look like a flower garden," he said.

Indeed they did; Rose in yellow calico, Letty in sky-blue chambray, Barbara in sateen the same color as her silver-gray eyes, and Madelaine in apricot gingham. Jerry spread out the blue-and-white-checked oilcloth he was carrying and the women put down a huge bowl of cole slaw, a platter of ham, two pans of gingerbread, and a bowl of cream whipped into rich peaks.

"You ought to see the tent!" he said. His knees and elbows were neatly patched, his shirt had buttons, and his formerly snarled, shaggy yellow hair was becomingly trimmed and bright and fluffy as a new chick. "Each lady has a bedroom! And there's a pretty rug in the big room in the middle where you can eat or just sit, and there's what you call an *awning* that makes kind of a porch!"

"It's quite comfortable for now," said Rose, taking the plate Julie offered and helping herself to stew and cornbread before sitting down by the oilcloth. "We couldn't have found a big tent like that in Tyrone except that a family that had been living in it traded it in at the general store when they moved into their soddie. Of course, by winter we'll need a house."

Laban looked up from spearing a slice of ham and gazed toward a faint rumbling from the west. "Wagon coming."

Everyone looked. Rafe narrowed his eyes, then wheeled to his father and brother. "It sure looks like our womenfolk! I'm bound that's Lorena's pink sunbonnet in the middle!"

"And Millie's on the left!" Thad gripped his heaped plate in one hand and tugged at his mustache with the other.

"Reba's driving," Laban groaned. "She must've borrowed a wagon and team from Trace. Great sufferin' golliwogs!"

"Well, that's splendid!" Julie said. "It gives us all a chance to get acquainted and we can find out when Trace thinks he'll finish the well."

Laban nodded without enthusiasm. "Better eat fast, boys," he told his sons. "We'll need to talk a mile a minute when our women get here."

"I think we should go meet them," said Rafe.

"That's because you've not been married as long as we have," retorted Thad. Still, after a few bites, he sighed and got to his feet. "Might as well face the music."

The Hall men walked out to greet their wives, escorted them as the wagon grumbled along, and helped them down from the wooden seat. Julie held out her hand with a welcoming smile and, as they were introduced, clasped Reba's strong, stubby fingers, Millie's long, chapped ones, and Lorena's shapely and comparatively soft hands. Starting with Rose and ending with Jerry, Julie gave the names of each of the group around the oil-cloth and offered plates to the Hall women.

"Please join us. There's plenty, and to spare."

"Looks that way." Reba's shrewd hazel eyes took in the female settlers with one swift glance. She pushed her sunbonnet back to dangle by its ties as if defiantly revealing her gray hair which was pulled back in an uncompromising knot. She addressed herself to Julie. "We didn't want our men eating up your provender so we went to bakin' and borrowed that nice Mr. Riordan's wagon. He and Mr. Cibolo are helping our girls with the chores and we left their suppers in the warming oven. Mr. Riordan expects to hit water tomorrow so he says you can come the next morning and set up the windmill."

Before Julie could say yes, no, or maybe, the plump, rosy woman turned to her husband and sons. "Labe! Boys! Unload the boxes." They hustled to obey. "Six loaves of bread in that one." She indicated Laban's box and nodded at Thad's. "My special applesauce cake and Millie's burnt-sugar one. Rafe's box is plumb full of corn muffins and oatmeal cookies."

Most settlers used molasses for sweetening. To use precious sugar in baking proved the Hall wives' determination to show their new neighbors they were women to be reckoned with. "You needn't have done it," Julie said, "but you can bet we won't waste a crumb. Please help yourselves and sit down."

"I'll set out my cake first." Reba lifted the big glazed cake from the box and plunked it down in challenge between the pans of gingerbread. *Anyone can make gingerbread with molasses,* said her dismissive sniff.

She filled her plate with stew and cornbread, pointedly ignoring the ham and slaw. Not so Millie, who took generous helpings of everything before she slid like a blond iceberg between Thad and Madelaine.

Dark-haired Lorena was probably no older than Julie. She was heavy with child and somehow this made her seem even younger and quite defenseless. Her soft brown eyes fixed appealingly on Rafe, who gazed back tenderly and located a box for her to sit on before he selected food he thought would be to her taste and sat down at her feet.

"You *ladies* known each other long?" Reba fished.

"Long enough to know we'll be good neighbors," parried Rose with a pleasant smile.

"No offense," said Millie quite offensively, "but you don't look like you've ever been on a farm before."

"We all grew up on farms," Barbara remarked in a gentle tone. "Iowa, Missouri, and Letty and I come from east Texas."

Millie shook her head in commiseration. "You're used to good soil and decent rainfall. You may be real disappointed in farming out here."

Madelaine gave a slow, delicious chuckle that made Shan beam upon her. "We've been disappointed before, Mrs. Hall, but we intend to stick it out by the grace of a windmill and a fence around our crops."

Reba gave the newcomers a disparaging look. "Don't none of you look to me like you can hold a sod-breaking plow in a furrow."

"I've broke more sod than I like to remember, ma'am." Dan Shelton dropped his hand to Letty's shoulder. "But I'm marryin' this lady so I'm ready to get behind that plow again."

"Wonder if you'll sing that same song in a year or two," Reba said dourly. "Well, I wish you luck, I'm sure. I just never have held with the way some widders and single women expect other women's husbands to do their hard work."

"Oh, don't worry your head about that, Mrs. Hall." Rose's sweet tone held no hint of mockery though her dark eyes twinkled. "It's true that your husbands made a deal to help put up our fence, but we've paid cash into the Cap McCloud Cooperative that will pay for the posts and wire to fence *your* fields."

"We're mightily obliged to the cooperative, wife," Laban said hastily. "Without it, we sure wouldn't have any windmill or fences."

Reba *humph*ed. She swung her sharp eyes to Julie. "How can you and Mr. Riordan afford to do all this on credit?"

Involuntarily, Julie glanced toward Cap's grave. "I can't afford not to."

Reba flushed. "I'm sorry about your foster father, dear. Mr. Riordan told us. That Jess Chandless! Thinks he owns the earth!"

"We all want to show him that he doesn't," Julie said.

"You mean we've got to get along together," Reba frowned. Julie nodded.

"Well—" began Reba grudgingly.

"Just a minute." Rose's voice cut through the older woman's. "It's none of your business, really, all you Missuses Hall, but we'd rather tell you now than have you come squawking and squalling later." She spoke fast as if she had to get it out before she lost her courage. "We—entertained men in Carrizo but we're sick of it. We want to start over." She and her companions looked at the Hall wives unflinchingly, yet with hope. "Will you believe that?"

After a shocked, heart-stopping moment in which Reba's eyes examined each of the new women, she nodded. "Since you've told us straight and honest, I believe you. Lord knows that kind of life must've plumb disgusted you with men."

"Not all of them." Letty slipped her hand into Dan's.

"Good luck to you, child," Reba said. She took a piece of gingerbread and slathered it with cream. "Dee-licious! Finish your supper, girls; we need to be getting home."

Rafe led the team to water so they could drink their fill before starting back. The Hall women said their good-byes, got into the wagon with their husbands' extra-dutiful help, and drove away across the moon-washed plains.

"Whew!" breathed Laban. "I'm glad that's over!"

"So are we," said Rose in such a droll tone that everybody laughed.

Seven

The well was situated on a little slope so that water piped from it would have the advantage of flowing downhill. A pitch-daubed wooden storage tank waited hopefully nearby. The big wood trough the Halls had filled from the hand-dug well would be moved over once the windmill was erected.

As she had watched Cap do so often, Julie used his old steel tape measure to mark the distance from the top of the well casing to each corner and then the distance between each of them. Her eyes kept blurring and she had to keep swallowing a lump in her throat. *The first windmill raised without you, Cap. I can't believe you'll never be in charge again, making sure the anchor posts are exactly level so the tower legs will come together at the top, lifting the mill in place. . . .* She threw her head back, facing the wind, hoping that Cap somehow knew and approved.

This mill is for you, Cap. And so will all the others be that I have any hand in setting up. "Let me break the sod for you." Trace started for the location of her anchor hole, but she held up her hand.

"Everyone digs their own hole," she said.

"Even if we have to wait for you to finish?" His hazel eyes

were cold and his dark eyebrows pulled straight together above his nose.

"You won't wait long," she retorted, more hurt by his manner than she could have imagined. "You can have a cup of coffee while you're loafing."

Even with picks to drive into the sod and pry up the matted roots, it took awhile to reach a depth where a shovel could work. Julie welcomed the familiar labor. She had been so proud when Cap first let her dig a hole, so thrilled the first time he inspected one of hers and nodded instead of jumping in and leveling and squaring the bottom to suit his practiced eye.

The tools were laid out on the tarp according to Cap's precept. To Julie's relief, LeMoyne drowsed under the wagon she and Shan had driven to the Hall place this morning. When she coaxed and Shan whistled, LeMoyne had whined and acted as if he didn't know whether he should come or maintain his vigil. Then suddenly, as if at a command only he could hear, he rose from the grave by the plum thicket and trotted beside the wagon.

The Hall women had undertaken to feed the windmill crew, so the other wagon and the chuckbox had been left at the Collinses' for the use of the fence-builders. They had started stringing wire to the posts that morning. When they finished protecting the Collinses' field, they'd come home to fence their own growing corn and wheat before enclosing the five acres Dan Shelton had started plowing yesterday and should finish tonight or tomorrow.

A good many days before that, of course, the Kenton ladies' well and windmill should be in operation. At that point, the combined well/windmill outfit could move on, but as she considered that, Julie didn't see how *she* could, not when she'd supplied the means for the settlers to provoke Jess Chandless's wrath.

There was an obligation to them—and to Cap—to see that the windmills stayed up, that the fences weren't torn down. How could that be done?

It had to be talked over with Shan and Trace and Cibolo, but as she thought of leaving, she felt a pang she'd never experienced before when a job was finished and it was time to move on.

She didn't, for one thing, want to get too far, for too long, from Cap's grave. She wanted to make sure wildflowers grew there and weeds were kept away, and sometimes, if she was lucky, to feel his loving presence. Added to that, she longed to see the Collins boys grow up on their land, and she *had* to know how things worked out for Rose and Madelaine, Barbara and Letty and her Dan, and if the Halls prospered.

Thad and Millie's girls, plump nine-year-old Annie, with flaming curly hair and freckles, and fair, blue-eyed Ellen, who was a coltish thirteen, brought out coffee and hot cinnamon rolls while Shan was checking to see that the anchor posts were precisely level and square.

"I hope I can put up windmills or drill wells when I grow up," declared Annie. "It'd be more fun than milking cows or weeding the garden or having babies."

"It is sort of fun," said Julie. "But if no one had gardens or cows or families, they wouldn't need windmills."

"I'd rather put them up!"

Julie grinned. "Come see me if you still feel that way when you're strong enough."

"Whatever else you may do, young lady," said Shan, patting his stomach, "I hope you'll learn how to make cinnamon rolls this good."

The windmill and steel tower the Halls had traded their labor for had to be reassembled. Since the vertical boom of Trace's drilling rig could be used to raise it, instead of building the tower from the ground up, the crew put it together on the ground, breaking off for dinner and getting back to work without second cups of coffee. Blocks raised the lower side about a foot so tools could be used underneath. Trace and Cibolo were expert with wrenches and soon the opposite side was assembled on top of the lower one. The remaining two sides were bolted in place as twilight made it hard to see and Lorena called them for supper.

As they had done at noon, the men let Julie wash first in the basin set on a crate outside the door of the largest soddie. Far enough from the door to give it room for growth was a gaunt apple tree, obviously the recipient of water tossed from the basin and probably that used to rinse dishes and clothes.

The home of Thad, Millie, and the girls had a floor of hard-packed earth but rag rugs brightened it and the walls were plastered white with gypsum mud which made the most of the light from the two small windows. The roof was of cedar shakes, doubtless cut from the cedar- and scrub oak–studded hills near Kenton. Beside the door was a small but valiant climbing rosebush with the hint of buds among its new leaves.

"Maybe I'll get some blooms this year," Millie said, as she welcomed the crew.

Reba and Lorena had their own homes, but they were helping with the meals. Because the Halls had a laboriously tended garden, four black-and-white Holstein milk cows and several dozen hens lorded over by a Rhode Island Red rooster whose brilliant comb fell over his neck like a cavalier's plume, the women could concoct treats seldom found in this raw country. Lorena brought in a large bowl of creamed cottage cheese and Reba's dessert was melt-in-your-mouth custard.

Taking biscuits out of the oven of the kerosene stove, Millie told Julie, "We came from Missouri where there was plenty of wood. I just couldn't get used to burning cow chips so I saved my share of the butter and egg money till I could order this stove from Monkey Ward. The oven's made of Russia iron and bakes better than coal or wood."

"To each her own," shrugged Reba. "I like my old cast-iron range that'll cook all over the top and heat water in the reservoir at the same time. It was a wood floor I was set on, once we could afford glass for windows instead of oiled hide."

"I wanted curtains more than anything," Lorena said.

Reba snorted. "Nothing's going to peek in your windows out here excepting cows and coyotes!"

"Yes, but it's so dark outside."

"Of course it is." Reba gazed at her daughter-in-law in mystification. "You could look out and see our lamps if you didn't stay up so late."

"I suppose it's because I grew up in town." Lorena sounded apologetic. She sat down beside Julie, aproned belly pushing against the homemade table. "I'm so thrilled about having all the water we want! My family has a windmill on a little slope behind the house in Dodge City and it pumps water right into the house!"

"Even without anything that newfangled, it'll be the Lord's blessing not to have to draw up every bucket of water we need from the well our men dug by hand," nodded Millie, passing marble-sized new potatoes and peas rich with cream and butter. "Now we'll be able to grow a really big garden and plant an orchard."

Lorena smiled. "I won't feel like a criminal every time I take a bath or wash my hair. And it'll be so much easier to keep the baby fresh and clean."

"They're not very appetizin' when they stink from spit-up milk and dirty diapers," Reba nodded. "But," said the matriarch with a shake of a stubby finger, "the main thing is, we can water our critters and crops that'll be fenced in so's Chandless's cows can't eat 'em." Her hazel eyes, usually bright and piercing, seemed to moisten as she looked at Julie and the crew. "It's the difference in hangin' on by our toenails and getting a good, solid foothold. We won't ever forget your helpin'."

"You and Pa Laban were doing all right, Mother Reba," said Millie to her mother-in-law. "But the farm wasn't big enough for all of us to make a livin' from." She turned to the crew. "That's why Thad and Rafe and me decided to move out here."

"We couldn't stand being so far away from our children and grandchildren," Reba sighed. "But none of us had any notion of livin' miles from a creek or river where it may not rain for months."

"We'll hoist that windmill up tomorrow and you'll have sweet, pure water, and plenty of it," Trace promised.

"And we're going to keep it." Reba's jaw set. "That ornery Lute Hartman tries to tear down our windmill, I'll my own self dust him with buckshot."

"I'll help!" vowed Millie.

"I don't know if I could shoot at someone, even just with buckshot," Lorena pondered doubtfully. Then her soft eyes flashed. "I could, though, if they tried to hurt Rafe!"

Trace gave the young wife a reassuring look. "My guess is Chandless was pretty sobered when Hartman accidentally killed Cap McCloud. When he knows he's not dealing with just one family, kids at that, he may just make up his mind to sharing the land as long as he can keep the range with running water."

The women wanted Julie to sleep inside but she insisted, truthfully, that she liked to sleep outside as long as it wasn't raining.

"Not much danger of that," sniffed Reba. If she thought it improper for a young woman to sleep in the proximity of three men, she held her tongue, probably reflecting that Julie had grown up that way and worked all day alongside her male partners.

The moon washed the prairie, limned the dark shapes of the three houses, the sod barn, and chicken house. The day's heat had drained away with the sun but it was warm enough not to need a tarp over the bedroll, but Julie still positioned it with her feet to the wind. Shan and Cibolo already had their covers pulled over their heads but Trace stood by the windmill, gazing south.

Why had he been so distant that day, almost unfriendly? Julie was still dressed. She walked toward him. He turned. The pale light drenched the angles of his face, leaving shadows beneath his cheekbones. He watched her without smiling.

Had he taken a dislike to her? Perhaps he favored one of the Kenton women. Tensing at the thought, Julie wished she hadn't ventured near him, but she had. To cover her dismay, she asked, "Do you really think Chandless will pull in his horns?"

"We can hope."

"But do you believe he will?"

He hitched one shoulder up and let it drop. "I can't imagine a man who's held his land as long as he has giving way so easy."

"He can't shoot women."

"No. That's their strongest card. But if he kills the Hall men, I don't think the ladies would stay."

Julie shivered. In her resolve to avenge Cap, was she encouraging men to stay where they might lose their lives? "Even if he killed the Halls, there's Rose Kendall and her friends, and that teacher, Cora Oliver. Anyway, surely he wouldn't murder the Collins boys."

"Dave's old enough to shoot if he fires first. Chandless could send the other two to an orphanage or settle them in with one of his married hands."

"That would be about like shutting up two young wildcats."

"They could be whipped or starved till they wouldn't scratch much."

Trace's bleak tone made her wonder if something like that had happened to him. She knew little about him. Only that he'd grown up in Indian Territory, learned drilling on oil wells in Pennsylvania, was longtime partners with Cibolo, and had killed a friend of Jack Mallory's.

"If you wish you hadn't thrown in with Shan and me," she said in as indifferent a voice as she could manage, "you're free to go as soon as you dig Rose Kendall's well."

"Now wait a minute—"

"I'll find another ground man for our crew," she rushed on. "And I'll pay you for digging the Halls' well and helping raise the windmill and—"

Strong arms closed around her, brought her close. His hard, warm mouth found hers. The beat of his heart entered her blood, pulsed through her in wild, sweet tingling. When, gasping, he tried to draw away, she melted against him and clasped her hands behind his neck, hungering for the feel of him, longing to be so close to him that there'd be no telling where one began and the other left off.

"Julie, Julie!" He smoothed her hair, cradling her against him. "I never meant to do that!"

"I'm glad you did." *Oh, so glad!*

With what was almost a groan, he moved away and held her at his long arm's length. "I didn't mean to do it but I guess I might as well say I've wanted to from the minute I saw you with that shotgun, all proud and brave and scared and just plain beautiful. I—" He shook his head. "I'm sorry, Julie. It's not fair to let you know how I feel when I'm not likely to live through settlin' accounts with Mallory."

"Is that why you've been acting like a rattler with a toothache?"

"That bad?" He gave a rueful laugh and released her, stepping farther back. "Before I met you, I wouldn't have worried. Man has to die sometime. But now there's other things I'd rather do."

"Why are you so sure Mallory can kill you?"

Trace shrugged. "Mallory lives by his gun. I don't. Even if he waited till I had my pistol in my hand before he drew his, chances are he'd drop me while I was aiming."

"If you believe that, you're crazy to give him the chance!"

"We have an agreement."

"An agreement to let him murder you?"

"Oh, I won't just stand there. Might be my lucky day."

She made a rude sound and resolved to talk to Mallory herself or ask Rose to use her influence with him. Trace spoke softly. "I've got to hope you won't pay too much in grief for that kiss, Julie. I'm asking you to help me behave. Till things are square with Mallory, no more kissin', huggin', or honey words."

"It won't matter." Her breath caught in a sob. "Oh, Trace, forget Mallory! I don't know how I'd stand it if he killed you."

"I can't run."

There'd be no changing his mind, at least, not just yet. She swallowed and said raggedly, "I thought maybe Rose—"

He didn't pretend not to understand. "Miss Rose is sure pretty and quite some woman. I'll admit that once I'd have been pawin' up dust in her corral." Trace chuckled. "But I'm man-critter enough to want to teach my woman how to kiss rather than have her teachin' me."

Even if he wouldn't hold her, it was sweet to be with him. Julie cast around for a happier subject than his quarrel with Mallory. "Trace, what would you think about claiming land here, making it the outfit's headquarters?"

He considered. "Cibolo's been saying we should homestead while we can, and from the way Shan looks at Miss Madelaine, he'd favor the notion. If anything happens to me I'd like to know you have a homing place where folks care about you."

"Nothing's going to happen to you!"

"I hope you're right." Even though they weren't touching, achingly sweet awareness flowed between them. His voice was husky. "If the four of us took up claims, we'd have a section. We could get another section by filing timber claims."

"Then we'd have to plant trees, wouldn't we?"

"Sure, but cottonwoods aren't hard to grow from cuttings, especially when they can be watered."

She closed her eyes to imagine young trees that changed into a shady grove, a haven for the cattle and horses and mules that drank from a tank by the windmill. On the slope above, trees sheltered a house surrounded by flowers, a big garden, and fruit trees. She was picking apples when Trace came up and took her in his arms. . . .

His voice roused her. "Good night, Julie."

"Good night," she whispered.

She ached for him. It was going to be harder, much harder, now she knew the feel of his mouth, the tender strength of his arms. Yet how wonderful, how lucky, that he did care about her! She'd try to deserve that, work cheerfully, and be glad.

In spite of that determination, when LeMoyne rose in greeting from the foot of her bedroll, she threw her arms around him and buried her face and tears against his neck.

She had lost Cap. She couldn't lose Trace; she couldn't bear it.

Shan had nailed an old windmill crate back together to hold the apex end of the tower about four feet off the ground. Julie tried to ignore Trace's long muscular brown hands, his closeness, as the crew fitted in the wooden platform where someone would stand while oiling the mill or pulling the pump to change the leathers, a chore that needed to be done about every six months. Next, the head and vane assembly were lifted into place and attached, the task made easier by having four people instead of three. Since the mill was small, a six-foot Eclipse, the wheel, too, was fitted on.

"Artesian wells save all this fuss and are great—when you can find 'em." Trace helped Shan wire the wheel to the vane so it wouldn't spin as the tower was raised. Several times that morning Julie had caught him watching her. Each brief encounter sent lightning through her, though he'd glanced quickly away. She sensed that he was talking to dispel the mounting tension between them. "The army sure wasted a lot of time and money huntin' them before the uncivil war."

Julie guessed he was trying to ease the awkwardness between them. She couldn't watch him without remembering last night, couldn't look at his mouth without longing to feel it on hers. It must be as tormenting for him, so she asked, though she had little interest then or now, in the army, "Where were they looking for the wells?"

"Along the southern trail to California. It ran through the driest parts of this whole country, across the Llano Estacado and what became the New Mexico and Arizona Territories. The Gold Rush started folks to California and they kept on going."

"Yeah," put in Shan, "and with oxen needing five to ten gallons of water a day, and horses nearly as much, there's no way to haul enough barrels to last between watering spots."

"So poor old Captain John Pope—he got to be a general in the war—spent three years drillin' for water in southeastern New Mexico. They drilled wells as deep as eight hundred sixty-one feet with just a spring-pole and oak poles, but they never got one where the water overflowed at the top the way Pope's bosses wanted it to."

"Soldier boys had cave-ins and blue northers that near froze and blowed them off them lonesome plains." Cibolo shook his head in mock condolence. "Then Pope got hold of a steam boiler engine and did he have grief with that!"

"It only took a few days for that Pecos River water to clog the boiler flues with lime and sand," Trace explained. "Pope reflued it and put manheads in the boiler so it could be cleaned good every six days or so, but he was fightin' a war he couldn't win. The water completely ate up the boiler and sand cut the valves and plungers of the pump to pieces." He grinned at Cibolo. "We don't hanker to dig wells out there, do we, pard?"

Cibolo gave a long whistle. "I'd as soon drill in hell, and there's not a lot of difference exceptin' hell don't have cactus and rattlesnakes."

As they bantered, the crew fastened the upper tackle block

to the main pull-rope which was drawn over the top of the snubbing posts, a pair of crossed pipes bent toward the tower at about a thirty-degree angle, which supplied leverage. This end of the rope would be tied to the harness of the four mules, who, flicking ears and tails and munching a treat of grain, waited more or less patiently on their humans.

The other end of the pull rope passed through pulleys in the blocks and was firmly secured to another block and tackle on the ground. Guy lines fastened to both sides and the rear of the tower were held by Shan, Julie, and Trace. They would tighten these ropes or slacken them to keep the tower from tipping over as it was hoisted.

Shan and Julie carefully checked over the whole tower, the connections, supports, and ropes. "Slow and smooth and steady does it," Shan called to Cibolo who was directing the team. "I trained the lead mules, so just let 'em do their job."

Any sudden jerks could loosen parts of the windmill or tower. Julie held her breath at the critical moment when the rig rose from the support of the crate and great stress was placed on it and the ropes.

There was creaking and squeaking as the mules moved forward, but nothing buckled. "You're the best, smartest mules in the world," Cibolo praised. "Why, you're steppin' so light and pretty you wouldn't smash eggshells! Wouldn't swap you for any fancy horses that ever came down the pike. Just a tad more. . . . Just a hair. . . . Good babies! Whoa!"

The women and girls hurried out to cheer as all four legs settled into the anchor holes. While the pull rope and guy lines were still in place, the crew used crowbars to pry the legs to match the holes in the anchor posts. These were bolted into place and then the holes were filled in with earth tamped down frequently to pack it solid around the five feet of the tower legs that were underground.

"Now," said Julie, smiling at the excited Hall family while going to the tool tarp to choose a riveting hammer and her favorite wrench, which had an extra long handle to give her more leverage, "we tighten every nut and bolt on this windmill. Cap always said, nine times out of ten windmill problems come from nuts dropping off."

When every nut and bolt was tight as it would go, Shan whooped, "Now to get this outfit ready to pump!"

Cibolo and Trace already had pipe in the hole. While Cibolo unharnessed the mules with lavish praise, Shan and Julie attached the pumping cylinder to the bottom length of the sucker rod. Then Trace helped them screw cypress rods together, lowering the string of them down the pipe till the one with the pump rested beneath the water surface ninety feet below. When attached to the windmill head, the sucker rod would move up and down, pumping water up the pipe.

Now and then Trace's arm or hand brushed against Julie. They both reacted as if burned by sweet fire. Did the others guess? From the troubled sympathy in his blue eyes, she thought that Shan did. A final rod reached into the head. Standing on the platform, Shan and Julie connected it, to be powered by the up-and-down thrust created by the head from the rotary motion of the wheel.

While Julie climbed down the steel ladder, Shan slid down a tower leg, gripping it with his gloved hand, hooking his right leg lightly around the leg's outer edge, catching himself with his left foot just long enough at each horizontal girt to control the speed of his descent.

"Now, you ladies, be sure your husbands oil the head and any other parts that need it every week," he cautioned. "They need to check the nuts and bolts just as regular. And about every six months they'll probably need to put in new leathers."

"What are they?" Lorena asked.

"They're a set of molded leathers at the end of the sucker rod that form kind of a seal to keep water from running back out of the valve instead of going up the pipe. Going up and down inside the drop pipe wears the leathers out."

"So how do we change them?" Reba frowned. A windmill was a blessing but not one to be enjoyed without continuing effort.

"The sucker rod has to be pulled up. But first you unscrew the top rod from the lower ones and tie it out of the way. Then you pull up the rest of the rods, either with man power or using a horse and block and tackle, unscrewing them till you get to the one with the leathers."

"The bottom rods are slippery from being wet," put in Julie. "It's a good idea to wear gloves because all the rods get splintery."

Guy lines and pull ropes were taken off the tower. Trace fitted a pipe with a cross valve to the drop pipe, and attached a short pipe to spill water into the big wooden trough dragged over from the old well. Then Trace added the pipe to fill the storage tank. This would supply water on the rare occasions when the wind wasn't working hard enough.

"Here's how you turn the mill on," Julie told the Halls. Reba pulled the lever. The wheel, turning to catch the wind with its cypress slats, gave a sound like a giant drawing in a breath. It began to spin. The sucker rod pushed down, pulled up. In a few minutes, water sparkled like liquid diamonds as it poured from the pipe into the trough.

Long-drawn sighs came the Hall women. Tears ran down Reba's cheeks. "Prettiest sight I ever saw outside of my boys when they was born."

A surge of longing swept over Julie, a sense of loss for something she had never known. Had her mother thought she was pretty? And what was her mother like—and the young father? What had been their dreams and hopes? It made Julie ache to realize that they couldn't have been many years older than she was now when their lives had ended. Growing up safe and happy in the love of Cap and Shan, she hadn't thought too much about her parents, but as she grew older, she had wondered and felt sad for them.

"We'll get a hose to run to the garden," Millie planned. "I can't wait to see the tomatoes and peppers and beans and peas perk up!"

"We'll build a well-house as soon as we can," Reba beamed. "We'll have a trough to set the milk and cream in, and the water running through it can flow into a pipe that'll carry it to the orchard we're going to plant."

Lorena laughed joyously. "It'll be wonderful to take a bath without feeling guilty for using water that had to be drawn up from the well."

"We'll do a big wash in the morning," Reba said. "Scrub

the winter's grime out of the quilts so they'll be fresh and clean when we put them away till fall."

"Sounds like more work instead of less," said Ellen under her breath.

Her mother's sharp ears caught the grumble. She frowned at her daughter. "It may be more work but we'll have lots more good things to eat, even fruit when the trees get big enough. You ought to like that, even if you're scared you'll melt like sugar or salt if you take a bath."

Scenting the water, the mules came up to drink. "You deserve it," Reba told them. Her plump face widened in a smile as she turned to the crew. "Come have your dinner before you go."

"We've got two kinds of pie!" shrilled Annie, red frizz jouncing as she raced ahead.

"As long as we have a bite of food," said Millie, in a voice that caught, "you'll always be welcome to half of it."

Trace grinned at her. "I'll try to happen by when you're having roasting ears."

"Slathered with your fresh butter!" enthused Shan.

Julie looked up at the whirring blades and whispered to Cap's spirit, "Do you see how glad you've made them?" She thought he did. And she gave thanks that at least she and Trace could do such a good thing together, that they could share in bringing the water of life to humans, birds, and beasts, and growing things.

A meadowlark rose trilling from a tussock of grass. An eagle spiraled in joy of sun and air. The black-and-white cows came to drink and the rooster crowed his dominion from the edge of the tank.

"*O all ye Fowls of the Air, bless ye the Lord.*" The prayer Cap loved filled Julie's heart. "*O all ye Beasts and Cattle, praise ye the Lord: praise him and magnify him forever.*"

*E*ight

*O*n their way back to the Collins place, the crew met the Hall men with Dave and Jon riding in the back of the wagon amidst post-hole diggers, shovels, pry-bars, wire-stretchers, and half a bale of wire.

"The boys' fence is up, stretched good and tight," said Laban. He smiled approvingly at the sunburned youngsters. "Jerry allowed as to how he could hold down the farm while Dave and Jon help us with the fence. The ladies want to feed him and he sure likes that proposition." The farmer peered hopefully from under grizzled eyebrows. "Our windmill up and workin'?"

"You bet." Shan chuckled as he looked from Hall to Hall. "Your wives are tickled pink. Already got you buildin' a wellhouse and irrigatin' an orchard."

"First thing we've got to do is fence our crops," said Laban. "Don't want Chandless's cows feastin' off our corn and wheat like they did last year."

"Soon as we get the fence up and run irrigatin' pipe to the fields, we'll come back and build the ladies' fence," Rafe promised. He gave a relieved smile. "Miss Rose can midwife. The others say she's better'n most doctors because she scrubs her hands and boils the scissors and makes sure everything's clean."

"I doubt," said Laban dourly, "that your ma will want any help from the Kenton ladies."

Rafe stared. "Why, Pa, you ate three chunks of Miss Maddy's chocolate cake! You drank that willow tea Miss Rose gave you for your headache and swore it cured you! And—and you sat up listenin' to Miss Barbara sing and play her mandolin a good while after Cibolo quit playin' his harmonica and Thad and me hunted our covers."

The elder Hall crimsoned. "No call to blab everything you know, boy, 'specially not to your mama. How do you think Lorena would take it if she knew you dried dishes for Miss Maddy when you don't do it for her?"

"That's different! Lorena's my wife!"

"Sure," said his father. "Try tellin' her about it like that if you want to live in the doghouse permanent."

"I only ate two chunks of cake." Thad's expression was virtuous. "And I only listened to a couple of songs and never dried no dishes."

"That's on account of you're lazy!" Rafe shot back. "I bet Millie wasn't on your mind when you watched the ladies like a kid in a candy store."

Laban grinned. "Like old Ben Franklin said, we all better hang together or we'll sure hang separately." He sobered. "We can't thank you enough for the well and windmill and lending us cash for fencing. Dave and Jon can drive to Tyrone for it tomorrow whilst the rest of us start diggin' post holes."

"Wouldn't hurt to have Ellen or Annie climb up the tower once in a while to watch for dust," Trace said.

"You mean Hartman?"

"Him or anyone who might give you trouble. Send for us and we'll burn the wind gettin' here."

The Hall men exchanged glances. "If we have to fight to have water in this country, we'll fight," Laban said, more in resignation than anger.

Thad nodded. Rafe burst out, "Jess Chandless hogged the creeks and Dry Cimarrón. He can't claim the water under our land!"

"Let's hope he won't try, son," put in Shan. "But call us if he does."

"We're obliged," said Laban. "The same goes for us. If you run into grief, let us know and we'll come fast as we can." He clucked to the mules. "Good luck with the ladies' well."

Trace laughed and called over his shoulder, "Good luck with your wives!"

Julie felt a curious sense of homecoming as the wagons rolled into the gentle valley, and not only because of the new grave from the plum thicket. What she would always think of as Cap's windmill rose like a sentinel. Jerry, from the tower platform, waved his hat and yelled a greeting. Below, Barbara and Rose were busy at washtubs. Sheets and other white things fluttered from a line stretched from the west leg of the tower to a pry-bar driven into the ground. Since this end cleared the earth by less than five feet, only washcloths and frilly white camisoles and drawers hung there.

The blue-and-white-striped tent seemed to watch over the Collinses' dugout. Though the crew had only been gone two whole days and this was late morning of the third day, the vibrant green stalks of corn and wheat, ruffled by wind behind their four wire fence, seemed to have grown half a foot.

As the mules slowed near the windmill, LeMoyne jumped down and made for Cap's grave, but he did pause to sniff at Sunny and endure her ecstatic welcome, a series of wild loops galloped around him, with a scuffle at the end. LeMoyne trotted on to the mound but he carried his tail at a happier angle and when Sunny curled up by him, he touched her nose before he put his head between his paws.

Freezing halfway down the tower, Jerry cried, "Someone's coming!"

"How many?" called Trace.

"One. Just one. On a horse."

"Are you sure?"

"Sure I'm sure!"

"Is the horse a red roan?" Shan yelled. Julie knew he remembered that was the color of the horse Lute Hartman had ridden. Of course, riders used a number of horses, so the color didn't positively identify the rider.

Starting to clamber on down, Jerry said, "It's gray."

"Stay up there, just in case, son," Trace ordered. "If anyone else follows, let us know."

One rider wasn't much of a menace. Trace visibly relaxed and glanced up at the big crates between the tent and plowed land. "Looks like you collected your windmill," he said to the laundrywomen. "I'll drive the steam engine up there and we'll start your well just as soon as we've had dinner."

The women's faces were shadowed by their sunbonnets but that didn't conceal the dance of Rose's dark eyes and flash of her smile. "Is that a hint?" she teased. "I just put cornbread to bake. It'll be ready by the time you move your engine."

Her sleeves and Barbara's were rolled up, exposing graceful arms and, though their cotton dresses were simple and high-necked, no garment could hide the lushness of Rose's figure and the slender bloom of Barbara's.

How would I look in a dress? Julie wondered. It had never mattered before, but she wanted Trace to see her looking like a woman sometime, not a boy. She couldn't, of course, wear skirts while working with windmills, but—well, she thought for the first time in her life that it would be nice to have a dress.

Hefting down the box of butter, cream, and eggs, and the jug of buttermilk sent by the Hall women, Julie stayed in camp while Trace and Shan drove their wagons up to the prospective site of the women's well. It looked to Julie as if Danny had plowed the planned five acres. He, Letty, and Madelaine were dropping what must be seed corn into the clods and covering the grain with their feet.

Rose was scrubbing out boys' grimy clothes on the washboard and putting them through the hand-turned wringer which rolled them into the rinse tub. There Barbara swished them up and down and ran them through the wringer again before dropping them in a big willow basket.

"Shall I hang these up for you?" Julie asked.

"Thanks, but we're almost finished." Rose wiped her face with the edge of her apron and shielded her eyes. The horseman now bulked larger on the horizon. "Whoever that is, he's still alone, thank goodness! We'll have to invite him to dinner. Maybe you could throw a couple of cans of tomatoes in the rice and beans, Julie, and open up some peaches and pears. If you toss dried apples and apricots into the juice, it makes a pretty fair fruit salad."

"We can have butter on the cornbread," Julie said. "Reba Hall sent it along with eggs and cream. I can whip cream to put on the fruit. If there are potatoes left from breakfast, I'll fry them up with eggs and onions."

"Scrumptious!" Rose sighed as she held up torn and faded Levi's. "The boys don't have any clothes that aren't falling to shreds. If their poor mother could see them—"

"She'd be happy they've got neighbors like you," Julie said. "Next time we send Dave to town, Jon and Jerry can go along and all of them get some clothes."

"We'll pitch in for that," volunteered Barbara. "We're enjoying the boys." Her smile faded. "My kid brothers must be about ready to leave home by now. I haven't seen them since—since I left five years ago."

Why had she left? What had happened to bring her to a fancy house in Kenton? Did she know who had fathered the child she carried? Did she love him?

Rose touched the younger woman's arm in wordless comfort. "We've missed being around children, and the boys miss their folks, especially their mother, poor lady. It's fun playing aunt or big sister."

Julie nodded. She felt the same. Nothing could make up for losing Cap but it was good to have friends. As she went about the last touches to dinner, she allowed herself to dream again of the home she and Trace would build, of fields and an orchard, gardens, and children. . . .

Jerry slid down the tower leg in a monkeylike imitation of Shan. "It's Colonel Chandless! I remember the shaggy eyebrows and that humpy nose of his from when he tried to get us to sell out!"

The man behind Lute Hartman! The one really to blame for Cap's death! Blood roared in Julie's ears. Her knees would have given way beneath her if she hadn't steadied herself on the chuckbox. In spite of knowing Hartman had meant to scare Cap, not kill him, and that Cap wouldn't want another life wasted, her mouth tasted of bitter salt. The diffused hatred she had for bullies, those who'd trample the lives of people like the Halls and Collinses and the Kenton women, concentrated itself to focus on the man who smoothly halted his big gray horse with some secret communication of his body.

He took off his battered, once pearl-gray Stetson. There was more white than black in his hair, shaggy and kinked as a buffalo's topknot. The prominent hook of his nose gave him the look of an eagle. Sleet-gray eyes took Julie in and swept on to Rose and Barbara.

He gave the last two an unguarded, incredulous stare before he recovered with a bow that seemed a trifle exaggerated. "Ladies."

"Colonel." Rose's tone was coolly ironic.

His gaze, as if against his will, rested on Barbara. "I'm kind of surprised to find you in a washtub, Miss Galway." His mouth tucked down at the corners. "As I recall, when I asked you to be my—housekeeper, you turned me down cold."

Her fair skin colored. She picked up the basket and threw over her shoulder as she walked to the clothesline, "I'm not keeping anyone's house but mine, Colonel Chandless."

Again using that uncanny control, he eased his horse to the other side of the line so she'd have to face him or reverse the way she was standing. "If being a laundress suits you better, Miss Galway, I'm looking for a good one."

"So many are," she murmured, pegging up Jerry's raggedy pants. "I could use a laundress, too, sir. If you find one, please let me know."

In spite of her outrage, Julie almost laughed. Rose did. It was the colonel's turn to redden. Seizing on his discomfiture, Rose said, "Julie, I don't think you know Colonel Jess Chandless. Colonel, this is Miss Julie McCloud."

He turned from Barbara as if baffled at an abrupt change in the rules of a game he knew well and was used to winning. He had the sense not to smile. "Miss McCloud, I'm sorrier than I can say about Captain McCloud. He was, I'm told, your guardian."

"Yes." That was all Julie could trust herself to say. Cap wouldn't want her to cry or curse.

"My foreman was told not to shoot to kill unless he was fired upon."

"But you think it's fine to shoot to scare?"

"If that's what works."

"And if people don't scare?"

His face grooved into hard lines. "Whatever it takes, Miss McCloud." Before she could defy him, he raised his gauntleted hand. "Let's settle this before anyone else gets hurt."

"I just put up windmills," Julie said.

"Yep. And your partner digs wells and you put up cash for posts and that damned barbwire."

"It's the only way to keep your cattle out of people's crops."

"Cattle might as well get some good of the wheat and corn before grasshoppers do or the wind sears them down to the roots."

"Our corn looks real good." Jerry's indignation made him forget his manners and sass an elder. "Mama said this was the best corn land she ever saw!"

The rancher looked almost wistfully at the snub-nosed, yellow-haired boy. "The soil's rich, lad. But you don't have a corn sky." He swept his hand toward the brilliant, cloudless heavens.

"That's what windmills are for," Julie reminded him.

His jaw clamped tight. "Windmills just prolong the agony."

"Some could say that about your trying to stay in the cattle business." Julie ticked the major disasters off on her fingers. "There was the blizzard of 'eighty-three when cattle froze by tens of thousands along the drift fences. The blizzard that hit New Year's Day in 'eighty-six wiped out more than half the cattle on the plains. More died the next year in the bad drought. And then there's tick fever—"

"I reckon I know more about those times than you do, young lady!" Chandless gazed south as if he saw specters of starving, freezing herds. "Out of ten thousand head, less than a thousand lived. We skinned the dead ones and sold their hides. I mortgaged everything to restock my range. What with good calf crops, twelve thousand head wore my brand in 'eighty-six." His voice dropped. "After the blizzard, only four thousand did."

"But you stayed."

The shaggy head came up. "Since you know what I've been

through to hang on to my range, looks like you'd know I don't aim to lose it."

"You don't have to hog the whole country."

"Who's got a better right to it?"

"The Comanches and Kiowas might think they did, or the Cheyenne and Arapaho who hunted here, too. Or the sheepmen who brought their flocks out of New Mexico as early as the Civil War and freighted their wool up the old Santa Fe Trail to Missouri. Did you scare them off, kill them, or buy them out?"

"I paid the Bernal brothers to move their sheep."

"I suppose that was better than killing them."

He laughed. "They thought so." The winter eyes speared her. "We ought to cut a deal before anyone else gets hurt. I can use windmills—if you'll recall, you were supposed to put up a dozen for me. I'll pay you for putting up this one and the well and mill over at the Halls' place. Hell, I'll pay you for the well and mill it looks like you're fixin' to do for these ladies. I'll buy their claims at twice what they're worth—not that they're anything but squatters with no legal rights."

"And what are you?" Julie asked.

His heavy shoulders seemed to bulk larger. "I've stuck it out here for eighteen years through everything this country could throw at me. I reckon that gives me a better right than nesters who'll rip up the sod, ugly up the landscape, and head for easier living when things get tough."

"It's been tough on us, mister." Jerry's round chin lifted. "We ain't left!"

The rancher's eyes thawed a bit. "Son, you and your brothers are welcome anytime to come live with me."

Tears glittered in Jerry's eyes. "Not after you killed Cap!"

"We aren't leaving, Colonel." Rose smiled pleasantly as she brought crimson to his face by flaunting ruffly drawers as she hung them to the line. "I doubt if you can get your men to shoot us. Will you do it yourself?"

He watched her grimly. "The country'll take care of you, ma'am."

Arched black eyebrows rose. "Oh?"

"Wait'll your soft, pretty skin starts to get rough and leathery. Wait'll a late blizzard kills your critters and freezes your garden and crops. Wait—"

"*You* wait!" Barbara shook a beribboned camisole in his face, causing his horse to shy. "When No Man's Land opens up for legal settlement the way it's bound to in a year or so, we'll file our claims and we'll already be a good way toward proving up on them!"

With a whirl of skirts, she turned to peg up the garment. Chandless's eyes followed her as if drawn unwillingly, lingered on the sweet curves accentuated by her actions. He said harshly, "What the sodbusters that swarm in will learn is that this is God's country but few men's. And it's no woman's."

"We'll show you."

He grunted. "What you'll do is show the dratted home-steaders that you're on my range so they'll get the notion they can light there, too."

"They can." As Chandless stared, Rose continued in an amiable tone. "Justice will come along with legal settlement, sir. Lute Hartman's gun won't be the law anymore."

"This—this is a damned rebellion!"

" 'Rebellion' is rising up against authority," Barbara retorted. "You've got no authority to tell us what to do!"

Trace, Cibolo, and Shan had left the steam engine and supply wagon near the striped tent, unharnessing the mules before turning them loose. The men came down the slope now, Letty, Danny, and Madelaine close behind them.

Chandless sent his horse forward. It looked as if he were going to force the nervous gray right into the men but Trace kept coming. It was the rancher who let the horse stop.

"I'm Jess Chandless." From the side, he looked more than ever like a brooding eagle as his gaze flicked over the newcomers. He took off his hat and nodded to the ladies before he studied Trace. "Are you the well-digger Jack Mallory's sore at?"

Trace grinned. "News travels, seems like. I'm Trace Riordan. Yonder's my partner, Cibolo, and Mike Shanahan here's our new partner along with Miss McCloud. I reckon you've met."

"We have."

Trace smiled at Madelaine and Letty. "We're fixing to start on these ladies' well this afternoon. Let me acquaint you with Miss Thomas and Miss Sutherland. Maybe you know Dan Shelton."

"Heard of him." The rancher's tone was bleak. His eyes studied Dan in a way that made the young man flush. His Adam's apple bobbed as he moved protectively close to Letty.

"Me 'n Miss Sutherland are gettin' married. We've already claimed our land."

Chandless's thick brows forked together. "Claiming's easy, youngster. Keeping's another." He gave a bark of laughter. His side glance brought a rush of color to Letty's face. "Might be as true of your intended as it is of your land."

Danny's fists knotted. "Climb down off of that horse, you old buzzard!"

Letty caught his arm. "Danny! Pay him no mind!"

"Don't fret, ma'am. I don't fight boys." The cattleman shifted his attention to Trace. "Hope you've got better sense than your partner here, Riordan. You can head out of here with your rig and a nice profit or you can lose everything you've got, includin' your hide."

"Reckon we won't be leaving, Chandless." Trace's voice was lazily soft.

"What do you mean by that?"

Trace shrugged. "We're claiming land. We like the neighbors."

Veins stood out in the rancher's temples. His horse fidgeted. He brought it under control. Bulking in the saddle, he slewed his gaze to strike Julie like a freezing sudden wind. "Why? Why won't you go?"

Strange that such a quiet, almost-pleading tone could turn her bones to water, frighten her more than Hartman with all his men. Her spine chilled with a primal sense of his desperation, his cornered ruthlessness.

She couldn't trust her voice not to waver. She pointed to the raw grave by the blooming thicket.

Chandless's lips thinned as if formed by a chisel. His eyes swept from the Collins boys to the Kenton women and Danny. "Your claims aren't worth a match in hell but I'll buy you out."

Rose looked at her friends. Slowly, they shook their heads. Danny put a protective arm around Letty. Dave said, in a voice that cracked from deep to high, "We're not leavin', Colonel."

The rancher's glance touched Cibolo and Shan and halted on Trace and Julie. "Whatever happens, it's on your heads."

He spun the gray with the slightest hint of the reins against its neck. In spite of the heat of the sun, Julie shivered. More graves beside Cap's?

She turned to the women and boys. "Maybe you should—"

"Sell out?" Rose stared after the horseman with a bleak smile. "It'd likely be the same wherever we tried to homestead. Cattlemen think they own as much land as their cows can graze, and that's plenty in this country."

Madelaine's smile lingered on Shan. "Like you told the colonel, Trace, we like our neighbors." Her smile broadened into a mischievous grin. "Tell you what, soon as we're through planting, let's give a dance."

"A dance?" Julie echoed.

"Perfect!" Rose clapped her hands. "No cowboy will miss a dance!"

"And after they've dosey-doed with you ladies, they sure won't want to have a hand in running you out." Shan chuckled and sniffed. "Smells like the cornbread's ready for the butter."

"Come and get it," Julie invited. "There's a well to start this afternoon."

"And corn to plant," said Madelaine.

"And post holes to dig," groaned Dave.

No one put into words what was in all their minds. What would Chandless do now?

Trace said to Jerry, "Would you mind climbing the windmill tower every now and again, son, and having a good look around for anyone heading this way?"

Jerry swelled with importance. "You bet I will!"

"Get your dinner first," Trace said, but Jerry shook his yellow head.

"I'll go up right now, Trace. Maybe that nasty ol' colonel

103

has Lute Hartman holed up somewheres waitin' on him!" The boy sped up the vertical steel ladder without a pause, shaded his eyes, and warily studied the horizon. He slid to earth down a tower leg in a precarious imitation of Shan, and trotted up to the group filling their plates.

"There's a bunch of antelope to the north. The Halls' windmill's flashin' in the sun and I could make out the men diggin' post holes. Miz Oliver's got her laundry flappin' and there's cows along the river. But I never saw no riders outside of the colonel."

"Well done," praised Trace. "Now, you fill your plate and eat hearty so you'll have the ginger to keep climbing up there."

"Yessir!" Jerry furrowed his brow as he looked up at Trace. "It's important, bein' a sentry?"

Trace dropped a hand on the boy's thin shoulder. "The way things stand, son, there's nothing more important. If anyone's headin' this way, the sooner we know it, the better."

Julie feared it wasn't a question of *if* but of *when*.

$\mathcal{N}$ine

$\mathcal{G}$ray clouds roiled from the smokestack of the boiler. Cibolo shoveled more coal into the firebox and spread it carefully around. A heavy manila rope, attached to the crank on the band wheel, ran over a pulley at the top of the mast, and came back down to fasten to the rope socket, screwed to the weight bar which in turn was screwed to the spudding bit, a steel bar about four feet long, rounded on two sides, with a broad, blunt wedge at the bottom.

Trace straightened from adjusting the rope and signaled with his gloved hand. Cibolo started the engine. Trace held the rope steady and the twist in the rope made the tools turn slowly as the revolutions of the crank raised the bit and let it drop hard against the earth.

"We can drill without rods till we get to about three hundred feet," Trace explained to Julie above the racket. "I'm pretty sure we'll have water before that, judging from the Collinses' well."

"Can I help?" she asked, none too enthusiastically. The belching steam engine and whining rope with the huge bit made her more nervous than working on the highest windmill tower ever had.

Trace must have read her feelings. His eyes danced and he took one hand off the vibrating rope long enough to brush her arm. "Thanks, but Cib and me can handle it. What you could do is connect a hose down at the Collinses' mill and add on lengths to reach up here. I don't expect to hit any water till we're down a few hundred feet. We'll need water for the steam-engine boiler and to mix the shale and rock we hit in the hole so it can be sucked up by the bailer and dumped."

She hastened to rig the hoses. By the time she dragged the last length up to the rig, the bit had pulverized the sod and was pounding into the soil. "The bit raises and falls about fifty-five times a minute till some mud is mixed," Trace told her as she paused to watch. "That slows down the fall of the tools."

"How long do you think it'll take to reach some water?"

"Depends. The easiest drilling is through shale hard enough to stand up without crumbling but soft enough not to dull the bit real fast. We can make forty to a hundred feet a day in that. But sometimes you're lucky to make ten feet a day through hard limestone." Jerry watched, fascinated, as Trace guided the rope and the earth vibrated at the impact of each drop of the bit.

"Want to get the feel of it, son?" Trace asked. At the awed dip of Jerry's head, the driller said, "Put your hands just beneath mine on the rope. Right now we can see what the bit's doing, but once it's pounded itself out of sight, you can learn to tell a lot from how the rope acts."

"Whillikers!" breathed Jerry. He glanced sheepishly at Julie. "I still want to be a windmiller when I grow up but this is— is glory-awfulness!"

"You can do both," Julie said.

"Sure you can," Trace nodded. "Right now, when we get a little deeper, you can run in the water and help with the bailer. And you can be waterboy for Cib and learn how to keep that old steam up."

"Whillikers!" sighed Jerry beatifically. Remembering his prime duty, he squinted at the tower. "Is it time for me to climb up again?"

"Pretty soon." Trace smiled down at the boy who gazed at him worshipfully as they stood by the rope.

What a marvelous father Trace would make! Watching the play of hard muscles in his shoulders as he directed the bit and

106

rope, remembering the wonder of being in his arms, close to his beating heart, she was suffused with a melting, delicious tremor followed by dread.

They would soon have this well dug, the windmill up, and the fence done. Trace would then believe he had to give Jack Mallory a chance to kill him—and from what he'd said about their comparative skill with guns, it would be near murder.

She couldn't just wait and let that happen. Trace would never let her intercede for him. The same male pride that decreed he meet a professional gunman forbade that. But she'd be pleading for herself more than for him—for their life together, for children who'd be lucky to have Trace for their father.

I'll ask Mallory first myself, Julie decided. *Track him down as soon as we finish with the windmill. If he won't listen to me, maybe Rose will try, though he hasn't come calling the way she sort of made it plain that she hoped he would.*

Julie went to dig post holes around the broken sod where the Kenton women were still planting. "We're putting in some broom corn and castor beans, too," said Letty as she passed by. Her face was flushed and sweaty under the sunbonnet and her dress stuck wetly to her shoulders, but she beamed at Danny.

He smiled back, sending down the post-hole digger with all his strength. "We're gettin' married, Miss Julie," he said proudly. "Soon as this fence is up and I plow a fireguard around our quarter sections!"

"Let's make it Saturday. We have to track down Reverend Wardlaw and give time for the news to spread," called Rose. "After the wedding, we'll have our dance." She heeled in the seed corn she dropped from a canvas bag. "Rafe Hall can fiddle. And Cibolo, I've heard you play sweeter than a mockingbird on your harmonica. We'll serve homemade ice cream and cake and tell folks to bring covered dishes to share. It'll be the biggest, best dance ever held in No Man's Land!"

A dance? Mallory was sure to come to that. A thrill of danger shot through Julie. She would have to find him first. Then, remembering something else, her heart sank.

She didn't know how to dance. Oh, until just a few years

ago, she had loved to whirl and spin in the rain, arms spread to the sky, glorying in the wild play of lightning, laughing at the thunder. She had swirled and twirled, one with the wind and storm.

But she had never danced to a fiddler or with men—and she didn't have a one single solitary excuse of a dress. Her eyes stung at the thought of Trace swinging the beautifully gowned Kenton women and who-knew-what-other pretty girls.

Silly! she chided herself. *How can you worry about something like that when there could well be other graves beside Cap's before this is settled, even if you talk Jack Mallory out of pursuing his feud?* But it still mattered. *Maybe,* she thought with sudden hope, *Trace can teach me to dance.*

That still didn't solve the problem of a dress. She was sure any of the Kenton women would be glad to lend her a gown, but she was much taller than any of them and their bodices would sag emptily from her small, high breasts.

There wasn't time to order from Ward's. Madelaine had a sewing machine but Julie could scarcely abandon work to jaunter off in search of suitable material which might not be found closer than Dodge City.

She blinked back tears and lifted dirt from the hole, so parched and dry that it lacked the fragrance she loved, the rich, moist smell of nourishing earth. She felt arid as the soil, skinny as a beanpole, forlorn as Cinderella left home from the party, and though she chuckled grimly at these exaggerations, she felt like crying.

Two days later, good water flowed into the hole at one hundred eighty feet. "It's still diggin'," Shan said with a laugh, as he broke the sod of his anchor hole with a pick, "but I'd a sight rather do this than make postholes."

"Me too," said Julie. "I guess we're just windmillers, Shan."

With Trace and Cibolo helping, they assembled the tower on the ground and raised it with the vane and mill the way they had done the Halls' rig. Everyone gathered round to watch and cheer as water gushed from the pipe. Rose produced champagne and sarsaparilla.

"Here's to wells and windmills." She lifted a sparkling crystal goblet in salute. "But most of all, here's to the ones who dig deep and build high to bring us wind water!"

Danny grimaced and rubbed his back. "Yeah, and here's to post-hole diggers!"

"Chirk up, lad," comforted Shan. "Now the windmill's spinnin', we'll pitch in on makin' that fence."

"And then," caroled Letty, grasping her sweetheart's hand and pirouetting, "we'll get married and have our dance!"

Julie applauded along with the others but her smile was stiff. She could preside over the coffeepot and refreshments, of course, but she would *hate* watching Trace dance with other women. Far more important, though, was that he be alive to dance.

When the men were at work on the fence, she went to Rose. "Could I borrow Duke or Valentine and a saddle?"

"Of course, dear." Rose's dark eyebrows arched and she laughed. "Are you sure you don't want both horses? If you lured Trace away for an hour, I'll wager we could have a double wedding."

"Remember what Jack Mallory agreed on with Trace?"

Rose gasped, hand going to her shapely throat. "Good Lord, that's right!" She frowned and then said hopefully, "Jack lots of times heads off into New Mexico or Colorado for a while. Trace could just move on."

"He won't. If Jack doesn't come looking for him, he'll look for Jack."

"Thickheaded of him."

"That's why I'm going to try to find Mallory and talk to him. Without Trace knowing."

Rose squeezed her hand. "I'll go with you."

"You don't have to," Julie began, though she was vastly relieved at the offer.

"Of course I do. For one thing, I know where he raises horses when he's not raising Cain."

"Jack Mallory raises horses?"

"The best. Quarter horses that can plow all week and win a race on Sunday. I always hoped—" Her face masked and she hunched a shoulder before she let it fall. "Let's tell the others we're looking for Reverend Wardlaw to marry Letty and Dan.

He preaches all around No Man's Land so we might as well start hunting him in Kenton."

"I—I'd like to get a dress or some material."

Rose stared at Julie's Levi's. "Good gracious, child! None of us thought! But why would you have a dress? We've got more fancy clothes than we'll wear out if we live to be a hundred—"

She broke off as she surveyed Julie. "A flounce around the hem might work for length but I doubt if our styles would alter well enough to suit your willowy figure."

"Skinny, you mean."

"Willowy," insisted Rose. "With those deep green eyes and glorious tawny hair, you have a special beauty. Your dress can't be ready-made. It needs to be simple yet elegant, flowing as wind and water." Her eyes widened and she laughed in delight. "I know just the thing! My dream dress!"

"Your what?"

Rose regarded her quizzically. "Don't you believe women in my former line of work might need to dream?"

Julie blushed. Rose patted her hand. "That's all right, Julie. How would you know? Most of us do have a dream dress, one we never wear. It's the one we plan to be buried in."

"Oh! But you're young!"

"Lots of us die young, quite a few by poison." Rose gazed back in time and shook her head. "I've seen a dozen of my friends buried in wedding gowns—lovely dresses hidden at the bottom of their trunks. Letty has one. Thank God, her bridegroom won't be death."

Sobered by this glimpse into a life that had always seemed exciting and glamorous though wicked, Julie nodded heartfelt agreement. "It's sweet of you, Rose, but I can't wear your dream dress."

Rose grinned crookedly, "I've got another dream now, honey. Even if it never comes true, I've got a lot more to look forward to than an early funeral."

"But—"

"The dress in my trunk isn't a wedding gown, and it's as different as it can be from what I used to have to wear. Nuns at the convent in Las Vegas in New Mexico made it for me. Come in the tent and I'll show you."

Rose's small, partitioned "room" had a cot, a chair, and a large brass-bound trunk. Delving to the bottom, Rose brought up folds of snowy white cloth so sheer and soft it looked like silk.

"India linen," she explained, inviting Julie to feel it. "It's not linen at all, but finest South Sea cotton woven like lawn but smoother-finished. Nothing's further from brocades and satins and taffetas."

She shook out the almost transparent cloud. "See, it has an Empire waist that lets the cloth fall without a break to the floor. I'm sure there's enough material left over for Maddy to lengthen the dress with an insertion beneath the breasts. The lower seam of the insert can be covered with this foam-green gauze sash that'll add to the floating, airy effect."

The flowing sleeves looked as if they would end at Rose's wrists but would leave three or four inches of Julie's lower arm exposed. Rose studied the problem intently, then smiled. "We'll cut the sleeves off at the elbow, gather the cut-off bottoms to make flounces, and sew them on so that you'll have sort of Juliet sleeves that end in the middle of the forearm. Very graceful."

It really did seem possible. Then Julie remembered her heavy laced boots and peered at them in horror.

"Now, don't be fretting about shoes. The four of us have so many that something's bound to fit, but I'm hoping you can wear some pale green satin slippers of mine with Spanish embroidery. They'd be perfect with this."

She rummaged in the trunk and unwrapped tissue from around exquisite slippers with one-inch heels. Mesmerized, Julie obeyed Rose. She sat down, unlaced a boot, apprehensively drew on one foot of the superfine white lisle hose Rose offered, and snugged on the slipper.

"It fits!"

"Better than it does me," Rose laughed. "Let's see now. You'll need a corset."

Aghast, Julie demanded, "Those things with laces and metal or bone strips?"

Rose eyed her appraisingly. "You can do without, I think. But you will need a chemise, an underskirt, and either garters or supporters for your hose. I assume," she added kindly, "that you do wear drawers?"

"You bet I do!" yelped Julie. "White muslin with Hamburg embroidered edging. I order them at nine dollars a dozen from Monkey Ward."

"Splendid," chuckled Rose. "Let's show Maddy what to do with the dress. She's got a good lamp and can work on it at night so she won't miss out on the planting. And then let's find John Jack Mallory!"

Julie was not an expert rider. Her traveling had been mostly in the windmiller wagons, though she had occasionally ridden one of the mules to town to pick up a few supplies. Intimidated by the sideways prong on the sidesaddle, she borrowed the Collins boys' old saddle, and Duke graciously allowed her to cinch it snugly without puffing out his satiny-cream sides.

He single-footed at a smooth, easy gait as if inviting Valentine, Rose's high-strung pale golden mare, to relax and enjoy the trip instead of shying at imagined rattlesnakes and other menaces.

"I'll have to ride this one more often," Rose declared as Valentine skittered at a meadowlark winging up from the buffalo grass. "I used to ride her every morning in Kenton but I've been too busy here."

Had she ridden with Jack Mallory? Had he given or sold her the horses? Julie wondered but held her tongue. She sensed that Rose was chagrined that he hadn't accepted her invitation to come calling and that this proud, beautiful woman was glad of an errand that gave her the chance to see the laggard without appearing to drop her conditions.

Wagons and mules going back and forth to the Hall place had scuffed the beginnings of a road which Rose regarded pensively. "I suppose the Santa Fe Trail started like this," she mused. "Just a few pack trains and wagons at first when Santa Fe was still part of Old Mexico; then by 1860 they say three thousand wagons, seven thousand men, and sixty thousand mules passed over it. Have you ever seen the trail?"

"No, but all my life, our outfit's traveled back and forth across the Chisholm Trail, the Western Trail from San Antonio to Dodge, and the Goodnight-Loving Trail that takes off from San Angelo to run out through New Mexico up to Colorado." It was Julie's turn to be pensive. "I've seen dust churn up from all the trails from the hoofs of thousands of cattle. But that's all over now with the railroad loading cows at Tyrone and the Atchison, Topeka, and Santa Fe Company, and the Missouri, Kansas, and Texas Railway Company building to Texas through the Indian Nations and Unassigned Lands. I grew up with the trail drives, Rose. It's hard to believe they're finished."

"Poor baby!" teased Rose. "But I guess that's right. The big trail-driving times only lasted twenty years and that's about how old you are, isn't it? God willing, though, we'll always have this." She gazed up at an eagle circling toward the sun and then at a badger poking his striped nose from his hole near a flowering soapweed yucca. The plant stalk rose from a daggered rosette of tough, spiky leaves but the luxuriant white blossoms blessed the prairie in all directions, and in the distance pronghorns nibbled the succulent petals.

As was prudent, the Halls had plowed a fireguard of six furrows around their claim. This broken soil would help check a prairie fire unless it was whipped with relentless winds—as such fires often were.

Approaching the Hall farm, Julie could see the men building fence while sunbonneted women were busy at tubs set on benches near the windmill. Lorena, who looked as if her baby might come anytime, stirred a steaming copper boiler set over a fire smoldering in a pit. Coltish young Ellen hung dark socks and clothes, the last things to be washed, on a wire stretched from one tower leg to a spike driven in the frame of the barn door.

Reba straightened from a washboard and came forward in welcome. Millie joined her after running some overalls through the hand-turned wringer clamped to a rinse tub. Annie, tightly kinked red hair blazing in the sun, hurried down from the platform of the windmill tower. "I knew you weren't men from a long way off!" she shrilled. "You're riding a straddle, Julie, but I know the way you hold your head. Besides, the lady's riding sideways with her skirt spread out like a peacock's tail!"

"You're a good lookout," Julie praised.

"Yes, I saw Colonel Chandless coming the other day, so Mama and Daddy and everybody was ready when he rode up."

At Julie's concerned glance, Reb's plump face tightened. "He offered to buy us out at a decent price. Said the windmill would be handy for watering his stock."

"And he said the climate's healthier in Colorado," put in Millie. "We told him we like it here just fine." From the shadow of her bonnet, gray eyes flicked warily over Rose's handsome, dark green riding habit, but she remembered her manners. "Won't you come in and have some cold buttermilk? There's a big jar of it keeping cool in the water tank."

"That sounds wonderful," Julie accepted. "But we could just drink it right here and not keep you from your work."

Reba wiped her face with her apron and laughed. "You wouldn't exactly be keepin' us from our favorite entertainment. Anyhow I just scrubbed out the last pair of overalls. We'll have a drink, too. Annie child, fetch some cups. Ellen, trot over and bring the jar." The matriarch squinted at Rose's voluminous skirts. "Think you can climb down if we overturn a tub for you?"

"Thanks for offering," said Rose in a pleasant tone. "It's less fuss to stay put."

Annie returned from her raid on all three houses with seven stoneware cups nestled in a dish towel in a kettle. She held each cup as her mother poured.

"Nothing better than cool buttermilk on a hot day." Rose thanked Ellen for her cup and took a grateful sip. "I used to not mind churning because Mama made such wonderful buttermilk biscuits."

"You grew up on a farm?" Reba's tone softened as if anyone who had churned for a mother who made good biscuits must not be utterly depraved.

Rose nodded. "Couldn't wait to get away, but these past few years, I've wanted nothing more than to get back."

Millie eyed the beautifully tailored riding outfit and straw hat trimmed with a rakish green bow. "Maybe you've forgotten how hard it is on a farm."

"Planting corn the last few days refreshed my memory." Rose rubbed her back. "But it reminded me, too, of how hopeful and fresh plants look pushing out of the earth—and if there's anything better than fresh roasting ears with fresh butter, I've never tasted it."

"I favor new potatoes creamed with peas," allowed Reba.

"Yes, and let's not talk about when hail beats down the crops or droughts shrivel them," added Millie.

"At least cows won't be eating them once the fence is up," put in Lorena. "And it's wonderful to have plenty of pure, sweet water."

"That's not all we're gettin' from that windmill." Reba pointed at a framework of old barrel staves built beneath the windmill. It held a wooden churn attached to the windmill that revolved with the motion of the blades. "Laban rigged that up. Churns grand butter in two-thirds of the time it takes by hand—and frees those hands to do something else."

"We've almost saved up enough butter and egg money for a washing machine." Millie's gray eyes shone. "Thad and Rafe claim they can rig up a way to make the windmill work the lever. Imagine that! No more washboards!"

"Before winter, the men are going to build a washhouse on one side of the windmill," put in Lorena, resting on the end of a bench. "That way we'll only have to carry water a few steps, and the fire used to heat it and boil white things will keep us nice and warm."

"Laban says he'll fix a drainpipe on the wash machine so we won't have to carry the water away and dump it." Reba shook her head in delighted wonder. "Why, there won't hardly be any work left to washin'! Girls, do you remember how we all cried when the clothesline blew down last month?"

"It was something to cry about," retorted Millie. "All those sheets and clothes to be rinsed a couple of times and every drop of water drawn up in a bucket and toted to the tubs."

"Yes, but at least we had a well," pointed out Lorena. "That was lots better than hauling water from the creek." She smiled timidly at Rose. "Is it true you're a midwife?"

"I've helped quite a few babies into this world, dear. You just send for me when you start having pains."

"With a first baby, she could have pains a good day or so before anything happens," Reba said. "Probably be time enough to call you when the pains are ten minutes or so apart."

"Send for me when you get the first honest-to-goodness pain, honey," commanded Rose. "I'd rather be here a day early than five minutes late."

Lorena's thin face brightened with color that made her dark eyes seem larger and softer. "Thanks, Miss Kendall. I don't want to be a nuisance but I can't tell you how much better that makes me feel."

Lorena's hardworking mother-in-law and sister-in-law might have been less than thrilled when Rafe brought home a town girl unused to farm chores and hardscrabble living. Probably she would have liked to ask her own mother to come to stay a few weeks and help with the baby, but that might insult Reba and Millie.

Thanking Ellen as she handed back the cup, Rose said, "We're looking for the preacher to marry Letty and Dan this Saturday, and we'll have a dance with ice cream and cake. Will Rafe bring his fiddle?"

"He'll be glad to," Lorena said. She glanced ruefully at the mound beneath her apron. "I'm usually sorry he's the fiddler because he doesn't get to dance, but since I can't, either, it'll be nice to sit by him."

"Come over as soon as you've done your chores and bring a covered dish for supper," Rose invited. "We need all the ladies we can find to dance with Chandless's cowboys."

"You're inviting them?"

"Word'll get around."

"Shouldn't think Chandless would want his hands getting friendly with folks he wants to run out of the country."

"He may not like it but I've never met a cowboy you could tell to stay home from a frolic." Rose's smile broadened to show a dimple. "That's part of the reason we're having the dance. Most men don't want to tear down fences and windmills of folks they've got to know a little, women they've danced with, and men they've joked with."

"Can I come, Mama?" begged Annie.

Millie smoothed the riotous curls of her youngest daughter. "We wouldn't dare leave you home. Last time we did, Ellen tried to lower you out of an upstairs window in a bushel basket."

"Mama!" squirmed Ellen. "That was back in Missouri when I was younger than Carrot-top is now!"

"I'm not a carrot-top!" squealed Annie, sticking out her tongue at her sister. "I—I'm a strawberry blond!"

"You may be someday," retorted Ellen loftily. "Right now, you're just a redheaded brat."

"Girls!" rebuked Millie. "Take these cups to the house, stir the beans, and put some chips in the stove." As they departed, she gave an exasperated sigh. "Let's hope you have a boy, Lorena, to keep the farm going. That pair will probably marry cowboys."

"Cowboys do turn farmer," Rose said. "We'll see you Saturday."

Julie mounted. She and Rose waved and called a greeting to the husbands stretching wire from post to post, but wisely, Julie thought, Rose didn't stop to visit.

*T*en

*B*looming soapweeds were the glory of the plains, but white and pale-pink evening primroses peeped from the grass, locoweed grew in frondy mats with tiny violet flowerets, and larkspur reared purple spikes as high as orange globe mallow.

As a shadow glided over them, a roadrunner streaked into a plum thicket a whisker ahead of the talons of a red-tailed hawk. The baffled hawk rose high enough to spot its quarry and plunged right into the thicket. As it disentangled itself, the roadrunner darted from the other end of the thicket and completely disappeared in a huge clump of grayish saltbush.

"Mr. Roadrunner was lucky that time," said Rose.

"Yes, but of course he's hunting a nice lizard or a little snake to take home to his babies," remarked Julie.

Not long after leaving the Halls', Rose pointed out what looked like a darker rim of the horizon, Black Mesa. "There's not a break or pass in all its sixty miles," she said. "The lava on top's kept it from wearing away."

The plains broke as if smashed by a giant hand into craggy, gully-scarred slopes strewn with stunted cedar, oak, and piñon. These descended to a broad valley spreading out of sight in the distance, the hills and buttes on the south side deeply riven with canyons. Prickly pear, cholla cactus, and soapweed studded the valley. Cattle grazed whatever grass they could find and luxuriated in soapweed blossoms. Chandless's cows?

A wide, shallow riverbed writhed through the valley to the north, traced by the early-summer bright green of willows and cottonwoods. It was crossed by three deep, broad ruts that snaked through the valley like giant reddish serpents. Julie rose in her stirrups and gave a long low whistle. "Is that the trail?"

"Nothing but—at least the Cimarrón Cutoff. It took days off the journey and avoided the Colorado mountains but there wasn't any reliable water for sixty miles." Rose waved a disgustedly affectionate hand toward the parched watercourse. "The Dry Cimarrón's generally flooding like crazy or dry as a bone."

"Why are there three tracks?"

"In Indian country, wagon trains traveled three or four abreast to make a compact mass that was harder to attack. In case of trouble, the columns formed a square, made a barricade of the wagons, and put the oxen or mules inside the square. That's how the freighters camped at night, too, because if the teams got spooked or stolen, the wagons weren't going anywhere."

"What do you suppose all the freighters did when the railroads took away their business?"

Rose shrugged. "Same as the buffalo hunters, beaver trappers, and other folks whose line of work dried up. Of course, there's still a lot of short distance freighting to and from railroads. Things have changed so fast in this part of the country that when you talk about the good old days, you have to figure out which ones you mean."

"And who they were good for," Julie grinned.

"Sure. The Comanches and Kiowas, Cheyennes and Arapahos enjoyed roaming here after the buffalo long before the Santa Fe Trail crossed through. When it did, all those wagons full of exciting things must have seemed like a parade of stores where you didn't have to pay for anything."

"But the Indians must have hated having all those white men coming through their hunting grounds."

"I suppose they did, but I'll bet they had fun with a lot of the stuff the wagons carried. And there were those mules that were good to ride or eat, and the chance for warriors to win honors. The trail had its entertainment side for the Indians. Railroads didn't. They were pure racket and aggravation, they sliced up the Great Plains, and worst of all, they brought in people who stayed."

Julie looked away from the trail and tried to imagine Indians coursing buffalo but instead she thought she heard the rumble of ghost wagons along the old ruts. "Where are we heading?" she asked.

"The trail takes us within a mile of Camp Nichols, which is the most likely place to find Jack Mallory."

"Kit Carson built Camp Nichols, didn't he?"

"He did, in the spring of 1865, with rocks from Carrizo Creek, but it was abandoned that fall before it was completely finished." Duke and Valentine carefully picked their way through rocks and stunted trees as they angled down the slope toward the wagon ruts. "Ten feet deep and twenty feet wide," Rose sighed. "They'll last a hundred years, I'll bet. They're so washed out it's probably easier to ride beside them than in them."

Stub-tailed prairie-dog sentries barked as the riders edged past mounds that covered many acres. At the far edge of the village, a hawk sailed down. There was a flurry of dust. In seconds, the hawk winged off with its struggling prey.

"Wonder if that was the same hawk that missed the road-runner," Julie mused.

She felt sorry for the perky little ground squirrel, but the hawk had to eat and was likely feeding young as well. This rugged hidden valley seemed a world apart, so different from the high, unbroken plains, guarded by palisaded canyons and the length of the great mesa.

The rumbling she had thought was imagination increased now. She and Rose exchanged glances and took cover behind a weirdly carved sandstone ledge. Ordinarily, one wouldn't think of hiding from someone in a wagon but these weren't ordinary times. Rose reached inside the folds of her skirt and produced a derringer. It had a a pearl stock, fancy engraving, and would fit in the palm of Rose's hand, but Julie knew from

Cap's tales of gamblers and men on both sides of the law who carried the hideout gun, that its .41-caliber slug could be deadly at distances up to thirty feet.

Two cream-colored oxen clopped into sight, sun glancing off the brass knobs on the tips of their horns. They pulled a ramshackle wagon laden with all manner of implements and furnishings. These were tied down with wire and rope laced over a ragged tarp.

The driver was as skinny and unkempt as his oxen were sleek and burnished, but Rose slipped the derringer back in its hiding place and edged Valentine from behind the ledge. Julie let Duke follow.

"Seth Owens!" Rose greeted. "Where are you heading?"

"The Smoky Hills up in Kansas, Miss Rosie." He yanked off a frayed hat of indeterminate hue to reveal sparse locks of gray hair, and nodded gallantly as Julie was introduced. "Pleased to meet you, ma'am," he said in a rusty voice before he looked fondly at Rose. "I'm tickled to have the chance to tell you good-bye, Miss Rosie. When I stopped in town, they told me you'd gone off to take up land." He squinted at her. "Hope you ain't claimed any of what Jess Chandless thinks is his'n."

"Lordy, Seth," Rose grimaced with a wry grin. "That would take in most of No Man's Land and a good chunk of Texas!" Her tone darkened. "Are you leaving on account of him? Your corn was coming up so pretty and you'd finally got your field fenced."

"Lute Hartman stopped by several days ago. He allowed as how the fence might get blown down and the corn with it, maybe my soddie, too. Then he offered me five hundred dollars cash to pack up and git."

"I guess you didn't have a lot of choice," said Rose slowly.

"It rankles to get pushed," shrugged the farmer, "but I was glad to get the money. Since my big sister Bessie's husband died last year, she's been after me to come help with their farm but I didn't like goin' empty-handed. Bessie's got a good heart but a sharp tongue." Seth shifted his tobacco but mercifully didn't spit. "Now I can pay for a windmill, buy some cows, be a real partner—and tell Bessie where to head in if she don't like my feedin' Sarge and Knobby the corn it takes to keep 'em glossy and fat."

"They always got their grain." Rose smiled.

"They earned it. Freightin' and breakin' sod is hard work. I gave 'em a feast yesterday, turned 'em in on the corn. Better them that plowed the field than Chandless's cows." He shook his head regretfully. "Guess I won't be haulin' cases of champagne and French wine to you no more, Miss Rosie. I 'preciated the way you'd give me a snort of the bubbly—and pour it into one of them thin gobblers—"

"Goblets, Seth." Rose twinkled. "I'll pour you all you want if you ever come our way, but I wish you—and Knobby and Sarge—the best of luck in the Smoky Hills."

"Thank you kindly." He pulled on the scruffy hat. Faded blue eyes touched Rose with affectionate concern. "I wish you all the luck in the world, too, Miss Rosie. You deserve it for bein' so purty and so sweet to old coots like me." He hesitated, then blurted, "I'm mighty glad you're startin' over."

Rose inclined her head. There was a mist in her eyes. "Thanks, Seth. *Vaya con Dios,* as they say in New Mexico."

"God go with you, too, honey." Seth spoke to the oxen who moved off with a rippling of muscles under smooth hide. "Nice to meet you, Miss McCloud," he called over his shoulder. "I've heard what a windmiller Cap was. Wisht I'd had the money to have him set up a mill, though I reckon now it's just as well I didn't. It's hard to leave a place with good water and plenty of it."

Their last farewells met on the wind and vanished in the grind of wheels. Neither woman spoke till they passed a soddie and sod barn next to a trampled cornfield. "Seth had every reason to go and none to stay," said Rose. "I'll miss him, though."

"You wouldn't see him often."

"No, but it's sort of company to know people you like are somewhere around. Makes the air friendlier." Rose pointed to a stone tower rising above stone ramparts on a distant knoll. "There's Camp Nichols. If Jack's home, you can bet he's watching us through his spyglass."

"Will Chandless try to run him out?"

"Not unless he fancies chasing dust devils. If Jack was raising cattle or putting up fences, they'd tangle, but Jack's horse operation isn't big enough to be a problem and his being here keeps out rustlers."

"He isn't—" Julie began, and broke off.

Unperturbed, Rose chuckled. "I suspect he eats Chandless beef and it might not be good manners to inquire much into his past, but when Jack and his friends need more money than the horses bring in, they dig up monster bones."

"Monsters?"

"Dinosaurs. They must have been thick around here millions of years ago. Giant lizards and critters whose names all end in 'saurus.' That means 'lizard,' too, Jack says. Only one I can remember is 'brontosaurus.' "

"Jack sells the bones?"

"Hauls them to the railroad and ships them to museums and rich folks who want their own private dinosaur skeleton."

Julie shook her head. "How did he get started at this?" she asked in bemusement.

"He was working for Charles Goodnight in the Texas Panhandle about four years ago when a dude scientist came to stay in an old line shack and prowl the country. He needed someone to drive his wagon so Goodnight let him hire Jack. They found this place where wind and rain had already done quite a bit of excavating. Jack rounded up some friends and they spent the rest of the summer digging out bones with the dude teaching them how to do it. The *pale—paleo*—whatever he was—went east with a boxcar full of pieces he put together for a big museum. He can find buyers for all the skeletons Jack ships him."

"It doesn't seem quite right for our dinosaur bones to wind up somewhere else."

"There'll be plenty left if the Territories ever have a museum," soothed Rose. "There's so many skeletons in that one place that the dude reckoned it might have been sort of a place they went to die. Or maybe they were caught when a volcano erupted."

They were nearing the creek that flowed beneath the knoll

where the abandoned camp stood silent vigil. "If Mallory digs up bones and raises horses for a living," puzzled Julie, "how come he has such a reputation? Trace says he's lightning with a gun."

"He is. Some say he was an outlaw before he worked for Goodnight, some say he was a sheriff."

"What does he say?"

"He doesn't. The only thing I know is that he may not live by the gun these days but he's kept in practice. At least two men who thought they could outshoot him are buried in Carrizo."

"What about his friends?"

"No one knows anything about Wyatt Mabry, the gray-haired one, except that he's fast with a gun. He and Billy Lincoln, the yellow-headed kid, hang out at Jack's and help him when they're not off freighting supplies to Carrizo from Trinidad up in Colorado."

Or robbing trains or banks? Julie decided not to ask. It wasn't good manners, or even safe, to be too curious about someone's past or their means of livelihood.

The horses splashed across the creek below the fortification, pausing to drink, and followed a trail past the sentry tower on the eastern side, passing through a gap where a gate had once been, into a two-hundred-foot square. In the center, long walls stood open to the sky except for the south end which was covered with corrugated-iron roofing. The same red-painted metal walled off the exposed part of the structure from the protected side. Flashing blue-black above and cinnamon beneath, fork-tailed barn swallows twittered as they flew in and out.

"That was the stable," Rose explained, with a smile of appreciation for the swallows. "Bill fixed the south end to shelter his horses in bad weather. In Kit Carson's time, three hundred horses were kept there at night to mount three hundred soldiers. The officers' half-dugouts were just outside the south wall. Soldiers and ten Indian scouts slept inside the walls in tents and dugouts. The hospital's over there; that's the commissary; and—"

Valentine's nostrils quivered. He pricked up his ears and whickered. Duke joined in. A jubilant response came from behind the only building with an intact roof, and Jack Mallory's big bay trotted around the walls to stretch out his neck with a soft nicker.

"Good afternoon, Ro—Miss Kendall, Miss McCloud." Jack Mallory stepped out the door. His horse came to nuzzle his arm. The tall, black-haired man caressed him and laughed. "Haven't forgot your old pals, have you, Blaze?" His smile faded as his dark eyes scanned Rose. "Have you, Miss Kendall?"

"Have I what?"

"Forgot your friends."

Her color heightened and her eyebrows arched. "I've been planting corn, Mr. Mallory. I doubt you've been doing anything that constructive."

His teeth flashed and he nodded toward horses grazing in a fenced pasture opening into the tumbled north side of the wall. "Gentling colts is all. Of course, I've been to Carrizo a couple of times."

"Of course!"

Mockery vanished from his tone and hard-angled face. "There's no one like you."

Her gaze dropped. "Then why—"

"Why haven't I come courting you like a greenhorn boy?" He stepped forward, calming Valentine with a word and a pat, and closed his hand over the woman's as it rested on the saddlehorn. "We're not kids, Rose. Isn't it kind of silly to pretend we just met each other at a Sunday-school picnic?"

She reined away from him. "It's not silly to want to—to be treated differently!"

"Why don't we talk about it?" He offered Rose a hand. Almost as if mesmerized, she let him help her down. "You ladies go inside. I'll hitch the horses in the shade. They can visit with Blaze while we have some—" He glanced at Julie. "—some root beer? I just mixed up a gallon from Hires' Extract."

"That sounds good," Julie said. Unaccustomed to riding, her thigh muscles complained as she dismounted. She was glad to give the reins to Mallory and tried not to limp as she followed Rose to the roofed building.

A mourning dove alighted in some grass a stone's-throw

away. Immediately, two doves that were almost as large as the parent rose up with beaks open wide.

"The parent's feeding the young ones pigeon milk," said Rose, smiling as she stopped to watch. "It's a mix of bugs, seeds, and whatever the big bird eats and digests. See, it brings it up from its crop and puts it in the babies' mouths."

"How would you know a thing like that?" Mallory had come up so quietly that they jumped.

Turning her back, Rose entered the building. "I watched birds a lot when I was a child."

"You've been here before and never mentioned the doves."

"Neither did you," she retorted.

He sounded rueful, a trifle shamed. "I guess I didn't."

"That," Rose informed him, "is the kind of thing people talk about when they're—when they're courting. Little things. Things they'd be afraid would bore most people. That's how they get to know each other."

Jack said in a hard, flat tone, "I guess I don't want anyone to know me all that well."

Rose's back stiffened visibly. She pivoted on the doorsill to confront her host, then squealed and ducked as a small, brown-yellow bird with black-and-white wings and a jaunty black cap undulated past her. It winged off singing, almost bounding in the air.

"A goldfinch!" Rose straightened her hat and dignity but didn't try to conceal her delight in the tuneful little bird. "It must just be starting to molt." She added to Julie, "He'll be gorgeous when he gets his summer plumage."

Turning again, she surveyed the long room. The end with a fireplace held three quilt-covered cots, a crude table and chairs, and a cupboard made of stacked crates. The bottom crate was anchored with five-pound tins of marmalade, apple, quince, and plum butters. The upper shelves held coffee, cocoa, sugar, baking powder, salt, bottles of catsup, horseradish, Lea & Perrins Worcestershire sauce, Durkee's salad dressing, Tabasco sauce, olive oil, a jug of mustard, tins of sardines, oysters, clams, potted ham and salmon, soups and condensed milk, and two-pound cans of strawberries, pineapple, cherries, apples, peaches, pears, corn, string beans, lima beans, peas, Boston baked beans, and tomatoes, and smaller tins of imported mushrooms. A wooden box purported to hold a wheel of cheddar. On top of it was a round of tinfoil-wrapped Edam.

Fifteen-pound kegs of sauerkraut, pickles, and white Holland onions stood in a corner next to a hundred-pound barrel of corned beef, a pail of spiced herring, a barrel of soda crackers, big boxes of graham crackers and gingersnaps, and stacked twenty-five-pound boxes of dried apricots, peaches, and apples, and a smaller box of figs. A fifty-pound can of lard occupied the coolest corner beside big sacks of beans, one of hominy, a hundred-pound bag of roasted peanuts, and a two-hundred-pound barrel of cornmeal.

"Looks like you don't intend to starve anytime soon," Rose said with a straight face.

"Came close to it once," Mallory shrugged. "All this stuff will keep except the cornmeal, but I make a Dutch oven of cornbread every day. What the boys and I don't eat, the birds do. Have a seat, ladies, while I get the root beer."

"Thank you," said Rose primly. "I think we prefer to stand."

After two hours in the saddle, Julie certainly did. When Mallory stepped out the back door, she and Rose wandered about the room. The opulent store of food contrasted with the sparse furnishings and cracked, whitewashed plaster of the walls. An eroded mirror hung above a barrel that held a tin washbasin and water bucket. Part of the barrel was cut away to reveal a shelf holding shaving mugs and brushes and bars of pine-tar soap and fragrant bay-rum soap.

Sheepskin coats, ponchos, clothing, an array of hats, bridles, halters, and ropes dangled from spikes. The bridles and halters were well oiled, however, as were the saddles resting on a long sawhorse, and the gray felt saddle blankets had no worn places. Shelves near the door held a number of curry combs, brushes, saddle soap, harness dressing, awls, hoof picks and hoof dressing, liniments and salves, everything for repairing riding equipment and tending horses except for horseshoes and nails and a forge and anvil. These must be in the stable. Judging from the supplies, Jack Mallory wouldn't trust anyone else to shoe his horses.

"Look at this!" Rose pointed triumphantly at a huge covered bin. "Birdseed! Look at the millet and hemp spilled on the floor! John Jack Mallory, terror of No Man's Land, Texas, and the Territories, actually buys birdseed!"

"What of it?" demanded that person defensively, crossing the room to hand them engraved glass tumblers. "Wasn't against the law last I heard about it."

"Not that you'd care," shot back Rose. "But look over there, Julie, at the weed garden! Bad Jack Mallory doesn't grow geraniums or petunias inside—he raises thistles and dandelions for his goldfinches!"

Indeed, the stone paving of the floor seemed to have been pried up from a long space beneath a window, and piled up to hold soil on which thrived blooming dandelions and fresh green thistles, just starting to bud, amidst the dead stalks of last summer's growth.

Most of the thistle heads had been picked bare but some wispily feathered seeds awaited gleaning. "Your finches nested in here, too," Rose added smugly, touching a small, densely constructed nest lined with thistle-down that was still coated with the lime of the nestlings' excrement. "Did you hatch the eggs for them?"

Mallory crimsoned from the open collar of his plaid shirt to the widow's peak of his wavy hair. "I reckon, Miss Kendall, that you know doggone well that finches weave such a tight nest that it'll hold water in a downpour and the babies can drown."

"The thistles soak up water and hold it," she returned. "But it does make a nice, soft nest. Lucky finches don't nest till the thistle-down is ready."

"And till the cowbirds have quit leaving their eggs for hardworking parents to hatch and feed," said Mallory, scoring his point with a grin. "Now then, ladies, I'm not conceited enough to think you rode out here for my company. Why did you?"

The cool abruptness of the question sent a wave of alarm through Julie. It was as if he knew their mission and was resolved not to yield. With the slightest hint of a warning frown at Julie, Rose said airily, "We came to invite you to Letty and Dan's wedding this Saturday and a covered-dish supper and dance afterwards."

"I'll sure have to come and wish the kids luck." His eyes touched Rose with an intimacy that made Julie feel very out of place. "Save me a lot of dances. But you could have sent Dan to tell me the news."

Julie looked into his eyes. They were as unreadable as his angular face. "Please, Mr. Mallory," she blurted. "Please drop your quarrel with Trace."

His lips drew tighter though she thought his eyes held pity or regret. "I'm sorry, Miss McCloud. To come all this way, you must love him."

"I don't love him," said Rose, "but I'm asking, too, Jack. Trace killed your friend in a fair fight. Let it go."

"I wish I could, but I wouldn't stand here today if Owen hadn't saved my neck. May not be worth much, but it's all I've got."

"It's murder!" Julie fought back tears. "You're a gunman. Trace isn't."

"He was gunman enough to kill Owen."

Julie blinked back tears. "It's still not fair!"

"It certainly isn't!" cried Rose.

Mallory threw up his hands. "Ladies, you're talking to the wrong man."

"What do you mean?" In spite of her puzzlement, Julie felt a glimmer of hope.

"If Riordan disappears, I won't hunt him."

Julie's heart sank. "He won't do that."

"You've already asked him?"

She flushed and looked at the floor. "Yes."

Mallory sighed but there was a gleam of approval in his eyes. "Ask him again, girl. He may do it for you if not to save his skin."

Rose stared at the dark-haired man. "Would *you* run, Jack?"

"You know I wouldn't. A man who runs isn't a man—"

"And that's what you'd do to Trace!" Julie burst out. "You

both have the same stupid notions. You know if he went away, he'd be shamed! So shamed his pride would break."

"He'd be alive." Mallory's voice gentled. "And he'd have you. Ask him again."

"What else can I do?" Julie turned her back so Mallory wouldn't see her tears.

*E*leven

*R*everend Jim Wardlaw was a genial, long-jawed former cowboy whose eyes and hair were the color of sere grass in his weathered face. They found him in one of Kenton's saloons, arranging to hold a service there.

"Don't worry, Jim," promised the bartender, with a jerk of his head at the voluptuous, almost-nude painting behind him. "I'll drape sheets plumb over the bottles and the gypsy queen." He nodded to the women standing by the swinging half-doors. "Howdy, Miss Kendall. What can I do for you?"

"You can tell everyone Dan Shelton and Letty Sutherland are getting married Saturday and there's going to be a dance." She smiled at the preacher. "Would you perform the ceremony, Reverend Wardlaw?"

"Ruther marry than bury any day, ma'am," he drawled, with a twinkle that made Julie like him at once. "Where's all this jubilatin' going to be?"

She gave details and she and Julie rode out of Kenton as soon as they'd watered the horses at a trough by the town well which still depended on a hand pump to bring up the water. There was little in the hamlet to tempt a woman to stay—a few rock or adobe shacks, one general store, a dozen saloons, a livery stable, blacksmith, harness shop, and the most imposing building in town and the only one with curtains, a two-story rock house on the outskirts.

A blowsy woman in a tight satin dress called from the balcony, "The boys miss you, Rosie. When you comin' home?"

"I'm going home now, Corinne." Rose's tone was pleasant but positive. "Letty's getting married to Dan Shelton Saturday. You're welcome to come."

"Married, is it?" Corinne raised a plump shoulder and let it fall. "Wish her luck for me, more than I've had. Wait a minute! You know why I won't be at the wedding, apart from not wantin' to jiggle-jaggle that far in a buggy, but I want to give the child something."

She vanished from the balcony, emerging in a few minutes from the front door. She pressed a small packet into Rose's hand. "Take care not to lose it. It's my mother's wedding ring. Save them buyin' one."

"But Corinne—"

"I've got no child to give it to," the woman said harshly. "And if you're thinkin' it's not good enough for Letty, let me tell you that my mother was the finest, sweetest lady you could know!"

"It's really kind of you, Corinne." Rose took her hand. "Letty will be happy you thought that much of her."

"I guess it's my mother I'm thinking of. I'm not fit to have her ring." Corinne stepped back and added with weary scorn, "I wouldn't trade my life for hers, though—married to a man who never let her step out the door except to go to church, having a baby 'most every year and losing two of them before she died birthing her seventh child. I was ten when that happened; twelve when my stepmother made things so hard I ran away."

"You could claim land out by us, Corinne," Rose offered.

Corinne shook her frizzy auburn head. "It's not for me, Rosie. I got a bit put by and I never got a drug or drink habit, praise be. When I'm too long in the tooth for this, I'll buy a nice little house in a nice little town. I'll have calico cats, a flower garden and lilac bushes, and I'll make cookies for the neighborhood kids, maybe join the Ladies' Aid if I can stand the excitement." She made a laughing face at Rose. "Now you hug Letty for me and wish her the happiest bride in the world."

"I'll do that." Rose tucked the small package into a pocket of her dress. "Thank you, Corinne. Take care of yourself."

"You do the same, Rosie. Who knows? Maybe you can train John Jack Mallory to double harness!" Giggling, she went inside and they rode on.

"Maybe Trace will listen to you this time," Rose said hopefully.

"I doubt it, but I'll try." Julie gave a bitter laugh. "As I said to Jack Mallory, what else can I do?"

Twilight was deepening as they approached camp. LeMoyne rose from Cap's grave, stretched, and came to meet them. As she greeted him, something unfamiliar caught Julie's eye. A white stone rested at the head of Cap's mound, a stone like the one above Mrs. Collins.

"I'll be along in a minute," Julie told Rose. "Would you take Duke with you?"

"Of course," said Rose.

Dismounting, Julie patted Duke's satiny neck. "Thanks for the ride, boy." As Rose and the horses moved off, Julie knelt by the big white rock.

Cap's name was chiseled on it with the dates of his birth and death. Under that, in smaller letters, were words from the prayer Shan must have told the carver was Cap's favorite: *"O ye Winds of God, praise ye the Lord."*

Thankfulness that Cap had the kind of marker he would like mixed with a fresh surge of grief. Julie sobbed, face against the stone, one arm around LeMoyne who whined and tried to lick her cheek. She kept busy at the work Cap would have done, and much of the time she could feel as if he was still with her, but there was a great aching wound in her that tore open when something like this took her by surprise. It was a relief to ease this by weeping.

When she got to her feet, Trace was waiting. She wanted to run into his arms, seek comfort there, plead with him not to throw his life away and leave her doubly bereaved, but he leaned down to pat LeMoyne and kept the dog between them.

Why, why, are you so stiff-necked? Swallowing to get control of her voice, she said, "The stone's beautiful, Trace. And the prayer—"

"Shan got it out of Cap's prayer book. Dave and Jon went with me to get the stone, and Cibolo carved it."

She looked down, clenching her jaws to keep from crying again, felt rather than saw his motion toward her, the way he checked himself.

"So," he asked, "did you find the preacher?"

"Yes. He'll come."

She summoned her courage. They were alone, as was rarely the case. There wasn't any right time to implore him to act in a way he'd think dishonorable but this was as good a chance as any. Even though he tried to evade her, she caught his hands. "Trace, we went to see Jack Mallory."

"Oh, did you? I guess Rose wanted to invite him to the wedding."

"She did." How hard it was to speak against his forbidding calm! "We asked him to forget his feud with you."

Trace withdrew his hands from her pleading grip. It was too dark now to see his face but she flinched from the anger in his voice. "I know you meant well, Julie, but you shouldn't have done that. I'd a sight rather be shot than have him think I'm hiding behind a woman's skirts."

"I'm not wearing skirts, and he didn't think that!"

"What did he think?"

"He thinks he's honor-bound to kill you."

"Sure. I reckon he would."

Julie plunged. "But he did say if you left the country he wouldn't look for you."

Trace laughed softly. "Mighty big of him."

"Oh, Trace!"

"Come up to the fire and get your supper." He turned and strode away.

She got in front him, desperate. This was the last time she could try. "If you won't save your life for your own sake, do it for me. Don't make me bury you here by Cap."

The darkness between them seemed to thicken into a wall through which words passed, but no understanding. "Julie, if I could, I would. My life means a sight more to me now than

134

it did before I—knew you. But if I ran, I'd shrivel up inside. You couldn't think much of what'd be left."

"I would!"

"We won't be finding out. If I live, I'll be a whole man for you. If I die, you'll mourn that man, but by and by, you'll love and marry a good man who deserves you."

"And name my first son after you?" she hurled at him. "What about my pride, Trace? I asked Mallory for your life. I've begged you! How is it women can beg and no one worries about how that feels, but men can't use a little common sense?"

He laughed in surprise, then sobered. "You women can beg for someone else because you're strong. Men aren't that brave." He slipped his hand beneath her arm. "Come along, Julie. The corn bread's getting cold."

Letty and Madelaine drove into Tyrone to spread word of the wedding dance and buy necessities for the new household, including Letty's main gift from her Kenton friends, a kerosene stove. They also stocked up on food and drink for the occasion. Charlie Shaw, the storekeeper, promised, as a wedding gift and contribution to the feast, to order ice shipped by rail from Dodge City. Enterprising businessmen cut great blocks of it in the winter and stored it in sawdust in well-insulated sheds where it would last well into summer. The Halls had an ice-cream freezer, Madelaine bought one, and the Shaws would bring their big machine and round up enough others to make ice cream for a crowd.

"Charlie can fiddle and he's the best caller this side of Wichita," Letty said, as the supplies were unloaded. "So he and Rafe Hall can spell each other." She offered her hand to Danny and led him in a happy little dance. "We need two fiddlers, and Barbara's mandolin, and Cibolo's harmonica, because we're going to dance all night!"

"Aw, honey!" protested the bridegroom.

"We'll have lots of nights, Danny, weeks and months and years of them," she consoled as she pirouetted around him. "We can dance the first one!"

"Might as well stay up," Shan advised, chuckling. "I bet

folks can hear the racket we'll make at your shivaree all the way to Beaver and Tyrone."

Dan sighed resignedly. "At least it's too far to the creek for you to toss me in."

"We can sure turn you loose in the cactus," Shan teased.

"Just remember, your time's coming." Dan cast a significant glance from Shan to Madelaine that made them blush. "Whatever you dream up for me, I promise you'll get back in spades."

Shan stole an adoring look at Madelaine. In spite of wearing a sunbonnet when in the sun, her face had tanned to a honey gold that made blue brilliance of her eyes. Her once-manicured fingernails were short and broken, her cuticles rough, and her hands chapped, but she radiated happiness, especially when she looked at Shan.

Bashful as he was, he probably hadn't said much, but it all shone in his eyes. "Let me marry the lady I want," he said gruffly, "and you can throw me in the Cimarrón's quicksand for all I care, laddie. I'll be so joyful-hearted that I'll float right to the top."

Julie was glad for him but the thought of him marrying sent a lonesome pang through her. It didn't bear thinking about a world without Trace, but if he were gone, no matter what he predicted, she didn't think there would ever be another man for her.

While the men and boys finished the fence and plowed fireguards around the claims, the women thoroughly cleaned the Collins dugout. The boys were sleeping near the wagons anyway and Dave had suggested the newlyweds use the shelter till they could build a dwelling of their own.

When the place was as clean as a dirt floor and sod walls and roof allowed, the women whitewashed the walls and covered the ceiling with cheesecloth to at least impede the descent of bugs, earth, and crumbling roots.

Letty's trunk, cot, and rug were brought from the tent along with two chairs, an etched-brass-stand lamp, and dishes and pans to augment what she'd bought in Tyrone. Madelaine's machine whirred as she hemmed blue plaid curtains for the window and crate cupboards and made a matching tablecloth. Letty arranged this on the large crate table, carefully placed a white pitcher of sunflowers and a reddish purple Mexican hat in the center, and stepped back to admire the result.

"It's beautiful!" she sighed, glancing with possessive pride at the well-stocked cupboard and shiny new teakettle. "I'm not going to let Danny peek till our wedding night! Now then, Julie, let's see how your dress looks."

Madelaine had skillfully lengthened Rose's dream dress. The women gathered around as Julie tried it on with the embroidered slippers. Barbara looped her hair into a French knot secured with sidecombs and hairpins artfully concealed by a hairbow of green velvet and white chiffon. Letty contributed a pendant and earrings set with tiny sparkling stones.

"They're supposed to be real emeralds," she said, and laughed. "Maybe they are; they're little enough."

Julie regarded herself in Rose's large mirror and was overcome. If Trace loved her in her jeans and plain braid, what would he think of this? "I can't believe it's me!" She took a few experimental steps. "But skirts feel so strange! Like an umbrella the wind might turn inside out and blow up around your ears!"

"Oh, it won't do that," Madelaine assured her. "I've sewed little weights in the hem. Nothing short of a cyclone's going to flip those skirts above your ankle."

"But I still don't know how to dance!"

"You don't have to, dear," soothed Rose. "Just let your partner swing you around and do what the caller says. We can't get too fancy without a dance floor. It'll mostly be play-party tunes like 'Weevily Wheat' and 'Jolly is the Miller Boy'— the kind you played at school."

"I never went to school!"

"Oh." Barbara pondered. "Well, you have had a sort of different bringing up, but don't get in a swivet. Your work's trained your body to move fast where you want it to. You'll be fine."

"It was dear of Corinne to give us her mother's ring," Letty said. "She used to bring me ginger tea and hot-water bottles when I was having my monthlies, and when I first came to Kenton, she tried to talk me into going home till I told her what kind of a home it was, my stepfather pawing me and my mother slapping me and screeching that I was a born hussy who led him on." She added fiercely, "If—if Danny ever dies and we have a little girl, I won't marry any man on earth till she's grown up!"

"My father was wonderful," said Madelaine. "It was Mother who made my life pure misery. She never swore—too religious for that—but her tongue blistered worse than a mule-skinner's whip."

"My parents loved me," said Barbara. "I was so ashamed when I got into trouble that I ran away. Something was wrong with the way the baby came. The woman who helped couldn't get it to breathe. But I couldn't go back to my folks." Her hand brushed the slight rounding of her belly. "If this baby's born healthy, though, I've been thinking that I'll go home on a visit so my parents can see their grandchild. I'll invent a husband who got killed in some accident."

"Maybe you won't have to invent him," Julie said.

Barbara shrugged. "I will unless I find a man who'll love my baby like his own." She smiled at her circle of friends. "A lot worse things could happen to a child than to be raised around three aunts like you."

"Make it four," said Julie. At their surprised looks, she asked Madelaine, "Hasn't Shan told you we're claiming land here?"

"You are?" Madelaine's delight took on an edge of irritation. "Shan watches me a lot but when we're alone for a few minutes, he acts like I might bite him."

"Dance a lot with him," advised Julie. "When he finds out how nice it is to have his arms around you, he'll never want to let you go." She hoped it would be that way for Trace, though she feared she'd be so awkward that he'd be all too ready to pass her on to the next partner—just as he seemed so quick to do in real life.

Starting Friday morning, Letty's kerosene oven baked eight cakes: two applesauce, two sour-cream chocolate, German chocolate, burnt sugar, raisin spice, and shredded coconut. The dense raisin spice cake lost a corner when the pan was turned upside down, but Rose patched it with frosting.

"It'll just make it better," she said cheerfully.

Loaf after loaf of tangy sourdough bread was set to cool before being stored in the wash boiler covered with a board weighted with sadirons to keep out hungry mice and smaller foragers. On Saturday, so the juices wouldn't have time to make crusts soggy, all manner of dried- and canned-fruit pies emerged from the oven golden and fragrantly steaming.

The men let down the tailgates of two wagons so the back of the beds could hold milk cans of lemonade made from bottled clarified lemon juice, a wild-cherry drink made from phosphate, and root beer. There'd be coffee, of course, and the Halls were bringing buttermilk and lots of sweet milk and eggs for the ice cream.

The largest available crates were ranged a safe distance from the fire and covered with sheets held down at the corners with canned food and pan lids. Jerry and Jon stowed enough cow chips and dried stalks to burn all night beneath the windmillers' supply wagon. Everything that could be sat or perched on—kegs, boxes, benches, stools, and chairs—formed a semicircle beyond the tables. The men tied two lanterns to the windmill, one to the drilling rig, and secured another to the gate post of the Collinses' cornfield. Cow chips tended to smolder rather than flame so the lanterns would be needed in addition to the fire.

Late in the afternoon, Reverend Wardlaw jogged in on a durable little spotted Indian pony. The boys took care of his horse and the women took care of him, adding plenty of condensed milk and sugar to his coffee and allowing him his pick of the food that was ready. He passed up ham and corned beef to fill his plate with cornbread hot from the Dutch oven and beans that had simmered to succulent firmness. He topped this off with half a raspberry pie.

"That's enough for now," he said, beaming at his hostesses. "Don't want to spoil my appetite for supper." He looked shrewdly at the women who were still in their everyday clothes. "Bless your hearts, ladies, you don't have to fuss over me. Go ahead and get yourselves ready. I'm going to catch a little snooze in the shade of the wagon."

The women gratefully hurried to the tents. Even though

four people weren't needed to dress the bride, they all helped, happy to share her joy. Julie and Madelaine carried in the tin bathtub that had been filled and left in the sun. The water wasn't hot but it was comfortably warm.

Julie knelt to unlace Letty's plain work shoes while Madelaine and Barbara helped Letty disrobe, pin up her hair, and step quickly into the frothy perfumed suds Rose had produced from a bar of lilac soap.

Julie had never seen an unclothed woman and was grateful for the rainbow sparkle foaming over Letty's breasts. Averting her eyes when Letty stepped from the tub into a thick towel held by Rose, Julie used a smaller towel to carefully dry Letty's slender, high-arched feet and buff the toenails to a glow.

After Parisian cream was smoothed over face, throat, arms, and legs, Barbara fluffed on lilac-scented bath powder. Then, to Julie's relief, Letty stepped swiftly into lace-trimmed drawers of finest lawn. Rose fastened the hooks of the white open-work corset.

"Oof!" Letty explosively let out her breath. "I'd forgotten how miserable these stays are! After today, this goes to the bottom of the trunk where my bustle already is."

Barbara dropped a lace corset-cover over Letty's shoulders. While Letty sat on her cot, Madelaine and Julie pulled on white silk stockings and Rose adjusted garters of blue ruffled satin and elastic. Letty had forsaken her bustle, but her cambric petticoat had tiers of cascading lace-trimmed ruffles down the back.

"Now for the dress!" lilted Rose.

She reached into the open trunk, laid white satin slippers and a filmy veil on the cot, and then lifted out folds of shimmering ivory satin and lace. "Stand on the rug, dear," Rose adjured. "We don't want the hem to get dirty. In fact, unless you want to ruin your dress, you'd better slip back here as soon as everyone's kissed the bride and put on another dress."

"I never expected to wear this dress till I was buried," Letty said. "I don't care if it falls to ribbons afterwards, just so I can wear it tonight."

She bent, yellow hair sweeping down, holding out her arms so her friends could help her into the exquisite gown. Lace medallions and embroidered violets edged the skirt. A chain of violets and leaves was embroidered down one side and violets were strewn over the fitted bodice.

Hooking the dress in the back, Rose said, "The rest of you had better get ready yourselves. I'll fix Letty's hair."

Julie stole a look at the mysterious array on the polished dresser: ornate cut-glass bottles of perfume and Rouge Oriental, Crème Rivière, Lotus Crème, Poudre Merveilleux, assorted brushes, small pencils, silver-handled mirror, comb and brush.

Julie did use castile soap and rubbed Vaseline on her hands at night, and used it on her lips to keep them from chapping, but she brushed her teeth with baking powder, and her only other beauty aids were a comb and brush.

"I'll do your face," offered Barbara. "A whisper of powder, just a touch of eyebrow pencil and rouge."

"And I'll fix your hair," said Madelaine.

There was no time for them to bathe but they washed, splashed on Barbara's fragrant Florida water, and put on fresh undergarments. Julie hooked her friends' corsets, and then surrendered to their deft ministrations.

Again, the French knot and tiered bow of green and white worked magic with Julie's tawny hair while Barbara's art subdued freckles and sunburn, accented Julie's green eyes, and ripened her mouth.

"Trace will melt right down into the ground when he sees you," Madelaine predicted. "And the men'll cluster 'round like bees after honey."

"I look better than I ever dreamed I could," Julie admitted, fluffing her green sash and admiring the embroidered slippers that peeked from beneath her flowing skirt. "But you're the ones the men will fall all over each other to dance with."

Madelaine critically scanned her mirrored reflection and brushed off rouge till satisfied with the natural-looking result. She had filled in the low-cut neck of her blue taffeta dress with blue lace that exactly matched her eyes. "There's only one man I want to dance with. I'm afraid he's too bashful to ask."

"I'll make him," Julie promised. She turned to Barbara and gazed in awed admiration. Barbara's pale blond hair and crystalline eyes made her look like a snow queen in her gown of ice-blue gauze. "You look like you're wrapped up in moonbeams!" Julie breathed.

"I wish I felt that cool." Barbara's whimsical tone sobered. "I'd better enjoy this dance. It's probably my last one till after the baby comes."

Madelaine frowned slightly. "Jess Chandless was riding over to see you real often all spring, Barbara. Do you think—"

"I *know* he wants a son to inherit his land and cattle." Barbara's voice frayed. "He'll size up the mother the way he would a prize heifer—and on top of having stamina, perfect conformation, and good bones for calving, you can bet she'll be a virgin."

Madelaine's frown deepened. "If you think it's his, and you told him—"

"That's the first stupid thing I ever heard you say, Maddy!" Barbara touched perfume behind her ears and picked up a fan. "Come on! I hear a wagon."

Twelve

The sun was setting when Reverend Jim pronounced Letty and Dan man and wife and Danny fumbled Corinne's ring onto Letty's finger. "Now it's true there's no law hereabouts," the minister said. "There's no power vested in me by the State of Texas, Kansas, Colorado, New Mexico, or even the Territory of Cimarrón the good folks of Beaver have tried to get going. But, dearly beloved, folks I marry better stay that way." He kissed the bride and shook Dan's hand. "God bless you now and all your lives. I look forward to baptizin' your kiddies."

There were loud cheers. Cowboys' wide-brimmed hats flourished in the air beside farmers' more prosaic ones. Women dabbed at their eyes; besides the Halls and Cora Oliver, storekeeper Charlie Shaw's plump wife and daughter were there, with two pretty, dark-haired cousins who'd come by train from Trinidad for the festivity.

Women, of course, were far outnumbered by a score of cowboys, bachelor Tyrone businessmen and freighters, half a dozen homesteaders Julie had never seen before, the male Halls, and the windmill/well outfit. They crowded around to slap Dan on the shoulder, congratulate him, and kiss the bride as shyly or as boldly as their temperaments and Letty allowed.

Rose, bewitching in airy yellow muslin, kept watching the

northwest rim of the plains. Jack Mallory had said he'd come. Julie hoped he wouldn't. Neither he nor Trace would look for trouble on Letty and Dan's festive night, but things could always get out of hand.

Reba and Millie Hall beat eggs into quantities of cream and milk they had brought, blending these with sugar and vanilla contributed by Julie. Stocky, redheaded Charlie Shaw broke ice in a sack by pounding it with a sledgehammer and chipping off smaller pieces with an ice pick. After the custard was poured into the freezer cans and the lid fastened, Charlie and Hank Trevor, the skinny, balding livery owner, packed ice around the cans, and added rock salt.

"You fellers are gonna want some of this ice cream," Charlie yelled at the bachelors. "Get yourselves over here and churn it. When the cream starts to get slushy in this fifteen-quart freezer of mine, it's gonna take a heavy guy to sit on top of it and keep it from jouncing clean out of the country!"

Cowboys and farmers answered his call, joking as they knelt or hunkered on their heels to turn the handles of Charlie's huge freezer, the Halls' ten-quart, and the Kenton women's eight-quart one. Charlie and Hank kept chipping ice, delegating the chore of feeding it into the freezer, along with more salt, to the Collins boys.

"I never had any ice cream," Jerry said, watching the revolving cans with eager eyes.

"Yes, you did," corrected Dave. "It was at a church social. But you were only three so you don't remember."

"I do," bragged Jon. "It had fresh peaches in it."

"And you ate so much you got sick when were driving home in the wagon," Dave added with the formidable recall of an older brother. "Mind you don't make a hog of yourself tonight. Just because our folks are dead, we don't need to act like we never had any raising."

While the men and boys attended to the ice cream, the women set out food on the sheet-covered crates, wedging bowls and kettles so tight there was no space between them. Besides cakes, bread, pies, and the beans simmering on the fire, the hostesses had made a dishpan of potato salad. The Halls, besides dairy ingredients for ice cream, a can of buttermilk for

144

drinking, and butter, put out a crock of cottage cheese, a platter of deviled eggs, and a kettle of stewed wild greens.

Most of the cowboys brought candy or tinned delicacies like oysters, clams, or sardines. Bachelor settlers produced fried jackrabbit, prairie chicken, and quail or cans of whatever vegetables or fruits they could spare, and livery owner Hank Trevor contributed a large smoked ham.

Mary Shaw, a pleasant-faced chubby woman with merry brown eyes, placed a dishpan of sugar cookies and gingersnaps on the back end of a wagon between milk cans of wild-cherry drink, lemonade, and root beer. Charlie had dropped slivered ice into the beverages and each held a dipper for filling the assortment of glasses and cups ranged around them.

"Making cookies kept the girls busy," Mary smiled. "As it was, they nigh drove us wild with their curling irons heating over the lamp and their prinking and fussing." The fond way she watched the young women belied her complaint. "Pauline doesn't see much of other young folks. It's a treat to have Beulah and Betsy come, but they've already started pestering me to let her go with them when they head home next week. Maybe we will. I could travel up later to visit my sister in a week or two and bring Pauline back with me. Sure is wonderful to have the train." She looked with concern at Lorena Hall, who was the only woman sitting down. "Are you feeling all right, honey? You look kind of frazzled."

"It's just the heat, Mrs. Shaw." Perspiration dewed Lorena's face and plastered tendrils of dark hair to her forehead. "I suppose I shouldn't have come, but—"

"Gracious, child, you need a little jollification," said the older woman kindly, patting Lorena's hand. "Just take it easy and let your man or one of us wait on you—and be sure you're out of the way of these heavy-footed galoots when they start prancin' and dancin'."

Cora Oliver contrived to maneuver jars of pickles and relishes among the dishes. No strand of gray-streaked black escaped from the tight knot at the back of the tall, rawboned woman's head. She acknowledged Julie's introduction of her new female neighbors with a frosty nod, but her handsome black eyes softened as she spoke quietly to Julie. "I was sure sorry to hear about Captain McCloud, my dear. He was a fine man. I'm glad to see that you've put up a stone for him."

"Trace and Cibolo and the boys did that," Julie said, swallowing the lump in her throat. "I—I wish Cap could be here. This was the kind of get-together he'd have loved."

"Yes, and the kind Jess Chandless hates because it shows he's losing his grip on some of the land he's hogged."

"Has he been to see you?"

"He sent Lute Hartman." Cora's thin nostrils flared. "No way will I sell my place! Especially now I've got plenty of water in spite of the colonel's hogging all the land close to the creek and river." She glanced toward the Kenton women with a bit more tolerance. "Now there's a little bunch of us pretty close together, it won't be so easy for him to run us out."

"If he tries, we ought to see him coming in time to get ready," Julie said. "One of the boys skins up the tower every hour or so to watch for dust. If we see any, we'll send you word. Maybe you ought to come over here if there's trouble."

"Only way I'll leave my claim is when I'm carried out in my coffin." Cora's lips pressed together. "I took care of my parents when they got old, all the time teaching school. Mama outlived Daddy by ten years. Couldn't leave her bed the last year. But she left the farm and all to my brother who hadn't done a blessed thing but come to see her a few hours every other Sunday."

Julie could think of no honest comfort to offer at the bleak memory. Cora's lips thinned even more as she watched Letty smiling up at Dan. "The Bible says the wages of sin is death, but it looks more like it's having men fall all over themselves to do your work."

"The women from Kenton have worked hard," Julie defended. "Take a look at their hands when you get close enough."

Cora's eyes sparked. "I never thought I'd live to neighbor with—"

"They *are* neighbors, Miss Oliver. My goodness, look at how hard it's getting to turn the freezer handles! Even with

Jerry sitting on it, the eight-quart one is jumping and bumping."

"The ones who aren't churning might as well fill their plates," said Rose. "Bride and groom first, then you, Reverend Wardlaw. Will you bless the food?"

"Proud to, ma'am." The lanky parson doffed his travel-stained hat. "Let go of them freezer handles a minute," he bellowed, "and let us praise the Lord!"

The laborers hastily straightened their backs and bowed their heads. "O Lord," intoned the preacher, "we thank Thee for these scrumptious and plentiful eats and the wholesome drinks with ice in 'em. If any polecat don't appreciate these healthy, decent ways to quench a thirst and has a pint hid away, Lord, we beseech thee to send a lightning bolt through the bottle and singe the miscreant a little whilst you're at it. Bless the hands that prepared this food and bless it to the nourishment of our bodies. We thank thee special for the ice cream which we couldn't have if you hadn't froze ice on the river, and made the hens to lay, and the cows to give milk. We ask thy blessing on this young couple and pray that their life together will be long and joyful. We ask—"

He paused. Charlie Shaw muttered, "If you don't get a move on, Reverend Jim, the ice cream's gonna melt."

"Thank thee, Lord," concluded the minister. "Amen." He picked up an enamel plate and got in line behind the bridal pair.

Rose's vigil was finally rewarded. Three horsemen came over the slope and rounded the newly fenced and planted field. They watered, unsaddled, and rubbed down their mounts, and hobbled them where they could graze with the other mules and horses beyond the Halls' wagon and the buggies belonging to Charlie Shaw, Hank Trevor, and Cora Oliver.

Followed by boyish, yellow-headed Billy Lincoln and Wyatt Mabry with his wary eyes the color of cold ash, Jack Mallory approached with a sack he'd taken from his saddlebag. His companions also carried bags.

Taking off his hat to the women, Jack said to the newlyweds, "Sorry we missed the ceremony, Miss Letty—I mean, *Mrs.*

Shelton—but we had to ride clear into Texas to find champagne for you."

"Champagne!" roared Reverend Wardlaw. "Guzzle the devil's brew till it rots your guts, John Jack Mallory, but don't be temptin' these young folks—"

"Now, Reverend Jim." Mallory's tone was one of respectful and earnest curiosity. "Wasn't it Jesus himself who livened up the wedding at Cana by turning water into wine?"

"That wine was just grape juice!"

"So's this." Jack sunnily produced four paper-wrapped bottles from his sack and his companions did the same. "It's just set a little longer is all."

" *'Look not upon the wine when it is red*—' " thundered Reverend Jim.

"It's not red." Mallory held a bottle aloft. "Not even pink."

" *'Wine is a mocker!'* "

"Well, anyone who doesn't want to be mocked sure can leave their share to me."

Reverend Jim blanched at such levity. "I beseech you, Brother John Jack, to repent while you can. Don't you know you may be called at any moment, in the twinkling of an eye?"

"Sure, Reverend Jim," chuckled Mallory. "But once I bluffed three guys into throwing in their hands when I called, and I only had a busted flush."

The minister turned away, despairing, while Mabry added tins of deviled crab and lobster to the food and Mallory and Billy threaded their way through the crowd, splashing dollops of fizzing amber into proffered cups and glasses. Julie didn't extend her cup but Mallory grinned at her and poured in a little anyway.

He served Trace without the flicker of an eyelid. "Evening, Riordan."

Trace nodded. "Evening, Mallory."

Cora Oliver and Reverend Jim were the only ones who held their glasses well away from the champagne. "Here's to Letty and Dan!" Mallory raised high an almost-emptied bottle. "May their grain and livestock and kids grow high!"

"Here's to 'em!" the toast resounded, from cowboys, townfolk, and homesteaders alike.

The grinding squeak of ice-cream freezers and the ceremony of toasting had kept anyone from noticing the new arrivals till Jess Chandless dismounted and tossed his reins to Lute Hartman.

"I'm too late to drink the toast to these young folks but I wish them well just as much as the rest of you do." Broad shoulders slightly hunched as if braced against a mighty wind, the rancher strode toward the couple. There was a hesitation in his gait, almost a limp. He handed a document to Letty. "Here's a deed to a quarter section with half of it good Arkansas River bottomland." He handed her an envelope. "This check's for a start there and to make up for what you've done here."

Letty stood as if paralyzed. Dan went scarlet. "If that land's so great, Colonel, how come you're not using it?"

"It's no good for ranching now," Chandless said. "Farmers and fences on every side of it."

Recovering her poise, Letty slipped a restraining hand over her husband's. "Thank you very much, Colonel Chandless." She handed back the document and check. "It's kind of you to worry about our success, but we're staying here."

Momentarily speechless, Chandless aimed a scornful hand toward the smaller tent beside the big one. "It's not like you had a house built and a lot of work done on the place. Have some sense, girl!"

Dan stepped between his wife and the cowman. "Don't talk to my wife that way, Chandless! Show her respect or—"

"Respect?" Chandless laughed. "Wasn't long ago that she was more interested in getting her price—"

Dan lunged at the rancher. Before his fist could strike Chandless's jeering mouth, Lute Hartman brought the barrel of his revolver down on the young man's head. Dan crumpled.

Blood seeped through his hair and down his forehead to the dust. With a cry, Letty dropped on her knees beside him. It was a good thing she'd changed out of her wedding dress or it would have been stained with Dan's blood when she tried to lift him.

As Julie and the Kenton women ran to help Letty, Trace swiftly brought the side of his hand down on Hartman's wrist.

The foreman swore as the six-shooter dropped from his fingers. Trace caught it up and held it trained on its furious owner.

"Get out of here, Hartman. You too, Chandless."

The foreman's heavy shoulders hunched. "Give me back my gun!" He dived at Trace.

Trace sidestepped. He gave Hartman his own medicine, creasing his skull, knocking him senseless. By now Jack Mallory, Wyatt Mabry, and Billy Lincoln had their guns out and ready.

"Ride, Chandless," Trace said. He handed over the six-shooter. "You can give this to Lute when he wakes up."

"Shorty! Jake!" Chandless called at a couple of his cowboys. "Get Lute in his saddle."

Several of Chandless's men hurried to wipe blood off Hartman's forehead and bandage the gash with bandannas before hauling him into the saddle and holding him there. His head drooped but consciousness seemed to be returning.

"Any of you boys who want to be working for me tomorrow," said Chandless, "saddle up and get back to the ranch."

"Aw, boss!" protested the wiry young hand who was obviously Shorty. "We ain't started to dance yet!"

"Dance all you want and pick up your time tomorrow." Chandless wheeled away, not troubling to see if Hartman could stay in the saddle.

The cowboys steadied Hartman till he roused enough to hold the reins looped over the saddlehorn. Shorty slapped the horse on the rump and it moved slowly off. The Chandless cowboys eyed each other.

"Hell!" said Shorty. "Uh—excuse me, ladies, that just slipped out. There's other jobs, I reckon, but only one dance tonight. Me, I'm dancin'!"

"Me too," said handsome, curly-haired Jake, grinning at Julie.

"I was lookin' for a job when I found this one," shrugged a freckle-faced redhead. "No man's gonna tell me I can't go to a dance."

Amid the cowboys' chorus of agreement, two older men exchanged glances. "I been with Jess through thick and thin," said one. "I'm kinda stove-up but he ain't hinted at me to hit the road."

"He was trail boss on my first drive north," said the other graying cowboy. "Pulled me and my horse out of quicksand at the Cimarrón." He turned to Letty and her bridegroom, who was starting to rouse and mutter. "I'm sorry, ma'am," said the aging man. His tone left no doubt that he was. "Sorry about the trouble, sorry to miss your dance. But I sure do wish you well, you and your husband."

"Me too, ma'am," said the other Chandless supporter. They went after their horses.

Julie had brought a clean, wet, dish towel. Letty took it from her and possessively cleaned away the blood from Dan's face and head. "What—" he began, trying to sit up.

Jack Mallory examined the wound with deft fingers. "You'll have a permanent part in your hair, Danny, but your brains aren't leaking out, such as they are."

Danny moved his head woozily. "I sure got a headache."

"So does Lute Hartman," comforted Jack. He took another clean towel from Rose, tore off a wide strip, and expertly made a pad that he bandaged over the gash with the rest of the towel. "Do you see two of me, kid?"

"One's plenty," grunted Dan. "Give me a hand up, Jack."

"Are you all right, Danny?" Letty still looked scared and angry.

He winced as he got to his feet, but after a moment, he stepped free of Trace's and Jack's sustaining hands, and took his wife's, drawing her to him. "Honey," he said, "soon as I wrap myself around some of that dandy grub, we're goin' to lead the dance!"

By the time everyone had feasted, spirits had risen, though the threat of Chandless must loom in all their thoughts. Now that his efforts to buy out or intimidate had failed, what would he do? He couldn't do anything tonight, most likely, so the wedding guests clearly resolved to make the most of their party.

The last ice cream was scraped from the pails, and the Collins boys and Annie and Ellen Hall blissfully licked the dashers. Dishes and food were cleared away, except for cake and cookies left beside the drinks. Charlie Shaw and Rafe Hall got their fiddles, Cibolo his harmonica, and Barbara her mandolin. After a brief consultation and tuning up, Charlie Shaw ran his bow thrillingly across the strings.

"All right, gents!" he called. "Grab your partners for the Varsouvienne—if you don't know what that is, down in Texas they call it, 'Put Your Little Foot Right Out.' "

Julie was seized by the discharged cowboy Shorty, who had been watching her like a starved chicken hawk. The odor of cloves on his breath made her suspect that he'd tippled more than the toast of champagne. Surprisingly, he was a good dancer. By the end of the sprite number, Julie found herself responding easily to Shorty's lead and the caller's instructions.

"Now the Virginia Reel!" yelled Charlie. "Or 'Weevily Wheat,' if that's the name you know it by! Don't complain about the grass, folks. Wear it out and we'll have a better dance floor! Swing around the circle! Balance all!"

Julie was as tall or taller than some of the men who looped their arms through hers but that didn't keep them from murmuring compliments in the few seconds they danced together. She located Trace in the next set. Was he keeping away from her deliberately?

Her suspicions grew as she whirled through quadrilles, schottisches, polkas, and galops without once encountering him, though he danced at least once, as was etiquette, with every other woman there, including Cora Oliver and Ellen Hall. As he partnered Madelaine for a third time, Julie heard Billy Lincoln growl morosely, "If Maddy was still my girl, I'd teach that well-digger to scoop a deeper hole! Don't he know you don't dance three times with the same lady 'less she is your gal or you're huntin' a fight with her beau?"

At the stab of jealousy twisted deeper by Billy's words, Julie reminded herself that Madelaine had danced a lot more than three times with Shan. And what a dancer Shan proved to be! Julie had never guessed. Another surprise was Hank Trevor, the amiable Tyrone livery owner, who bowed to Cora Oliver and swept her gallantly into the dance.

Julie didn't too much mind Trace's keeping Lorena Hall company, as he now moved to do. It couldn't be much fun for

Lorena, heavy with child, to sit alone and watch others frolic, especially now that Rafe had joined the dancing till Charlie should want to be spelled. But when Barbara came to share Lorena's bench, Trace no longer had the excuse of entertaining a lonely mother-to-be.

Barbara, of course, was also expecting, but her full skirts concealed any hint. Even though Julie told herself Trace was avoiding her because he believed that was in her best interest, he didn't need to laugh so delightedly at Barbara's remarks, did he?—or watch her *that* admiringly.

Charlie announced the Blue Danube. Rose had coached Julie in the steps. It wasn't a dance she cared to do with anyone but Trace. Shorty was heading for her, a grin on his face and a glint in his eye. And Trace!—he had hunkered down on his heels the better to chat with Barbara!

Julie ran through the assembling couples and stopped just short of stepping on her laggard sweetheart's toes. "Trace!" She wasn't in a mood to "please" or wait for him to offer. "Dance with me!"

He got up slowly—reluctantly, she thought. "I don't know how to waltz, Julie."

"There's nothing to it," she urged recklessly. "It's just one-two-three, one-two-three. Anyway, it's my feet you'll step on. Come along."

He had to comply. Other men were making the most of this chance to put an arm around a woman but Trace tried to keep far too much space between them. "Not like that!" Julie hissed. "Hold me the way Jack Mallory's holding Rose! Or even the way Hank Trevor's hugging Cora Oliver!"

"Julie—"

She blinked back tears of vexation. "You've danced with everyone else," she accused. "Why can't you dance with me?"

"You know why I'm trying to—"

"I don't care why! Dance with me!"

His hand tightened on her back. "All right," he said. "We'll dance."

He had either fibbed about not knowing the waltz or was remarkably apt. He swept her in a glide so deep she would have stumbled except for his arm and guiding hand. They were at the edge of the dancers, the edge of the light. She felt luminous and fluid as water following the channel of music and the magic of being close to him. So close . . .

She shut her eyes, savoring the bliss of being held by him, so long denied. When she opened her eyes, he was watching her in a way that pierced her with ineffably sweet pain.

Without thinking, when they dipped again and his face was bent above her, she kissed him on the mouth. For a blinding instant their mouths clung. Then he righted them, almost wrenching away from the kiss.

"Julie! We can't—"

"Maybe you can't!" She battled tears of frustration. "But I didn't make any silly, noble promises, Trace Riordan! I—"

Jack Mallory veered around them, laughing with Rose. Barbara darted from the shadows and caught Rose's shoulder. "Rose, hurry! Lorena needs you!"

There could only be one reason for that. Julie slipped out of Trace's arms and hurried after the women.

Thirteen

*R*afe, his mother, sister-in-law, Madelaine, Barbara, and Cora Oliver had helped Lorena to the big tent. She lay propped on a cot fetched from one of the cubicles. They had taken off her shoes and Reba and Millie were helping her off with her skirts and underwear.

She clung to Rafe's arm, dark eyes wide with fear, and grimaced as a pain wrenched her swollen body. "I want to go home!" she said in a scared, breaking voice. "Please, Rafe! I want to have our baby at home—"

"You can't go jouncing over those roads," decreed Reba.

"But this is my first baby," Lorena gasped. "Don't they take a long time to come?"

"I don't think yours will," Reba said. "Not as close together as your pains are. Rafe, you get out of here. If you want to do something useful, get some water heating on the stove and then go outside and wait till we call you."

Rose added, "Madelaine, can we boil your scissors?"

Madelaine nodded, picked them up from her sewing machine, and dropped them in a kettle which she set over a burner.

Rafe brushed a quick shy kiss on his wife's perspiring forehead. "I won't get far away, honey." He gave his mother an anguished look. "Mama, are you sure—"

"I'm sure this is how it goes when a mortal's born into the world," his mother said. "Now get that water on."

He retreated, taking the kitchen water buckets with him. Rose slipped on an apron and scrubbed her hands with lilac-smelling soap. She emptied the basin outside the tent and laid out towels. Without being told, the other women washed. Rose doubled a clean sheet several times and placed it under Lorena's bottom.

"Flex your knees, dear, and keep your feet flat on the cot," Rose instructed. She draped a folded sheet over each knee and as she worked briskly, she was watching the opening from which the baby would come. She pressed her lips together.

Oh Lord! Something's wrong.

Millie went to hold Lorena's hand. "You'll do fine," she comforted. "Go ahead and yell when it hurts bad. I don't know why, but that helps."

"I—I wish my mother was here," Lorena whispered. She added hastily, "Not that you aren't real good to me, Mama Reba. But—"

"I know, child." Reba wiped Lorena's face with a damp towel. "I wanted my mother when my boys came and was lucky enough to have her for Thad." She smiled reassuringly. "After the baby's here, Rafe can go to Tyrone and send a telegram. He can just wait there till your mother comes in on the train."

Lucky there was a telegraph and train. If Rafe had fetched his mother-in-law from Dodge City by wagon, the round-trip would have consumed the time when Lorena most needed her mother.

"Lorena," said Rose, "you've been having pains for a while, haven't you?"

The young woman nodded reluctantly. "They started this afternoon, but they weren't much. I've always heard first babies take a long time. I didn't want to make everyone else miss the wedding and I—I wanted to come myself." She caught in her breath with a moan, then tried to sit up. "I feel like I need to go to the privy!"

"That's just the baby, dear," soothed Rose. "Don't worry

about a thing but getting your son or daughter out in the world."

"Should I bear down?"

"No, not unless your body does it without your telling it to. Just pant when a pain comes."

"Don't fight it," Reba advised. "Just try to go with it. The pains are what will bring the baby, they're helping you."

Lorena panted and grunted and groaned. She gripped Reba's hand and clenched her teeth with contractions that now had only a minute or so between them. Julie took the damp towel and wiped her face and neck and arms.

"Scream, honey." Millie took her other hand and endured its vise without flinching. "Scream. We all do."

"But Rafe—"

"It won't hurt him a bit to hear you," said his mother. She laughed grimly. "Maybe he'll appreciate me a little bit more."

Lorena screamed.

Rafe poked his curly head through the tent door. "Mama! Is she all right?"

"She's doing what women do." Reba's tone was irritable. "I've always said it was too bad you men didn't have every other baby! Wouldn't any family have more than two."

"Can I do anything?"

"Yes! Scat out of here!"

He vanished.

"I feel like I'm breaking apart!" his wife breathed. "Why—why won't it come?"

"The baby's buttocks are coming first," Rose said. She sounded calmer than she looked.

"A breech?" cried Lorena.

It was a good thing she couldn't see the horror on Reba's and Millie's faces. Even Julie had heard of breech births and knew they were dreaded.

"That's all right," Rose comforted, standing near Lorena's drawn-up knees. "I've brought two breech babies. They did fine and so did their mamas."

Minutes crawled. If Lorena's cries ripped through Julie, they must have reverberated with real physical impact in the women who'd given birth. Would it never end?

"I—I—can't—" Lorena choked. A wrenching cry tore from her.

"You did!"

Rose slipped her arm beneath the tiny emerging buttocks so that as soon as the infant's trunk followed, she supported it with bowed little bluish legs dangling down on either side of her arm. "Now then, honey—just let the head slip out! You've got a dandy big boy!"

"He—he's all right?"

"Got all his fingers and toes. Come on, Lorena. Just breathe out his head."

It didn't come in spite of Lorena's panting. Reba and Millie exchanged terrified looks. "The baby'll die if he can't breathe," Reba said under her breath. "The cord's squeezed against the bone so blood's not flowing through it to the baby." She looked imploringly at Rose. "Can you pull him out?"

Rose shook her head. "I have to make a space where he can breathe."

Gently as Rose moved her free fingers inside Lorena, the young woman shrieked. "Lorena!" Rose spoke loudly to penetrate be the other's agony. "I'm pressing the wall of your vagina away from the baby's face and keeping a finger in his mouth to hold it open. Now go ahead with bringing him."

The women looked at each, sick with apprehension. What if the head was too big to come? What if the baby died wedged inside his mother? Would Lorena die, too?

The head slipped out.

A sigh of held breaths filled the room. "He's here!" Rose laughed, keeping a firm grip on the newborn as she cleaned his mouth and nostrils of mucus. "He's here, Lorena, all of him! What a beautiful baby!"

He was, in Julie's view, a pathetic scrap with flattened nose, eyelids and ears, streaked with blood and secretions. He gave a protesting yell followed by lusty wails. As he drew the air of his new planet into his lungs, the scary blue tinge pinked to a healthy glow except for the incredibly perfect feet and hands which remained somewhat dusky.

That pink, Julie admitted, was beautiful!

"Let me see him!" Lorena pleaded. "If he's fine and all here, why am I still having cramps?"

"Bless you, dear, that's the afterbirth," Reba said, getting ready to attend to it.

"Here's your son, Lorena. He's a darling!" Rose held the howling little boy so his mother could see him before starting to clean him up. Julie was frightened at the gush of blood that followed the liverish-looking mass of the afterbirth, but Reba gently rubbed the lump in Lorena's abdomen with a circular motion and the blood soon stopped.

Rose kept a good grip on the baby while Cora held a basin and Millie washed off the remnants of the mysterious hidden life he'd had while growing in the womb.

Without being told, Barbara brought the well-boiled scissors and tore two strips off a clean cloth. Her silvery eyes glistened. Was she thinking about her own baby who'd be born in five months or so? Was she contrasting the fatherless birth with this one, Lorena surrounded by her husband's family with him in earshot?

Barbara had obviously helped Rose before. What had happened to those babies? Letty was probably too young to have had one, but what about Madelaine, Barbara, and Rose herself? That was something Julie would never, ever ask, and something the women might never tell her.

"What's taking so long?" Lorena demanded.

"You can hold him in just a minute." Rose tied one band of cloth about eight inches from the baby's navel, drawing the square knot down carefully against the cord. She tied the next knot about two inches closer to the baby and cut between the knots.

Julie repressed a sigh of wonder mingled with joy and regret He was no longer part of his mother, nourished by her blood and breath. All the rest of his life he would be separate, in some ways inevitably alone. The only brief joining with another mortal would be in the act of love, the act that brought him into being.

But now his mother could hold him. Now she could gaze proudly, dotingly, at his wee face. Millie and Barbara had helped her out of her waist and chemise and washed her blue-veined breasts. "You won't have milk for a few days," Reba said, looking almost as proud as the mother. "But the clear yellowish stuff in your breasts has lots of good things in it and will fill his little tummy. Besides, his sucking will help your uterus get back to normal."

Touching, marvelous, the way the small mouth nuzzled at and found its mark, the way tiny hands pushed rhythmically at the nourishing flesh. Tears filled Julie's eyes. Cap's Morning Prayer needed words for this transcendent moment. *Child born of woman,* she thought, *praise life, the miracle; praise it and make your own life worthy.*

Reba turned to Rose. "I wouldn't have known to do what you did to help the baby breathe," she said. "Without you, he and his mama both might be dead this minute. There's no way to pay you back."

Rose smiled and shook her head. "I expect there will be, Mrs. Hall. We're going to be neighbors a mighty long time."

"All you have to do is call on us," Reba vowed. "Or just look our direction." She squeezed Rose's skillful hands in her own, work-reddened ones. "My name's Reba. Will you let me call you Rose?"

"I'd like that." Rose's glance included the other women. "After being through this together, I think we could all use first names. Don't you, Miss Oliver?"

"Cora," requested that lady. Gathered around the mother and child, these very different women shared a moment of accomplishment before they bathed Lorena and cleaned up the room.

As soon as this was done, Millie went for Rafe. He hurried in, dropping on his knees to circle his wife and son in one arm and laughed with glee when the baby gripped his finger. Julie glimpsed the forlorn expression on Barbara's face and hastily turned to Rafe.

"Look at that!" bragged the father. "How'd he get so strong? How'd he get so smart?"

"He's yours," Lorena murmured. She looked tired but proud as a triumphant warrior. "Rafe, do you think Reverend

Wardlaw would stay overnight and baptize our boy in the morning?"

"Gracious, I'd almost forgot you were raised Methodist!" Reba stared in dismay at her daughter-in-law. "We're Baptists, you know. We don't hold with infant baptism."

"Well, I do!" The usually gentle Lorena held her baby closer. "I carried this child and bore him and I want him baptized!"

Rafe, caught between the two most important women in his life, looked unhappy. "Don't see how it can hurt to sprinkle him," he told his mother.

"Won't help him, either," she sniffed. "For a baptism that counts, the person's got to be old enough to know what they're doing and they need to be dunked clean under."

"I wasn't," retorted Lorena.

"There's always time."

Fire kindled in Lorena's dark eyes. "Not that much! If you're going to be so mean about it, I—I'll just turn Episcopalian!"

Reba paled and shuddered. "Epis—Episcopalian!" she moaned. "Why, they're just the same as Catholics except they don't put any stock in the Pope!"

Julie thought it lucky that Shan wasn't there to blaze up in defense of his religion, cruelly persecuted in his homeland. Before harder words could explode, Rafe said hastily, "I'll ask Reverend Wardlaw, honey." He added to his mother, "When the boy's old enough, Mama, he can always get dunked if he wants."

Reba began to cry. "Aw, Mama!" Rafe protested.

At their distress, Lorena looked miserable, too. After a few dreadful moments, she touched Reba's hand. "How about this, Mama Reba? We'll baptize the baby like a Methodist but we'll ask Reverend Wardlaw to dip him under—real fast—like a Baptist."

"Honey, that's a great idea!" praised Rafe.

Reba wiped her eyes and blew her nose into a bandanna. "I suppose the good Lord won't hold what you do against the baby," she grudged. "Especially if he gets immersed good and proper."

Fortunately, before Lorena could frame a retort, Laban and Thad came to admire the latest Hall man, and Shan, Trace, Cibolo, and the Collins boys were allowed to peek in briefly and congratulate Lorena. Back outside, Jerry whispered to his brothers, "I didn't look like that, did I?"

"You looked a sight worse," Dave said crushingly. "Your head slanted to one side and you stayed red as a beet for ages."

"Yeah," said Jon, doing his part to keep the younger brother in his place. "What's more, you had colic and hollered all the time. Let's go see if there's any cookies left!"

As the boys streaked back to the festivities, Trace grinned at Julie. "Big doin's for one night! A wedding and a brand-new baby!"

And a fight that may lead to a regular war. Looming behind that threat was Mallory's vendetta with Trace. Presumably, after tonight's truce, Mallory would press the quarrel the first time he and Trace met in a suitable place for a gunfight. A fight that would, barring a fluke, be the same as murder.

Why were men so stubborn? Julie looked despairingly at this one she cared for before she slipped her arm through his. She was going to squeeze all she could into this night. "We're not needed here," she said. "Let's get back to the dancing."

To her relief, he didn't argue. "Sure," he said. "I want to pass the hat for the new little settler." Absorbed in savoring his closeness and the play, beneath her fingers, of the hard muscles in his arm, Julie didn't notice what was going on among the merrymakers till Trace made a sound of annoyed surprise.

"Look who beat me to passing his Stetson!"

Jack Mallory moved through the crowd with his hat. "Lots of room in there," he exhorted as silver dollars mingled with other coins and greenbacks. "The musicians said not to take up a collection for them tonight so we won't hit you up twice."

Trace chunked in a gold piece. Julie went to the windmillers' wagon and got a twenty-dollar bill. As she dropped it in the hat, Mallory laughed. "Ought to be enough here to buy the little feller whatever he needs and get him a cow to start his herd!"

Julie nodded and moved away before she shamed Trace

with an outburst. *How can you be so nice in some ways, John Jack Mallory, and so cruel in others?*

As if he read her feelings, Mallory drew her out of the lantern-light. "Riordan has time to melt away if he wants, Miss McCloud. I'm going to build Rose a house."

"Does she know that?"

He grinned crookedly. "No, but I reckon she won't plumb run me off unless I rile her by shooting your friend first."

Julie frowned though her heart beat fast with relief, temporary as that might be. "It seems to me, Mr. Mallory," she ventured, "that you hope Trace *will* go away and you won't have to kill him. Rose will have a soddie by winter."

Did Mallory redden in the dim light? "A soddie?" he growled. "I can't stand to think of Rose living in a dirt house with snakes and centipedes rainin' down on her and muddy water dripping all over everything when it rains!"

"A good soddie's not like that."

"Have *you* ever kept house in one, ma'am?"

Julie, truth to tell, had never kept house. "No, but I've been in quite a few of them."

"Visiting or sitting down to a dinner someone else cooked is a long shot from living in one. Rose is going to have a proper house, a rock one."

"Where'll you get the rocks?"

"I'll haul them from the creek." He chuckled. "More likely, I'll hire the Halls or someone else to do that."

"Have you ever built a house?"

"What kind do you want?" he countered gaily. "I've helped build soddies, log cabins, rock houses, brick ones, even some from milled lumber."

Julie stared. "Were you a house builder?"

"In a way. My dad was the kind to hanker for greener grass about the time Mother got curtains up and rugs down."

"But you couldn't have lived in that many houses!"

He counted. "Two log cabins in Texas. Two soddies and one brick house in Kansas, plus the wood-frame one in Topeka where Mother will probably live the rest of her life since Dad broke his neck in a horse race fifteen years ago."

This was even more startling than his traffic in dinosaur

bones—which must be paying well for him to speak of hiring men to do his hauling. "All right," conceded Julie. "But where'd you build a rock house?"

"They weren't regular houses," he admitted. "Just a couple of line shacks on the first ranch I worked for."

"What if Rose won't let you put up her house?"

"How's she going to stop me?"

Julie gasped. "You can't just build a house on somebody's land!"

"Why not?"

"Because—because—you just can't!"

"Oh," he smiled, eyes dancing, very handsome, "I reckon I can."

Mulling over this cheerful effrontery, Julie said, "Why don't you ask Rose to marry you? Then she'd be glad for you to build the best house you can."

His tone hardened. "Rose is a loyal soul."

"That's good, isn't it?"

He shrugged. "She thinks a lot of your outfit, especially you. If you can't persuade Riordan to pull up stakes, I'll have to kill him. You won't be the only one to hate me then. Rose will, too."

"It's all so crazy! Your friend's dead in a fair fight. From all accounts he wasn't much loss—"

"He saved my life. I owe him one. Riordan's."

The dogged sadness of his tone was worse than anger, stifling Julie's rush of hope. "So you'll not only kill the man I love," she said slowly. "You'll give up Rose."

Still, Julie seized on the glimmer of a possible way out of this fateful death trap created by two strong, bullheaded men's weird notions of honor. During the course of the evening, she'd heard Trace and Shan discussing wells and windmills with prospective customers. Those would keep Trace around for a while but when the jobs were done, perhaps she could convince him that it wasn't running to journey elsewhere for work.

But would he court her till it was settled once and for all? And what of her dream of living near these people she had come to regard almost as family? She felt close to Cap here, not so much because of his grave with the white stone, but because he had died while bringing these people water. In this region, he would never be forgotten.

She had begged Mallory once to drop the feud. She didn't ask now in words, but she looked at him.

Slowly, regretfully, he shook his head. "It's up to you to talk him into taking his chance, Miss McCloud. Giving him one is more than I ever thought I'd do."

With a nod, he moved up the slope toward the tent with his merrily clinking hat. Charlie Shaw called, "All right, folks! Grab your partners for a quadrille!"

Trace stood in the shadows talking with one of the bachelors, a gaunt, black-bearded young man. "Julie," Trace said, as she came up, "Milt Quinn lives a couple of miles out of Tyrone. Reckon we can dig him a well and put up a windmill?"

Julie offered her hand in a firm shake. "We'd be glad to do that, Mr. Quinn. Let's work it out before you leave. Right now, I want to dance."

"Sure," he said wistfully. "Go right ahead."

"Some businesswoman you are!" Trace chided as she urged him toward the dance. "Do you always treat cash customers that way?"

"Only," she laughed as they took their places, "when there's a wedding, a birthing, and a dance! Not to mention a baptism in the morning!"

She hoped it would be a long time before there was another funeral.

*F*ourteen

*N*ext morning, the neighborhood assembled at the water tank beneath the shining, spinning blades of Rose's windmill. The Collins boys wore the new clothes Trace had bought them and had scrubbed their faces and slicked down their yellow hair for the occasion. They looked a lot different from the skinny ragged orphans that had approached the windmillers' camp a month ago. Dave turned pink when Ellen Hall just happened to stand next to him. In the blue gingham dress she'd worn to the wedding, with her fair hair caught back with a big ribbon instead of swinging in a braid, she gave a glimpse of the woman she would be. Jon fled at Annie's approach. She consoled herself by making terrible faces at Jerry when she thought no adults were watching.

Millie and Thad had borrowed Rose's wagon and mules and gone home last night so they could tend to the milking and chores this morning. So had Cora Oliver, but since she didn't live far away, she had ridden over for the ceremony and the big breakfast that would send Reverend Wardlaw on his way well fortified.

Lorena's cot had been carried outside. It was considered risky for a mother to be up and around in less than a week or so after childbirth and her hostesses insisted that she stay with them till she was strong enough for the bumpy ride home. Rafe took the baby from her arms and stood by the preacher.

"Dearly beloved," boomed Reverend Jim, "you are gathered to witness the baptism of this innocent babe into the holy faith. Remember that Jesus said, 'Suffer the little children to come unto me, and forbid them not; for of such is the kingdom of heaven.' Do you promise, family, friends, and neighbors, in so far as it's in your power, to help this child renounce the devil and all his works, and grow in favor with God and man?"

There was a murmur of assent, mostly from the Halls and Cora. The Kenton women and the well/windmill crew probably didn't feel qualified to take on such a responsibility. "We'll teach him to help folks, work hard, pay his debts and be honest, preacher," Shan offered diffidently. "Will that do?"

The old cowboy briefly superseded the preacher. "Shucks, if you can do that—" The preacher hurriedly took control. "Act accordin' to your abilities, Brother Shan. The Lord's merciful. He knows you got to ride a gentle horse before you can stick to a bronc."

Leaving the blanket in Rafe's grasp, Reverend Jim almost enveloped the diaper-clad baby in his large brown hands. "How do you name this child?"

"John Laban McCloud Hall," said Rafe with a proud smile at Lorena and a nod at the startled Julie. "We're calling him after both our daddies and Cap McCloud. We never had the chance to know him, but he had to be a fine man."

"Thank you." Julie had trouble speaking through the lump in her throat. "Cap would be honored—and Shan and I are."

As she ducked her head to smudge away her tears, Julie noticed Barbara's set face. She must be thinking how different her child's naming would be. Who was the father? Somehow, Julie suspected that Barbara knew.

"I baptize thee John Laban McCloud Hall in the Name of the Father, the Son, and the Holy Ghost," proclaimed the minister.

He dipped the infant so quickly that the water scarcely closed over his head but the baby howled and kicked at the outrage. Reverend Jim hastily gave him to the father who just as speedily placed him against his mother's breast. There he found solace, discreetly sheltered by a towel.

Missing no chances, the minister scanned his audience. "Any of you dear brothers and sisters feel moved by the spirit to have your sins washed away while we're so close to good clean water?"

No one stepped forward. He sighed at the stony ground it was his task to cultivate, but brightened as Rose said, "I'm sure the biscuits are ready. Shall we eat?"

After a sumptuous meal, the minister set off with enough good food in his saddlebag to last him a couple of days. As they waved farewell, Shan said admiringly, "You got to give him credit for scourin' the country for a sorry lot of mavericks and culls. You know the old sayin' when the weather's awful: 'Nobody's out today but crows and Methodist preachers.' "

Cibolo squinted at John Laban McCloud Hall, blissfully asleep in his mother's arms. "Do you reckon this boy is a Methodist-Baptist or the other way around? Wouldn't it be something if this way of baptizin' caught on and settled their fuss over whether to sprinkle or dunk?"

"Don't hold your breath till it happens," warned Trace. He turned to Julie and Shan. From his brisk manner and unreadable eyes, Julie doubted that he was remembering, as she was, the way they had danced last night, dipped and glided, the way they had kissed—or rather, the way she'd kissed him. "Well, partners," he said. "Do you want to go with Cib and me while we dig Milt Quinn's well, or would you rather follow in a couple of days? He said he'd go to Tyrone today and pick up his mill so it'll be waiting for you. And then Hank Trevor wants a well and windmill at his claim five miles southwest of Tyrone."

Julie hadn't yet told him about Mallory's intention to build Rose a house, or her conviction that he'd be glad if Trace disappeared. Her best hope, Julie thought, was to try to steer their work away from No Man's Land so that, before Trace knew it, he'd be out of the region where Mallory felt impelled to seek vengeance.

But that region was where she wanted them to live—here,

among their friends. *I'll look for a place,* thought Julie. *Someday, somehow, it may work out. Even if doesn't, I'll have something to dream on.*

Besides, she wanted to be on hand when Mallory started the rock house. That should be something! She had seen him talking to the Hall men last night and they'd shaken hands so there'd been a deal. Most likely, he had sworn them to silence.

"I'll stay here," she said to Trace, and looked at Shan. "How about you?"

"No use breaking up the team." His glance at Madelaine was a dead giveaway. "The ladies are kind of worried about tornadoes. Dave says he and the boys'll help me dig a cellar they can all head for if they see a funnel, and Dan'll help, too, even once he and Letty build on their claim, this'll be too far away for them to use."

Reba nodded approval. "I got Laban to make a cellar before we built our house," she said. "I'm scared to death of tornadoes. Anyhow, you need a cellar for storing canned goods and potatoes and onions and turnips."

"Far as I'm concerned," muttered her youngest son, "they can leave the turnips stored in the ground!"

"You may see the day you'll be glad to have a turnip," chided his mother. She surveyed her remaining family. "We'd better head for home so Thad can bring back your wagon and team, Rosie."

Rosie! That was a far cry from the stiff "Miss Kendall" of only yesterday! Lorena and her son were carried back into the tent. Cora departed and in half an hour, the Halls drove away, Ellen and Annie waving furiously till they were out of sight. Cibolo and Trace soon followed.

He didn't even try to see me alone for a minute! Julie thought resentfully. She added with swift gratitude, *At least he's still alive! And we danced last night. We danced.*

After the celebrations, the workaday world closed in. Sheets and towels used for the birthing were soaked in cold water. While the other women washed dishes and put the tent to rights, Julie filled the washtubs, and shaved soap into the one heated with kettles of water from the stove. Next she filled the big copper boiler, and helped Madelaine lift it on the burners to heat.

"Will you get your measuring tape and help me mark the corners of the cellar?" Shan called from where Rose and Madelaine were deciding on the location.

"We can build our soddie big enough for you boys," Rose said as Julie came up. "We hate to think of you in that dugout."

"Whillikers!" cried Jerry. Jon looked as eager, but Dave shook his head.

"Thank you kindly, ma'am, but we better stay on our own land. It's real good to be close to you ladies," he added hastily, "but all the same—"

"You're probably right," Rose said with an understanding smile. "Your mother would like for you to live on the land she picked out for you."

Shan looked up from assembling the digging tools on the canvas bag, just as if they were fixing to dig anchor holes. "I'll bet we can help you laddies build you a soddie before snow flies," he said. Straightening, he slapped Dave's shoulder. "You'll be getting married in five or six years, son. Thinkin' already that you'll need your own house?"

"He's sweet on Ellen Hall!" crowed Jerry. "Did you see her feedin' him ice cream last night?"

Dave colored to the edge of his bright hair. "That's got nothing to do with it," he said, the dignity of his tone belied by the swat he took at his brother. "Ladies, we've got pretty fair shelter from tornadoes in that dugout. The cellar ought to be closer to you than us."

"How's about here?" Shan indicated a small slope just beyond Letty and Dan's tent. "The lads can sprint here in less'n a minute, I'm guessing, if they see a funnel."

The site was approved. Julie unfurled Cap's metal tape and began to measure.

By dinnertime, the clothesline was hung with laundry snowy-white from scrubbing, boiling, and a final rinse with bluing. "I'm sorry to have caused you all so much trouble," Lorena murmured when Julie brought her a plate of delicious leftovers from the wedding.

"With neighbors, there's always a time to pay back," Julie reminded.

Lorena's mouth quivered. "I know it's silly but I—I feel all weak and weepy."

"You miss your nice husband," Barbara said. She smiled though it must have hurt to say the comforting words. "He'll just be all the happier to see you. Besides, I've heard that most new mothers feel like crying a lot—and it's my opinion they should cry if they want."

Had she heard that or did she know firsthand? Was regret for a child she'd given away responsible for her decision to have this one? Or was it that she loved the father?

With Dan, Dave, and Jon helping Shan dig the cellar, Julie wasn't needed. Jerry got in the way so much that he was ordered to gather cow chips in between his scurries up the windmill tower to watch for visitors. By mid-afternoon, the chores Julie could help with were done and she felt entitled to borrow Duke and a saddle and hunt for the land she'd claim if ever it were possible to live here.

Trace should be with her, but she was sure he wouldn't encourage this chasing a dream that he feared could never come true. If—if what he expected happened, if she failed to get him to follow their work to a new region, life without him would be a world without sun, but people don't die of broken hearts. They bleed slowly. After a time, the wound closes though it will always ache.

If she lost Trace, she would take up land here and use it as a home base. Shan could claim, too. Should he and Madelaine marry, they'd have half a section of land, a nice start, and could add to it with timber claims.

These were 160 acres, the same as a homestead, so as Julie explored, she found the survey markers that would include such claims for Rose and her friends adjacent to the three quarter-sections outlined by plowed fireguards.

Circling north of these, she halted Duke frequently to picture a house on this knoll or that. Each prospect gave unbounded views of rolling plains spiked with flowering yucca and here and there the dark clump of a plum thicket. Under this vast sky, softened today by scudding clouds that shadowed the earth, the sweep of land was awesome to Julie, beautiful, but she could understand why, to women used to trees and gentler country, this could seem stark and unhospitable.

What was it Chandless had said? "God's country, No Man's Land, and certainly no woman's"? It would always be God's country, that of hawks and eagles, but she hoped that through her life she might have the use of a small part of it, with Trace. If God granted that, whatever else befell her, she would feel blessed beyond measure.

As she was blessed now, as she rode by the fleeting drift of pronghorns over a slope, the dazzling spirals of a hawk, and a coyote melting into the grass. The most unusual sight was a mother badger, bowlegged and white-cheeked, with a long white stripe from nose to stubby tail, trundling along with four pigeon-toed babies behind her. Already their front claws showed why badgers could swiftly dig out burrowing prey. If cornered, a badger would charge a man or dog and fight with such desperate ferocity that dogs three times their weight had been known to turn tail.

Beyond Letty and Dan's land, Cora Oliver's windmill tower glittered from a long way off. It set on the northeast corner of her claim, about a hundred feet from the soddie she'd inherited from the previous owners who'd gladly sold to her and gone to make the Run that spring. The roof was shingled with cedar shakes from the slopes above the valley of the Dry Cimarrón.

Julie knew, because Cora had invited the windmillers in for peach pie and coffee, that the walls were whitewashed and the hard-packed earth floor was covered with mottled-green hemp carpet and several braided rag rugs. Cora was lucky to have found such a good house but there was no luck about the way deep tree wells had been dug for her orchard and the weeded, cultivated small garden. It used the longest side of the house for one wall but Cora had somehow dug postholes and fenced the other three sides herself. The woven wire sagged a bit here and there, but from the verdure of the plants, few rodents or other hungry creatures were getting in.

A Jersey cow and her big-eared, soft-eyed calf browsed near a dugout that served as their barn. A big red rooster with iridescent green-and-black tail feathers strutted among his hens, who seemed too intent on pecking finds from the earth to admire him. Their home was a miniature soddie with a grassy roof that sprouted flowers.

Cora's was the last well Cap had recorded. The outfit had gone on to the Collinses and . . . Tears blurred Julie's vision, just as they had when she'd written down the three mills erected since then. She doubted if she'd ever be able to record a mill without a pang of grief and loss, but at least she knew Cap would be glad she was carrying on his work.

The former schoolteacher had coupled a number of hoses to reach from the windmill to the first rows of cottonwood limbs planted beyond the fireguard of her home place. The hoses couldn't, of course, reach many of the forty acres of potential saplings. Cora filled buckets from the hose and left it running down the furrow in which a row had been planted while she carried the life-giving water to the distant trees.

"That's a real job!" Julie called.

Cora turned and set her buckets down. She had changed from the blue polka-dot voile she'd worn to the baptism. She had, in fact, abandoned skirts altogether in favor of blue denim overalls. An old waist, heavy gloves, laced work shoes, and a sunbonnet completed her attire.

"Thank goodness it's you!" She nodded at Julie's trousers. "There's no one here but God and me for weeks on end. When you were helping put up that windmill, I watched you getting around so free and easy without skirts that I just up and ordered two pair of overalls from Ward's. Out riding for pleasure?"

"I'd like to claim land here someday."

Cora eyed her keenly. "With Trace Riordan?"

Julie felt a blush spread to her face and toes. Of course, after the brazen way she'd forced him to dance last night, it was probably all over No Man's Land, from the Kansas border to the Texas one, from New Mexico to the Cherokee Strip, that Trace had Julie McCloud after him.

She didn't care, at least not much. The dance was worth it.

She looked straight at Cora. "I hope Trace and I can marry and live here. Whether we can or not, I—I just wanted to choose a place."

"To dream on?" Cora smiled and sighed. "Nothing wrong with that, dear. I'm still stiff from last night—haven't danced in years—but I'd dance at your wedding if it was this very night!"

"It won't be," said Julie. "I'll just be glad if it happens at all." Before Cora could probe, Julie said, "If you've got more buckets, I'll help you water the trees."

Cora drew herself up as if about to proudly refuse. Then she relaxed. "Let's have a glass of lemonade and a chunk of gingerbread," she proposed. "Then you could help me for a while. An hour should do it."

Julie tethered Duke in the shade of the house and followed Cora in. In spite of her brother's avarice, Cora had some splendid antiques. The curtain partitioning off the bedroom was drawn to reveal an elegant four-poster and carved armoire. A tall, glass-doored bookshelf and rolltop desk served to further divide off the sleeping area.

Crystal and gold-rimmed dishes filled a mahogany china cabinet. The heating stove was thoroughly blacked and the white enamel of the kerosene cook stove gleamed. The water bucket and washbasin stood on a marble-topped stand and the polished round table's clawed feet gripped large glass balls.

Cora washed and dried her hands on a clean roller-towel. Ample squares of gingerbread were served on porcelain saucers and lemonade poured from a crystal pitcher into crystal glasses. The forks were heavy silver and the napkins linen.

"That was quick thinking, the way Rose Kendall kept the baby breathing," Cora said. "And Letty and Danny Shelton seem like nice young people. I'd be glad to share my well with them if Danny would do my plowing."

"You plowed the furrows for the cottonwoods?"

Cora grimaced. "Yes. I put the cuttings in the furrows with their tops sticking out and then plowed another furrow to cover them. I was too tuckered out by then to plow a field for corn or wheat." She sighed. "Of course, it's not much use planting if a field's not fenced. If wild creatures don't nibble the stalks, Chandless's cows will. I wonder what he'll try next to get us out of here."

"Maybe he'll see that he can't keep people out."

"He's not the kind that sees what he doesn't want to."

"Jerry Collins climbs the tower every hour or so to watch for anyone coming," Julie said. "Someone'll warn you if a bunch of riders are heading this way. You might want to come fort up with the neighbors."

"Fort up in a tent?"

"The Collins dugout would work."

Cora looked around at her treasures. "It would about kill me to lose these things my grandmother left me, especially after the way my parents willed everything to my brother." She brooded. "Of course, there's no one to pass them on to."

"I thought that nice Mr. Trevor from the livery stable in Tyrone asked you to dance every chance he got."

Cora blushed. It made her look almost pretty. Indeed, with the usual strict bun of her hair mussed by the sunbonnet, errant wisps curling around forehead and ears softened the severe angles of her face. Healthy color from outdoor work brightened her lips and cheeks and brought out the magnificence of her black eyes.

"Mr. Trevor told me he was lonesome," Cora admitted. "It's all right during the day while folks come and go at the stable, but at night there's nowhere to go for company except saloons. He's not a drinking man."

"He could use one of his own buggies and come see you."

Blushing an even deeper rosy red, Cora admitted, "He said he would Sunday if he can get Mr. Shaw to keep an eye on the stable. They help each other out that way." She added with shy pleasure, "He's not after my land. Mrs. Shaw told me the livery does lots of business and Mr. Trevor built a nice frame house for his wife. Poor lady, she died two years ago before she got to enjoy it."

"They had children?"

Cora lowered her voice and glanced around as if someone might hear. "She had *female* problems."

That was what doctors said when they couldn't figure out what was wrong with a woman, as if she were to blame for having complicated innards. Julie thought Cora was still of childbearing years but it would be impertinent to ask.

"Would you want to move to town, Cora?"

The momentary softness fled Cora's features. "I'm not giving up this place for any man in the world, even if he's gold-plated toenails to whiskers. More lemonade?"

"Thanks, but I'd better help with the watering and be on my way." Julie flashed a grin to cover the pang she felt. "I think the next wedding we celebrate around here will likely be yours."

"We'll see." Cora surveyed her home and looked proudly out at her windmill and the acres of cuttings that should grow into a shady grove. "I don't have to marry to get along. Never hurts a man to know that." She gave a most uncharacteristic chuckle. "It's sort of like playing poker with four aces in your hand."

Even though the last furrow of young trees was watered in less than an hour, Julie's arms and shoulders ached from many trips carrying a two-gallon bucket in each hand. Cora insisted she have another glass of lemonade, and after watering the patient Duke at the tank, Julie rode south.

If Mr. Trevor might claim land next to Cora, there was no use going over it, and her neighborly chore hadn't left time to loiter though supper would only be a matter of finishing up the leftovers.

The westerly breeze blew stronger and ruffled the buffalo grass, changing its color like rumpled pale-green velvet with shadows of rose. A jackrabbit bounded from their path. Duke, luckily, considered shying at such things beneath his dignity but he did jig for a second and loop wide to avoid a rattlesnake sounding its warning from the scant shade of a soapweed.

Most people Julie knew killed every rattler they could, but Cap had always said, "They're scareder of you than you are of them. Give 'em half a chance and they'll get out of your way."

Cap! Cap . . . Most times I try not to think about it, that I'll never see you again, not on this earth you loved so well. When I do, it hurts so much I can't stand it. But I've danced, and

I've laughed. I've kissed a man and held a new baby in my arms.

That's how it should be, honey. She could almost see Cap's smile, the twinkle in his eyes, and she remembered what he had once told her. *"It's your bounden duty, child, to be as happy as you can, be a bright spirit in a world that's often dark. Cry when you have to, sure, but laugh when you can."*

She was riding along the broad gentle slope that curved into the wide, shallow valley where the Collinses had settled. They would doubtless take the rest of the basin for a timber claim. Involuntarily, she glanced north, to the windmill and growing corn. The sun blazed out past a racing cloud and shone with brilliance on Cap's white stone by the dark green of the plum thicket.

LeMoyne, thank goodness, wasn't stretched on the mound. Peering from under her hat, Julie located him and Sunny resting near the cellar-diggers as if supervising their progress. Without Sunny, LeMoyne might have pined away. Not for the first time, Julie gave thanks for the gangling, frisky half coyote.

Jerry waved and yelled from the windmill tower. She waved back, smiling at his vigilance, yet incensed that it was necessary. Chandless already had the prize land along the creeks and river. Why couldn't he be content with that and the cattle he could graze there?

Looking all around, Julie was surprised at the difference this slight elevation made in the shimmering vistas. It was like gazing into forever. A house could nestle partway down the south slope, windmill above it, garden and orchard and fields below. This would be a good place to live, just a short walk to be in sight of Cap's grave but not where she would have to pass it every day.

If only, only, she could build that home with Trace. . . . She could dream anyway. She let Duke pick his way down the slope and watched for survey markers while hunting a place level enough to build on, found this on a shoulder of the knoll so gradual that a plow and shovels could even the ground.

She envisioned the house. Cedar shake shingles whether the walls were rock or sod, windows with real glass, a long, roofed porch . . . Or would they build Texas-style in two parts and have the roofed porch in between? They'd plant trees right away for shade and beauty. The windmill would set higher and troughs in the well-house would keep milk deliciously cool.

Duke looked back and whinnied. Roused from her dreaming, Julie turned in the saddle. A lone horseman was approaching. She recognized the slight hunch of his broad shoulders before she could make out his face.

It was Jess Chandless.

*F*ifteen

*P*rimeval fear of an enemy made Julie's skin prickle, chilled the nape of her neck. This was why Jerry had waved and gestured so wildly. He'd seen the rider and tried to alert her. She willed her face to be expressionless but there was nothing she could do about the tightness in her throat that made her voice husky.

"Hello, Colonel Chandless."

"Miss McCloud." He touched the rim of his hat. The hump of his nose between chill gray eyes gave him the look of a hawk.

"What brings you out our way?"

His jaw clamped. "It's my way, young lady. I've given you lots of slack because of how your foster daddy was killed, but I've hit the end of the rope."

Tingling spread to the base of her spine. He didn't sound any happier about it than she felt, but there was no mistaking the dogged resolve in his tone.

"There's a new baby at the Halls', and two little girls. There's three boys trying to hang on to what their mother died for."

"I offered to take the boys."

"And their land."

"Don't amount to shucks and you know it. Hell, woman, I don't like fighting females and babies! You're making it damned tough on me."

"Colonel, you must see times are changing. You can't keep people from coming any more than the sheepmen could stop you or the Indians could stop them." She leaned forward. "You have the choice land along the living waters. Be content with that."

"Don't tell me to be content, girl. I've been here since you were knee-high to a grasshopper. I—" He broke off and cleared his throat. "Maybe you can tell me something."

"What?"

"Is Barbara—" He gulped, then blurted. "Is she in the family way?"

Stunned, Julie hesitated. She shouldn't discuss Barbara's private affairs, but if it would soften Chandless . . .

"She is!" he exclaimed.

"I never said that."

"If she wasn't, you'd have said no right off." A queer, almost bashful eagerness tinged his voice. "Do you know—has she said—who's the daddy?"

Could he think *he* was? Mind flashing back to his remarks about Letty and the way he'd seemed to know the Kenton women, Julie wondered what could come of this.

"Colonel Chandless, may I ask why it's any of your business?" She met his hard stare directly.

After a moment, he gave a harsh laugh. "Since you ask, I'll tell you. I've had—dealings with the lady. If she hadn't been where she was—" He shrugged. "I'm old enough to please myself, and Barbara Galway pleases me."

"Do you please her?"

"Sometimes I've thought so. Look, Miss McCloud, I need a son, even a daughter, to carry on what I've built. Not much sense in it otherwise. That was one reason I offered the Collins kids a home, to see if they'd be fit heirs, but no, they'd rather live in that dugout and plow up the grass!" He paused. "If Barbara's carrying my child, I'm of a mind to marry her."

He sounded so confident, so magnanimous, that Julie smiled sweetly. "If she'll have you?"

"Why wouldn't she?" he asked in real shock.

"Maybe she's sick of men. Maybe she'd rather raise her baby with her friends to help."

The veins in his forehead swelled. "I never heard such crazy talk!"

"Well then, Colonel, why don't you go talk to her?"

"I don't crave to get shot at by a covey of women I can't draw a gun on."

"They wouldn't shoot you without good reason, and some men are there, too." Julie hoped she was doing the right thing. "I'm going home. You can ride with me if—"

She broke off as Shan, Dave, and Danny came over the slope with Barbara close behind. Shan and Dave carried shotguns, Danny a rifle and revolver, Barbara a derringer.

Chandless laughed. "Well, look at this! How in the world—"

"Jerry Collins climbs the tower pretty often." Julie didn't much hope the rancher would be deterred by sentinels, but perhaps it would show him the settlers were determined, too. "I saw him motioning but thought he was just waving at me."

"Won't be any use to see who's coming if you can't stop them," he said dryly. He nudged his horse forward, reaching neither for the rifle in its scabbard nor the revolver at his hip. "Hunting a lobo?" he asked the men. "I reckon I've pretty much cleaned 'em out of the country. Can't get rid of coyotes, though. They just breed more pups."

Dan went deep crimson. "Are you comparin' homesteaders to coyotes, Colonel?"

"Don't think I mentioned homesteaders at all." Chandless turned his back on the men and took off his hat to Barbara. "Miss Bar—Galway—I'd appreciate a word with you. Private."

In spite of the courteous phrasing, it was a command. And something more. The hint of a plea? Barbara tucked the derringer into her apron pocket. "I'm listening, Colonel."

He glanced at the others, thick eyebrows arching imperiously. "It's all right," Barbara told her friends. "I'll be along in a minute."

Shan frowned. "You sure, Miss Barbara?"

She nodded, but as they started off, Chandless called, "There's something you need to know."

"What's that?" Shan asked.

"Instead of regular cowboys, I'm replacing the hands who stayed for your dance with men who're good with guns."

Dan's head jerked up. His fingers tightened on his rifle but Shan placed a hand on his arm. "That's lookin' for trouble, Chandless."

The rancher shook his head. "That's what I'm not. I don't want to war on women and kids. I've thought it over and reckon I can live with the little knot of you wedged in next to each other with passage for my cattle between you and the Halls." He drew himself up, no hint of slouch to the massive shoulders. An old buffalo bull might have looked like that, cornered by wolves.

"You've taken all the land I'll stand for. Anyone else moves onto my range, I'm movin' them out, pronto—and I don't care if they're old ladies, babes in arms, or gunfighters."

"You know they'll come," Shan said quietly.

"And they'll go!" Chandless glared at the men with an edge left over for Julie. "If you have any notions of trying to help them, best way is to warn them to move right along."

"Don't see how we could hardly do that," said Dan.

Chandless shrugged. "Suit yourself. Just don't try to help them when Lute comes to run 'em off." He climbed from his horse, somewhat stiffly, and limped the slightest bit as he led his horse and walked the other way with Barbara.

Dan let out an explosive breath. "Even if one of Lute's raids don't just accidentally spill over on us, how can we stand around and let him run other folks off their claims?"

"By his lights," Shan pointed out, "he's being real forgiving to let all of you, Miss Cora, and the Halls stay."

"Maybe no one else will come till No Man's Land is opened up to legal homesteading." Julie tried to sound more hopeful than she felt. "That's bound to happen in a year or two, and there'll be law then. Real law."

"Probably what he has in mind is keeping the land open till

182

then and havin' his cowboys take homesteads," said Dan. "They can prove up and deed the places over to him for a few extra dollars."

"That's happened in a lot of places," Shan agreed. "He'd wind up owning legal what he holds now with guns." He glanced toward Cap's headstone, dazzling in the late-afternoon sun. His good-natured face hardened. "I was of a mind to take up a claim here and make Hartman kill me to get me off it. But now with Chandless sayin' he'll leave you folks alone, I don't want to kick up trouble."

"Do what you want." Dan's freckled young face was changing into a man's just as his thin body was taking on heft. "We'll back you."

"I appreciate that, Dan." The older man didn't remind the younger that they were the only grown men in the Collins-Kenton-Oliver cluster. Even adding Trace and Cibolo, that wasn't many to battle a force of out-and-out gunmen. "But I won't be the one to start a war. Laban and Rafe and Thad would think they had to help us. They've got wives and kids."

"I've got a wife," reminded Dan with a grin of pride.

"You sure do." Shan punched his friend's shoulder. "And you know what? You plumb got out of a shivaree your wedding night because of Lorena's baby!"

"Doggone!" Dan chuckled. "I'm sure sorry!" He glanced over his shoulder. "Here comes Barbara. She looks mad as fire!"

Julie got down from Duke to walk with Barbara some distance from the others. The young woman's light complexion was indeed flushed and her rapid breathing didn't seem entirely due to walking fast.

"The nerve of him!"

Julie waited. Barbara swallowed and ducked her head to wipe her eyes on her apron. "He—he asked whose baby I'm going to have!"

Cautiously, Julie said, "You can sort of understand that, Barbara, since he wants to marry you."

"He acted so—so godlike!" Barbara raged. "As if he were lifting me out of the mud! I lifted myself! I don't need his wedding ring to be a decent woman."

"You turned him down?"

"Not at first." Barbara swallowed and brushed a sleeve across her eyes. "Not till he asked me if the baby's his. I'm sure it is but I wasn't about to tell him so!"

"Why, Barbara?" From the way her friend looked and sounded, Julie believed she did love the burly rancher.

"If he wouldn't be a good father to my child, no matter whose it is, I don't want him." Barbara gulped before her tone went steely. "I said to him, 'It could be yours.' And when he looked all excited, I added, 'Or any other man's I slept with about then.' "

"Oh, Barbara!" Julie was no advocate of Chandless's, but it did seem perverse to hurt and provoke the man you loved. "I can understand your needing him to accept your child, regardless of the father, but did you have to put it that way?"

"Yes!" Barbara clenched her hands. "He has to want *me*, not just an heir to his cattle and land."

"He does want you," Julie assured her. "And he wants your baby and his. Goodness, if all he wanted was a child by any healthy woman, he could find plenty who'd marry him. Not just for his ranch, either."

Barbara listened hungrily to that, but shook her head. "How can I marry him if he might try to run all of you out of the country?"

"He said he'd leave us alone," Dan said.

"Yes, but other settlers are bound to come," argued Barbara. Again, she scrubbed away tears.

Dave halted and looked northeastward. "Sounds like a wagon."

"You're right," said Dan, peering. "There it is, just coming over the slope from the Halls' place."

Could the men already have collected a load of rocks? Mallory, Billy Lincoln, and Wyatt Mabry had left after the dance. Mallory wouldn't expect the rocks to be delivered so soon, but being a carefree bachelor, he must not have reckoned on the eagerness of the Halls to earn cash money for their families.

Julie felt amused sympathy for whichever of the Halls would have to explain the rocks to Rose. What if she refused to let

184

them unload? Mallory should have been on hand—but that might have really pitched the fat into the fire.

Rafe and Thad rumbled up by the big tent at about the same time Julie, Barbara, and their party got there. Rose, Madelaine, and Letty poured outside and stared at the wagon. Rafe sprang down, hurrying toward the tent.

"How's Lorena and little Johnny, Miss Rose?"

"Go see for yourself." In spite of puzzlement over the rocks, Rose gestured him in with a smile. "They're sleeping but Lorena won't mind your waking her up."

While Rafe admired his family, Rose advanced on Thad. "Are you taking the rocks to Cora?"

Thad's black mustache seemed to droop lower in astonishment. "Uh—no, Miss Rose," he floundered. "Don't you— I mean—"

Rafe came out, beaming. "Lorena says Johnny's a good baby. Don't see how he could be much else since I reckon all he does is sleep and eat."

"He could howl with colic," Rose told him. She pointed at the wagon. "What about this?"

Rafe's bewilderment mirrored Thad's. He scanned the onlookers. "Where's Jack Mallory?"

"Where, indeed?" counterqueried Rose. "Has he got something to do with this?"

The brothers exchanged bemused glances. "Didn't he tell you, Miss Rose?" Rafe asked, as if each word burned his tongue.

"Tell me what?"

"He—uh—" Rafe's eyes implored his older brother for help but Thad was busy examining his shoe. "Well, it's like this, ma'am. He—uh—wants to build you a house."

Rose fell back as if pushed by an invisible hand, then advanced on the men and wagon. "John Jack Mallory is *not* building my house. You can just take those rocks back to the creek and dump them!"

"But Miss Rose!" protested Rafe. "If we don't unload 'em here, we won't get paid."

"Yeah," said Thad, addressing his shoe. "And Jack hired us

to help lay up the walls." He didn't have to say how much cash wages would mean to all three Hall families, but he shot a quick glance at Julie. "We were planning on paying you and Trace for the well and windmill."

"You don't have to worry about that," Julie assured him. "We're a cooperative, remember. You got credits for building the fence here. When I claim my land, you can pay off the balance by helping build the house."

Rose consulted briefly with Barbara and Madelaine. "I've got a bone to pick with John Jack," she told the Halls. "But I don't want to keep you from earning some money. Haul all the rocks he asked for and dump them yonder." She indicated a location north of the windmill, and smiled grimly. "Then John Jack—or whoever wants the rocks—can hire you to haul them to wherever they'll be used. The money you make on double hauling ought to help make up for losing house-building wages. Or maybe whoever takes the rocks will hire you to make something out of them."

Rafe and Thad grinned at the reprieve. "We're much obliged, Miss Rose. Of course, when Jack finds out you won't let him build a house—"

"By the time he comes around to face me, you may be through hauling." Her tone was grim and she frowned in a way that meant Jack Mallory would get dragged thoroughly over the coals and left to fry a bit. "Leave him to me."

"Glad to, ma'am," nodded Rafe, and clucked the team toward the indicated site.

"When you're through unloading," called Rose, "have supper with us before you head home." She turned to Julie and those who had encountered Chandless. Her dark eyes probed Barbara, who still looked angry. "What went on over there anyway? Who was the horseman Jerry spotted?"

Julie left the story to her friends. She unsaddled Duke, rubbed him down, and gave him a chunk of leftover cornbread she got from the tent.

Already she was missing Trace. She promised herself that when they all returned from erecting Hank Trevor's windmill, she'd get Trace to look at the other side of the gentle slope bounding what she was starting to think of as Cap's Valley.

She couldn't claim land there now that it would touch off fighting, but someday—someday.

Two mornings later, Shan and Julie were preparing to follow Trace and Cibolo to Hank Trevor's when Mallory drove up with a wagon full of lumber, windows, and cedar shake shingles. Ranging beside the wagon was a buckskin colt the color of pulled taffy. His tail and mane were still crimped, like hair released from a tight braid. From the way one mare kept a proud and anxious eye on his cavorting, she was his mother.

Jerry ran to hold the team, eyes ashine. He still worshiped Trace, but no boy—and few grown-ups—could resist Jack Mallory. "Thanks, son." Giving the boy's yellow hair a friendly tousle, Mallory took off his hat to the ladies. "How's my namesake?" he asked before Rose could assail him.

"*Your* namesake?" she gasped. "Little John Laban Mc-Cloud Hall is named for his grandpas and Cap McCloud!"

"His name's still John, same as mine," shrugged Mallory. "I'm giving him that colt, the likeliest any of my mares dropped this spring, soon as it's gentled for riding in about four years."

"Go see the baby for yourself," Rose said, stepping away from the tent door. "And then you can come back out here and explain yourself."

Julie whispered to Shan. "Take your time hitching up. I want to hear this."

"Me too," Shan said with a wide grin. "He's a fast talker but I don't know if he can make Miss Rose listen."

Julie and Shan weren't the only ones to eavesdrop shamelessly when Mallory emerged to face Rose. Madelaine and Barbara followed him out, Letty came out of her tent, and Dan, Jon, and Dave paused in their work on the cellar which, with Shan's help, was close to being excavated.

"Before you start in on me, I've got a few things Corinne sent Letty." He went to the wagon, lifted a tarp, and produced a package which he placed in Letty's hands. "Corinne took laudanum in her whiskey-and-soda night before last. She left a note that she wanted you to have this." He looked somberly at the other women. "She wished you all good luck."

The women shrank together. Rose went so pale that Mallory steadied her. "Poor Corinne! I never thought she'd be one to do this—"

"A customer knocked out some teeth and broke her nose," Jack said. "Wyatt Mabry and I saw to it she was buried decent in the white dress she'd laid out."

Letty read a note tucked in the wrappings of Corinne's bequest.

"Dear Girls:

My looks are gone and I'm tired out. All I want to do is sleep. I bought the baby doll, Letty, when I knew I'd never have kids of my own. I called her Annie. Sometimes when I'd had enough to drink, she seemed to talk to me. Please, when you have a little girl of your own, give her Annie to love. Good-bye, and Letty, I'm glad you got married with my mother's ring."

Letty's hands shook. Madelaine helped her unwrap an elegant, life-size doll with golden ringlets, a bisque head, and realistic-looking teeth showing through the parted rosebud lips. "Corinne set a lot of store by this doll," Rose said, touching the lace edge of the pale blue gown.

"I wish she hadn't sent it to me!" Letty sobbed. "I couldn't let a baby of mine play with it, ever!"

Rose put her hands on the younger woman's shoulders. "Corinne loved Annie, dear. She didn't want her thrown away and didn't know anyone else to leave her to."

"I'm sure she'd be pleased if you find a little girl who'd take good care of Annie," Madelaine comforted.

Everyone was silent. More than likely, thought Julie as she made her own silent prayer, they were all hoping Corinne's sleep was peaceful. When Letty, still sobbing, had taken the doll into her tent, Rose straightened her back and fixed a stern gaze on Mallory.

"All right, Jack. What's this about a house?"

" 'This is the cow with the crumpled horn / Who tossed the dog who worried the cat.' "

Rose interrupted his bland recital of the old nursery rhyme. "There isn't going to be any 'House that Jack Built.' Not on my land anyway."

"Now, Rose—"

"You thought you could get around me by hiring the Halls," she thrust, eyes glinting. "I didn't want to knock them out of a job. They can unload here. Then, when you decide where you want the rocks, you can pay again to get them delivered! I'm building a soddie."

He said just as fiercely, "I won't have you living in a dirt shanty!"

"What business is it of yours?"

"I love you, damn it!"

Her hand went to her throat. "Then why—"

He took a long stride and captured her hands, heedless of onlookers. "Let me build you a good house, Rose. One that'll protect you from northers and high winds and shut out the heat in summer."

"Jack—"

"I'd keep you safe in my arms if I could. Since I can't, let me build walls that will."

She watched him with her heart in her eyes. "But Jack, if you love me. Why don't we—" She broke off.

He finished for her. "If you'd have me, I'd marry you in a minute. But you won't have me, will you, if I kill Trace Riordan?"

Julie gasped, as if pierced by a thin swift blade. Shan put his arm around her as Rose drew her hands away from Mallory. "No. I wouldn't have you."

"So let me build your house."

This time she caught him by the arms and shook him. "From all I've heard about your friend, Trace is worth a hundred of him. Can't you let it go?"

Praying, Julie held her breath. He wouldn't listen to her but maybe he would to Rose.

"Not and be a man," he said.

Rose shook her head in sorrowful anger. "You'll be a man by killing a good one, by bringing grief to Julie and Cibolo and everyone who cares about him?"

"Maybe he'll kill me."

I hope he does! thought Julie, and then remembered Rose would weep. Besides, in spite of everything, Julie couldn't keep from liking Mallory. The world would be dimmer and duller without him.

Rose gave a bitter laugh. "Is that supposed to make me feel better?" She whirled away, face buried in her arm. He took a short step and gathered her to him.

"Rose, Rosie," he murmured against her black hair. "Please. Do it for me. Let me do something I can feel good about."

Her whisper barely carried to the others. "All right, Jack. Build me a house."

Sixteen

*I*t was something to see, dashing Jack Mallory using Cap's tape measure, with Jerry's eager help, to mark the dimensions of the house which the women had decided should be situated a little lower than the windmill. Fortunately, that wasn't far from the unloaded rocks.

"I couldn't get cement in Kenton," he said. "Guess I'll have to make a trip to Tyrone."

"I can fetch it for you, Jack," offered Dan, peering out of the cellar. "We want to cement the sides and floor of this, make some steps coming down, and we need door lumber and roof poles."

"Fine, if you're going anyway," said Jack. "I'll be leveling the site and digging out for the foundation."

How could he act so ordinary when he intended to kill Trace? Julie wondered, sick with helplessness. And Trace was just as stubborn! Unless she could prevail on him to gradually work their way out of No Man's Land, there'd be a killing. Whichever way it went, a woman would mourn her love.

She poured this out to Shan as they journeyed that afternoon toward the Trevor place. "That's men for you, honey." Shan patted her hand. "But you'll notice Mallory keeps puttin' it off. He don't really want to kill Trace, he just reckons he has to."

"That's crazy!"

"Well, men are whenever it comes to whatever it is makes us men." Shan gave her a wry grin. "If Mallory kills Trace, naturally I'll have to try to kill him."

She hadn't thought about this. "Oh, Shan!" She gripped his wrist. "Not you, too!"

"Yeah, Julie." Shan's jaw hardened. "Me, too. Though there's a chance Cib might beat me to it."

"And then," she blazed, close to tears, "I suppose if one of you kill Mallory, Wyatt Mabry and Billy Lincoln will have to avenge *their* friend—and so on, till you're all dead!"

"That's how it goes, honey. You expect us to crawl away from a friend's body with our tails between our legs?"

"What about Madelaine?"

He sighed. "I can't ask her to marry me till all this settles down."

"What'll be settling is the ground on someone's grave!"

"More than likely."

Julie groaned with frustration. "With Chandless hiring killers, it looks like you men who are more or less on the same side could fight him instead of each other."

"Reckon we will if he starts anything."

"Maybe he'll be smarter than you and wait till you kill each other off."

"We'll see."

Shan's tolerant smile set her teeth on edge. She didn't answer for fear of being crosser than she should with Cap's longtime companion who was like her own uncle. She watched the long ears of Columbine and Absalom flop rhythmically as they followed the tracks that were becoming a rough sort of road, what with the horses, wagons, and buggies that had traveled that way for the wedding.

Above the squeaks and whines of their own wagon, Julie heard the rumble of what sounded like another. "Danny must have decided to go for the cement," she said, and looked around.

Sure enough, he was driving Rose's mules. Dave sat beside him. They gained quickly with the unloaded wagon and pulled out wide around the windmillers, grinning and waving.

"See you later!" Dave yelled. "Tell Trace and Cib howdy for us!"

Julie shouted back, "Be careful!"

"Remember you're a married man now, Danny!" yelled Shan.

They rattled on with a flourish of hats. "I'm glad the Collins boys have some men around," Julie reflected. "I wonder how much longer they could have gone on living like a litter of wild things."

"They've filled out like possums in a corn-crib," nodded Shan. "Maddy's cut their hair and Rose sees to it that they wash up before meals. But you know, Julie, I reckon they'd have made it anyway, havin' each other, and set as they were on hanging onto their mama's land. She'd be proud of them."

A lump rose in Julie's throat. "I hope she is." And she hoped that somehow, beneath the prairie earth by the plum thicket, Cap and Mrs. Collins could keep each other company. Certainly she herself felt better that Cap rested near another person. It didn't seem so lonely.

And Cap, she told him silently, *we're putting up another windmill for you—and we'll try to do it just as well as you would.*

It was like old times to camp that night along the way, except that Cap wasn't there and LeMoyne had been left with Sunny. Next morning, and the next one, too, Julie roused slowly, thinking he was grinding the coffee, but when she opened her eyes, it was Shan turning the handle of the mill. She had to bury her face in the pillow and shed hot tears before she dressed inside her bedroll and got up to make biscuits.

They crossed two creeks on Chandless range. Near the ford of the first one, a caved-in soddie was sinking back into the earth. "Chandless probably helped them leave," Shan said. "They were too close to his water."

A corral was built near each stream some distance from the track, and cowboys were at work. "Expect they're branding calves they missed in the main roundup last month," Shan speculated. "Probably they're doctorin' for screwworms, too.

193

Durn things are 'specially bad to get in the bags of calves that just got turned into steers."

"Looks like Chandless's new hands can handle ropes and cattle as well as guns." Seeing them at ordinary ranchwork was vastly reassuring to Julie. "Maybe Chandless didn't really hire gunfighters."

"Don't bank on it," Shan warned. "Our best chance is for no one else to claim land close to Cap's Valley till the whole shebang gets tacked onto some other state or territory." He squinted at Julie. "Don't think I've seen that shirt before. Pretty fancy for windmillin'."

"Madelaine sewed it out of scraps," Julie explained briefly.

The cloth was left over from a bronze-and-green dress commissioned, with blushes, by Cora Oliver the day after the dance when she'd come over for Johnny's baptism. The shirt had ruffles down the front and Julie considered it quite fetching.

"Mm-hm," grinned Shan. "You gals stick together, don't you?"

"We'd better. After you men get through killing each other, we won't have anyone else!"

If Shan, usually blind to such things, noticed the shirt, maybe Trace would. It seemed a long time since she'd seen him though it had only been five days. How awful it would be to never see him again—yet that could happen.

Trevor's claim was supposed to be located about five miles southwest of Tyrone along the dim track, but the travelers began to encounter other ruts leading off in several directions. They followed what seemed the most-used road, but as the day wore on, Shan said, "Seems like we should be getting there. Hope we shouldn't have taken one of the other tracks."

"This was the clearest one." Julie scanned the way ahead. "Look! I think that's sun flashing off glass."

"Yep." Shan sounded as relieved as she was. "Hank Trevor's got two windows in his soddie. And there's the rig."

Julie's heart raced. She could hardly wait for the team to pull up near the pipe sticking up from the ground. "You're just in time!" Trace gave her a hand off the wagon and held hers a breath longer than he had to.

Warm tingling thrilled up her arm and radiated through her. Their eyes locked. If he felt the same tantalizing shock, the same delicious hunger, he didn't show it. He stepped away from her. "That's sure a pretty shirt. Or blouse or waist, whatever you ladies call it." Before she could thank him for the compliment, he turned to Shan.

"We hit good water at ninety feet. Everything's ready to set up the mill." Trace nodded toward the unopened windmill crate, the vane, and bundled tower sections.

Cibolo finished banking the Dutch oven with coals. "We even made a start on the anchor holes," he said, pouring coffee for Julie and Shan. "How's little John Laban McCloud? He better get big fast to tote all those names!"

Shan drained his coffee before attending to the team while Julie reported on the baby, the encounter with Chandless, and Mallory's house-building.

"Sounds like plenty's happened," Trace said as they sat down to eat. "Beats all about Chandless wanting to marry Barbara, especially her turning him down. What curls my toes, though, is Jack Mallory putting his back into raising a house."

"From what he says, he's pretty experienced." Julie didn't tell Trace about Mallory's unbending intent to kill him. "Even with the Collins boys, Dan and the Halls helping, the house should keep him busy for a while."

Shan turned the subject. "The biggest, best surprise to me is Chandless's letting folks keep their claims."

"*He* may," Trace allowed. "Lute Hartman may see things different."

"But Hartman works for Chandless," Julie said.

"For the time being."

"What are you getting at, partner?" growled Shan.

"Hartman stopped by here at noon on his way to Tyrone. He bragged that Chandless is making him his heir."

Julie froze. "Chandless is adopting him?"

"No, but Chandless knows Hartman will keep the JC brand going on this range." Trace considered. "Sounds like after Barbara turned Chandless down, he went home and talked turkey with Lute."

"A brand's not alive!" Julie burst out. Was there no end to masculine conceit?

"A brand's not a living son," Trace agreed. "But since Chandless can't have one, he must reckon the next best thing is to keep his brand going."

Julie pondered this disastrous turn of affairs. "Did Hartman say he'd honor Chandless's promise to leave present settlers alone?"

"He allowed as how that was one of the conditions of the colonel's making out a will in his favor."

"But," put in Cibolo, "he grinned kind of nasty when he said it."

"Chandless can't be over fifty," Shan reminded them. "If he don't break his neck from holding it so stiff, he ought to be around long past the day law comes to No Man's Land."

Still, Julie was filled with foreboding. Men who prized their honor were a trial but she didn't think Hartman had any.

The anchor-post holes were dug and, shortly before noon, the tower was being assembled, when Hank Trevor drove up in what a startled Julie realized was the Kenton women's former opulent spring wagon. The crimson paint was a bit dingier, the leather seats scuffed, and black striping chipped here and there, yet the fringed canopy swayed gaily as ever.

Hank did his best to live up to his equipage. Hot as it was, he wore a three-button cutaway frock coat and pants in a tiny blue-and-gray check. A gold chain looped to the pocket of his gray vest. The stylishly curled-up brim of his gray fedora hadn't protected his nose. It shone fiery red. Still, he was the picture of heavyset fashion and the gilt-paper box beside him could only hold fancy chocolates.

"Going to a wedding or a funeral?" Trace asked. "You're dressed for either one."

"Just paying a little call on Miss Oliver." The livery owner's face colored to match his nose.

" 'Little call'?" Shan teased. "If you camp in her yard as long as it takes you to get there, you'll be gone a week."

"Except for the wedding last Saturday, I haven't been away from the stable since I opened it." Hank spoke as if he were being accused of sloth and dillydallying. "Charlie Shaw's looking after my business—and he owes me plenty of days because he and his family are always hopping on the train to go hither and yon."

"I'm sure Cora will be glad to see you," Julie soothed.

"Do you think so?" He gave Julie a shy, eager smile that made him almost handsome. "Has she said anything that makes you think she might be willing to move?"

Julie shook her head. "It'll take crowbars and dynamite to get her off that claim."

"Drat it, what'll I do about my business? And this place, now I've got a well?"

"You'll have to talk it over with Cora." Julie wanted to remind him not to take Cora for granted. "Did you see Dan Shelton and young Dave Collins in town?"

"Let 'em sleep on hay in my barn last night. When I left this morning they were headed to Liberal because Charlie didn't have as much cement as they needed. By the way, several families around Tyrone want wells and windmills. Charlie's keeping a list and can tell you who they are."

"Much obliged," said Trace. "We'll do our best for them."

Hank's warm hazel eyes twinkled. "Say, is it true that Jack Mallory's puttin' up a rock house for those—"

He searched for a word. Julie supplied it. "For those ladies? Yes, he is."

Hank gave a soft whistle. "Next thing we know, rattlesnakes'll be coilin' around baby rabbits to protect them!" He refused politely to stay for dinner, clucked to his bays, and trundled off.

Julie wished him and Cora luck but as she tightened another bolt, she thought the couple were much more likely to solve their problems than were she and Trace. As they worked, the sweetness of being near him was tainted with worry.

Would Lute Hartman abide by Chandless's word, or would he try to force her friends off their land? If something happened to Chandless, then what? And even if the homesteaders were left in peace, could the old score between Mallory and Trace be settled without the death of one or the other?

That night after supper, Cibolo played haunting tunes on his harmonica, lonesome as the thin sliver of moon sinking in the western sky. Summoning her courage, Julie asked Trace to go for a walk.

"Better not. Rattlers like to wander around and do their hunting in the cool."

It was a sensible answer. He was right. But that wasn't the real reason he refused. Julie got into her bedroll that night with a sore heart.

They finished putting the tower together next morning and attached the head, wheel, and vane since this was a small mill. "We're in luck," Shan observed. "Not hardly any wind today." That did make raising a tower and mill much easier, but Julie wished their luck could extend to more serious matters.

After dinner, they hoisted the tower into place with the wheel wired to the vane so it wouldn't spin off. They were tightening bolts when a reverberating sound of wheels made them look up.

"Could be Dan and Dave," Trace said. He glanced at the lowering sun. "They can't go much farther tonight. Might as well have supper with us and bed down here."

When she had tightened the last bolt on her side of the tower, Julie straightened, stretched, and gazed in the direction of the approaching wagon.

She shaded her eyes and peered again. "There's only one person. And those are sorrels, not Rose's team. It must not be Dan and Dave."

They all watched. There was nothing unusual about a wagon traveling along, but Julie's stomach began to twist and knot even before Trace said, "That's Dave."

What could it mean? The crew exchanged anxious looks and started forward to meet the wagon that jounced along the ruts, wheels sometimes in the air. Whatever it held, it wasn't cement. Far behind it, barely in sight, another wagon followed.

Dave halted the sorrel horses. He tried to speak but no words came. "What is it, son?" asked Trace in a calming tone.

The boy jerked his head toward the wagon bed and the edge of a wooden box that stuck out from under a tarp. The box looked about the length and size to hold a man. Dread numbed Julie. "Is—is it Dan?"

Dave nodded.

Trace's voice knifed the stunned silence. "How?"

"Lute Hartman—" Dave's thin shoulders heaved. He rubbed his sleeve across his face and swallowed hard. "We'd got back from Liberal and were loading more cement at Charlie Shaw's—wanted to give him all the business we could. Lute Hartman came out of a saloon with another man. Hartman laughed and told his pal Dan had married a—a—"

Again, Dave broke off. Trace put a steadying hand on his arm. Dave gulped and hurried to finish. "Hartman called Letty a bad name. Dan pulled his six-shooter. Hartman didn't draw. He grinned and asked Dan if he couldn't take a joke. Dan—Dan said if he didn't draw, he'd kill him like a snake."

"So Hartman drew."

Dave nodded. "Dan's bullet grazed Hartman's shoulder. Hartman got Dan in the chest, maybe the heart. We got him into the store. He died as we were lifting him onto a counter."

Dave began to shake uncontrollably. "Mrs. Shaw and another lady washed him and put on a clean shirt. They poured embalming fluid over him and the blanket they laid him on. Charlie Shaw loaned me this team from the livery and said he'd bring the cement—wouldn't be respectful to bundle Dan on top of the load."

"What about Hartman?" Shan demanded.

Dave gave his head an angry, helpless shake. "Even if there was any law here, Charlie Shaw said Dan made Hartman fight."

"But Hartman insulted Letty!" Julie cried.

Trace sighed. "Sorry, but plenty of folks would think Hartman was just calling a spade a spade. And no one can fault him for drawing after what Dan threatened."

"What Hartman should've done," growled Shan, "was wing the kid and take his gun away. But when you draw on someone like that—" His voice trailed off as he watched the blanketed form of the young man who had been a bridegroom less than a week ago.

Julie tried to hold back scalding tears but a few ran down her face. "So Hartman will get away with this?"

"I'd like to blow his head off with a shotgun!" Dave cried in a raw voice.

"You won't." Trace gave him a shake, none too gentle. "You'd get yourself killed, and where would your brothers be?" Trace turned to Julie. "If Letty wants it, I'll find Hartman and do my best to kill him. For now, though, we need to eat supper."

"I'm not hungry," Dave muttered.

"Take a few bites and you will be," Trace advised.

Charlie Shaw arrived in time for supper. "An awful thing." He ran his fingers through his thinning red hair. "Married less than a week. Hartman shouldn't have shot off his mouth, but the kid didn't leave him any choice."

It was a somber meal, eaten to fuel their bodies, not from gusto. "We have to hook up the sucker rod and pipes tomorrow, but two of us can do it," Trace said. "Dave, you can stay here if you don't feel like driving on tonight. We need to get Dan home as quick as we can."

He didn't need to explain that even a body soaked in embalming fluid would start to smell in a few days, an added horror for Letty.

"I'll drive," Dave said after a moment. "Letty'll want to know—everything."

"I'll go with you, Dave." Julie shrank from the task but she thought Dave might be able to talk to her more easily than he could to the men, for whom—again, that male pride—he would feel he had to put on an act. "We can travel till it's too dark to see," she said. "Grain the horses good, and start in the morning as soon as we can tell where we're going."

"I may leave the engine here," Trace said, "since it sounds like we have some jobs around Tyrone. As soon as we're finished here, Cib and I will come in our other wagon." He touched her cheek. His fingers were so warm and strong that it was hard to believe the crash of a bullet could turn them cold and lifeless. "We won't be far behind," he added softly. "You're a brave lady."

I'm scared. Scared of what this will do to Letty, to Dave—

to all of us. Still, Julie managed some kind of smile for him and went to get grain from her wagon to carry for the sorrels. It wasn't far to Pony Creek. They could water there instead of from the barrels carried for the well/windmill teams.

"Ready, Dave?" she asked, after, trying not to look at the coffin, she'd stowed her bedroll and belongings in the wagon. "Shall I drive?"

"Let me. Gives me something to think about except—" He broke off and unhitched the team from a post near the soddie.

Trace gave Julie a hand up. "We'll be along as soon as we can," he promised.

She nodded, unable to speak. Dave started to the horses. The wagon rolled off toward the fading sunset but Julie's heart yearned back to Trace.

Seventeen

They watered and rested the sorrels at Pony Creek and decided to follow the crescent moon till it sank beneath the prairie rim. Traveling at night was cool and would tire the horses less. Dave kept going over those few minutes outside the store, searching for something that might have made a difference.

"Maybe if I'd grabbed the shotgun—"

"There might be two of you dead." "Supposing you were lucky and shot Hartman? How would you be feeling now?"

"Not as bad as I do." His young man's voice cracked. "What'll Letty think of me? I—I should of done something!"

"Dave, it wouldn't help Letty for you to be filling another coffin. Besides, you have to look after your brothers."

He didn't answer. Even in the dim light she could see the despondent droop of his head and shoulders and it tugged at her heart. Resting her hand over his on the lines, she used her most persuasive tone.

"You and your brothers can help Letty a lot, Dave, especially if she moves over on her claim. She's going to need all her friends."

"We could build her house if some of the men'll help," Dave said eagerly. "We can plow for her and help plant and harvest." He straightened a bit. "Maybe now she'll build on the corner of her land that's close to us and Miss Rose. I hope she will! The other ladies are nice but Letty—well, she's like a big sister."

Julie suspected that he also had a boy's worship for an older woman, but this was not the time to tease him. "She'll need a well if she decides not to share Cora's," Julie thought aloud. "We can dig it and put up a windmill before we work our way east."

Dave jerked erect. "You—you're leaving?"

"Outfits like ours have to find new customers, Dave."

"I—I guess so, but, aw, Julie—"

She squeezed his arm. "I'm going to claim that land I was looking at the other day when Chandless came along. It can be home, our headquarters."

"Are you going to put up windmills all your life?" he asked dubiously.

"Why not, as long as I can climb a tower and dig an anchor hole."

He mulled this over. "Don't you sort of like Trace?"

"More than sort of."

"Well, if you get married and have babies, I don't see how you can chase all over the country to set up windmills."

Julie's experience of babies was limited to Lorena and little Johnny, but even that made her suspect that windmilling with small children might be difficult. "Maybe I can't go all the time," she admitted, "but we could have a covered wagon and take the kids when they're old enough. LeMoyne can help watch them."

"I bet Trace will want you to stay home," Dave said, so sagely that Julie had to chuckle.

"We'll worry about all that later, Dave. Right now, I'm just praying to keep Trace and Jack Mallory from fighting."

"That'd be plumb awful!"

"It would, and that's another reason to head east."

"But you want to claim land next to us!"

"In order not to start a war with Chandless, that'll have to wait till Congress opens up No Man's Land to legal home-steading."

"I wish there were enough of us to run Chandless and Hartman right out of the country!" Dave burst out. "The way Hartman killed Dan—" His shoulders heaved. "How'm I going to tell Letty I just stood there?"

"By all accounts, Dan was good with guns." So strange to realize he was really dead; all that was left of his earthly being contained in the crude box behind them. "Hartman was dead wrong to provoke him but Dan didn't leave him any way out."

"I'd still rather be beat within an inch of my life than tell Letty."

"She won't blame you, Dave."

"*I* do!"

Terrified that he would brood and do something fatal, Julie shook him hard. "Listen! You couldn't do anything but get yourself killed!"

"But—"

"It wasn't your fight. Dan had more than a fair chance."

The boy's only answer was a groan. "Your mother counted on you to raise your brothers." Julie used her best weapon relentlessly. "Do that right, Dave, and you'll be more of a man than the toughest gunfighter that ever walked."

They drove in silence till the scythe moon reached the edge of the horizon. As it slipped lower, Dave unhitched the horses and rubbed them down while Julie put their grain in nosebags. The horses were hobbled, Dave and Julie got their bedrolls from the wagon, spread them, and got under their tarps with feet to the wind.

Dave said, "Dan won't ever be hot or cold again, or hungry or thirsty, either. He won't care if it hails or comes a blizzard or don't rain for months. But I wonder what it is like, Julie. What it's like to be dead."

"I don't know, Dave." Julie tried to be as comforting as she could, in honesty. "I think it's good. I'm sure it's peace."

"Do you think dead folks know what's happening here?"

"Sometimes I've had the feeling Cap was close—that he was glad when we finished putting up a windmill."

Dave sighed. "I used to dream Mama was still alive. She was so real. . . . Then I'd wake up."

"There's lots we don't know, dear, but I believe your mother still loves you and her love can help you. Let it help you now. And listen, I'll say Cap's favorite prayer."

By the time she reached, " *'O ye Light and Darkness, bless ye the Lord . . .,'* " Dave gave another sigh, but this one sounded drowsy. In a little while, his breathing deepened.

If you can, Julie besought his mother's spirit, *comfort him tonight.* She wept as she prayed for Letty and for Dan. Then, to solace herself, she envisioned Cap, remembered his wisdom and kindness and laughter. Oddly, on this mournful night, she could for the first time remember him without tears. With a sense of his closeness warming her, she fell asleep.

Waking when it was just light enough to see, Julie couldn't remember for a moment where she was. Then she saw the top of Dave's bright head above his covers. Everything flooded back. Though she usually relished snuggling into her pillow for a few luxurious moments, that was impossible.

She dressed in her bedroll, collected cow chips and dead soapweed stalks, and got a fire going. Dave and Dan had provisions, including ground coffee, a coffeepot, frying pan, and Dutch oven. Julie put on coffee, made biscuits, and sliced potatoes into the frying pan with wild onions and greens she'd found while gathering fuel. Next, she picked over beans and set them among coals so they'd be soft enough to finish cooking at their noon rest.

Dave began to move restlessly and made sounds of protest. Julie started to bend down and rouse him from what she feared was a nightmare when he sat up abruptly.

"Dan!" he cried, fighting the covers off. "Dan!"

Julie knelt down and gripped his shoulders. "Wake up, Dave. Wake up! It's Julie."

His eyes flew open. He stared at her, bewildered. His gaze veered to the livery wagon, the grazing sorrels. His muscles tightened under her hands.

"It's true," he mumbled.

He began to tremble. Julie put her arms around him and held him while he sobbed, murmuring his name and making consoling sounds as she wept, too. After a time, he pulled away, rubbing his sleeve across his eyes.

"You must think I'm a big baby!"

"To cry because you've lost a friend? There'd be something wrong if you didn't cry, if you didn't care."

"Men don't cry."

"Cap did. More than once."

"He did?"

"You bet."

"Cap was sure a man."

"More of a man because he could cry." Julie moved toward the fire. "Ready for some coffee?"

Off well before sunrise, they reached the next creek about noon and forded the shallow stream by the abandoned soddie, perhaps a mile from a corral where cowboys were working. They sheltered in a welcoming stand of cottonwoods, grained the sorrels and put on hobbles so they could enjoy the rich mixture of grama and buffalo grass.

Taking advantage of fallen branches and fibrous bark, Dave got a fire going. Julie put on coffee and beans and mixed up cornbread, enough to have plenty left for supper. After a brief hesitation, Julie put dried apples to stew in the frying pan. When they were juicy, she made biscuit dough to pat thin and form a sort of a crust for a dessert.

Dave was boy enough to be cheered by treats like that; making him do without wouldn't help Dan. After hours of jostling along in the wagon, it felt wonderful to move and stretch, in spite of the pang of realizing that Dan, little older than she was, would never flex his muscles again or fill his lungs with sweet air.

Julie gathered more wild onions to flavor the beans while Dave filled the bottom of the wagon with limbs and bark. The moon would be a little fuller and set later that night. They'd travel as long as they could, but would rest the horses this hottest part of the day.

Dave's eyes were swollen and he didn't talk much but after a few tentative bites, he ate heartily and polished off the better part of Julie's skillet cobbler.

"We'll leave the beans in the ashes till we're ready to go," she said. "It won't take so long to warm them tonight and we'll make a quick supper." Dave looked tired. She herself was weary. "Why don't we spread our bedrolls and get a little rest?"

Julie, lying on top of her bedding, didn't quite go to sleep in spite of the soothing rustle of the cottonwood leaves, but she was close to slumber when one of the horses nickered.

An answering whinny brought her fully awake. Sitting up, she looked east. Riders were coming toward them. "Dave! Someone's headed this way!"

Hastily, she pulled on her work boots and laced them up. Dave did the same. He waited close to the wagon, in easy reach of the shotgun under the seat. "Don't start anything, Dave," she implored under her breath.

"Depends on them." His young voice started deep and changed to high.

Julie went out to meet the horsemen. The three were well mounted on horses wearing the JC brand. They had well-used ropes coiled at their saddlehorns, but there was something about them that was different from most cowboys. Beside scabbarded rifles, each wore a revolver in a holster molded to the gun like an expensive glove to a hand. This kind of fit, Cap had once told her, came from the holster-maker soaking the leather and shaping it to the gun. Ordinary cowboys seldom bothered with such refinement. They generally left their six-guns in the bunkhouse or chuck wagon.

The approaching men looked tough and weathered as rawhide. The stockiest, dark one had a clipped black mustache, another a sandy stubble, and the third had a bleached scraggly mustache and longish hair the color of frayed rope.

The dark man's eyes widened at Julie before they slitted again. "Ma'am," he said, touching the brim of his hat. The others did the same but in a perfunctory way that showed no real respect. "You was stopped here so long we thought maybe your wagon had broke down."

"Our wagon's fine," said Julie.

"You folks passin' through?"

She longed to tell him it was none of his business, but with

Dave on trigger-edge, it was no time to defy Chandless's gun-men, which is what she was sure these three were. "We're going to the Collins place," she said.

The men exchanged glances. "Reckon you'd be the Miss Julie McCloud with the windmill outfit?"

"I would. This is Dave Collins. I suppose you work for Colonel Chandless?"

The dark man nodded. "I'm Chance Rivers, ma'am. Shell Harris is the feller that needs a shave and Ote Langley looks like the mice been at his moustache."

Julie didn't like the way Langley and Harris watched her. "It was nice of you to ride over, Mr. Rivers, but we don't need any help."

"That's good, ma'am. We got orders to help any new nesters right on out of the country but the colonel says to leave the ones already here alone."

Langley spat tobacco from the side of his mouth. "He's makin' a mistake there. It's like leavin' a log in a creek. If it don't wash away quick, it catches all the trash and pretty soon the creek has to run around it."

"If you're calling us trash—" Dave began.

Rivers frowned at Langley, then said coolly to Dave, "No one jerked your chain, sonny." Again, he touched his hat to Julie. "We won't be keeping you, Miss McCloud. Guess you want to be on your way."

"Sure!" Dave blurted. "We just can't wait to take a dead man home to the lady he just married! A man Lute Hartman killed!"

"What's this?" demanded Rivers. He jerked his head toward the wagon. "You got a coffin under that tarp?"

"And a dead young man," said Julie.

"Lute ain't back from Tyrone yet," Harris mused. "Sounds like he's havin' himself a spree."

"A spree?" Julie choked with outrage. "Is that what you call it when a man—no, more of a boy—gets killed?"

"Did this man-boy of yours have his gun out when Lute shot him?" asked Langley.

"Yes, but Hartman provoked him."

Rivers shrugged. "Well, ma'am, if your boy was man

enough to draw a gun on Lute Hartman, don't see you've got much kick comin'."

Afraid that an even younger man-boy might grab the shotgun any minute, Julie moved back beside Dave. "We do have to get the body home."

"Sorry he left a widow." Rivers's dark eyes touched Dave. "Young pups need to be careful. They light into an old he-dog, they'll get trounced every time." He turned his horse. "So long, folks. Hope you make it home all right."

The three rode off at a lazy pace. Dave let out an explosive breath. "So there's Chandless's new hands! Calling us trash and me a pup!"

"Dave, it doesn't matter."

"It sure does!" He blinked but tears glinted in his eyes. "Just because they can shoot faster than me, do I have to put up with their sneering around and—"

"Seems like a pretty good reason to me," Julie said. "We don't need two funerals, Dave. You just remember that."

He was still trembling with bottled-up fury. "If we'd been new settlers, they'd have run us off."

"Yes. That's what Chandless said he'd do."

"He's got no right!"

"He's got the guns."

Dave stared at her. "I can't believe you said that, Julie!"

"It's true, Dave."

"So if someone new takes up land, you think we should roll over and play dead while Hartman chouses them out or kills them?"

"I never said that!" Julie's temper soared but she clamped down on it. Dave had been through a lot since yesterday—and a lot before that, too. Good grief! As touchy as males were, it was a wonder any of them ever lived to full growth! In the most reasonable tone she could manage, she said, "We're hoping no one does claim land till there's law to back them up. If somebody does—well, we'll just have to do what seems the best thing."

"For us?" Dave asked bitterly. "Or for them?"

Julie looked at him, so wounded that no words came. After a moment, Dave hugged her and buried his face against her shoulder. "I—I'm sorry, Julie. I didn't mean it. After all you've done—"

She kissed his cheek and smoothed his hair. "It's all right, Dave. Let's get moving."

Late that afternoon, they met Hank Trevor driving the fringe-canopied wagon back from his visit to Cora. He shook his head woefully at their news. "What a shame! And him just married! Don't be in a rush to get the team and wagon back. There won't be a charge."

"Charlie Shaw's following in Rose's wagon with a load of cement," Julie explained. "He can bring your wagon back, if that's all right."

"Fine by me." Trevor hesitated. "I'd come back for the burying but what with Charlie gone, too, that throws both the store and livery on his wife and girls. They don't know beans about horses. Do you think Mrs. Shelton will think bad of me for not coming?"

"I'm sure she won't," Julie assured him. "She really will appreciate your being so kind about the team and wagon."

"Charlie knew I'd want him to help," Trevor said. "Tell that poor little girl I sure am sorry. If there's anything I can do—"

He touched his hat and drove on, not so jauntily.

Julie didn't like pushing horses this hard, but the load was light, they were grained at each halt, and they weren't traveling in the main heat of the day. A little after noon on Saturday, one week from his wedding day, they brought Dan Shelton home.

"Lordy Lord!" breathed Dave as he turned the sorrels up Cap's Valley. "I'd give anything not to be doing this!"

Julie, too, was sick at the thought of Letty's heartbreak, but she squeezed Dave's hand. "It's a lot better that friends are bringing him, Dave. Be pretty awful if some strangers did."

"I guess."

The team slowed as if they, too, were reluctant to end their mission. Dave didn't urge them on. "We've got to dig the grave." He glanced toward the plum thicket where tiny fruits replaced the snowy flowers that had dropped on Cap's mound and Dave's mother's. "Look, Julie! Isn't that Reverend Jim's paint horse behind us?"

"Looks like it. Maybe he heard about Dan."

That proved to be so. The minister caught up with them as they started up the slope where everyone had left their work and come to meet them—the Hall men, Jack Mallory, Jon, and the women. "I was preaching in Liberal when I heard," Reverend Jim said huskily. He shook his head. "To think I married him to that pretty young wife just one short week ago! Truly, the Lord giveth and he taketh away."

"Please don't tell Letty that, Reverend Jim," begged Julie.

Dave said grimly, "The Lord didn't take Dan. Lute Hartman did. And I hope it's not long before someone takes him!"

"Son, son!" the minister reproved. " 'Vengeance is mine, saith the Lord.' "

"Well, I hope he gets to it pretty fast!" Dave muttered.

"I saw you from a long way off!" Jerry shrilled, running to meet them with LeMoyne and Sunny at his heels. "How come you're drivin' those sorrels, Dave?"

Dave hung his head. Julie took a long breath as she glanced around at the alarmed faces and Mallory's curious one. She slipped off the seat, made her way to Letty, and took her by the shoulders. Oh God, how could she say it?

"Letty, dearest—"

"What?" Letty's voice climbed and she caught Julie's arms. "What's the matter?"

"Dan—" Julie broke off, unable to go on.

Reverend Jim turned his horse over to Jon. He stepped up to Letty and took her hands with gentle firmness. "Child, your husband's dead."

Letty gave an unearthly shriek. "Danny? He—he can't be! It's a mistake!"

"I wish it were," Julie said through trembling lips. "We've brought him home."

Tearing away from Julie and Reverend Jim, Letty ran to the wagon, dragged the tarp aside and clawed at the coffin. "I don't believe it! It's someone else!"

"It's him, Letty." Dave gave the lines to Rafe Hall and tried to pull the distraught young woman away from the coffin. "I—I saw it. It's Dan, and I—I don't think you better look in the coffin. We came fast as we could but—"

As suddenly as she had gone to pieces, Letty went still. In a way, that was worse. She stepped free of Dave and watched him with eyes so dilated the blue scarcely showed. "What happened?"

Miserably, Dave said, "Lute Hartman shot him."

"Why?"

"They—they had words."

"Why?"

"It don't matter, Letty!" Dave growled. "Dan drew his gun first. Even if there was any law here, a jury would call it self-defense."

Letty's eyes glittered. "Why did Danny pull his gun?"

Dave shook his head. Letty gripped Julie's wrist with biting fingers. "Why did it happen? Tell me!"

What was best? For Letty to think her husband died over nothing or because of a slur on her name? Julie decided Danny deserved the truth. It would place a heavy burden on Letty, she was bound to feel guilty, but at least she would know how much Danny prized her.

"Lute may have been drinking. He made some off-color remark about you."

Letty paled. Her grasp loosened but Julie took her hands and held them between hers, looking her in the eye. "Danny pulled his gun. Lute tried to pass it off, but Danny told him if he didn't draw his gun, he'd kill him anyway."

"So it *was* because of me!" Letty wrenched away from Julie and clung to the rough wood. "Oh, Danny! Danny—"

No one knew what to do to help her. There wasn't any help. But after a moment, Rose came and put her arm around Letty, bending down beside the fair head pressed against the coffin. "Dan loved you a lot, darling. We'll all mourn him, you most of all. But he'd want you to go ahead and have a good life."

Letty raised up a little. "How can I when I'm to blame for his dying?"

"He thought you were worth it," Rose said. "Prove he was right."

Shuddering, Letty pulled herself straight. With a defiant glance at Reverend Jim, she said, "I'm pretty sure I'm going to have his baby. Since we—we'd known each other before, it didn't make sense to wait till we were married."

Barbara gave her a hug. "That's wonderful, dear! Our babies will be almost like twins and little John Laban McCloud Hall will be just older enough to keep an eye on them when he's not leading them into mischief."

"I'll prove up our land for the baby," Letty said, steel in her usually soft voice. "I want Danny buried there. In a way, he died for it."

That was healthy, her realizing that Lute's slur had literally triggered Danny's death, but was not the underlying cause.

"Show us where you want his grave," Jack Mallory said.

"Maybe now you'd like to build on the corner next to Miss Rose and us," Dave urged. "That way Jon and Jerry and me can help with your chores."

"And we'll build your house," the Hall men and Mallory declared in a chorus.

Letty moved her head as if to clear it. "We were going to share Cora's windmill—"

"We'll put one up for you." Julie was glad to be able to promise something leading to the future. "No hurry about paying."

"I can pay," Letty said with pride. "The doll Corinne left me—there were four twenty-dollar bills pinned inside her petticoat."

Dave tried to help her to the wagon seat but she huddled on a tarp by the coffin, steadying it as the sorrels resumed their task. "You're going to get a good rest and a nice bag of oats," Julie told the horses as she walked alongside. Rose had climbed in beside Letty but Madelaine and Barbara walked.

"Thank goodness Lorena and Johnny went home yesterday," Barbara said. "This wouldn't be good for her milk and Johnny's got kind of a delicate digestion."

Reverend Jim followed on his paint, but the other men walked, even Jack Mallory, carrying shovels and picks. They crossed the Collinses' quarter section. The northwest corner, marked by the plowed fireguard that continued north along

Rose's boundary, lifted to a slight plateau that put them in sight of Cora Oliver's windmill, as well as those at the Collinses' and Rose's.

Surely that would be a cheering, neighborly view, and welcome to Cora Oliver, in spite of that redoubtable lady's independence. It occurred to Julie that the two women could work out a signal, perhaps a white towel tied to a higher part of the tower, to show they needed help.

Even without such a device, Cora Oliver came up while Letty was walking around the plateau. "Oh, the poor child!" She looked genuinely shocked and sorry when Julie quietly explained. "Letty can still use my well, though, even if Dan won't be here to do my plowing and such."

"That's really kind of you," Julie said, "but the Collins boys want to help her. They can do that easier if she's on this end of her claim."

Cora studied Dave and Jon appraisingly. "They are shooting up, aren't they, though they've got plenty of filling out to do. If they don't get too busy, maybe I can hire them to work some for me."

"I'm sure you can. And I imagine Rafe and Thad Hall will always be glad to earn some cash."

"I've already talked to them. They want to plow as a neighborly favor." Cora's strong jaw set. "I can't allow that since I can't trade work."

"Why not?" Julie had a sudden inspiration. "They've got two girls who ought to be in school. The Collins boys could study in the winter. You could teach and get work done instead of wages."

Cora shook her head. "I've offered to teach the Collins lads for free but they weren't interested."

Julie shot Dave a grim look. "I think after all of us give them scoldings, especially Trace and Jack Mallory, they'll be glad to study, Cora."

Cora grinned. "You may be right." She sobered instantly as Letty paused, looked all around, and nodded. "Poor girl," Cora murmured. "A bride last Saturday, a widow today. We never know what life has in store."

214

"No, but lots of times it's good and happy. We met Hank Trevor yesterday. Did you have a nice visit?"

Cora's face turned a becoming pink. "He said he'd never tasted such good bread or such delicious dried-peach pie. But I told him it was ridiculous, his riding all this way to spend just a day with me—and it was just a day!" she added. "He wouldn't hear to sleeping outside my house, even, because of my reputation." She brooded. "If he hadn't just got that windmill on his claim—"

"He can sell it along with his squatter's-rights claim if he decides to move here," Julie encouraged. "It'll work out."

"Land alive!" Cora's cheeks grew pinker. "It's early days to be jumping that far ahead. But I do miss teaching school."

She looked compassionately at Letty, who stood among her friends by her husband's coffin. Dave had unharnessed and hobbled the horses, giving them a reward of oats before he joined in digging the grave near a stand of soapweeds that were still in glorious white bloom. It was hot, hard work, but all the men wanted to help, and took turns, even Jon and Reverend Jim.

"Wouldn't it be a mercy," Cora thought aloud, "if Letty could have young Shelton's baby? That way, he wouldn't really die."

"Maybe she will." Cora had made miraculous strides in tolerance but Julie saw no use in straining her charity.

"I suppose it's best not to open the coffin," Cora reflected. "But my uncle was killed at Gettysburg and since he was buried there and they never saw his body, my poor grandparents never quite believed he was dead."

"I'm just glad the embalming fluid's kept there from being a horrible smell," Julie said. "It's good Reverend Jim turned up. Letty may feel better with a real service."

It wouldn't have helped Julie with Cap, but the gravestone and flowering plum thicket had. As soon as possible, there must be a stone for Danny. Cibolo would carve it beautifully.

In one way, it was heartbreaking to watch the grave dug. In another, it was a kind of solemn observance that gave Letty time to begin to accept the reality.

Trace, Cibolo, and Shan must have pushed their horses after finishing the well connections, for they drove up in the windmillers' wagon just when Reverend Jim wiped his hands on his bandanna, put on his black frock coat, and got his Bible out of his saddlebag.

"Dearly beloved," he began, "we are gathered to mourn the death of our dear young brother. Indeed, we are exceeding sorrowful. Just one week ago, Daniel Shelton was joined in holy wedlock to Leticia Sutherland. We danced at their wedding. Now, such a pitifully short time later, we grieve at his funeral.

"Father in heaven, we do not know why thou hast called Danny to thee in the bloom of his youth and the pride of young manhood. We do not know, and we weep.

"Yet all the same, Lord, we know your own dear mother wept for you, and you, having a care for her even on your cross, told John, your beloved disciple, to be a son to her. And don't we have your promise, Lord?: 'Blessed are they that mourn for they shall be comforted.' So you, who were mortal like us and died a cruel death, you, Lord, who dwell at the right hand of the Father, we beseech you to be with Letty in her time of loss, and help us all to live as if each hour and day might be our last."

Reverend Jim called on the mourners to join in the Shepherd's Psalm. Cibolo got out his harmonica and played "Streets of Laredo." While the grave was being dug, Madelaine and Barbara had gathered wildflowers. They shared these around. Everyone followed Letty to drop a few flowers on the coffin.

Letty moaned when the first shovel of earth thudded on the wood but she refused to leave. When the grave was mounded and Barbara and Madelaine strewed over it the last of the daisies, blue flax, and black-eyed Susans, Letty said, "Please— all of you go home. I want to stay awhile with Danny."

"I'll stay, too," offered Rose.

Letty shook her head. "Thank you but I—I need to be alone with him." As her friends watched her with concern, she gave a faint smile. "Don't worry. I'll come along after I've said good-bye."

After some discussion, the livery wagon was left to be hitched up to the grazing sorrels when Charlie Shaw was ready to take them back to Tyrone. Julie hated to leave Letty alone but understood her need for a private farewell.

Not that it would be final. Letty would surely visit the grave many times, as Julie went to Cap's. Somehow, though you knew the spirit was not in the ground, being there made the loved one seem closer.

The men tossed their picks and shovels in Shan's and Trace's wagons and helped the women up; they themselves walked back toward Cap's Valley. Seated next to Julie on a bedroll, Rose gazed back at Letty who had sunk beside her Danny.

"Thank God she has a baby to think about. All the same, if she's not home by supper, I'll go after her." She sighed. "For now, humans that we are, we'd better fix some dinner."

Eighteen

The women cleared away after a meal eaten in subdued silence. The Halls hitched up their team and departed for another load of rock. "We'll spend the night at home and come back tomorrow." Laban shook his head. "Our women sure will be sorry. If there's any way to help—"

"We'll let you know if there is," Rose said. "Later on, when Lorena's strong enough to bring Johnny over, it would certainly cheer Letty up."

"She'll come soon as she can," Rafe promised.

As the Halls rattled off, Reverend Jim said he was expected at Beaver to perform a double marriage, so he'd better be on his way. Generously provisioned for supper, he was barely out of sight on his paint horse when Jack Mallory, who had disappeared after his third cup of coffee, rode up on his blaze-faced bay.

"I've got errands in Tyrone," he said. "Be back as soon as I can. After Shaw brings the cement, the Halls and you Collins lads can go ahead and finish the cellar. I want to lay the foundation of Rose's house."

That lady arched dark eyebrows. "Why didn't you ride with Reverend Jim? You could camp together tonight before he has to turn off to Beaver."

Mallory shrugged. "For a preacher, Reverend Jim's just fine. That was a good service he did for Dan, not ravin' on about how he that takes the sword shall perish by the sword and all that. But I still don't feel like hours and hours of his telling me to repent my sins."

"Is that because you intend to commit some more sins?" Rose asked with a deepening frown.

Mallory gave her a bland stare. "Oh, I reckon I'll have a few drinks, maybe play some poker."

"Are you hunting for Lute Hartman?"

Mallory reined his horse away. "Never know who you may run into."

Rose took a few steps after him. "Jack! Listen—"

He kept riding.

Those who were left watched after him. Trace gave a deep sigh. "Cib, we've got those wells to dig around Liberal but our mules need to rest before we start back. Why don't we go locate the best place to make Letty's well? She's already showed us where she wants her house."

They wouldn't intrude on Letty but now she'd had time alone to let out her grief, seeing them pick a well site should remind her that she had a future, that her life must go on for the sake of the new one growing within her.

"Do you think Mallory's looking for Hartman?" Julie asked Rose as they did the dishes.

"I'm sure he is." Rose scoured a pan long after it was clean. "Jack can beat almost anyone in a fair fight—but who says it'll be fair?"

"I wish Reverend Jim would spot him and wait for him to catch up," said Julie. "Maybe he could talk him out of it."

"No one ever talked John Jack out of anything." Rose added despairingly, "Considering his quarrel with Trace, Julie, you should be hoping Hartman will win."

"But I can't," Julie said. They looked at each, sympathy and foreboding flowing between them. There was little to be said when it was possible that both of the men they loved might die, one at the hand of the other. Julie and Rose touched each other, smiled shakily, and went back to their work.

* * *

Sand was needed to mix with the cement. Dave knew of a sandy streambed—one of those that ran only after torrential rains—a little north of Rose's. Using both the Collinses' old wheelbarrow and Rose's new one, they trundled loads of sand and dumped them near the cellar.

Trace and Cibolo returned in a few hours but it was sunset when Letty came slowly toward the tent she'd shared with her husband for just one week. The women had debated changing the sheets and taking his clothes away but had decided that though seeing Dan's things would pain Letty, it was her right to touch these intimate things and decide what to do with them.

It was the right decision. When Letty came out of her dwelling to join the others, who were all eating that night outside Rose's tent, she said, "I'm glad you left Danny's things alone. After a while, I'll wash and mend them and put them away till Dave grows into them, but right now—" She broke off, wavering on her feet.

"You sit down," Rose commanded, making the younger woman have a seat on a box, and hurrying to fill her a plate. "Why, you haven't had a bite since breakfast!"

Letty smiled faintly. "Well, yes, I did. Cora brought a big bowl of rice pudding and a jar of tea. She stood over me till I ate and drank it all. Just like a schoolteacher making sure a pupil did a lesson."

"Good for Cora," said Rose. She handed Letty a plate.

"I—I'm not hungry."

"Your baby is," said Barbara. "Take your time. It'll taste better after you've had a few bites."

No one told Letty that Mallory had gone off on "errands" that probably included avenging Danny. No one, in fact, had much to say at all. However, after the dishes were done, Cibolo got out his harmonica and Barbara, her mandolin.

The music was sad and lonesome to begin with, but at the end it was serene as the moon, a little fuller than it had shone on Dave and Julie—and Danny's coffin—the night before. *He's home now, home forever,* the music said. *But he'll live on in your hearts and his baby.*

"Guess I'll turn in." Trace rose with a yawning stretch. "We need to make an early start in the morning."

"When shall we come?" Julie asked.

"Better make it three days. We have to pick up the steam engine and journey on. You can meet us at Caleb White's homestead two miles northeast of Liberal along the railroad."

"These customers will have windmill parts on the site?"

"They're supposed to. I understand Caleb White wants a wooden tower. You can build one?"

"That's all there ever used to be," Shan pointed out. "Quite a few folks still like 'em better than steel."

"Cap favored them, provided the owner would keep them painted and oiled," Julie said. "He said a good, well-maintained wooden tower would outlast three steel ones."

"Wood's easier and cheaper to repair," Shan agreed. "But owners tend to forget to paint wood mills, and steel's a lot cheaper, especially out here on the plains."

Trace went over to Letty and dropped on a knee beside her, taking her slender hand in his big ones. "You're not alone, you know, Letty. You've got all of us."

She nodded. "I don't know what I'd do without you." Her eyes moved around the friends dimly lit by lampglow from the big tent, and rested on Dave's serious young face. "But I'll try not to be a burden."

"You're not a burden, Letty," Dave assured her earnestly.

Julie caught up with Trace on the way to their camp below the Collinses' dugout. "Trace, if you meet Mallory you won't get into a fight, will you?"

"Not unless he starts it."

She let out an exasperated sigh. "With Danny killed, Mallory after Hartman, and whatever happens because of that, we've got enough trouble!"

"Seems that way to me."

She sensed a grin it was too dark to see. Nerving herself for a repulse, she reached for his hand. It was warm and strong, able to do so many things. Able to dig wells in a dry land, able to love her. . . . Her whole being rebelled at knowing a bullet could waste all that, turn these living fingers as cold and useless as Danny's—as Cap's.

Without asking, she moved into his startled arms, put hers behind his neck, and found his lips. With a sharp intake of breath, he gathered her close. His mouth claimed hers, sweetly, wildly.

When at last he drew away, steadying her, she whispered, "Oh Trace, can't we . . . If anything happens to you—"

"That's why we won't." His voice was stern. "I love you for feeling that way, darlin', but it'd make it harder on you if Mallory puts me underground. Look at poor little Letty—"

"At least she's going to have Danny's baby!"

"Well, you're not having mine till we're married."

"All right. Let's catch up with Reverend Jim and—"

"Not till things are settled."

"Why," she demanded, "did I have to love such a stubborn man?"

Trace laughed and brushed back her hair. "One thing, honey. I'll be just as stubborn in loving you."

"Well," she conceded, "that's a blessing—I think."

She went back to the tent to press Letty's hand. How could you wish a good-night to a woman who'd just buried her husband? Madelaine came out with a fragrant steaming tea.

"What is it?" Letty asked suspiciously.

"Prickly poppy and wild oats to help you sleep. Ginger for flavoring and to settle your stomach. Drink up."

Letty did, but not quickly. "Shall I stay with you tonight?" Rose asked.

"No, but I thank you. Thank you all. . . ."

Finishing the tea, Letty went toward her tent, the bed still molded to the body of her husband, and the bedding full of the scent of him.

The other women stood together in a silent moment of shared grief. "The baby will get her through this," Rose said. Her tone gave no hint of the dread she herself must feel for Mallory's safety.

"We'll help all we can," Barbara said. "But it's like the song. Everybody's got to walk that lonesome valley by themselves."

The women went off to their beds, but after Julie got into her blankets, she prayed for Letty's solace until she fell asleep, glad for the company of LeMoyne snuggled at her feet.

Trace and Cibolo rolled off after an early breakfast. Shan and Julie looked at each other. They had been so busy putting up windmills that to have a few days for other work seemed a luxury. "Let's see what the ladies are hankering after," Shan suggested.

"A chicken-house," said Madelaine promptly. "Reba Hall's promised us some setting hens as soon as we have a place to keep them."

Shan scratched his ear. "Don't think there'll be that much lumber left from what Charlie Shaw delivers for the cellar door."

"It won't take much wood," Madelaine told him. "Just make a little dugout in the slope. We can build up the front with rocks. If there's not enough lumber for a door, we should be able to make one out of the side of a packing crate."

Even a swollen-eyed Letty joined in selecting the right place. Dave and Jon took turns swinging a pick alongside Shan and Julie and pushing a hand cultivator between their rows of burgeoning of corn. How much the stalks had grown, with water from the windmill, since Julie first saw the struggling little blades in late April, over six weeks ago!

Yes, and since then, two men had died because of Chandless's land-greed. Julie's eyes blurred, and she swung her pick with the force of anger.

Over by the windmill, the Kenton women were filling laundry tubs and the big copper boiler heating over a fire built in a trench. They would be washing the better part of the day since they had extra laundry from Lorena and Johnny and had insisted on doing Julie's and Shan's things as well as the Collinses'. Letty took her turn scrubbing on the washboard, turning the hand wringer, rinsing once in clear water, once with blueing, and wringing a final time, but about mid-morning, she drifted over the slope like a blown leaf and everyone knew where she was going.

By noon, when Charlie Shaw and the Halls drove up within minutes of each other and took care of their teams, laundry filled the clotheslines, fluttered from the rungs of the windmill, and overalls and Levi's dried on the fence, carefully positioned to avoid barbs. The diggers had excavated a goodly oblong space in the side of the slope.

"Apple crates filled with dry grass will make pretty good nests," Shan said as they stripped off their gloves and went to wash up before dinner. "If the biddies are shut up for a couple of days till they figger out this is where they get nice scraps and grain, they should stick around pretty close."

"Mm-hm." Julie's mind was not on chicken safety. She got over to Charlie Shaw as fast as she could. "Did you meet Trace Riordan and Cibolo or Jack Mallory along the way, Mr. Shaw?"

"I met Mallory yesterday a couple hours this side of the old soddie crossing. He wanted to know if I'd seen Lute Hartman, which I hadn't. Sounds like there'll be trouble when they do cross trails. Then I stopped to talk with Trace and Cibolo about mid-morning." The blocky, redheaded storekeeper's voice turned gruff. "How's that poor little girl holdin' up?"

"About as well as anyone could hope." Julie saw no need to tell him about the baby. When the child was born, shame on any curious soul who wanted to count months. She shaded her eyes. "Here she comes now. She knew we'd worry if she didn't turn up for dinner."

The Hall women's evidence of loving sympathy was a crock of cottage cheese, a bowl of butter, a jug of buttermilk, several loaves of bread, three apple pies, and a bundle of green onions. Perhaps the most touching gift was the rose Thad gave to Letty.

"Millie wants you to have it, ma'am." The piratical flourish of his black mustache was belied by the care with which he presented the fragrant little bloom in its jar of water. "It's the first rose from that bush she's fussed over like it was one of her kiddies."

Letty's eyes brimmed. "Thank her for me, Mr. Hall. And thank you, very much, for taking such care of it on that bumpy road."

"Wish you'd call me Thad," he said. "Seein' as how we hope to be neighbors for the rest of our lives."

"And I'm Rafe," said his younger brother.

Her fleeting smile was like sun shining through a rift in a cloud before again being obscured. "I'm Letty."

She set the rose on the packing crate by the beans, coffee, and cornbread brought from the kitchen, and the Halls' offerings that had turned a sparse washday dinner into a feast.

After dinner, the men unloaded cement, lumber, and poles to support the roof from Rose's wagon, and the Halls started mixing cement with sand and water in an old barrel. Jerry and Jon brought the sorrels to the livery wagon. Charlie Shaw hitched up and was on his way. Julie washed dishes while Madelaine dried and Letty put away. Rose and Barbara attacked the last and dirtiest work clothes that had been soaking during the meal.

Julie left cementing the walls of the cellar to the Halls and Dave. Shan joined them after he made a frame for the crate-side door of the chicken-house, sinking the legs of the frame in cement. Jon and Jerry helped Julie carry rocks to wall in the front of the chicken-house. To make the walls more solid, Jon filched several buckets of mixed cement to fill the bigger cracks.

"Now for the roof!" said Julie. "I hope those hens appreciate this and lay a lot of eggs!"

After some pondering, Dave split a crate into boards and nailed them end-to-end to span the top of the dugout. Julie and Jerry took a wheelbarrow and ranged out hunting for dried soapweed stalks and thistles that hadn't been gathered for fuel. These were placed crosswise, then lengthwise, on the boards, and held down with a thick layer of grass and sod-covered roots since the boards weren't strong enough to support chunks of heavy sod. An old tarp covered everything, weighted down with rocks at the sides.

"Be good to get a metal roof on here," said Jon, stepping back to survey their creation. "But I bet this'n leaks less than the one on our dugout."

"If we sell enough corn, Dave says we'll buy a corr—corrugated sheet-iron roof that won't leak a drop." Jerry thrust out his lower lip. "I'd ruther have an air rifle, though."

"Not me!" said Jon. "I purely hate it when you move around all night looking for a dry spot and you can't find a square inch that's not mud!"

"Still rather have a rifle," Jerry muttered.

The Halls left in time to get home before dark, saying they'd catch up on some work at home and bring another load of rock in a few days. "Mallory should be back by then to lay the foundation," said Laban. "We'll plan on at least two of us stayin' here to work on the house till it's finished or it's time to get our wheat planted, whichever comes first."

As the Halls drove off, Rose voiced what everyone was probably thinking. "Jack may not come back in shape to do much of anything." Her tone frayed, betraying the fear she'd hid beneath busy cheer. "By now he should have found Hartman. By now it ought to be settled, one way or the other. It's awful not to know!"

"I don't see how he'd get back earlier than tomorrow or next day." Julie added hesitantly, "If Jack gets—hurt, Trace and Cibolo should hear about it in Tyrone or Liberal. Quick as they did, one of them would come tell us."

"If we don't hear anything tomorrow, next morning I'm saddling Valentine and I won't be back till I find Jack," vowed Rose.

"I'll ride with you," Julie said. "Shan can take our wagon to that farm outside Liberal."

In the remaining light, Letty took the cherished rose and disappeared in the direction of Danny's grave. Shan and the boys poured cement steps going down into the cellar. While the other women collected the far-flung laundry, and sorted and folded it, Julie volunteered to make biscuits. For a treat, she chopped up the remaining green onions to fry with potatoes.

In spite of sadness for Dan and anxiety for Jack Mallory, they had all worked hard and ate with appetite. Having work to do was a saving grace, Julie thought, remembering those terrible days after Cap's death. It made you hungry, it helped you sleep, it made the day pass with a sense of accomplishment that made you feel you weren't completely helpless.

After dishes were done, Rose shared out laundered clothes—mostly the Collins boys', that needed patching or mending. Shan had a rich tenor and regaled them with songs since Barbara's finger plied a needle instead of her mandolin. His gaze seldom leaving Madelaine, he sang romantic songs like "Drink to Me Only with Thine Eyes," "Aura Lee," and "I Dream of Jeannie," but after a time, Jon and Jerry grew restive. "I'll sing one," Jon offered.

> *"Pickin' up bones to keep from starving,*
> *Pickin' up chips to keep from freezing,*
> *Pickin' up courage to keep from leaving,*
> *Way out in No Man's Land . . ."*

Barbara proposed that each person recite a poem or sing or tell a story. This went on till the last pair of overalls was patched. "I'll make your tea," Madelaine said to Letty, but the younger woman shook her yellow head, rising.

"Thanks, Maddy, but I think I'll sleep all right."

Weary though she was, Julie felt a need to visit Cap and pour out her worries. She didn't want Mallory dead, but what if he or Trace met on the road and guns were drawn? LeMoyne followed her and lay down beside the stone that shone white in the last moonlight.

Hair stirred by the night wind, Julie silently told Cap all that had happened and all she feared. Then she prayed for her love, and Mallory, too, and for Letty to be comforted. LeMoyne escorted her back to camp, curled up on the tarp of her bedroll, and soon they were both asleep.

Nineteen

I roning! Julie hated it beyond all household chores. In fact, when the windmillers were living out of their wagon, they scrubbed their clothes in the big bucket that also served as their bathtub, rinsed them, wrung them, and dried them on whatever was handy, bushes, windmills, the sides of the wagon. Ironing was out of the question.

Here, there was no evading it. Two proper ironing boards took up all the free space in the kitchen. Two burners of the kerosene stove heated two sad irons apiece and a contraption that looked like an instrument of torture, while the day's beans cooked on the middle burner. Before breakfast, Julie had glumly sprinkled her shirts and Shan's and a share of the Collins boys'. She was *not* battling overalls and Levi's. Wearing them would shake out the lumps and bumps, or put new ones in. Nor had her things been dipped in starch as had the women's dresses and aprons.

She would a lot rather have been helping Shan and the boys lay the cellar roof poles, spread tar paper over them, and arrange the sod blocks, cut much thinner than for walls. It didn't seem fair, though, to leave her ironing to her friends when she wasn't really needed to help with the small roof.

Pulling on the metal catch of the wood handle to set it in

the matching holes in the top of the sad iron, Julie started with her new gold-and-green shirt. The iron weighed close to six pounds; it didn't rely on just heat to smooth out the wrinkles.

Wrinkles that would just form again when the garment was worn. It struck Julie that what she detested about most housework was that it didn't last, it had to be done over and over. Cooking she didn't mind because she liked to eat. Clean dishes were necessary. But to sweep and mop floors that were quickly dirty again, wash lamp flues that would be sooty in a day or two, dust furniture that would show fingerprints almost immediately . . .

Julie watched in horror as Madelaine took the peculiar contrivance from the middle burner by its handle, set it on a metal base, spread the ruffle of a fancy blouse on the lower rippled surface, and brought the rippled curved top down with a rocking motion.

"What is that?"

"A fluter." Madelaine admired the tiny, perfect creases as she continued her labor. "Such a time-saver! I don't know how people managed without them."

"They didn't flute," Julie grumbled.

"Would you like to try it on that pretty shirt?"

"Not on your life!"

"They're wonderful for men's fancy shirts."

"As far as I'm concerned," declared Julie, ironing in a long wrinkle and scowling as she had to dampen the place and press it again, "any man who wants his shirts fluted can do it himself!"

Would Trace? Not likely, but he'd expect his shirts to be ironed, possibly even starched. If they had a house—and she did want one, whatever the drawbacks—she would have to sweep the floor, clean the lamps, make up real beds instead of tossing a bedroll in the wagon. Once they had children—and she wanted them! Drat it! Why did she have to want exactly the things that would be so much trouble? Once they had children, especially once they were school age, how could she ramble off windmilling?

The iron had cooled. She set it on the burner and picked up

a hot one. Right now, if undertaking to flute stacks of shirts, starched ones, and scrub floors every day would keep Trace alive and well, how glad she'd be to strike the bargain!

Shaking out a plaid shirt, she measured the arm with hers. "This looks too big for Dave."

"It's Danny's. Letty wants to put his best things away for Dave or Jon."

Julie ironed it with special care although her eyes kept misting. Several hours later, neck and shoulders aching from pushing the heavy iron around, she gladly yielded the ironing board to Rose, carefully folded her ironing, and departed with all of it except two shirts of Danny's. These would be stored in a chest till needed.

Cap's clothes, kept in a box in the dugout, would fit Dave now, but when Julie imagined seeing them worn, she shrank and involuntarily shook her head. She wasn't ready yet.

Clothes piled to her chin, she stopped first at the dugout to put the boys' shirts in the crate that served as their bureau. Before winter, the front walls needed to be rechinked, the ceiling covered with fresh cheesecloth, the inner walls brightened with gypsum plaster. A few days' work would make the shelter much more snug and cheery. Cora Oliver might donate one of her many rag rugs.

Julie was stuffing Shan's things into his canvas bag when LeMoyne and Sunny ran out from under the wagon and barked as they ran for the ruts that led toward Tyrone. It was a welcoming bark, a joyful heralding. It must be—

Trace! Trace and Cibolo. Or possibly Jack Mallory, though Julie didn't think the dogs had grown that fond of him yet. But if it was Trace, why? If he traveled at a normal clip, he wouldn't reach Liberal till tomorrow night.

She tried to shut off the chilling fear but it persisted, knotting her stomach into a tight ball. If Trace had found Mallory's body, he'd more than likely bring it here. Being buried by friends was more important than getting embalmed.

Thrusting Shan's painfully ironed shirts in the bag with more haste than care, Julie ran along the track as Jerry, who had just scrambled up the tower, yelled from the platform, "It's

Trace and Cibolo. Mr. Mallory's bay is tied to the wagon. Looks like someone's stretched out in the back!"

Julie had a considerable lead but Rose passed her a hundred yards from the wagon. The others hurried from tent and cellar. Cibolo halted the team. Trace's left arm was in a sling secured to his chest by a ratty-looking strip of tarp.

"What—" Julie gasped.

Rose scrambled into the wagon bed, moved away the hat shading Mallory's pallid face. "Jack!" She caught his limp hands. A little fresh blood showed in the brown stain that had soaked through the bandage swathed over the dressing on his chest. The bandage was made from a shirt and the dressing looked like underwear. Mallory's breath came fast and shallow but at least he breathed.

"Jack!" Rose implored. "Oh, Jack, please!"

His eyelids wavered, opened slowly. "Rosie?" He mumbled something. His eyes closed again.

Rose whirled toward the men on the seat. "Hartman?"

"He don't fight his own battles anymore," shrugged Cibolo.

Trace nodded. "Quite a ways from the old soddie crossing, we heard shots so we left the team and wagon, took our rifles and revolvers, and eased along to the soddie, taking as much cover as we could from the cottonwoods. Hartman and three others were firing at the soddie, trying to close in, but Mallory kept 'em guessing where he was, shooting from the window and then from chinks in the walls. He could have shot their mounts out from under them but I've heard he has a soft spot for horses. In spite of that, he'd winged one fellow and knocked one out of the saddle."

"We figgered we'd even up things." Cibolo turned his head. A graze left a skinned trail along the right side of his skull. An inch or so lower and he wouldn't be driving a team. "We each found a big tree and opened up from two directions. They didn't know how many of us there was so they grabbed their downed pal—looked like a scalp wound—and skedaddled."

"Mallory had propped himself by the window," Trace said. "Reckon he'd lost too much blood to keep moving, but he sure meant to give them a run for their money."

"Could he tell you what happened?"

"From what we pieced together, he met the four of them a little beyond the soddie. Told Hartman he wanted to see if he was as good at killing men as he was at shooting kids after he'd insulted their wives. The other JC hands moved away. Mallory thought they were leaving him and Hartman to have it out, but instead they started shooting before he drew his gun."

"Sound like pretty poor shots for hired gunfighters," marveled Shan.

"Well, Mallory sure didn't just sit there. When he saw what they were up to, he made for the soddie, firing back at them. He got his bay inside in the safest corner and held them off all day."

"Good thing he had plenty of cartridges," Cibolo added. "Didn't have any water, though. That made losin' blood harder on him. Charlie Shaw came along when we were making camp last night and gave us some whiskey. We poured some down him and the rest on the wound."

"Let's get him to bed," said Rose, settling herself with his head in her lap. "Madelaine, can you fix something for him?"

Madelaine nodded and ran ahead, calling over her shoulder, "Dave, go find four of the biggest, fattest prickly-pear pads you can and cut off the skin. Be sure you get all the spines off."

"I hope Mallory pulls through," Julie murmured to Shan as they followed the wagon.

"His cashin'-in would solve your worries about him killin' Trace," Shan reminded.

"How could he still want to shoot Trace when he'd be dead if Trace and Cibolo hadn't come along?"

"He won't *want* to, honey. He may still think he *has* to."

"For the love of mud!" Julie wailed. "How can even a man be that hardheaded?"

Rose had Mallory placed on her bed. The men got off his boots and undressed him to his drawers. Madelaine put water on to boil and disappeared into her partitioned space to return with a small muslin bag.

"It's a good thing purple coneflower grows all over the plains," she said. "It's the best healing plant I know. All the Indians used it. I learned about it from a doctor who swore it'll cure snakebite but I've never tried it for that."

She eyed Trace's disreputable sling. "Sit down, Trace. We'll take care of you, too. Shan, you could support his arm while Julie cuts off the sling. That'll jar him less than untying the knots. That strip of old tarp's not worth saving."

"I'm fine," protested Trace.

Julie shoved a chair against the back of his knees. "Sit down!" She looked around for scissors. Rose produced them from the mending basket and went back to her place by the man she loved as Dave returned with the skinned pale-green cactus pads.

"You can pour some of the hot water on a towel to soak loose that bandage," Madelaine said. "Then you can tie the cactus on the wound and leave it a couple of hours. It'll draw out the bad stuff but there's something in it, too, that lessens pain and helps flesh heal. Dave, cut a strip off one of the pads to put on that crease of Cibolo's."

While Julie, Shan, and Dave followed instructions, Madelaine put a handful of crumbled root into a bowl and another handful into a teapot. She then poured steaming water over the substance. "Tea for inside, the wash for outside," she explained. "Barbara, may I use some of that white flannel you got for baby clothes?"

"All you need."

Barbara vanished behind her canvas wall and returned with a folded snow-white cloth. "How large shall I cut the pieces?"

"Don't waste that on me." Trace had paled and broken into clammy sweat as they soaked off the blood-caked dressing. "Any old rag'll do."

"To fasten on the cactus, yes, so long as it's clean," ruled Madelaine. "But that won't do for the final dressing. Barbara, if you cut about three pieces a yard square, we can fold them to fit. You hush, Trace Riordan, and let Julie take care of you."

The shot had plowed through Trace's upper arm near the shoulder. The front was bad enough, the scabbing hole oozing bloody fluid, but the cartridge had exploded from the back with shredding force that left a cavity half the size of Julie's fist.

Clamping her jaws on a cry, Julie examined the mangled

flesh for bits of cloth or shattered bone, drew a deep breath when she saw nothing suspicious. If the bone was whole and no vital tendons or muscles severed, infection was the main worry.

Shan took two slabs of cactus from Dave and held them on both sides of the wound with one hand while holding Trace's forearm with the other. Julie took the pieces of ripped sheet Rose handed her and bandaged the pads in place, then used a triangular cloth to fasten a sling around Trace's neck, and another strip to secure the injured arm to his chest to lessen its movement.

"Thank you, ma'am." Trace managed a grin though he still looked pale.

Copper lights glinted in his dark brown hair. It was hard to tell whether his eyes were more green or gold than brown. If the cartridge had struck eight or ten inches to the right, he'd almost certainly be as dead as Danny and Cap. Full of love and fear for him, she poured him a cup of coffee, dosed it with Pet, and handed the same potion to Cibolo whose scalp wound and the cactus over it had been deftly bandaged by Barbara.

Madelaine carefully wet Mallory's stained bandage with the weaker coneflower brew at back and front. After a few minutes, the front part came loose, revealing a ragged hole about two inches in diameter. Rose made a stricken sound.

"It's not that large in back," Madelaine consoled. "And it can't have hit a lung or he'd be dead. It's lucky the slug didn't lodge in a rib but passed on through. If we can keep it clean, the main trouble is the blood he's lost. We'll give him all the fluids we can get down him, and soup and such when he's conscious."

Rose held the cactus pads front and back while Madelaine bound them in place with more of the torn sheet. "Now let's get some tea inside him. I'll put a little Jamaica Ginger in it to make it taste better." Madelaine got the essence from a box shelf and poured a dash into a cup along with the odiferous drink. "Rose, hold him up and we'll see if he's conscious enough to swallow. We can't just pour it down him or he'd choke."

At Rose's coaxing, he sipped and made a face. "Please, Jack," she urged. "It'll make you better."

"Or poison me complete." The grumble was nearly inaudible but the others exchanged relieved glances. It was somehow reassuring that he knew how vile the concoction was and could complain of it.

It took a long, patient time to get the cup down him but he thirstily drank most of a large glass of lemonade made from lemon sugar before he lapsed into sleep, or unconsciousness. Rose stayed beside him but the others went outside.

Dave said between clenched teeth, "I'm goin' to take my shotgun and—"

"No," said Trace.

"But—"

"Look, son." With a short laugh, Trace touched his sling, nodded at Cibolo's bandaged head, and pointed toward the tent. "In case you hadn't noticed, we're in no shape to go to war."

The boy's blue eyes widened. "You mean we aren't goin' to do a doggone thing? Not a single dratted cotton-pickin' thing?"

"Think it'd help for you to get yourself killed?"

Dave thrust out his young jaw. "Maybe I wouldn't."

"Maybe we'll have a blizzard next week." Trace dropped his free hand on Dave's arm. "We call this one a draw. Hartman was hit and one of his pals hurt, I don't know how bad. Cib's just going to have an interesting scar and I think my arm'll heal close to good as new though it's plumb inconvenient. Mallory sure ought to get well what with all the ladies fussin' over him—"

"If he don't strangle on that nasty weed tea," snorted Dave.

"It's a grand thing Maddy knows about cures." Shan defended his hoped-for sweetheart. "I'd a heap rather have her dose me than some doctor, even if there was one closer than three days' ride." He looked at Trace and Cibolo. "Well, partners, what do we do now?"

Trace leaned on the wagon. "There's a man named Caleb White a few miles from Liberal who must be wondering where in the world we are unless the word's spread around from Hank Trevor."

"You can't work with your arm like that," Julie objected.

Cibolo studied his friend. "You do look sort of puny, Trace."

"The team needs to rest and I'll own up to being ready to have a snooze. In the morning, though, I'm headin' for that job."

No use to argue. "A man is a brother to a mule," said Julie. "We'll come along. You, Trace Riordan, can tell us what to do, but you'll boss us from the wagon seat or a pile of bedrolls."

"Who's bossy?" chuckled Trace.

"After all, we're partners," Shan reminded.

He rummaged Trace's bedroll out of the wagon and spread it in the shade cast by the tent. Julie plumped the discouraged pillow but the ancient feathers refused to take on much loft. The measure of how weak Trace felt was that he lay down quickly and didn't protest when Julie and Dave unlaced and removed his work boots.

"A rest wouldn't hurt you, either, Cibolo," suggested Julie. "Does your head ache?"

"Some. Mostly, I'm wore out. We traveled late last night and were up before light this morning." He grinned. "Been quite a while since I swapped lead with anyone. Gettin' too old to purely enjoy that much excitement."

"I'll fetch your bag," Dave offered.

"And I'll come around in a few hours and take that cactus off your head," Julie promised.

She knelt beside Trace. His dark lashes, long as a girl's, rested on his cheek like the curve of wings, and she caught a flash of how he had looked as a child. She thought he was asleep but as if he felt her presence, he opened his eyes and smiled at her before the lashes fluttered to rest again.

Green eyes. How could she have wondered? There was much more green in them than gold, and more gold than brown. She would gladly have stayed by him for hours, watching the beloved face, the rise and fall of his breathing, but Shan and the boys were already starting back to work on the cellar and they'd be hungry at noon.

Allowing herself the softest brush of fingers on Trace's wavy hair, she went to the tent to see how Mallory fared, and confer on what to fix for dinner besides the ever-simmering beans.

Just before noon, Julie took off Cibolo's bandage and the cactus pad. "Looks good," she assured him. "Now I'll just pour on this coneflower tincture."

"Stinks so bad it must work." Cibolo warded off a strip of Barbara's immaculate flannel. "Thanks, Julie, but it'll heal faster with the air on it." He wrinkled his nose. "Do I smell pie?"

"Peach cobbler. Could you lift Trace up a little so I can get at the back of his arm?"

With Cibolo's help, she took off the sling and tossed away the prickly pear. "Thanks," said Trace. "Glad to see it go. I could feel it puckerin' up the raw spots." He asked hopefully, "All done?"

"Not by a long shot! If you're going to get into gunfights, you'll just have to take your medicine—or let me pour it on."

Following Madelaine's treatment of Mallory, Julie laved each side of the wound with coneflower fluid and asked Cibolo to hold the flannel dressings in place while she secured them with a bandage and the sling. The dressings were dampened enough with the remedy to keep them from sticking as the wounds crusted over.

"We'll wet the dressings from the outside every three or four hours." Madelaine had come out to check on the other patient. "The less we disturb the wounds, the better. How are you feeling, Trace?"

"Kittenish, ma'am." The corners of his eyes crinkled. "I'll be a tiger after I wrap myself around some decent grub. Cib's been cookin' since I got myself shot. His notion is to throw everything in a skillet and fry it till it begs for mercy."

"Huh!" retorted Cibolo. "You're the only man I ever knew who ruined every batch of beans he made. They're boiled to a mush or so hard they fair crack your teeth!" In a gentler tone, he asked, "Want I should bring your plate up here? Shucks, I'll even sacrifice and keep you company!"

"Big of you, but I need the exercise." Trace tried to get up and winced.

"Careful!" growled Cibolo. "You'll start bleedin' all over Miss Barbara's nice flannels. Let's rise up slow and easy." Stooping, he looped Trace's right arm around his neck and helped him stand.

Trace wavered, then got his balance. "Let's go, Cib! I'm hollow clear down to my toes."

"And up to the hair of your head," his partner scolded.

As they neared the tent and sat down on crates near the big one, Mallory's faint voice reached them. "This blamed stuff smells like mud out of a buffalo wallow a trail herd passed through—and it tastes a sight worse!"

"Wonderful!" exulted Rose. "You must be feeling good enough to have a second cup."

"Rosie! Awwr—" The complaint trailed off in an outraged sputter.

"That's the way," Rose encouraged. "Now for some rice with lots of Pet."

"Rice! I smell beans and cornbread!"

"Smell all you want, but it's rice you're getting."

"Maybe tomorrow or the next day if you don't run a fever," Madelaine soothed. "For today, though, you don't want to strain your digestive system."

"The devil I don't! If it squawks, I'll oil it with some whiskey."

"Rice," said Rose sweetly.

Twenty

Trace ate heartily but didn't argue when Cibolo steered him to the shade on the other side of the tent. Julie moistened his dressings, got a cup of the reviled brew down him, and went about preparations for leaving next morning. She felt a little as if they were deserting Mallory and the women, but retaliation from the JC seemed unlikely. Hartman might hope Mallory had bled to death, but as Trace said, the battle had been a draw—after he and Cibolo took a hand.

When Letty returned from her daily pilgrimage to Danny's grave, Cora Oliver walked with her, carrying a basket. "Nothing against your prickly pear and root juice, Madelaine." The former teacher took out a fancy stoppered bottle, a long pan, several large jars, and a smaller one which she showed Madelaine. "There's nothing like arnicated carbolic for wounds. I always kept a jar of it at school to put on chilblains, boils, fever sores, and burns, and I've doctored some bad, nasty cuts with it."

She unstoppered the bottle, produced a spoon, and advanced on Trace with a swish of starched skirts. "Carbolic's for the outside," she said. "Now for the inside, young man. Open up."

"You don't want to waste your good stuff on me, Miss

Cora." Trace tried to ward her off. "Jack Mallory's the one who needs it."

"Plenty to go around," she said briskly. "Come now, Mr. Riordan! Orange wine bitters taste good."

He swallowed and made a face. "Bitters is right!"

"Oh, that's the twenty-seven herbs that are so marvelously efficacious," she laughed.

"Yeah, well, thank you kindly, ma'am. Now you better go give Mallory his share."

She scanned Cibolo's creased head. "First I'll just spread some of this along that graze, Mr. Cibolo."

"Aw, ma'am—" Cibolo, backed against the tent, could retreat no farther.

Cora anointed him and swept inside with her bitters and salve. Madelaine let her administer the elixir but said firmly, "If you'll leave the carbolic, Cora, we'll apply it when the wound starts healing."

"But carbolic kills infection!"

"Yes, and it kills flesh right along with it. My goodness, is that custard in that pan?"

Diverted, Cora brought in the delicate yellow treat and handed it to Rose. "It'll build up your strength, Mr. Mallory," Cora promised.

He chuckled weakly. "You don't have to beg me into eating custard, ma'am. I like it better than ice cream."

"You can have some right now, then." Rose filled a bowl and knelt beside him.

Cora nodded approval and turned to Julie. "Why don't you give Mr. Riordan some?"

"His right hand's not hurt, but I'll hold the bowl for him." As Julie did this, Cora presented Madelaine with the bigger jars. "Noodle soup's excellent for invalids—"

"I'm no invalid!" yelped Mallory and Trace in chorus.

"And so is this oatmeal drink," went on Cora, unperturbed. "I pour boiling water over the oats and stir in molasses, ginger, and extract of lemon peel. I brought ginger and extract in case you don't have any. Letty wasn't sure."

"Ginger yes, extract no," said Madelaine. "It does sound

like a nourishing concoction and it's kind of you to take the trouble."

"What are friends for?" beamed Cora.

That she could regard her attractive neighbors without a hint of her former disdain might owe a lot to Hank Trevor's courtship, but more, Julie suspected, to having seen Letty and Dan married, a baby born and baptized, and Dan buried. Instead of a suspicious onlooker, Cora had become one of their small community.

"Won't you stay for supper?" Rose invited.

"Thanks, but I have to get home and milk Betsy." Cora picked up her basket and closed her hand over Letty's. "When you come to visit Danny, my dear, do stop in for a cup of tea." She blushed. "Even if Mr. Trevor's there."

"Love's a wonderful tonic," Barbara said as they watched the tall woman move along the slope. "Instead of kind of jerking along like a wind-up toy the way she used to, Cora almost glides."

"Maybe, in her mind, she's waltzing with Mr. Trevor," Julie smiled, and sat down by Trace with the custard.

Mallory was a little feverish next morning but lucid enough to carp about the taste of the tea Rose had given him every few hours during the night. "I'm going to turn into a dratted coneflower!" he muttered.

"Drink it and you can finish off the custard," bribed Rose shamelessly.

Trace's wound was red and swollen around the edges when Julie washed it with Madelaine's brew, but he insisted that he was able to travel and was leaving whether she did or not.

"Will you rest till after dinner?" she bargained. "Please?"

"We'll do that, Julie." Cibolo cast a reproving look at his partner. "If you got to be a fool, Trace, don't be a damfool!"

"You're ganging up on me!" Trace grumbled. But he lay back readily enough after he'd sipped a cup of oatmeal gruel made in Cora's flavorful way.

Julie and Dave finished the chicken shelter while Shan, Jon, and Cibolo made the cellar door and attached it to the sturdy frame with strong hinges. "Bet that stays put through any tornado," Shan boasted. "A prairie fire ought to just sweep over it without catching it aflame, and a blizzard can't break it down."

"We're in no hurry to find out," Madelaine assured him. "But it's great to have a safe place to go, especially till our house is built. We'll keep a lantern and canned food down there in case we have to stay awhile, maybe a couple of boxes to sit on." She glanced toward a distant reverberation. "That should be the Halls with another load of rocks."

It was, except Rafe's place on the seat was occupied by Lorena and Johnny while the youngest Hall man strode alongside. They were astonished to find Mallory and Trace wounded and Cibolo with a scabbing streak across his scalp.

Laban shook his graying head. "Guess we can always hope Hartman's hurt bad enough to keep him off the warpath for a while." He frowned in perplexity. "We brought Lorena to visit a few days while we work but it looks like Rafe better drive her home tonight."

"Please, Lorena, you and Johnny stay in my tent," Letty urged. She offered her finger to the dark-haired baby and crooned when he grasped it. "Isn't he a darling?"

"Yes," agreed the proud mother, "but he needs changing."

"Come with me." Letty took the baby and held him adoringly while Rafe helped his wife down. It was clear that Letty was imagining this was her own child, hers and Danny's. "We'll get you settled. When Johnny's dry and happy, you can show him off to Jack Mallory, who claims the baby's his namesake."

"Does he?" Lorena's dark eyes shone as she reclaimed her infant and cuddled him to her breast. "Johnny's got a lot to live up to."

"He'll do it," guaranteed Rafe, hefting an ancient carpetbag from in front of the seat and carrying it after his wife while his father and brother presented Rose with a basket of eggs, buttered to seal them airtight, buttermilk, cottage cheese, and several loaves of bread. "So's we won't eat you out of house and home," Thad grinned. "Tent and home, I mean."

Julie, Shan, Cibolo, and the Collins boys helped unload the

rocks while the hobbled mules wandered off in search of grass. "We'll start the foundation this afternoon," said Laban, wiping beaded sweat from his forehead and bushy eyebrows. "Jack's plumb aggravated that he can't do it himself, but even he allows it'll be weeks before he can do much but gripe and boss us."

After dinner, Julie's friend shooed her away from the dishes. "Since Trace is bound to go, get moving," Rose commanded. "But for heaven's sake, make him take care of that arm."

"I'll try." Julie thanked Madelaine for a bottle of coneflower fluid and a small jar of Cora's arnicated carbolic. Barbara contributed two more soft flannel dressings wrapped in a clean pillowcase.

The boys had helped Shan harness Absalom and Columbine to the windmill wagon and the horses to the well-diggers' second wagon. Trace's bedroll was placed on top of their canvas bags and other bedrolls. Julie arranged all the pillows to support him comfortably and cushion his arm. Cibolo and Shan rigged a tarp to shade him. Madelaine held a draught of coneflower to his lips.

He sighed resignedly and drank it. "Thank you kindly, ma'am."

"Don't mention it," she said with a spark of laughter. "When will you be back?"

"Depends. We have three wells to dig close to Liberal and windmills to put up." Trace rested for a moment before he went on. "Probably more jobs will come our way when word gets around that we're there."

"We'll be back when we can," Julie promised. "I've got my eye on the land south of the Collinses'."

"And I'd like to roost east of that, south of Maddy," Shan added. His blue eyes searched her face. "Providin' you'd like that?"

Her color deepened. "Oh yes, Shan! There's no one I'd rather have for a—neighbor."

"When do I get to see this land you're partial to?" Trace's voice scarcely carried above the noise of two wagons.

"You can see it by turning your head," Julie called from her seat beside Shan. Once Shan and Cap would have taken turns driving. Would she ever stop having these sudden stabs of grief and loss when she remembered Cap was gone? They were passing his grave where the plum flowers had turned into small green fruits. By the time they ripened in August, would there be other graves?

Cupping her hand to her mouth, she explained to Trace, "The Collinses' boundary runs along the top of that slope. There's another gentle valley on the other side."

"When we come back—" The breeze carried away his faint words but her straining ears caught them. "You'll have to show me."

"I will." In spite of her confident tone, she wondered if that would happen.

About noon next day, they could see the cottonwoods along the creek. The corral east of Old Soddie Crossing was deserted though cattle grazed far as the eye could reach. The JC hands must have finished branding calves missed at the first roundup. Northwest of the crossing something white caught Julie's eye just as Shan exclaimed, "Be durned if that don't look like a covered wagon!"

He halted the team beside Cibolo's. "Think we should mosey up and warn those folks about Chandless? In case they're plannin' to stay?"

"Reckon we better." Cibolo glanced toward Trace. "No use jostlin' Trace over more ground than we have to. Why don't you and Julie go talk to them? I'll make noon camp and get coffee started."

Shan nodded and turned the mules toward the white patch. "They're most likely ordinary people, but be sure you can reach the shotgun easy."

She could, and a quick reach would put the rifle in Shan's grasp. It didn't seem likely that JC men would use a covered wagon, or outlaws, either, but it didn't hurt to be prepared.

Hobbled mules cropped grass beyond the wagon and a Dutch oven and coffeepot rested among coals. There was no other sign of life. Halting the team a good fifty yards away, Shan yelled, "Howdy! Anybody home?"

"What do you want?" came a woman's voice. Even shrill with nervousness, it was resonant.

"Just want to visit a little," Shan answered pleasantly.

Thinking it would reassure the woman to know one was outside, Julie called, "We're on our way to Liberal. We saw your wagon and wondered if you might need directions to any particular place."

The canvas flap was drawn aside. A slight woman stepped out. Her face was obscured by a sunbonnet but her figure was trim and her garments cleaner than those usually seen along the trail. "We're much obliged." The words were deep and soft with the intonation of east Texas where it blends into Louisiana. "But this spot looks just fine to us."

Julie and Shan exchanged glances of consternation. "You mean to live on it?" Julie asked.

"Of course. It's wide open."

Julie tried to think of a way to make a stranger to the region understand. "It's not exactly open, ma'am. Did you see that corral a couple of miles east of here?"

"Yes. But there's no houses anywhere except for that caved-in mud one by the crossing."

"There's a reason for that, ma'am," put in Shan. "The rancher who owns that corral claims all the land along the creeks, and he's said he'll run off any new settlers who try to move into this whole end of No Man's Land."

"*New* settlers? Does that mean there are some old ones?" The mellifluous voice took on a note of scornful suspicion. "Like you?"

"We're a well/windmill outfit," Julie said. The situation was too complicated to shout across a distance to this hostile woman. "But there are some families claiming land about twenty miles west of here. They're on the open prairie, miles from any creek."

"At that, two men have been killed and at least five wounded." Shan took the hurt of mentioning Cap's death from Julie. "Chandless—he's the rancher—decided not to fight women and kids, but while he was tellin' us that, he swore no one else would get away with claimin' land."

Even in the shade of the sunbonnet, Julie could see the woman's lip curl. "You're scared he'll run out your friends. They're safe, so you're warning everybody else to move along!"

"Ma'am," retorted Shan, "we're just trying to save you grief."

"We've had plenty of that," came a male voice. The edges of the flap had been twitching. Three more people emerged.

A woman, bonnetless, stood by the other. On either side of them, a man held a shotgun pointed downward. Julie tried not to gape. The young but mature woman had golden skin and bronze hair that curled where it escaped from a loose knot. The taller, strongly-built man was dark gold of skin and hair. It was too far to be sure, but Julie thought his eyes were green. The smaller man—small only in comparison to the other, for he must have matched Trace's six feet—had skin the color of a ripe plum, almost black with a sheen of blue. His black hair made a tight-curled cap.

"We're sick of not being welcome," he said. "We came way out here where there wouldn't be persnickety neighbors."

The other man nodded. "How do we know you're telling the truth?"

"I guess you don't." Could they be a family? They acted like it, yet their skin . . . Julie was tired of trying to reason at the top her of lungs. She slipped down from the wagon and walked toward the strangers. "You probably know this land isn't open yet to legal homesteading when claims will be protected by law, but it will be soon."

"How soon?" demanded the bonneted woman.

"As soon as Congress decides what state or territory to tack it onto. Within a year, I'd imagine."

"A year! What're we supposed to do until then?"

Julie made a helpless gesture. "Maybe you'll find a good homestead in Kansas or Colorado."

The woman pushed back her bonnet. It hung by the strings to reveal a mass of auburn hair, a creamy complexion, and tawny, wide-set hazel eyes. She looked at the men and the younger woman. "What do you say, children?"

The golden giant laughed and threw back his head. "I say No Man's Land is the right place for us, Mother."

"The rest of you would be all right without me." The black man's tone was matter-of-fact, not bitter.

The older woman slipped her arm through his. "Hush that, Marcus! I went through a lot to get us all together. Nothing's changing that!"

He spread his hand toward the rolling prairie. "If we can't live here at the world's end, where do we have a chance?"

The golden man nodded. "Listen, Mama. You and Sarita take the wagon and find you a homestead where you can do it all legal and proper. Marcus and me—well, we'll keep a shotgun and a shovel, make us a dugout in that slope yonder."

Julie's heart lurched. "Chandless's hands will kill you if you won't run!"

The men looked at each other. "We're sick of running."

The women moved protectively in front of the men and watched them with desperate love. "I won't leave you," said the mother.

Julie turned to Shan. After a moment, he nodded. Heavily aware of the risk to her friends, tormented by the possible consequences, she said, "I can't speak for the settlers, but they might be willing to let you live on one of their claims till No Man's Land comes under the law."

"These settlers white folks?" Marcus asked bluntly.

"Yes, but—"

"Sorry, lady, but I don't hardly see them chancin' trouble for the likes of us."

Julie was sure of the Kenton women and Collins boys; not so sure of the Halls and Cora who might understandably feel it was none of their affair and nothing to venture their claims over. "I said I can't speak for them," she admitted. "But even if you don't stay there, you'd be better off heading west toward the edge of Chandless's range and staying away from creeks and the Cimarrón. You might get away with that."

"What'll we do for water if this Chandless hogs the creeks?" demanded the mother.

"Our outfit will dig you a well and put up a windmill."

The sons looked hopeful but their mother said, "We don't have that kind of money."

"We want to homestead when we can do it without starting a war. There'll be a house and fences to build, trees to plant. It wouldn't take long to pay out the well and mill."

"Just so there's no cotton to pick," growled Marcus. "I'll do anything honest under the livin' sun but never again, 'less I'm starving, do I aim to bend over them cotton plants!"

"At least you never had to do it as a slave," his mother said. Wordless communication passed between her and her children. "We'll do it," she said, and shrugged. "Sounds like a better chance than we've got here."

"Here," Shan said, "you got no chance. Want to travel back with these folks, Julie? Likely you can borrow Duke and catch up with us at Caleb White's."

"No need to go to trouble for us." The small woman drew herself up. "Might be best if you don't, young lady. Your friends can say no a lot straighter if you're not there. Reckon they're at the end of these ruts?"

Julie wanted to take care of Trace but she knew Shan and Cibolo would do that. "I'll go with you."

The woman smiled for the first time. It hid fine lines at mouth and eyes and made her look almost as young as her daughter. "In that case, I'm Hester Free. You've probably figured out who Sarita and Damian and Marcus are."

Julie and Shan introduced themselves. Julie's bedroll and clothes bag was behind Trace but she got a tarp and grabbed canned fruit, Pet, and vegetables from the chuckbox. She didn't want to take time to catch up with the other wagon and get her things—or get into an argument with Trace, who probably wouldn't like the idea of her taking off across the plains with strangers.

Not having met the Frees and realized their desperation, he might well think it crazy for the present settlers to jeopardize themselves for people who could travel on till they did find a suitable place to homestead.

Shan sighed. "You be careful, Julie. Trace is goin' to—"

"Just give him more coneflower tea every time he opens his

mouth," Julie advised. "You be careful, too, Shan. I'll catch up by the time you get the well dug."

He turned the team reluctantly. Sarita helped Julie stow the tarp and cans in the wagon. "Cornbread's ready," said Hester. "Might as well eat."

Cornbread and coffee were it for dinner. Julie decided it would be more tactful to add her contributions to supper. Still, the cornbread was tasty and the coffee flavorful. Damian and Marcus got the mules and harnessed them to the wagon. Hester and her sons rode on the seat, Damian driving. Julie and Sarita found places on the jumble between the covered part of the wagon and the seat.

It was hard to talk above the grind of the wheels and rattle and creak of the wagon, but by the time they camped that night, Julie had told the Frees a little about the settlers, about Cap's death and Dan's, and the recent battle.

"It already sounds like a war!" Damian was almost gleeful. "If your friends let us stay in Cap's Valley, Marcus and me can sure hold up our end of a fight."

It wasn't till after supper, though, darkness masking her face as she sat some distance from the fire, that Hester told her story. "I expect you've guessed that I was born in slavery times. My mama was what they call 'high yellow,' a quadroon. Her master was my daddy. He was a bachelor—owned a plantation close by Caddo Lake in east Texas. I was brought up in his house. He called me his little girl and taught me to read and write though that was against the law, but I was a slave all the same. He died when I was thirteen, real sudden." After all these years, her face contorted with grief and anger. "He'd always told Mama he'd free us in his will, leave us enough to live on, but I guess he never got around to it. His nephew inherited Mama and me. His wife put us to work in the fields. Mama wasn't used to that, or living in a slave cabin. She took consumption and died.

"The master saw I was growing. He took a shine to me. He gave me work in the big house and a bed he came to. Damian and Sarita are his children. His wife worked up a hate at me. When the master broke his neck jumping his big horse over a fence, she sold away Damian and Sarita, and sent me back to the slave cabin. She sent a man, too, not for my husband, just to make a baby."

Sarita went to sit by her mother, taking her hand. Damian and Marcus listened impassively, but even in the flickering light, Julie could see Marcus's fist knot and a muscle jerk in Damian's smooth cheek.

"The mistress gave that baby to her oldest son. She didn't give Damian and Sarita to her children because she didn't want to remember her husband was their daddy. Three babies of mine she took away as soon as they were weaned, and sent them to her children in Tennessee, but she let me nurse them so I'd love them and feel it worse to lose them. Then she died." A deeper resonance in Hester's voice made Julie wonder if that death had been altogether natural. "But she kept after me even after she was dead," Hester brooded. "Her will said, 'Hester is to be kept with child till each of my children has one of hers to serve them, and then she will have a second child for each of mine, and so on until she is past the age.' "

Julie gasped at such implacable wickedness. Hester finished wearily, "The war ended. All the slaves went free. But I wasn't free, not in my heart, because of my lost babies. I went to Tennessee to them. The big houses of Old Miss's children were burned to the ground. Two of her sons were killed in the war but I couldn't find out what happened to my babies, except for Marcus who'd been taken in by some sharecroppers. He was only three years old." Hester shook her head. "My other daughter, my other son—did they die when the big old houses burned down? Are they still alive somehow, somewhere?"

"You found Damian and me, Mama," comforted Sarita. When Hester didn't explain, the daughter spoke in a softer echo of her mother's voice. "The family that bought us wanted us for house servants. We were brought up with the housekeeper's children, who made sport of us for being pale as frog bellies."

"That's what they called us—'frog bellies.' " Damian chuckled. "Only not where the white folks could hear."

"The master came home from war so staved up he just stayed in bed and stayed drunk till he died. Then the mistress sold out to a neighbor, took her children, and went to live with her brother in Louisiana." Sarita's brow puckered in remembrance. "Told the slaves we were free and could go where we wanted, only no one knew anyplace to go or how to set about being free."

"Some went off looking for President Lincoln even though we heard he was dead," resumed Damian. "Others heard about the Freedmen's Bureau that was supposed to help slaves get work and learn how to be free, and they went there. The housekeeper had her own family to worry about. She told us where our mother had lived, thirty miles along the road toward Jefferson, gave us a bundle of food and clothes, and started us off in that direction. I was almost seven and Sarita was five."

Julie looked her shock. Damian smiled. "Folks along the way were good to us. Fed us and made down pallets on their floor or let us sleep in their barns. A farmer took us a good piece in his wagon. But when we finally got to the plantation, an old slave woman who was still helping in the big house for her keep, told us mama had gone off to Tennessee to hunt for her little babies."

"We asked which way was Tennessee and went on walking," remembered Sarita.

"The old woman did say we could stay with her," said Damian. "She gave us all the food we could carry and a blanket."

"And that's how I found you." Hester shook her head. "I was in a swivet to find the littler ones and figured you'd be all right till I could fetch you. When I saw the two of you walking down the road, poor Sarita limping where she'd worn blisters—I knew it had to be you though I hadn't laid eyes on you since Damian was three and Sarita a year."

Damian took his mother's other hand and held it between his big ones. "It's all right, Mama. You brought Marcus."

Marcus nodded. "We've been together ever since."

"When the children were too little to work, I cooked or kept house just for our food and a place to live, maybe some old clothes," explained Hester. "Later, we worked at whatever we could find, mostly chopping and picking cotton. By the time he was five, Marcus was dragging his own little sack down the rows."

"When I was big enough to plow, we bought a team and sharecropped for several different farmers, but we never did better than break even," put in Damian. "We figured the only way we'd ever have a place of our own was to homestead."

"So we saved up for a good team and wagon and enough cash money for seed and getting started," said Hester. "But we found out the good land in Kansas was taken."

"We might have settled on some of the not-so-good land folks up and left when they made the Run in April." Marcus grinned hardily. "But we were too black for the white folks and too white for the black ones."

Almost certainly their educated speech had set them apart from most settlers of any hue, Julie thought. A good many former slaves had settled in Kansas in the 1870s under the leadership of Pap Singleton, renowned as "the Negro Moses." She had also heard there were towns where black people were afraid to spend the night, though Langston, a town for black folk only, was off to a good start near Guthrie in Oklahoma Territory.

Sarita's soft voice was wistful. "That's why No Man's Land sounded like just the place for us."

After what she had heard, Julie looked at the four of them and spoke from the depths of her heart. "I believe it will be." How good it was to be sure Trace would feel as she did, that he'd understand why, instead of looking after him, she'd come along with the Frees.

*T*wenty-one

*A*s they came in sight of Cap's Valley at noon the next day, Hester said, "We've thought on it, the children and I. We're agreed that it's not right to put your friends in the way of losing their claims. We'll head on west."

"As long as you stay on claimed land, I doubt Chandless will make trouble," Julie argued.

Marcus's jaw hardened. "No offense, Miss Julie, but we don't much want to be beholden to white folks."

"It's not beholden to be neighbors, helping each other out."

He gave a skeptical laugh. "We don't want you shaming them into it."

"I won't." Julie studied the taut faces. In spite of the variations in coloring, all three children favored their mother. She and Sarita could have passed for white. Damian might have been taken for part Indian or Mexican. Having Marcus with them proclaimed their race, though actually the elder two had only a trace of it. In the day she had known them, it had become important to Julie that they find their dreamed-of home among people who would be neighbors.

"Listen," she pleaded. "Camp here for a few days. Get to know my friends. Don't make up your minds ahead of time."

The Frees looked at each in that way they had of divining

each other's thoughts. With wariness that couldn't conceal hope, Hester said, "Reckon we have to camp someplace. If they act like we're welcome—"

Her children nodded.

The fact that Julie arrived with the Frees ensured them a warm greeting and invitation to dinner. When Julie explained that the family was looking for a place, Rose said immediately, "Why, claim land here—" and then caught herself. "We'd be glad to have good neighbors but I imagine Julie's told you about Jess Chandless."

"She has." Head atilt, Hester regarded Rose. "But tell the truth, lady. If it wasn't for him, would you want us living close?"

Rose returned the probing gaze. "Four of us—" She broke off, remembering the Collins boys, who stole fascinated glances at the strangers as they helped unharness the team. "Four of us aren't likely to look down at our noses at folks who want to make a new start. Julie wouldn't have left Trace to come with you if she hadn't thought you were good people."

Early to broach the subject, but the time seemed right. "I've told the Frees that Chandless said he'd leave the settlers alone who're already here. What I wondered—" Julie sought Rose's eyes "—is if they couldn't stay on one of your claims till No Man's Land comes under the law."

Rose glanced at Letty and Barbara. Madelaine must have been tending Mallory. "You could stay at my place," Letty said. "It doesn't have a windmill yet but maybe you could share Cora Oliver's."

"Cora's got a say in this," Rose cautioned. "Just in case Chandless or Hartman decide having another family here breaks the truce, Cora and the Halls have to be asked."

"We understand that." Hester was small but she made the most of her height as she gave Rose a weighing look. "Before we drag the other folks into it, why don't we just get better acquainted?" She swept a hand toward the rock walls going up beside the tent. "My sons can help with that. Working alongside people is the best way to get to know them."

"The Halls took Lorena and her baby home this morning," Rose said. "But they'll be back tomorrow with more rocks." She smiled at Hester. "Let's have dinner."

"How's Jack?" asked Julie.

"Cranky as a bear with a shot through him," Rose said cheerfully. "Means he's stronger. Goodness, it's time for more coneflower tea. Come along while I get it down him. Maybe he won't fuss as much in front of you."

A vain hope. Mallory complained at every swallow. When he had drained the cup, he scowled at Julie. "How come you're back? I thought—hoped—you were easin' Riordan out of the country."

Julie stared. "He and Cibolo saved your hide, John Jack Mallory!"

"I never asked them to."

"Good grief! The reason you're after Trace is because he killed your friend who saved your life. Doesn't Trace's doing the same thing even things up?"

Mallory tried to sit up, winced and lay back. "It does sort of complicate things, but I still don't hardly see how I can let him off the hook." He glared at her. "Well-diggers and wind-millers have to keep on the move. Looks like you could just be sure you move in the right direction."

"We want a home base. Here." She held his gaze till it wavered.

"Yeah." His eyes closed wearily. He was still pale, had thinned down, and she could see he was a long way from battle-ready. "Lord knows you're entitled to a place here. I'm sorry, girl—"

Over his bed, Rose and Julie looked at each other. Men and their notions of honor! "I'm sorrier," Rose said. "Of all the mule-stubborn—"

Julie shrugged. "Would you let me borrow Duke? I have to catch up with the outfit."

"Keep him as long as you need him. Is Trace doing all right?"

"Seemed to be when I last saw him. I bet it'll be hard, though, to keep him resting while we dig a well."

Rose grinned. "Come eat and keep up your strength!"

Julie set out on Duke early that afternoon, clad in clean overalls and socks borrowed from Dave, and a shirtwaist and drawers of Madelaine's. The saddlebag held a small coffeepot, skillet, and food. A borrowed pillow and blankets were rolled in the old tarp along with her dirty clothes. By the time she caught up with the crew, she'd have to do a wash for all of them. Thank goodness, Shan always helped with that chore.

"I don't like your striking off alone on a three-day trip," Rose worried. "Dave could take Valentine and go with you."

"No sense in anyone traveling a hundred and fifty miles to keep me company." Julie sounded brisker than she felt. She had slept out on the plains more nights of her life than she'd slept indoors, but Cap or Shan, usually both, had always been there. "Anyhow, I think it's safer for no lone male critters to be jogging across Chandless's range."

"At a distance," Barbara warned, "you'll be taken for a man."

"I don't think Chandless has told his hands to shoot at folks who're just riding along," Julie said.

"Take our shotgun," Dave urged. "Even if you don't need it for the JC, you might see a rattler."

"I might, but I don't kill them."

Dave's eyes weren't the only ones to widen. "Why," he choked, "everybody's supposed to kill any rattler they see!"

"Cap didn't. They always get away if you give them a chance, Dave. Anyhow, they warn you before they strike, which is more than you can say for most humans."

She waved and rode away. Duke was rested and eager. He cocked an ear back to listen to her as his swift, steady gait ate up the distance. It was wonderfully mind-clearing to tell Duke all her worries and dreams. When she asked him if he thought the Halls and Cora would welcome the Frees, he batted his ears in an encouraging way. When she asked him why Trace and Mallory were equally stubborn, he heaved a horse-sigh of sympathy.

They reached Old Soddie Crossing at twilight without having encountered a human, but it hadn't been lonely. Meadowlarks rose singing. Julie caught a motion that betrayed a huddle of tiny prairie chickens in a grass-lined scrape in the sand. A burrowing owl with a big spider in its beak dodged into what looked like an old badger hole. It must be feeding young that wouldn't venture outside for several more weeks.

Glimpsing some wild onions, she pulled them up, shook off the roots, and put them in the saddlebag. As she stretched mightily and put a foot in the stirrup, a rattler sounded off grouchily from a nearby soapweed, making Duke skitter. For a minute, she clung to him sideways before she drew herself upright by the saddlehorn and got her other foot in its stirrup.

"You're lucky I'm not Dave," she called back to the still-whirring reptile, but the flash of danger quickly faded. A coyote flashed through the grass after a rabbit. Pronghorns drifted along a distant ridge, and several hawks and an eagle plunged from the sky after prey.

All these lives and thousands more passed from birth to death between prairie and sky, each following its ordained pattern. *"O ye Light and Darkness, praise ye the Lord . . ."* She made camp by lifting the saddle and bedroll off Duke, rubbing him down and hobbling him, and building the smallest of usable fires.

While coffee simmered, she filled Duke's nosebag with oats. He munched contentedly while she fried and ate cold boiled potatoes with somewhat wilted but piquant wild onions. She topped this off with coffee that was half Pet, and a can of peaches.

Coyotes soloed and chorused from the distance as the full moon cast shadows from the trees and flooded the plains beyond. A shrill, catlike scream made Julie's scalp crawl before she realized it was the hunger cry of a great horned owl. Still a trifle jumpy, she treated Duke to a few peach slices.

"If you don't mind," she told him, "stay pretty close tonight—but don't step on me, mind."

His soft lip captured the last of the peach juice. She washed the stickiness off in the creek and splashed the dust off her face and neck. Calmed by the sound of Duke's grazing, she sank blissfully into sleep.

The tracks that were becoming a road led by Hank Trevor's new windmill. It flashed in the sun from miles away. It was late afternoon of her third day's traveling and she debated whether to camp at the windmill or push on.

She was anxious to see Trace and know how he fared. There'd be moonlight. It shouldn't be hard to follow the railroad tracks out of Liberal and locate Caleb White's place. "If you don't act too tired, boy," she said to the attentive ear, "you can water at the tank, graze an hour, and we'll go on." She peered from under her hand. "What *is* that heap of stuff? It's scattered all around. Trace wouldn't leave a mess like that."

As if sensing her anxiety, Duke quickened his gait. Even when she saw the ripped smokestack and boiler amidst the shattered mast, wagon, and wheels, she couldn't believe it. Circling the wreckage, she fought down terror.

The outfit had been through at this well before the men had followed Dave and Julie home with Dan's body. There was no reason to have fired up the boiler before hauling it to their job at White's.

What had happened? Where were they? Julie got a tight grip on herself. There was no damage to the windmill, tank, or soddie as far as she could see, no signs of a skirmish or recent burials.

"Sorry, Duke." Julie slipped from the saddle and led him to the tank. "Water and oats will have to do for now." Duke was trained to stand with the reins trailed in front of him. She did this and peered inside the soddie.

No one was there. She gave Duke his oats. When he finished, she stowed the bag and glimpsed what looked like a piece of paper sticking out from under an edge of the exploded boiler.

It was a ruled sheet from Cap's record book. *Julie—We're fine, don't know what happened to the engine. We'll use a spring-pole to drill at Whites'. See you there.*

They were all right! Relief surged through Julie, but she was still eager to find her partners. She mounted Duke and they set off in the last blaze of the sun.

Lamps burned in the thriving little town of Liberal as she rode through. Platted by the Rock Island Railroad a year ago in April, it was the hub of business for southwest Kansas and points south. It boasted stores of all kinds, many wooden buildings and a handsome brick school. Julie passed the railroad depot, and headed out of town.

Moonlight glinted on the rails and turned the soapweeds into pale ghosts. Dogs barked protectively from several farmhouses—none of which had windmills. Julie didn't know much about drilling with a spring-pole but it was sure to be slower and more laborious. Surely Trace intended to order another steam engine. If he was short on cash, there was still a healthy balance in Cap's bank, and they were partners, so if he put up an argument—

Duke imbibed the wind, raised his head higher, and whickered. He got several delighted answers from the direction of a soddie that showed no lamp but was silvered by the moon. "Trace and Cibolo's teams," Julie told Duke. "This must be Caleb White's."

A campfire smoldered beside a metal tank situated a little higher than the house. A tripod of long poles towered on the other side of the tank and another long pole slanted up from a fulcrum, its other end attached to a kind of hinged platform. Beyond the wagons, the hobbled horses and mules were coming to greet Duke. "Julie?" Shan rose from the fire. "We didn't expect you earlier than tomorrow, honey. Did you leave the Frees in Cap's Valley?"

"Yes. I think they're going to get along fine with the boys and ladies, but it wouldn't be fair not to give Cora Oliver and the Halls a say. How's Trace?"

"Glad you're here!" came his voice from the shadow of a wagon. It strengthened with annoyance. "Doggone it, Julie, how come someone didn't ride with you?"

"Because I wouldn't let them. There wasn't any need and—"

"Go argufy while I take care of Duke." Shan helped her down.

Julie hurried to Trace and dropped to her knees. "How

does your arm feel? Have you been drinking your tea?"

"Guzzling it," he retorted. "My arm feels like a cartridge tore through it but Shan keeps swamping it out with that stinking coneflower stuff so I don't see how any poor old germ's got a chance."

"It's healing good," called Shan from where he was rubbing Duke down. "But it'd heal better if somebody I won't hang a name on would use the sense God gave a goose and not be fidgetin' around."

"That's right," put in Cibolo, with a chuckle. "You'd think nobody else ever drilled with a spring-pole."

Julie interposed, "What happened to the boiler? It's blown to smithereens! Scared me to death when I saw it."

"It sure didn't do it by itself," Shan said dryly. "Somebody either built up steam and got out of the way, or blew it up with dynamite."

"We stopped in Tyrone and asked Hank Trevor if he knew about it," Cibolo added. "He didn't."

"Well, it had to be Chandless's men!" Julie gulped to control her wrath.

"To be fair, it seems more like a bright idea of Hartman's than his boss's." Trace sounded so tired that it wrung Julie's heart.

"We can buy another boiler—"

"No use tempting them. We'll use the spring-pole till this mess gets settled."

"But—are we just going to let them get away with it?"

"Want we should go shoot some JC cattle?" asked Shan. "Burn their corrals? Start a prairie fire?"

"Shan! Of course not!"

"Well then, honey, we'd best tend to our work. How's Mallory doing?"

"Grumpy as Trace." Julie laughed and realized that she was voraciously hungry. "Is there anything left to eat?"

"Mulligan stew and biscuits," said Shan. "May even be some cobbler."

She brought her plate over by Trace. In spite of the ruined boiler and concern for the wounded men and the Frees, being near him was warm joy and comfort.

As long as we're together, she thought, *there's nothing we can't handle.* She coaxed and scolded a cup of coneflower tea down him and spread her bedroll where she'd rouse to hear if he needed something in the night. How wonderful to be that close!

Next morning, Shan and Cibolo took turns working the treadles of the platform by shifting their weight from one side to the other. One treadle sent the drill and rods down the iron casing to the bottom of the hole. Stepping on the other treadle helped the twenty-eight-foot-long spring-pole raise them. "Lucky we could salvage the drills and rods," Cibolo told Julie as he yielded the treadles to Shan.

"And better luck that we could buy the spring-pole from a hardware store in Liberal," Shan puffed as he trod up and down. "To be any use, the pole needs to be a strong young sapling with plenty of bounce. Cottonwood's too brittle."

"How did the hardware man happen to have it?"

"Oh, he'd had the poles shipped from Missouri with a load of merchandise. Intended to drill wells as a sideline." Shan laughed. "He got his own well dug and decided to sell the outfit to anyone dumb enough to want it."

Cibolo hitched up a shoulder and let it fall. "Trace and me kicked down many a well before we got the engine, some five hundred feet down, and you can go deeper than that." He explained to Julie, "Instead of treadles, you can tie a rope with a loop or stirrup on the bottom end to the pole close to the drilling line. You put one foot in the stirrup and weigh the pole down."

"When the hole got so deep that the weight of the rods and tools kept the pole from springing back, you'd adjust the fulcrum," Trace said. "Sometimes, in order to get enough weight to send the drill to the bottom, both of us jigged in stirrups."

"The good old days." Cibolo's mouth quirked down.

"Lots of cuttings down there." Shan pulled up the drilling line and tools, grunting with exertion.

A hose ran from a pipe protruding from the tank which

White must have filled by hauling barrels from some creek, or even the Cimarrón River. Cibolo cleared out the cuttings from the last run of the bit. After cleaning the hole, he turned the valve and ran water into the hole for the next drilling run before lowering the bailer with the sandline that ran over a pulley fixed to the tripod.

Julie could run the sandline but she wasn't heavy enough to do much on the treadles. "Since you don't need me here, I'll be chief cook and bottle-washer," she said. "And if you'll scare up your dirty clothes, I'll wash them."

The beans were already cooking. As she brewed Trace's coneflower potion, he said grumpily, "How much longer do I have to drink that stuff?"

"This finishes up what we have. You don't have to drink absolutely all of it. I need enough to loosen the dressing on your wound."

"Why? It's doing fine."

She spoke sternly though she caught a glimpse of him as a child and yearned to ruffle his hair and hold him. "I want to see for myself. If it's healing well, we want it to scab over. I'll put arnicated carbolic on the new dressing so it won't stick. Then we can leave it alone as long as it doesn't start hurting as if it were infected."

Her caught her hand with his good one. Lovely, melting shock traveled up her arm and thrilled through all her body. His eyes burned warm gold with just a hint of green. "Oh, Julie, Julie," he said softly, "I'm so glad to be alive—so glad you're here. But it drives me wild to be plumb useless—"

"The well's getting drilled," she consoled. "It's a good thing to have partners. Drink the tea and you can have a cup of coffee to wash away the taste."

The wound was puckered around the edges but the flesh looked clean and healthy. Julie poured on the last drops of coneflower and let it dry while she got the last clean flannel dressings and smeared them with the pungent salve. Trace was still weak. He lay back as soon as she had bandaged the pads in place.

Before his eyes closed, he touched her throat where the blood pulsed.

Washing in camp wasn't as convenient as in Cap's Valley where she could use Rose's boiler and rinse-tub and heat water on the stove. However, Julie was grateful to be able to fill the windmillers' tub with the hose. It was already lukewarm from the sun.

Shaving soap into a kettle of boiling water, she poured that in the tub, putting white things to soak. She scrubbed them out on her washboard, wrung them by hand, and laid them on the endgate of the wagon. The bloody flannel dressings and bandages soaked in a bucket of water. Good flannel was not to be thrown away. Even if the stains never entirely came out, the soft flannel could be used for other things once they were no longer needed to cover Trace's wound.

While the dirty work-clothes soaked in the soapy water, Julie gathered cow chips and soapweed stalks to feed the fire. After shirts, overalls, and Levi's were scrubbed clean as she could get them, she emptied the tub and filled it again.

Every piece, from socks to flannel sheets, had to be rinsed twice and wrung out. Caleb White, a lanky, gray-haired bachelor with a sun-leathered face, came to see how his well was progressing and told Julie she was welcome to use the clothesline he had strung from between his barn and chicken-house.

Julie made cornbread and a canned-blackberry cobbler before finishing the whites and lights, hanging them on the clothesline, and calling the men to dinner, while the coloreds remained in the last rinse water. Trace could feed himself but needed someone to hold his plate. That, like anything she did for him, was pleasure, not a chore.

"Scrumptious cobbler," praised Shan as he savored a last bite. "Say, while our hands are clean, let us wring out those heavy overalls and pants."

He and Cibolo made quick work of that and returned to the hole. After Julie hung up the work clothes and carried the rinse water to several apple trees Caleb had hopefully planted near his soddie, she washed the flannel dressings, boiled them, and was through with the laundry—except, of course, for taking things off the line, folding them, and doing any necessary mending and sewing on of buttons.

Supper was easily planned. Dandelions grew thick around the barn and Mr. White had told her she was welcome to pick them for greens. For a change from cornbread and biscuits, she'd make fritters with canned corn. That would do it, with beans and cobbler left from dinner.

Trace was dozing. She watched him, loving the curve of his long mouth, the way dark lashes fringed his cheekbones. He was still pale but it looked as if he was going to be spared the sometimes fatal danger of infection. Bless Madelaine's coneflowers!

Water began to seep into the hole before the men quit for supper. Next morning, they drilled to a level that sent water up the hole.

"Now, Cib," grinned Shan, approaching the lumber White had waiting, "we'll show you how to hammer a wooden tower together after we run some casing in the hole to keep dirt and rocks from caving in."

"Can't hardly wait to learn," retorted Cibolo.

"First off, we don't dig anchor-post holes till the tower's settin' nice and pretty on a couple of six-by-sixes. Now, since our wheel is only ten feet in diameter, our tower will be thirty feet high. Four-by-fours will do fine for the legs."

Shan paused, then nodded approvingly. "Mr. White's already soaked the timbers with boiled linseed oil and he'll paint the tower once it's up. First, we'll lay the leg timbers beside each other."

Julie brought Cap's tape measure and carefully marked the legs for the position of the five belts that would connect them. Shan sawed the four belts that would support the platform near the top of the tower and nailed the first in place between two of the legs.

When this was done, Julie blocked the legs and sawed a belt to fit the second mark. She hammered it to the legs while Shan sawed and used it to measure the other three belts for that mark.

"See," he told Cibolo, "you make two of each set two inches longer so they'll overlap the other belts."

Belts nailed in place, the braces were sawed. These started

at the inside edge of one belt and ran to the inside edge of the next. The eight braces for each section had to be trimmed off so the outside corners were even with the outside of the legs.

Leaving the men hammering and sawing, Julie made fritters and greens and collected and folded the laundry. Her partners completed the first side of the tower by twilight and came to supper like ravening wolves.

"Doggone it," Trace growled. "It wears me to a frazzle watching you all work! Layin' around is the toughest job I ever had."

"Try not to get shot again," Julie told him severely.

When the last bit of cobbler was gone, and Shan was drying dishes for Julie, Cibolo got out his harmonica. The moon spilled over them and Julie settled beside Trace, tired but happy in spite of threatening troubles.

He was alive. They were together. She was unspeakably grateful for that. Caleb White called from his door to ask if he could join them.

"Sure beats coyotes," he chuckled, sitting down on the apple box he'd brought along. He gazed toward his new well and the start of the windmill with satisfaction. "That'll make right pretty music, too. Soon as it's singin', I'm marrying the nicest, prettiest widow in Liberal. Her first husband hauled water to their homestead and she allowed she'd never live on a farm again that didn't have a good windmill." He made an indignant sound. "It's a shame about your boiler, Mr. Riordan."

"We'll manage."

Cibolo played awhile longer, sweet and lonesome. When he stopped, White rose with a sigh. "Sure enjoyed that. Any chance you'll finish tomorrow?"

"Day after, most likely."

"Shuckin's! I was hopin' to go to town tomorrow and come home with a wife."

Shan laughed. "Why don't you go ahead, Mr. White, and have a honeymoon night at the hotel? You're not milkin' cows and we can shut up the chickens before dark. By the time you have a good breakfast and collect the first load of your wife's plunder, we should have the mill up and whirrin' away."

"Why, son, that's a grand notion! I'll do it, by jingo!" White departed with a bouncy step that denied his age. Seconds after his door closed, the others were in their bedrolls.

Twenty-two

Next day, Trace's wound, no longer laved with coneflower tincture, was starting to heal from the edges and crust over. It itched but it looked healthy. "One thing about that carbolic," he grumbled as Julie smeared it copiously on one of the laundered dressings, "is it'll run off any self-respecting rattlers and scorpions."

"Just so it runs off the germs." Julie scowled back at him with mock ferocity. She hated Trace's being hurt but tending him, learning that he could behave like a cranky sick child, had added a protective, almost motherly depth to her love for him.

By the time she joined Shan and Cibolo, they had laid the completed tower side facedown. Now they put the other side together directly on top of the first, matching belts and braces precisely. Then the base of the top was blocked up and the top horizontal belts of the sides nailed on.

While Cibolo and Shan sprang the top and bottom sides of the tower away from each other at the proper tension, Julie hammered on the rest of the horizontal belts and the men joined in adding the braces. They blocked up the apex, built the platform and ladder, and secured the mill, wheel, and vane assembly.

While Julie got dinner ready, her partners moved the tower to one side of the well, leveled the ground, and bolted the six-by-six sill board to the lower legs. Heavy steel spikes driven into the ground on both sides of the sill board would keep the tower from sliding or tipping as it was raised.

That afternoon, using both teams, blocks and tackle, and the sandline tripod for a snubbing post, the tower was carefully raised to rest on four six-by-sixes. With cables and guy ropes still attached, Julie measured from each leg to the well.

"That one needs to come forward an inch," she called to Shan; and to Cibolo, "This one is a half inch too close."

They adjusted the legs with iron bars. The measurements were equal this time but Julie employed Cap's old sash weight to make sure. She climbed up the ladder and hung the weight from the top of the tower. It dangled exactly above the well.

It was finally time to dig the anchor holes five feet deep beside each leg. "Mr. White got good cedar anchor posts that won't rot for a long time," Shan approved as he bolted a horizontal deadman to the bottom of each.

"Looks like it'd be better to set the posts in concrete," Cibolo frowned.

"Nope. Concrete traps any moisture around the wood and ruins it fast. Now let's fit the anchor posts snug against the tower legs."

The posts rose from their five-foot holes to parallel the legs for another five feet. Shan drilled three holes in each paired post and leg. One-inch bolts a foot long secured the pairs. The holes were filled, each shovelful tamped as hard as it would pack.

"Now we take away the space timbers," Shan said, lifting out one of the six-by-sixes that had held the tower off the ground.

Cibolo frowned again. "Aren't you going to fill in that six inches between the legs and the ground?"

"That's a good six inches," Shan grinned. "Helps keep termites and rot from gettin' at the legs. He squinted at the wheel in the gathering dusk. "Tomorrow we rig the sucker rod and she'll be ready to pump for Mr. White's bride."

The new Mrs. White's winsome smile broadened as she admired the windmill. "Oh, Caleb, it'll look so pretty painted a lovely blush rose," she enthused.

Sparkling blue eyes and smooth skin belied her gray hair and years on a homestead. Instead of a sunbonnet, she wore a straw hat trimmed with silk flowers and a big blue bow. Her blue floral waist brightened a navy skirt and her buttoned kid shoes were good quality and well kept.

Her bridegroom cleared his throat. "Uh—Lucy, I've already bought this barn red—"

"Surely you can use it on something else, dear, or trade it in on the blush rose."

Her husband turned the proposed color. "Lucy, I don't hardly see how I can tell Ezra at the hardware that I want some—some—"

"Then I'll do it," she said.

"How about a nice yellow-green?" White cajoled.

"Cow-patty green?" She laughed merrily at his shock and patted his cheek. "Caleb dear, you know I'm going to miss living in town. While I'm cooking good things in the kitchen, I'll be looking right at that windmill. Don't you want it to gladden my heart—make me happy I'm here?"

"Mmmm." He sighed and melted. "Well, sure, if you put it that way—"

They repaired to the house to unload the first of her belongings. The crew exchanged bemused grins. Trace slanted a quizzical look at Julie. "Hope this isn't giving you notions about a blush-rose tower."

"Why, no." She gave him an innocent smile. "I favor daffodil yellow myself."

"Julie!"

He saw her twinkle then, and they all burst out laughing though he had to be careful not to jar his arm. "The neighbor down the road comes next," he said. "Guess we might as well get over there and make a start."

By the time they dug two more wells and erected windmills over them, Trace was so improved that he insisted on helping with camp chores, and propped himself against whatever was handy to watch the crew.

"Tell you what my gran used to say," Cibolo remarked good-naturedly when Trace made his umpteenth suggestion in less than an hour. "Don't give either salt or advice till you're asked."

"My granddad was a carpenter," Shan put in with a laugh that took away any sting. "He always told me that if he took everyone's advice, he'd build a crooked house."

Trace glanced from Cibolo to Shan. His startled look changed to rueful amusement. "Okay, I'll stop casting my imitation pearls before genuine swine. I'll just sit here and stare at you till you wonder what you're doing wrong—"

"Nooo!" groaned Cibolo. "I'd rather you bossed us around!"

After that, Trace made a visible effort to hold his tongue but he was in that touchy stage when he was neither well enough to work nor weak enough to rest peacefully.

Their next job was west of town, Matt Quinn's place. "I think I'll ride Duke home and see how Mallory is and what's going on with the Frees," Julie said the night before they moved on. "If I could borrow one of your horses, Trace, I can ride him back and be at the next location in time to help with the windmill."

Trace's eyebrows drew together. "I don't like your riding alone that far through Chandless's range." He raised his arm experimentally. "If we tied this up good and tight—"

"No," said Julie. "Absolutely not! We don't want you tearing anything loose now you're healing so well."

"You just take it easy a few days longer," Cibolo told his partner. "If we can stand it, you can!"

Leading Smoky, the blue roan Trace recommended as the best saddlehorse, Julie started for Cap's Valley next morning at the same time the wagons rolled, Trace still unwillingly ensconced on the bedrolls. As she topped a rise, she turned to wave. He lifted his good arm and she rode on with a glow in her heart.

The wrecked steam engine and boiler were still scattered around near Trevor's windmill but the wheel hummed in the breeze and a dozen cows drank from the full tank or grazed contentedly nearby. Trace had said that as soon as they bought a new wagon, they'd salvage anything they could from the engine and haul the rest to Tyrone or Liberal to sell for scrap.

By now, she was getting used to camping at Pony Creek and Old Soddie Crossing. Nothing was going on at the corrals upstream; in fact, she never glimpsed another human till she rode into Cap's Valley and Jerry came sliding down the tower leg to greet her. Dave and Jon had been chopping weeds out of their corn but they'd leaned their hoes against the fence and ran to take her horses' reins.

"How's Trace?" they clamored as Dave gave her a hand down.

"Grouchy as a diamondback that's lost his rattles, but he's doing fine. How's Mr. Mallory?"

"About the same," Dave grinned. "He can get around but he can't use his arm or hand too good. The cartridge must have torn up some muscles and tendons that run from his chest to his shoulder. See, he's up there bossin' the Halls. He's calmed down quite a bit since they told him if they can't lay a rock without him hollerin', they'll quit and he can do the job himself when he's able."

It sounded so much like Trace that Julie chuckled as she glanced toward the rising walls beyond the big tent and was relieved to see the Free brothers. "Looks like Marcus and Damian are helping, too."

"Yep. They're real good at building—at most anything, really. They broke some sod at Letty's and planted corn and squash, though it's pretty late for that. Letty loaned them her tent and moved in with the ladies. She's made a deal with the Frees to build a good soddie, with her payin' for the windows and lumber. There'll be a wood floor and Damian and Marcus will go over to the valley of the Dry Cimarrón and cut cedars to split shakes for the roof."

"Sounds like the Halls and Cora Oliver decided it was all right with them for the Frees to stay."

Dave nodded. "Mr. Hall said he'd fought four years in the Civil War to put a stop to slavery and it would be hypo—hyper—"

"Hypocritical for him to keep the Frees from claimin' land the same as him," finished Jon.

"Miss Cora said she'd taught all her life that everybody should get an even start in this country," Jerry contributed. "She says that's what makes us different from places where you can't expect to do any better than your parents did and where other folks don't like it if you try. She hopes when they can homestead legal they'll be her neighbors."

Julie drew in a grateful breath. This welcome from the Halls and Cora in spite of the risk to themselves was based on solid convictions as well as sympathy. She untied her bedroll and belongings, and leaving the horses to the boys, walked up the slope to her friends.

Jack Mallory could sit in a chair but his arm was still in a sling in order to keep his shoulder as motionless as possible. Julie had already told everyone about the exploded boiler but that night after supper, Mallory brought it up again to the comparatively small group left after Damian and Marcus went home to supper and the Halls departed. They needed to catch up on work at their places and then would return with more rock.

"Sounds to me more like Lute Hartman than Chandless, sneakin' in to blow it up when nobody was around," Mallory said. "From all I know of Chandless, he tackles things head on."

"I doubt if Hartman was in much shape to be setting off dynamite back when it happened over two weeks ago," Julie protested.

"I don't mean he necessarily did it himself. He could've given that little chore to some of the gunmen the JC hired when Chandless fired his regular hands for comin' to the wedding dance."

"Can't see it makes much difference," Julie shrugged.

"It could, if Hartman's tricks begin to stick in Chandless's craw," mused Jack. "Chandless made Hartman his heir but he sure never meant for Hartman to take over."

Rose leaned forward. "What are you getting at, Jack?"

"I reckon Chandless needs to know what his pet heir and foreman's up to."

Julie digested this. "You mean someone should go tell him about the steam engine?"

Mallory nodded. "I'd do it myself—"

"Except I won't let you ride yet!" Rose finished. "Besides, aren't you satisfied with being ganged up on once by Hartman and his buddies?"

Barbara spoke up suddenly. "I'll go."

They all regarded her dubiously. What Chandless's trained eye had detected before it was more than a bloom on her, now showed gently beneath her apron to anyone who looked. "Jouncing around in the saddle or on a wagon might not be good for you." Madelaine voiced everyone's concern.

"I feel just fine," maintained the fragile-looking woman who certainly did her share of the work.

"You made Chandless pretty mad last time you met," Julie pointed out.

Barbara flushed to the edges of her silvery blond hair. "All the same, I think Jess will at least listen to what I have to say."

"I'll go with you," Julie said. "Do you know the way?"

Barbara colored again. "I was never there."

"If you get an early start and ride in late, you can go and come in a day," Mallory assured them. "Head out like you were going to Tyrone, but when you get to the start of Big Goff Creek, don't follow the track to Old Soddie Crossing, but turn south. It's maybe four miles to JC headquarters on Tepee Creek."

"Sounds like he's plunked himself down between two good creeks," Rafe Hall said enviously.

"Well, sure, a man looks for all the living water he can get." Mallory grinned crookedly. "If he had his druthers, he'd claim everything between Beaver Creek and the Cimarrón as far as Tyrone on the east and New Mexico on the west."

"Why, that'd be better than half of No Man's Land!" Rose cried.

"What surprises me is his softening up enough to let you ladies and the boys here and the Halls and Miss Oliver stay.

When and if he gets wind of the Frees, he'll likely think you broke your part of the bargain."

"We never made a bargain," Rose argued. "He just said he'd run out anyone else who tried to claim land, and we'd better not help them."

"So?"

"The Frees aren't claiming land yet," Julie said.

"No, but they'll be ready to soon as the land's opened. They're all old enough to claim separately, so there goes a whole section. Timber claims make another. That's one thousand two hundred and eighty acres—grass that would feed thirty, forty JC cows with their calves."

"He's got thousands of cattle!" Julie burst out. "Thousands of acres!"

"He's not a land hog," Mallory grinned. "All he wants is the land next to his."

Barbara squared her shoulders. "Anyway, it can't hurt to tell him about the boiler." She turned to Julie. "Drilling with a spring-pole sounds awfully hard."

"Trace says he and Cibolo have drilled wells with no pole to help—just suspended the tools from a bar between two tall poles. They took turns raising the drilling rope and bit by hand, then let it fall. *That's* work!"

She regaled them with the new Mrs. White's desire for a blush-pink windmill tower, and, amidst chuckles, they said good-night.

The trip to the JC didn't require much preparation. Julie and Barbara had canteens and lunch for themselves and oats for Duke and Valentine in their saddlebags, and ponchos tied behind the cantles in case of rain. Rose insisted they take a shotgun; it was in a scabbard on Julie's saddle.

They were off at dawn, Barbara very pretty riding sidesaddle in a pale green lawn and curve-brimmed straw hat with matching ribbon. An ecru lace shawl gracefully concealed her figure. There was a glow in her crystalline eyes, an eagerness in her expression. Julie suspected she was glad to have this excuse to see the man she loved even if mutual stubbornness seemed likely to keep them apart.

Glancing from Barbara's flounced skirts to her own faded Levi's, Julie sighed. Would she ever look like a lady? Did she want to? Some of the time, she decided. It would be foolhardy to swish around in skirts while digging wells or setting up windmills, but at home it would be nice to put on a pretty dress.

There was something about skirts, the flow and swirl and whisper of them, that made one *feel* feminine. Julie knew that from wearing Rose's lovely one at Letty's wedding. Poor Letty! She had dyed her bright clothes black.

"Do you think Chandless objects to black people?" Julie asked. "It's strange to call Hester that. She's fairer-skinned than I am."

Barbara considered. "One good thing about Jess, I've never heard him slur anyone for being black, Indian, Mexican, Chinese, Irish, Catholic, Jew, or polka-dot." She laughed, a sound as silver as her hair. "He hates homesteaders, that's all."

At Goff Creek, they watered and rested themselves and the horses. There was enough cottonwood bark to make a fire and have coffee to go with their fried-egg sandwiches, canned pears, and Madelaine's gingersnaps.

"I'm always hungry," Barbara said. "But that's better than losing my socks every morning the way I did for a month or so."

"Do you want a boy or a girl?"

"How about twins?" Barbara's smile dimmed. "I'd like that. I don't hold with raising an only child, but I doubt I'll have more."

"Gracious, Barbara! You'll have lots of chances to marry."

Barbara drew her shawl closer. "The only chance I wanted couldn't work."

"Chandless?"

Barbara nodded. Racking her brain for some reasonable hope, Julie said, "When the baby's born, if it looks like him—"

"He'll never know it!" Barbara's usually gentle tone was fierce.

"Maybe you're too hard on him. It's natural for a man to—" Julie groped for words. Barbara supplied some.

"For us to marry, Jess would have to act unnatural. He couldn't be throwing my past up at me or be afraid I'd go back to—that. So if he can't accept my baby without worrying about the father, we wouldn't have a prayer."

"Oh, Barbara!"

Tears glittered in those beautiful eyes, silver with a sheen of gray. "I love Jess," she said softly. "I always have and I always will."

They were tightening their horses' cinches when a lone rider came in view. Apparently seeing them, he veered from his straight course and jogged toward them. Those heavy shoulders, the arrogant yet embattled set of the head . . .

"Jess!" Barbara sucked in her breath. "Well, after all, we are within an hour or so of his house."

"Ladies." He took off his hat. Wind blew through his thickly curling gray hair and his eyes cut into them like sleet. "Let me take you wherever you're going. The JC has a bunch of new hands who might get a little too enthusiastic about protecting my range." His gaze rested entirely now on the older woman, the chill of his eyes warming. "How are you, Barbara?"

"Splendid, thank you, Colonel." How calm she sounded! But Julie saw the fluttering pulse in her throat and was sure the rancher did. "We were coming to see you, so you don't need to take us anyplace."

Shaggy eyebrows lifted. "I'm honored. What can I do for you?"

"A lot, if you would," said Barbara.

The magic between the two flashed almost as visibly as lightning. The rancher's face darkened then. "I've heard something that I have to ask you folks about. I was on my way to see you. But first tell me what you want."

Julie told him about the blasted steam engine and boiler. The rancher's solid shoulders bent as if against a bitter wind. "Maybe someone came by, got curious, and tried to get up steam."

"Jess," said Barbara, "you know you don't think that."

"I don't think anything. Trevor's place is close to Tyrone.

Maybe someone who doesn't like him thought the outfit was his."

Barbara's tone was dry. "You don't believe that, either."

"What I *know* is I didn't order it."

Julie's temper reached a boil. "You didn't order Hartman to kill Cap McCloud, either, but he did."

"That was an accident."

"Sure. The gun just up and fired itself. Are you saying, Colonel Chandless, that you're not responsible for what your foreman does?"

Pulses throbbed in Chandless's temples. "Now, you just hold on, young lady! I—"

"If you're not responsible for what your men do, that means you're not in control," Julie hammered. "Is that it? Is Lute Hartman the real boss of the JC?"

"While I live, I'm the boss. Maybe Lute has got carried away. But he's loyal to the brand, he's given it all he's got, and he's my heir."

"So you're not doing anything about that ruined boiler?"

"Prove JC men did it and I'll pay Riordan for a new one— as long as he doesn't drill for nesters on my range."

"You know we can't prove it."

Chandless shrugged. "Well, then."

"How about this?" Julie demanded. "Hartman and another JC hand must have come in shot-up. Did they tell you how that happened?"

"Lute said Jack Mallory, Trace Riordan, and that Cibolo fellow jumped them over Letty's husband. I couldn't blame them too much for that—figgered we'd call it a draw."

"What really happened," Julie blazed, "is that Mallory— by himself—looked for Hartman and called him. Your other hands joined in. Mallory holed up in the old soddie and stood Hartman and his pals off till Trace and Cibolo came along on their way to the next job." She paused for breath. "It was fairly even at the last, Colonel Chandless, but it didn't start that way."

Chandless's eyes dilated but he gave a hitch of his shoulder. "You'd believe your men. I'll believe Lute."

Trailing the reins in front of his horse to make him stand, he got down stiffly—again Julie thought of a beleaguered old buffalo bull who couldn't too much longer fight off the wolves and coyotes. He helped Barbara mount and arranged her skirt when it caught on the cantle. "I'll see you ladies home."

Julie swung into the saddle before he could touch her. "Why were you coming to see us, Colonel?"

He sighed. "I hear you folks have taken in a whole passel of colored people. I told you plain that if anyone else squatted on my range, I'd run them out."

"The Frees haven't taken any land, Jess," said Barbara. "They're living at Letty's place."

He gave her a wintry stare. "You've always told the truth, Barbara, maybe too much sometimes. So look me in the eye and say they don't figger on claiming homesteads as soon as it's legal."

"Plenty of people are going to do that," Julie thrust.

"Not on my prime range. My hands will all stake claims and timber claims and I have other folks agreed to claim land and sell later to me. What little I don't get title to that way, I'll buy cheap when the sodbusters burn out, blow out, or freeze out."

"Jess," reasoned Barbara, "it wouldn't matter that much to you for the Frees to homestead next to us."

"It matters plenty." His square jaw set. "I gave you people a break and this is what I get for it!"

"We never made you any promises!" Julie flashed.

"You know damn well it was understood."

"We didn't go hunt up the Frees," Barbara defended. "They haven't been able to find homesteads where they felt welcome—"

"And you welcomed them!" Chandless roared. "Great God in heaven, woman! The way Lute ripped me up about that—said I was gettin' foolish and foolish men can't hold on to what's theirs!" His eyes narrowed at a sudden thought. "Did the Halls and that old-maid schoolteacher go along with this?"

"They thought it was the right thing to do," shot back Julie. "And it is!"

Chandless cast her grim look. "Either you tell them to head out of my range, or you're all going."

Julie's heart thudded fast. "Now how will you do that?"

He didn't look any happier than she felt but his tone was dogged. "By the time those windmills get torn down, the wells filled in, the fences ripped out, and those pitiful little plots of corn trampled, I reckon we won't have to do much more to make everybody decide they'll do better somewhere else. Most anywhere else."

Barbara looked at him in horror. Shocked past anger, Julie couldn't speak for a moment. When she could, she said, "God help you! It must be terrible to be willing to do such things to hold on to land that's not yours in the first place."

His head seemed sunk between his shoulders. His face was a dull, painful red. "You've driven me to it. I gave in and gave in, but there's got to be a stop. Those new folks move on or you all do."

"We'll fight you." Barbara's voice cut like a knife.

"With Mallory and Riordan staved up, you won't have much show."

Barbara smiled. "How will your gunmen like shooting at women?"

He checked his horse. "What?"

"We've talked it over. Our windmills make good watch-towers, you know. We can see you coming from a long way off. If you send your hands to cause us grief, we women will use our shotguns and rifles—and we can kill a man as dead as you can."

"I never heard such craziness!"

"You've heard it now." As he stared, Barbara counted. "There's Cora, Letty, Hester, and Sarita Free, Madelaine, Rose, three Hall women, and me."

"You?"

"Of course me." Her smile deepened. She looked as deadly as she did beautiful. "It was my idea." She looked at Julie, who was wondering why she hadn't heard about this council of war. "We didn't want to drag you into it, Julie. You and your part-ners have done a lot for us already. There's no reason why you should fight to defend our claims."

"I will. You should know I will."

"But Julie—"

"Cap's buried there. It's my land, too."

Chandless regarded them as if they had sprouted two heads. "Sodbusters tend to be no account, but when they let women fight for them—"

"Most of us don't have men," Barbara reminded him. "Those that do, don't want them killed or hurt."

"You think I won't call your bluff!"

Barbara's eyes flashed bright steel. "It's not a bluff."

His jaw clamped so hard Julie thought he was grinding his teeth. "I'm going to talk to that Free family," he growled at last. "I'm betting they've got more sense than you. They'll go."

Drawing in a long breath, Barbara said, "Yes, probably they will. When we talked over what to do if you caused trouble, they wanted to leave."

"So let them!"

"They deserve a home. We couldn't be happy with ours knowing that we kept them by letting you run out the Frees."

Chandless reined in. "Barbara, you and me are heading back to the JC."

"You're out of your mind!"

He touched the rope at his saddlehorn. "You're coming if I have to tie you."

"Why?"

His rugged face went red. "I don't want you getting killed or hurt." He glanced at Julie. "I don't want any woman hurt but I'm not backing down on this. Come on, Barbara."

He turned back to stare at the little derringer held in a hand that didn't waver. "I'm not going, Jess. We've had quite enough of your company. Good-bye."

He reached for the rope. A shot made the horses dance and took off the top of his saddlehorn. He gazed at Barbara in astonishment, then suddenly wrinkled his nostrils and looked behind them.

Julie looked, too, and froze. "Ride like hell!" yelled Chandless. "Prairie fire!"

Twenty-three

*P*rairie fires raged most fiercely in late summer and autumn when the grass was driest, but it hadn't rained now in weeks. The grass was dry enough to erupt at a spark. Julie took one look at the ocean of fire, the billows of flame, and bent low over Duke's neck, urging him onward.

The fire was miles behind them but it traveled with the wind that was blowing west to Cap's Valley. There was no creek or river between, only the fireguards plowed around the claims. A wind-driven fire could leap those, but thank God there was plenty of water. The fire was bound to be seen in time for her friends to soak their dwellings and the areas around them. Soddies, even undamped, usually protected against the swift-moving flames but if those cedar shake roofs weren't doused, it could be disastrous. *Thank God for the windmills. Thank God and Cap.*

Even soaked, the tents would probably burn, but there was the dugout, the new cellar, and the partially-raised rock walls. With great luck, no one would die.

Except them. Julie glanced back. The fire was gaining. It blazed and writhed against the sky, flickering tongues like myriad ravening fiery beasts. She groaned and in a flash remembered the one time Cap's outfit had been trapped by a fire five years ago on the Staked Plains of Texas.

"We've got matches!" she shouted. "Let's burn off a place to wait while the fire sweeps by!"

"Looks like our only chance." Chandless slowed his horse, trailed the reins, and fumbled in his vest as he hit the ground. Julie tried to quiet Duke but he was terrified.

"You hold the horses, Barbara!" Julie cried. "I'll start a backfire on this other side." She got matches from the saddlebag, took a second to toss her poncho over Duke's head, and ran forward on a level with Chandless.

Lighting and tossing matches, she ran north while he ran south. It was a terrible thing to set fire to the grass and know it would burn toward Cap's Valley, but flames running from their safety island would be soon be devoured by the greater blaze, and it was the only chance for the three of them and their horses.

And other creatures, too. Most burrowing animals, prairie dogs, mice, rabbits, and badgers, sought refuge underground. If the fire passed over them quickly, many would survive, but others would suffocate or bake to death.

Meadowlarks were the first to fly into the charred haven as Julie led Duke, head still covered, away from the advancing firestorm—and a storm it was, roiling black clouds above writhing torrents of crimson-orange, smothering the sun. Beneath a steady thunderous roar, it hissed and crackled, spitting ash and sparks.

Holding and soothing their blindfolded horses, the three humans stood together. They wet bandannas from canteens— Chandless gave Barbara an extra—and tied them over the lower half of their faces.

"We look like bank robbers," Julie tried to joke, but she had never been so scared as the flaming avalanche swelled toward them.

Prairie chickens scuttled into the burned stretch. Coyotes panted to safety, not even chasing jackrabbits and cottontails that must have been unable to reach their holes. A drift of pronghorns floated past and stopped a distance from the track of the fire Chandless and Julie had set. Roadrunners and doves found sanctuary, and a family of dainty, swift foxes.

"The foxes and coyotes aren't killing anything," Barbara marveled. "It's as if the fire caused a truce."

"What I can't understand is why my hands aren't out fighting this," Chandless rumbled.

"Maybe they are—wherever it started," Julie coughed.

"It had to start after I left home—came fast. Good thing Lute's been moving the cattle east off this range."

"He's up and around?"

"Cusses every time he gets up or sits down. Got a hunk of thigh shot away." Chandless grinned, even in that taut moment. "Lucky it hit him on the outside instead of in." Bristling gray eyebrows knit together. "He may not be up to fighting fire but the other hands should be here. Standing orders at the JC are to drop everything when a fire's sighted and go fight it with whatever you've got—brooms, feed sacks, chaps, and saddle blankets." Julie suspected Chandless kept talking in spite of his gasps in order to steady her and Barbara. "The best thing is to kill cows and split them open to make drags you pull along the fireline with horses. A drag made of a big bull can put out more fire than fifty men using blankets and such." He went into a fit of coughing. "Where in hell is the JC?"

The lead fire hurled itself at the burned patch, snarled and shrieked, vomiting embers and ash. Would it find a pocket of unburned brush, would it belch sparks to catch their garments?

Closing her stinging eyes, choking on smoke, Julie stroked the trembling Duke. "Good boy, good boy. You'll be fine."

Back turned to the scorching, deafening blast, Chandless blocked the worst of it from the women, but the heat was so intense it seemed it must surely ignite their clothing. Chandless held his horse with one hand but his free arm went around Barbara. Humans and horses huddled together as the baffled fire lurched around the burned land, licked hungrily from the sides, and raced to catch the set fire.

It seemed forever, though it could only have been a few minutes. As the searing heat and turbulent din lessened, Julie looked cautiously around, blinking at cinders that made it dark as deep twilight. The fire had passed them.

She breathed a prayer for her friends and the creatures in its path, but took comfort from the certainty it would be seen in time to take shelter, and there was plenty of water to fend it away from the dwellings.

In their island that now merged with the charred prairie, every living thing was black. Sable pronghorns bounded in the direction away from the fire. Sooty birds winged away or, like prairie chickens and roadrunners, scuttled through the devastated stubs of burned grass. Here and there, soapweed smoldered. Blackened coyotes, rabbits, and foxes streaked away, quickly lost in the murk.

Barbara took off her hat and shook it. The straw hadn't kept fine ash from coating her hair. Chandless raised a big hand and clumsily tried to brush away the cinders. "Looks like you dyed your hair," he said, and dug a third bandanna from his pocket.

He tried to wipe her face as a father might tidy his child, but only smudged it. She smiled at him, though. Those moments of terror made shared life an intimate bond that shrunk differences.

"Ladies," he said, "there's nothing you can do to help your friends, but if they use sense at all, they'll be all right, 'specially with those damn windmills. I'm heading back to find my men and get them on this fire. Maybe we can stop it before it reaches your valley."

Your valley? Barbara and Julie exchanged startled looks. Had he really said that?

"Right now, you'd better ride along with me." The rancher futilely dusted Barbara's skirts as if it pained him to see her so bedraggled, cleaned the saddle as best he could with the bandanna, and helped her mount. "You can clean up at headquarters and stay there till things quiet down."

"But Rose and the others will worry!" Barbara protested.

"Soon as I can, I'll tell them you're all right."

"Are you—" Barbara broke off and looked at him imploringly.

His face set in hard planes. "I'm still going to talk to the Frees."

"Oh, Jess!" Barbara's voice, raw from smoke, vibrated with

outraged shock. She turned her face from him. Tears splashed on her ruined dress.

The large, blackened hands closed over hers. "Sweetheart, I'm going to offer them a hundred apiece to move on. They'll find land. And then—listen, I'm hoping clear down to my toenails you'll marry me."

Sooty as it was, joy lit Barbara's face for an instant before it dimmed. "What about my baby?"

He gulped. "It's your baby, honey. That's what matters."

"What if it doesn't look like you at all? What if you can't pretend it's yours?"

He winced as if she had lashed him, but his eyes never left hers. "The baby's part of you, Barbara. Standing in the middle of that fire made me know life can't have any sweetness without you. I'll love your baby just like it was my own—and it will be, on account of no matter who started that little one, I'll be the one to take care of it and raise it."

She freed one of her hands to brush his cheek. "It is your baby, Jess. It is. I know for sure."

He roared with pride and gladness, but then he chewed his lip and frowned. "Why didn't you say so at Letty's wedding? Why'd you put me through this?"

"To be sure you loved me." She met his probing gaze steadfastly. "To be sure you wouldn't throw my life in Kenton up to me."

Shaking his head in bemusement, he started for his horse. Barbara checked him. "Jess! Let the Frees stay!"

"Honey girl, better they go. Not because of me, but on account of Lute."

"Lute?"

"I made him my heir. I'll change that now, of course, so *our* baby'll inherit the JC, but Lute'll be my foreman." Chandless rubbed his face against his sleeve and didn't improve the looks of either. "Lute hates colored folks. Purely hates them. I can order him to leave those folks alone but something's bound to come up."

"Why don't you fire him?" Barbara stabbed. "He's no good, Jess! Can't you see that? Maybe killing Cap McCloud was an accident, but he killed Danny Shelton after blackguarding Letty so the boy had to draw on him. He wouldn't fight Jack Mallory fair, and you know perfectly well he was behind blowing up Trace's boiler. He—"

"Lute's my foreman, Barbara. He's worked his guts out for the JC." Chandless spread his hands. "Let's not fight about this, honey. Hell, I'll give the Frees a thousand dollars! They can't turn that down—"

"You're sure throwin' money around, Colonel!"

Julie, the rancher, and Barbara whirled toward the rasping voice. Taking on solid shape, half a dozen men rode out of the ashes and smoke, faces masked with black dust. Julie recognized Lute Hartman from his gangly build and flab at his jaw and waist.

"You were supposed to die in the fire, Colonel," the JC foreman drawled. "But if you're burned enough, no one will see the bullet hole." His pale eyes, eerie in that dark mask, flicked to Julie and Barbara. "Too bad you ladies got caught in the same fire."

Chandless's voice cracked with disbelief. "Lute! You must be funning!"

"It's fun, sure enough, you old buzzard, after all these years of askin', 'How high?' when you said 'Jump!' " Hartman laughed coarsely. "I'm gonna shoot out them cold gray eyes, see if I can't make you beg before I finish you."

Chandless's rifle was in the scabbard on the far side of his horse. He wasn't wearing a revolver. Through the shrouding ash and smoke, Lute raised his six-shooter.

Hartman's men watched him and Chandless. Keeping her body as still as possible, Julie pulled the shotgun from the scabbard. She swung it up and fired. Barbara's derringer barked a second faster, in time to spoil his shot at Chandless though it was Julie's blast that tore off the top of his head—

Hartman threw up his arms, gurgled, and slid from the saddle. Barbara and Julie fired at the other horsemen who were shooting wildly as their horses snorted and pranced. Chandless's rifle sent another man flip-flopping.

There was the beat of hoofs from the north, from Old Soddie Crossing. Three horsemen, rifles spitting, took shape in the smoky fog and thundered toward the renegade hands. One screamed, grabbed his arm, and reeled in the saddle, managing to hold on.

"Come on, boys!" he yelled. "Let's clear out of here!" Then he and the other three galloped into the obscuring haze.

Shaking, Julie leaned against Duke. She had killed a man, blown his head half off! *Oh Cap, Cap! He killed you, I ought to be glad, but this—this is awful. . . .*

A strong arm closed around her. "Julie! Julie, are you hurt?"

"Trace!" She threw her arms around him before she realized she was pressing against his arm that was still in a sling. She pulled back. "What are you doing riding around like this? If you've hurt yourself—"

"Will you pour more coneflower juice down me?"

"Oh, Trace!"

He gathered her close. If it hurt, he didn't show it. He stroked her hair and held her till she quit sobbing. "How—how did you know—" She gestured toward Hartman without looking. She had already seen more than she wanted of what had happened.

"A couple of Chandless's gunmen had too much to drink in Tyrone. When they picked up their horses at the livery stable, they hinted to Hank Trevor that blowing up the boiler wasn't a patch on what was about to happen."

"They said the bunch of squatters in Cap's Valley were goin' to get burned out," added Shan. "Hank drove out to where we were workin' to tell us, and brought along some saddles so we could toss them on the horses and get going."

"Goff Creek stopped the fire," said Trace, still holding Julie as if he'd never let her go. "We saw it start from a long way off and were sure surprised, since we'd figgered Hartman would start the burn a lot closer to Cap's Valley."

Glancing at Hartman's body and looking away, Chandless said huskily, "When Lute saw the chance to catch me in the fire, I reckon he thought burning this part of the JC was worth it. He could graze east and south till summer thunderstorms or fall rains brought back the grass, and be rid of me and the settlers all at once."

Julie peered through the cinder-filled air. Far away, the sea of flames flickered dimly like a blazing sunset muffled by a black dust storm. There was no chance, never had been, that they could reach Cap's Valley in time to help, unless the wind changed. The fire, speeding faster than any racehorse, only gained strength as it ran.

"Let's go see what happens in Cap's Valley," she said, then frowned at Trace. "Why don't you rest at Old Soddie?"

His teeth flashed in his ash-stained face. "Because I don't want to. Cib, give me a hand up, will you?"

"I'll come, too." Chandless jerked his head toward Hartman and his crony without looking at them again. "I'll send some men to bury them later. If anything's left."

Barbara laid her hand on his arm. "Jess, you—you won't—"

He raised her hands to his face. "I owe you my life, sweetheart, you and Julie. The Frees can stay."

"Jess!" The tears that dropped to her breast this time were as happy as those washing Julie's eyes free of grit.

The rancher sighed. "I want to see how much damage the fire does to you folks. I'll pay for it, if I have to ship cattle early." Mounting stiffly, he warned, "Don't ride too fast and get where the ground's so hot it'll damage the horse's hoofs. About all they can stand when pulling a drag through hot embers is half an hour. More than that, and it takes a good year for their hoofs to grow out. It'll all be over before we get there, so there's no use to hurry."

They followed the wake of the fiery ocean through a charred wasteland. A badger peered cautiously from its hole. Farther along, a jackrabbit poked his head from his burrow and twitched his ears. Here and there they passed sad little burned bodies—birds with feathers singed off, crisped rabbits, gophers, a few coyotes. They had died in the fire Julie helped set and it didn't ease her heart to think that Hartman's fire would have caught them anyway. She took some comfort from remembering, with fresh wonder now the danger was past, how foxes and coyotes had refuged with pronghorns and rabbits and doves.

No birds sang, but a song of gratitude grew in Julie's heart, filled it to bursting with the miracle of escaping death, of riding along with her dear love. And Chandless had dropped his war. There would be peace in Cap's Valley.

If there was anything left. . . . Well, no lives should be lost. Anything else could be rebuilt. Then she remembered Jack Mallory. She rode up to Trace.

"Trace, after all this—" She swept her hand wide. "Enough men are dead. Can't you and Mallory call it even?"

In his smutted face, Trace's eyes were a greener gold than ever. "Depends on him."

"Just tell him you won't draw your gun. He'd never shoot."

Trace didn't answer except with silence.

Twenty-four

ook!" cried Barbara as they came in hazy sight of Cap's Valley. "The fire jumped the fireguard on this end but it looks like it died at the western fireguard or they managed to put it out. The tent's gone, though."

The door of the Collinses' dugout was shut, not burned away, and the cellar door was covered with ash but seemed intact and wasn't smoldering. The thinner crate door of the dugout chicken-house had burned completely. There was nothing left of the tent but stakes and fallen metal poles.

Where was the kerosene stove? Had the other furniture burned to piles of ash? Hoses running from the inky windmills to the various structures gave the answer for the survival of the doors. Another hose ran to the Collinses' cornfield—probably the boys had wet down the corn—and the irrigation pipes were running water that had soaked the chunks of rotting sod. The fence posts, however, that had taken such work to bury deep, were many of them burned off from the ground to the first wire or so, and were still smoldering.

Amazingly, most of the waist-high corn shimmered green and hopeful, though the fervent heat had crisped the plants nearest the fire as it swarmed around the wet earth.

Through the smoke, there did indeed seem to be grass on

the far side of the west fireguard. Beyond the Collinses' claim, the east fireguard had checked the flames for at least as far as could be seen through the dimness. Cora's and Letty's places may have escaped. As if the wind had veered, the fire had burned to the north, towards the Halls'. "If it kept on in that direction," Chandless said, "it may have already been stopped at the big northwest bend of the creek a couple miles north of your neighbors."

Duke pricked his ears and whickered. Rose—at least the dusky figure moved like Rose—emerged from the sooted walls of her unfinished home, removing a blindfold from one of her mules. She slipped the halter off and gave her a slap on the rump. Madelaine brought out the other mule. Jon and Dave led out theirs. Humans and animals alike looked as if they'd been rolled in powdered charcoal.

In the same moment, Jerry opened the family's dugout. Sunny and LeMoyne, pitch-black, broke past him, sniffing this strange new world, barking a joyful welcome. "Gol-lee!" Jerry shouted, racing to the newcomers. "Gol-lee! We were scared for you, Julie, Aunt Barbie! Trace! Cibolo! How'd you get in it?" His eyes went wide as he stared at the rancher. "That you, Colonel? Gol-lee!"

"Is all you can say, 'Gol-lee'?" demanded Jon. He whirled at a dull thumping from the cellar.

"Let me out of here!" came a muffled roar. "These damn chickens!"

"Gracious!" cried Rose. She and Dave hastened to lift the cellar door.

Another flurry of squawking hens. Then Letty and Mallory appeared. Ironically, since cinders wouldn't have shown on Letty's mourning, they were the cleanest of all the relieved assembly.

"Stupid hens!" Mallory scrubbed the back of his pants with a bandanna.

"What's the matter, Jack?" asked Rose.

"One of those old biddies laid an egg and I sat on it! Why they couldn't stay in their dugout—"

"We weren't sure that crate door and framing wouldn't dry

out fast and catch fire," Rose chided. "You may not like to sit in eggs, but you certainly like to eat them!"

The riders dismounted and led their horses to the water tank, sloshing out the layer of sludge. Amidst laughter, louder because they were glad to be alive, and glad to see their friends were, the reunited told their stories of survival. No one laughed, though, to learn how the fire was set.

"So Hartman got in such a hurry to heir the JC he was willin' to burn off a big chunk of it," said Mallory.

"The way his man told it in Tyrone, he was just going to burn out Cap's Valley, Cora Oliver, and the Halls," said Trace. "But when he saw the colonel ridin' off with the wind in the right direction, he must have reckoned it was a good way to get rid of him."

Dave blinked. "But he'd have burned Julie and Barbara!"

Mallory glared at his bandaged chest and arm. "If I'd shot decent that day at Old Soddie Crossing, this mess wouldn't have happened."

Chandler grinned crookedly. "Sure, but if you'd killed my foreman, the man I counted on to carry on my brand, I'd have had to do my best to shoot you."

Mallory shrugged, winced at what that did to his wound, and gazed at Trace. "That kind of gettin' even can go on and on when folks might better be about their work." He glanced at Rose. "And their lovin'. Riordan, whilst I was down in the cellar with those blamed hens, I had time to think about what a fix we'd have been in if you hadn't dug the wells that let us douse the wood doors and sod walls and wet down around and inside the rock walls and all the furniture we piled in there."

"The water kept our corn from roastin' before it had any ears!" whooped Jerry.

"Digging wells is my business," Trace said.

"It's a better business than guns." Mallory offered his free hand to Trace. "I'd rather have one live friend, Trace, than two dead ones."

Trace took Mallory's hand in his unimpeded one. "Sounds good to me. But don't forget it takes Julie's windmills to fetch up the water fast and steady."

292

So relieved she could scarcely speak, Julie said, "Cap's windmills." Wouldn't he rejoice that her love and Rose's wouldn't kill or maim each other in some senseless, implacable rite of male honor?

She looked toward the two scorched stones by the plum thicket. Leaves and fruit and twigs were gone but some larger branches remained and weren't smoldering.

"I played the hose over the bushes," Dave told her. "I think they'll come up good from the roots and what's left."

Julie kissed him, begrimed as they both were. His mother and Cap would have blossoms again next spring. "Thanks, Dave."

Rose surveyed the field she and her friends had planted so laboriously. The irrigating water had been on but the plants were too small and far apart to resist the flaming onslaught unless some of the shriveled corn and castor beans in the middle could recover. "We were lucky. Lucky."

"It looks like the fireguard stopped the blaze south of here," said Julie. "But we ought to find out how the Halls came through."

Except for Chandless's, all the horses were exhausted. He said, "I'll ride over." His eyes touched Barbara. "If the folks are all right, I'll head for the ranch and bring a buckboard back for anyone who wants to stay at the JC till the worst of the char settles or blows out of here."

Barbara shook her head. "We've got work to do here."

"Where are you going to stay?" he objected. "You can't all sleep in that dugout and the cellar even when they are cleaned up."

"If my place didn't burn, we can camp out there," Letty said. "We threw rugs and tarps over our bedding—piled it all in the wagon and got it inside the walls."

Mallory moved his shoulder experimentally and grimaced. "Won't be too long till I can help with building the rock house. It'll be done well before cold weather."

"I'm going to have to hire some new hands," Chandless said. "I'll locate some who won't sull up at building fence or helping with the house. My foreman caused this. I aim to make it as right as I can." He took Barbara's hand. "You won't need to build a room for this lady, though. We're gettin' married."

"Oh, Barbara!" Her Kenton friends hugged her and Rose glanced at Mallory.

He cleared his throat and put his free arm around her. "So are we—aren't we, Rosie?"

"Yes, since you've decided to act like a grown-up man."

Trace turned to Julie. "Will you still have me, honey?"

Laughing through tears, she wiped his face with her bandanna. "Yes! And let's do it before you can think up another excuse!"

Shan raised a begrimed eyebrow at Madelaine. "Maddy, we could just about make it the biggest wedding Reverend Jim ever had and save him a whole lot of travelin'!"

She slipped her arm through his. "I thought I was going to have to ask you, Mike Shanahan!"

Though Letty smiled bravely at this volley of engagements, she looked terribly alone. Dave moved over to stand by her, still a boy, but growing. She gripped his hand and he looked down at her with protective adoration.

"Shuckin's!" lamented Jerry. "Why don't you get married one pair at a time? That way we'd have ice cream and a dandy spread four times 'stead of just once!"

Chandless ruffled hair that was going to need a lot of soap and water before it was yellow again. "Son, when you're old enough, you'll know why we all want to get married as quick as we can—me most of all, on account of I've got no time to waste." He kissed Barbara's ashy forehead. "I'm off to Halls and then home."

"You shouldn't ride after dark," she protested.

"Bless your heart, my horse can find his way home from anywhere a hundred miles around. I'll be back tomorrow with some hands and fence posts. I was goin' to fence what I kind of figure is my east boundary, but that can wait."

He glanced around at the darker shadows in the gathering twilight and cinder-filled air. "Sure you'll be all right?"

"We'll be fine," Rose assured him. "And don't worry, we won't let Barbara overdo."

"Jess, you need to eat," worried Barbara.

"I've got biscuits and smoked turkey," he assured her. "Don't fret about me, honey. Just take care of yourself." He disappeared in the deepening haze. Julie was so blissful that she would have been content to stay as she was, hand in Trace's, close to him, but Rose said, "Let's hose the wagon off, dry it the best we can, hitch up the mules, and load up bedding and what we'll need to camp out." She sighed. "Oh Lord, the laundry we'll have till these ashes and char are gone!"

Mallory laughed. "Better that than make charcoal ourselves, Rosie."

"Sure!" Shan's tone was exuberant. "Just keep it in mind that we're goin' to have the biggest wedding ever held between the Red River and the Missouri!"

"Yeah," murmured Jon, "but right now I'd settle for a cold biscuit."

"Sooner we move, sooner we eat," Rose encouraged. "The beans are already cooked, at least, and stowed under the wagon."

Moving more by memory than sight, they followed Rose's plan, Trace and Mallory grumbling because they couldn't use both hands. When the wagon was heaped high and covered with the cleanest tarp they had, Barbara was elected to drive and Mallory was threatened and scolded by Rose till he reluctantly got up on the seat.

"You get up here, too, Trace," he implored, "so's I won't feel like such a blame sissy!"

"Please," Julie seconded, giving his hand a squeeze. "The sooner you get well, the more you can help." She suddenly remembered. "How about the well you were working on? And the windmill?"

"The well went faster than we'd expected. We'd got the tower and mill up and the pump working when Trevor came. Maybe, since we're not much good for anything else, Mallory and I can ride up and bring back the wagons and your mules and my other horse."

"Don't we have some more jobs up there?"

"A couple, but they haven't settled on what kind of towers and windmills they want, so there's no almighty rush." He laughed softly and kissed her ear as he obeyed and got up beside Mallory. "We'll invite them to the wedding."

Julie was bone-tired. Her eyes stung and her lungs and nose and throat burned. As she trudged along between Shan and Dave, when she wasn't actively thinking of something else, the turbulent lake of fire glared beneath her eyelids. She saw again the small still forms seared of fur or feathers. These haunted her much more than Hartman's nightmarish fall from the saddle, though she was glad that neither she nor Barbara knew which one had killed him.

If Chandless was able to figure it out, she doubted that he'd tell them. It was strange, reprehensible maybe, but she, who had never killed a rattlesnake, after that first shocked recoil, felt no guilt or regret. If she had to do it over again, there was no other real choice.

Suddenly Delilah brayed in her inquiring way. A neigh came from the distance along with the sound of approaching hoofs and another wagon.

Two wagons. Barbara drove across the south fireguard of Rose's claim onto the unburned grass of Letty's. "Who's that?" came Cora Oliver's voice.

"All of us except the Halls," Rose called back. "The fire miss you, Cora?"

"Yes, praise be! The Frees helped me wet down the soddie and get the cows and chickens inside."

"It was a mite snug," came Hester's rich voice. "But we were sure glad to have those thick walls between us and that fire, even if it never got real close."

"We were coming to see how you were," said Cora. "Brought food and blankets and such. It looked like the fire burned your way."

"It did, but we're all right," Rose said. "Our tent burned. Everything's a mess, including us. We thought we'd camp out over here till the house is finished. Maybe we could wash off out by your water tank."

"It's not cold. That might be the best way to get the worst off, but then you'll need hot water and soap. We'll get buckets and kettles heating." With an experienced teacher's skill at seeing quickly what needed to be done, Cora took charge. "No one needs to sleep out unless they'd rather. The menfolk can have Letty's tent—if that's all right with you, dear, and with Hester? There's room in my house for us women if we make up pallets. Come along. I baked bread today. There's cottage cheese and I'll scramble some eggs with green onions."

"We've got a kettle of Indian pudding," said Hester. That old-fashioned dessert, flavored with ginger, was made of cornmeal, molasses, and milk and eggs when available.

"And we've got beans," laughed Rose.

It was close to midnight when the survivors had scrubbed off the worst grime, washed their hair, put on the cleanest garments they could locate, and devoured the last crumb and bean. Smoke had grayed the spotless whitewash of Cora's walls and fine ash coated the furnishings and floor.

"I'll be tracking in cinders for weeks to come," she sighed, "but that's not much compared to what could have happened. Thank goodness, there's plenty of water for washing everything from folks to floors."

"Most likely we brought this on you all," grieved Hester. She glanced around at her children. "Maybe we ought to move along. If we hadn't been here—"

"It'll be fine now," Julie promised. "Hartman wanted to get rid of his boss even more than he wanted to clear us out. *He* won't be setting any more fires."

Cibolo had scarcely taken his eyes off Sarita. "I've been waitin' to claim land till I found the right place," he said. "This looks like it to me." He glanced at Trace. "How are we going to prove up on our claims and run our business?"

"We'll need help," Trace allowed. "When this country opens up, there'll be lots of folks wanting wells and windmills." He looked at Damian and Marcus. "Would you maybe be interested in working some with a well/windmill outfit?"

The brothers exchanged pleased glances. "We sure would," said Damian. " 'Specially since we're going to need several wells and mills ourselves."

"Aw, Trace!" Dave looked crestfallen. "I was hopin' you'd let me work with you!"

"You can, sure, and Jon and Jerry when they grow some more. What we've got to figure out is how to keep the business goin' while we farm."

"Shouldn't be a problem if there's enough of us." Shan raised an eyebrow at Mallory.

"The plow was never made to fit my hand," John Jack shrugged. "And I'm a plumb loss at engines and such. 'Course, I'll help when a neighbor needs it but when it comes to making a living, I'll stick to raising horses and digging up dinosaurs when I'm short of cash."

"Wow!" gasped Jerry. "Can I help with that?"

"Why not? Just so you work it out with your brothers."

Hoofbeats sounded. "Howdy!" called a familiar voice.

"That's Rafe!" The Collins boys hustled out to take care of his mule.

Black from hat to boots, Rafe paused in the door. "Don't look so scared, Miss Cora, I'm not comin' in—nor washin', either, 'cause I just have to ride back through the burn. The fire's out—wind had died down by the time it reached the creek and it couldn't jump across."

"Thank goodness!" Cora said. "All you folks and your livestock all right?"

"Fine, 'cept for a couple of hens we couldn't catch before the fire got close. We wet down the soddies and brought the blindfolded mules and cows inside. Lost our garden and corn but Colonel Chandless says he'll make that up, and we'll plant wheat this fall."

"Have you had supper?" Cora asked.

"Yes'm." Rafe's teeth showed white in a face as dark as his hair. "I hope cinders are good for a body. We ate enough of 'em. The women are nigh distracted, but we sloshed out the wood-floored soddie pretty good. We'll all stay in it till we get the others cleaned out. I imagine it'll be three or four days till we can get back to work on the rock house."

Rose poured a mug of coffee and laced it with Pet. "Drink this before you go, Rafe. We're glad to know for sure you're all right. If you need anything we might have, let us know."

"You do the same." Rafe drank gratefully, then grinned from Trace and Julie, Shan and Madelaine, to Mallory and Rose and Barbara. "From what the colonel says, we're in for quite some fandango!"

Cora chuckled. "By the time little John Laban McCloud Hall's in second grade, there ought to be a good crop starting first! We'll have to build a school where none of the kiddies have to walk too far."

"I won't need my claim now," said Barbara. "I'll give it to the Cap's Valley school district. After a couple of acres are set aside for the school grounds, the rest can be sold or leased to benefit the school."

"We'll dig a well for it," said Trace.

"And raise a windmill," added Julie.

"We'll all pitch in to build the school," said Rafe. "Thad and Millie's girls need to be learning' now."

"They can come to the classes I'm having for the Collins boys this fall," Cora invited.

"They'll be tickled to hear that, Miss Cora." Rafe had another mug of creamed coffee and departed.

Julie had never been so tired, and thought Barbara must be even more exhausted. "Can't we let the dishes go till morning?"

"Indeed not!" Cora added in a kindlier tone, "Hester, Sarita, and I haven't had the day the rest of you have. We'll do the dishes. Make up your pallets where we won't step on you!"

"We'll sleep in the wagon with the dogs." Dave spoke for his brothers.

Stretching, Shan declared, "I don't care where I fall just so it's down and not on fire!" Marcus lit a lantern and the six men said their good-nights.

Trace let his hand rest a moment on Julie's. From the warm golden sheen of his eyes, she knew he was thinking what she was—that soon, come night, their bed would be the same, and that most sweetly melted her as she spread her bedroll against the wall.

The horror of the fire surrounded her again as she started to dream and woke, stifling a scream. *It's over,* she told herself. *It's over and we're alive.* She willed Trace's smile to come between her and the flames, and sank into sleep.

The air had cleared considerably next morning though the blackened earth beyond Letty's place and east of Rose's fireguard stretched bleakly as far as the eye could see. After a huge breakfast, Trace and Mallory set off on horseback to bring back the well/windmill wagons left near Tyrone. Cora, Barbara, Hester, and Sarita said they could manage cleaning out the soddie, would get a start on laundry, and would have supper ready for everyone that night.

That left Rose, Madelaine, Letty, the Collins boys, Damian, Marcus, Cibolo, Shan, and Julie to tackle the work in Cap's Valley. They cleaned out the Collins dugout, hosed down the surroundings to settle the ash, and brought Rose's cookstove down where it would be sheltered just outside the dugout. Furnishings not stored in the dugout or cellar had been covered with tarps inside the rock walls. They were placed against the dugout wall and covered again for protection against sun and wind, which were certain, and rain, which should be coming any day now from the way clouds were building up every afternoon.

Damian and Marcus, having built with stone, were able to show Cibolo and Shan how to lay up the rocks, which they hosed off as much as possible. There was no need for Jerry to clamber up the tower every hour or so to look out for trouble, so he joined his older brothers in the laborious task of digging the fence-post stumps out of the ground. In a region where wood was scarce, there'd be many uses for these three-foot-long stumps, and what hadn't burned of the rest of the posts. Few would wind up in anyone's fireplace or stove.

Madelaine and Rose watered any corn and castor beans that weren't completely shriveled. Julie and Letty scrubbed the gravestones with soap and water till they were much cleaner, trimmed dead limbs off the plum bushes, and watered them again.

"I'm so glad I'm going to have Danny's baby," Letty said, straightening. "I—I still can't really believe he's dead. *Why* couldn't Chandless change his mind before Danny died, before all these awful things happened?"

"It's the awful things that made him change his mind." Starting with Cap. Julie swallowed the tight lump in her throat and searched for the most comforting thing she could think of.

"Danny will be alive in your baby. Isn't it strange and wonderful? We don't know whether you'll have a boy or girl or whether they'll favor you or Dan. It's a mystery! But then, just the way it was with little John Laban, the baby'll be here, himself or herself, a real person that couldn't have been anyone else! And—and you know we'll all love your baby and help."

Letty nodded. "I know. And it helps." She wiped her eyes on an apron that was already grimy. "Let's go scrub off the tubs and boiler so they'll be fit to wash things in. All the blankets and quilts are full of ashes. We might as well get started."

Like a blessing, the first summer storm raised towering thunderheads that afternoon. The women got in the drying blankets and quilts as the rain began to fall—pittering as the joking, breathless men and boys took cover with the women in the dugout, then pelting down in earnest, rinsing away char and cinders, washing the sky, cleansing the air, and charging it with fresh, tingling life.

Jerry whooped and ran out first, followed by Dave and Jon. They spun and cavorted, arms wide. Letty ran out with a bar of soap which she handed to Jerry.

"Wash yourself off!" she instructed.

Instead of returning, she loosed her hair, threw back her head and tasted the rain as she danced. Everyone followed, even Rose, who had managed to keep fairly clean.

Shan jigged with Madelaine while the rest clapped and laughed and whirled, taking turns with the soap, lathering hair and clothes as the rain poured. They had lived through fire, they were building, and now the rain itself was washing away the scars, soaking to living bits of root, nurturing new life.

Then wind and sun pushed away the clouds, so warm and drying that the women merely wrung out their skirts before toweling their hair. They went back to work with a lilt in their voices and movements.

That morning they had worked hard and doggedly though it seemed they'd never get rid of the pervading ash or grit that burned their eyes and throats, that the sky would never again be bright and blue. Now, washed with rain and dried with light and wind, they worked as hard, but it was joyful.

Twenty-five

By late July, more rains had sluiced the char away or silted it into cracks and crannies. Grass sprouted from old roots like green shadows on the prairie. The plum thicket spread leafing twigs over the gravestones. Protected by wire strung on new posts, the Collins boys' corn had formed tasseled ears that would soon be ready to boil lightly and munch with butter, that most delicious of fresh foods.

The rock house was finished, and though the stones retained traces of smoke, everyone said it gave the dwelling more character. Inside and outside, tables were laden with food. The wedding was being held Saturday noon so some guests could feast and dance and still get home in time to do their chores. People from Tyrone, Liberal, Beaver City, and Kenton had several days' journey each way and would have neighbors or friends take care of their tasks.

"I never married more than two couples at a time before," Reverend Jim muttered, fortifying himself with coffee as wagons, buggies, and horses continued to jounce, bounce, or trot into sight. "Four teams! Hope I don't get the names mixed up."

Shan and Trace sported new vests over white shirts and had shined their boots, but that was the extent of their wedding finery. Madelaine had been excused from all other work in order to make gowns for Julie and Barbara. Rose's long-treasured wedding gown—the one she'd lent Julie for Letty's wedding—had been altered back to fit her.

"Don't you worry about names, Reverend," grinned Mallory. "We know who's which and that's what matters."

The minister regarded him dourly. "If you drink much of that case of champagne I see coolin' in the tub, you may not even know who you are, John Jack."

"I won't drink more than a toast to my wife," Jack promised sunnily.

He and Trace had been rid of their slings for a week, able to help put the finishing touches to the house. Mallory looked dashing in a black serge Prince Albert coat and matching trousers and vest. Along with most of Kenton's population, his friends Wyatt Mabry and Billy Lincoln had come to wish him well. They watched Madelaine and Barbara rather wistfully. Madelaine, in palest yellow taffeta, and Barbara, in foamy, light blue-green chiffon, had never looked more beautiful. Letty, not wishing to remind her friends of what had happened so quickly after her wedding day, wore blue instead of mourning, but a glimmer of tears was there behind her smile.

Chandless couldn't take his eyes off Barbara. He was the oldest groom, but he looked ruggedly handsome in his gray pinstripe cutaway frock suit. He squinted at the clouds that were banking up early, blue-gray underneath, haloed at the edges with sunlight. "Never thought I'd hope rain would hold off," he said, "but I'm hopin' it now!" He twinkled in a devilish way at Barbara. "Once we're married—well, it can rain all it wants!"

"I hope we made enough custard for the ice cream," Reba Hall fretted. "Good gracious, there's more folks turning up every minute. Now you're sure, Rose, that Charlie Shaw's bringing the ice?"

"He ordered an extra six hundred pounds from Pueblo," Hank Trevor assured her. He and Cora were enjoying their courtship. It seemed likely that in time he might sell his business in Tyrone and claim land next to Cora's, but she said there was no hurry—that it was nice, after being an old maid, to have a man willing to travel so far to see her.

"That's Charlie comin' now with his wife and girls," Hank nodded. "He asked me to bring the rock salt and freezer. I put 'em over by the dugout. Oh, there's Caleb White with his practically brand-new missus." Hank shook his head. "That windmill tower of his! Blush pink! Can you beat it?"

Charlie turned his team over to the Collins boys, who rubbed down the horses and led them toward the better grass at Letty's before hobbling them. Since the guests would be staying for hours, all their horses and mules were being allowed to graze, but in order to keep the ground fit for walking and dancing, the animals were hobbled well to the south.

As he helped his womenfolk carry crocks of baked beans, potato salad, and rice pudding to a table, Charlie admitted sheepishly, "I sure am sorry, but no ice at all came in on the train. I sent a telegram. They wired back that they were plumb completely out—wouldn't have any till it came from Denver in a couple of days." His freckled face brightened. "I brought my fiddle, though, and I see Rafe Hall has his."

"No ice cream?" wailed Jerry.

Redheaded Annie Hall nudged him in the ribs. "Don't be a baby!" she scolded, but her own mouth trembled.

"Oh dear!" lamented Millie. She caught herself and tried to smile at poor Charlie. "Don't feel bad, Mr. Shaw. There's plenty of other delicious food."

"Of course there is!" said Rose. "Why, I'd rather have your wife's rice pudding any day than ice cream."

A relieved smile spread over his chubby face. He hurried to join his family as Reverend Jim put his fingers in his mouth and emitted a raucous whistle, followed by a second. At the third summons, everyone heard, and followed his beckoning toward the stone house. Begun while Madelaine and Barbara had intended to share it, it had three bedrooms and a big kitchen/living room. A porch ran the length of the south side. It was spread with carpets to protect the brides' skirts and it was here they and their grooms assembled with the minister while the guests watched from the yard.

"You look like an angel, Julie," Trace whispered. "Let's save that dress for our girls to get married in!"

"Maybe they won't feel as funny in skirts as I do," Julie whispered back. "I suppose when I'm not working on a well or windmill, I'll have to start wearing dresses."

"Not unless you want to," Trace said firmly. "But you sure do look scrumptious in that one."

Reverend Jim cleared his throat. "All right, if you grooms can quit moon' over your brides—" There was an immediate hush. "Dearly beloved," he intoned. "It's a happy but solemn occasion when any couple vows before God and man to join their lives. This day is four times as happy and four times as solemn, I guess, on account of four men and four women are getting married—but it's not goin' to take four times as long, I promise you! Our Lord himself loved weddings. He performed his first miracle at the one in Cana—though I still maintain the wine he made was grape juice—and I believe he's with us today." The lanky preacher shot Jack Mallory a warning glance. "Have a good time, but remember that."

Since he was preaching one sermon for four couples, he made it thorough and detailed but at last he asked the men if they would have the women as their wedded wives, and then asked the women if they would have the men.

"Now take each other's right hands," said Reverend Jim. "And repeat after me: 'I take thee to have and to hold from this day forward . . .' " *Cap, please know! Please be happy for us . . .*

"To love and cherish," Julie and Trace told each other, "till death do us part; and thereto I give thee my troth."

Reverend Jim produced four rings, fumbling a bit at the identifying tags which he took off as he distributed the plain gold bands. All the grooms echoed Reverend Jim, but Julie heard only Trace.

"With this ring I thee wed, with my body I thee worship. . ."

"You may kiss your brides," Reverend Jim concluded. "But don't all the rest of you fellas out there think you get to, or we'll never have dinner—and besides, it looks like it's goin' to rain!"

Despite this adjuration, Julie felt like she'd been kissed by every man, whiskered or smooth-faced, within a hundred miles, but none of their kisses dimmed the warm glow left by Trace's mouth, a glow that deepened into sweet fire within her.

This celebration was lovely, it was wonderful to feel such goodwill from so many, to at last feel she belonged to a particular place and its people. But oh, tonight—

Trace whispered in her ear. "Want to change out of that dress, sweetheart, so we can keep it for our girls? I'll go fill a plate for you."

When they could escape, all the brides changed into their prettiest regular clothes. It had been foreseen that Levi's would hardly do for Julie. She slipped into a dusty green dress of Rose's that had been altered for her.

"It does look like rain," she said to Trace as she joined him, with an apprehensive glance at the sky. "The house is big but I don't think everyone can crowd into it, much less dance."

"I don't think it'll amount to much if it does rain," Trace consoled. He cast a wary eye at the darkening clouds as he located an apple crate for her to sit on and hunkered on his heels beside her. "Folks better eat now and do their visiting later, though. Even a little shower won't help vittles."

Doubtless agreeing, people did circle the tables faster than usual and attended to the serious business of doing justice to the cooks' best efforts. The heartier eaters were on seconds or thirds when a large drop splashed on Julie's nose.

One hit Trace in the eye as he looked up. Another splatted on his boot. "Maybe it'll just sprinkle," Julie hoped.

Trace jumped up and caught her arm. "It's fixin' to pour, honey! Let's duck into the dugout and leave the house for company."

On Cora and Letty's heels, they sprinted into the dugout, followed by Hank Trevor, Rose, Mallory, the Collins boys, and the dogs. Peering out at the rain coming down in veritable sheets, Trace said, "Well, that'll wash the dishes! Good thing for whoever's on the porch that the rain's slantin' the other way."

Then suddenly it wasn't rain. Sharp, cracking sounds dinned furiously. Even within the thick-walled dugout, the air cooled.

Marble-sized balls of ice struck against those on the ground, eddied into drifts against walls or the crates used for seats.

"I hope this doesn't reach the horses and mules," Trace said. "Looks like the chickens had sense enough to get in their house."

"Yeah." Dave's voice shrilled. "But look at the corn! It's all beat down!"

"Oh, Dave!" Letty gave him a sympathetic hug. "It was so pretty and proud! You worked so hard, keeping the weeds out. I could already taste those roasting ears."

"Maybe the stalks are just bent over, not broken," Julie hoped as the roar started to abate.

The hail stopped. It rained a few more minutes. Then the sun burst through the clouds, glittering on the several inches of ice that whitened the ground and sparkled on the tables and hastily-covered food. Some guests had already stowed their plates and emptied dishes in boxes or baskets thrust under the tables or other sheltered spots, so comparatively few plates and bowls were cracked or broken.

The corn, though, was beaten into the ground. The barrage of hail had struck it relentlessly from the side, breaking the stalks, pounding the tender new kernels to a pulp within the husks.

Dave stared wordlessly at the ruin and scrubbed his arm across his eyes. "I'm sorry, son," Chandless said gruffly.

"You said we don't have a corn sky," Dave said. "I thought you meant we don't get enough rain."

"That," nodded the rancher and swept his hand toward the destroyed crop. "And things like this."

"Last year the hot wind blasted every single stalk," Dave said. "Now it's hail after a prairie fire. What's next?"

"Why, you can plant wheat this fall. Next summer may be your year to get fifty, sixty bushels to an acre and sell it for a dollar a bushel."

Dave's eyes lighted. "Well, sure, maybe—"

"I've seen my cows piled up high in the draws or against fences, froze stiff as boards," Chandless went on. "Skinned 'em for the little that brought, and bought more mother cows. When you ride around in spring and see the new little calves, you forget about the freeze-ups." He dropped his hand on the boy's shoulder. "Say, this corn'll make great fodder. What you and your neighbors can't use for winter feed, I'll buy off you. It's not like makin' a good crop, but it sure beats nothin'."

Dave gulped and nodded as Rafe Hall hurried from the direction of the hobbled mules and horses. "Not much hail over there!" he called. "Looks like none of the critters are hurt."

Letty clapped her hands. "Gracious! Here we are, up to our ankles in *ice*! Let's make ice cream!"

After a startled moment, the Hall women hurried to fetch their pails of mixed custard and the freezer while buckets and tubs and boxes were filled with the cleanest ice. Rose brought her freezer and the Shaws readied theirs.

While the freezers were churned by relays, people collected their dishes and tidied things up. Melting hail sparkled on the short, resilient new grass. Little John Laban McCloud Hall laughed in his mother's arms and reached for the gleaming jewels.

Rafe and Charlie began to tune up. West, where the storm had moved, a faint rainbow spanned the horizon. As it deepened to soft brilliance, another arch appeared below it.

Hand warm in Trace's, Julie thrilled to the beauty and promise. She felt Cap's presence, felt his blessing as his windmill whirred above them.

"Let's start with the Grand March!" Charlie called. "Newlyweds first!"

Trace's eyes, gold as the day, smiled down at Julie. "Dance with me, Mrs. Riordan?"

"Always," she said. "Always!"